P9-CEE-733

Growth of the Soil

Growth of the Soil

KNUT HAMSUN

Translated from the Norwegian by

W. W. WORSTER

VINTAGE BOOKS

A Division of Random House
New York

9B

BOOK ONE

CHAPTER I

THE LONG, long road over the moors and up into the forest—who trod it into being first of all? Man, a human being, the first that came here. There was no path before he came. Afterward, some beast or other, following the faint tracks over marsh and moorland, wearing them deeper; after these again some Lapp gained scent of the path, and took that way from field to field, looking to his reindeer. Thus was made the road through the great Almenning—the common tracts without an owner; no-man's-land.

The man comes, walking toward the north. He bears a sack, the first sack, carrying food and some few implements. A strong, coarse fellow, with a red iron beard, and little scars on face and hands; sites of old wounds—were they gained in toil or fight? Maybe the man has been in prison, and is looking for a place to hide; or a philosopher, maybe, in search of peace. This or that, he comes: the figure of a man in this great solitude. He trudges on; bird and beast are silent all about him; now and again he utters a word or two; speaking to himself. "Eyah—well, well"—so he speaks to himself. Here and there, where the moors give place to a kindlier spot, an open space in the midst of the forest, he lays down the sack and goes exploring; after a while he returns, heaves the sack to his shoulder again, and trudges on. So through the day, noting time by the sun;

night falls, and he throws himself down on the heather, resting on one arm.

A few hours' rest, and he is on the move again—"Eyah, well"—moving northward again, noting time by the sun; a meal of barley cakes and goats'-milk cheese, a drink of water from the stream, and on again. This day too he journeys, for there are many kindly spots in the woods to be explored. What is he seeking? A place, a patch of ground? An emigrant, maybe, from the homestead tracts; he keeps his eyes alert, looking out; now and again he climbs to the top of a hill, looking out. The sun goes down once more.

He moves along the western side of a valley; wooded ground, with leafy trees among the spruce and pine, and grass beneath. Hours of this, and twilight is falling, but his ear catches the faint purl of running water, and it heartens him like the voice of a living thing. He climbs the slope, and sees the valley half in darkness below; beyond, the sky to the south. He lies down to rest.

The morning shows him a range of pasture and woodland. He moves down, and there is a green hillside; far below, a glimpse of the stream, and a hare bounding across. The man nods his head, as it were approvingly—the stream is not so broad but that a hare may cross it at a bound. A white grouse sitting close upon its nest starts up at his feet with an angry hiss, and he nods again: feathered game and fur—a good spot this. Heather, bilberry, and cloudberry cover the ground; there are tiny ferns, and the seven-pointed star flowers of the wintergreen. Here and there he stops to dig with an iron tool, and finds good mold, or peaty soil, manured with the rotted wood and fallen leaves of a thousand years. He nods, to say that he has found himself a place to stay and live: aye, he will stay here and live. Two days he goes exploring the country round, returning each evening to the hillside. He sleeps at night on a bed of stacked pine; already he feels at home here, with a bed of pine beneath an overhanging rock.

The worst of his task had been to find the place; this no-man's place, but his. Now there was work to fill his days. He started at once, stripping birch bark in the woods farther off, while the sap was still in the trees. The bark he pressed and dried, and when he had gathered a heavy load, carried it all the miles back to the village, to be sold for building. Then back to the hillside, with new sacks of food and implements; flour and pork, a cooking-pot, a spade—out and back along the way he had come, carrying loads all the time. A born carrier of loads, a lumbering barge of a man in the forest—oh, as if he loved his calling, tramping long roads and carrying heavy burdens; as if life without a load upon one's shoulders were a miserable thing, no life for him.

One day he came up with more than the load he bore; came leading three goats in a leash. He was proud of his goats as if they had been horned cattle, and tended them kindly. Then came the first stranger passing, a nomad Lapp; at sight of the goats, he knew that this was a man who had come to stay, and spoke to him.

"You going to live here for good?"

"Aye," said the man.

"What's your name?"

"Isak. You don't know of a woman-body anywhere'd come and help?"

"No. But I'll say a word of it to all I meet."

"Aye, do that. Say I've creatures here, and none to look to them."

The Lapp went on his way. Isak—aye, he would say a word of that. The man on the hillside was no runaway; he had told his name. A runaway? He would have been found. Only a worker, and a hardy one. He set about cutting winter fodder for his goats, clearing the ground, digging a field, shifting stones, making a wall of stones. By the autumn he had built a house for himself, a hut of turf, sound and strong and warm; storms could not shake it, and nothing could burn it down. Here was a home; he could go inside and shut the door, and stay there; could stand outside on the door-slab, the owner of that house, if any should pass by. There were two rooms in the hut; for himself at the one end, and for his beasts at the other. Farthest in, against the wall of rock, was the hayloft. Everything was there.

Two more Lapps come by, father and son. They stand resting with both hands on their long staves, taking stock of the hut and the clearing, noting the sound of the goatbells up on the hillside.

"*Goddag*," say the Lapps. "And here's fine folk come to live." Lapps talk that way, with flattering words.

"You don't know of any woman hereabouts to help?" says Isak, thinking always of but one thing.

"Woman to help? No. But we'll say a word of it."

"Aye, if you'd be so good. That I've a house and a bit of ground here, and goats, but no woman to help. Say that."

Oh, he had sought about for a woman to help each time he had been down to the village with his loads of bark, but there was none to be found. They would look at him, a widow or an old unmarried one or so, but all afraid to offer, whatever might be in their minds. Isak couldn't tell why. Couldn't tell why? Who would go as help to live with a man in the wilds, ever so many miles away—a whole day's journey to the nearest neighbor? And the man himself was no way charming or pleasant by his looks, far from it; and when he spoke it was no tenor with eyes to heaven, but a coarse voice, something like a beast's.

Well, he would have to manage alone.

In winter he made great wooden troughs and sold them

in the village, carrying sacks of food and tools back through the snow; hard days when he was tied to a load. There were the goats, and none to look to them; he could not be away for long. And what did he do? Need made him wise; his brain was strong and little used; he trained it up to ever more and more. His first way was to let the goats loose before starting off himself, so that they could get a full feed among the undergrowth in the woods. But he found another plan. He took a bucket, a great vessel, and hung it up by the river so that a single drop fell in at a time, taking fourteen hours to fill it. When it was full to the brim, the weight was right; the bucket sank, and in doing so, pulled a line connected with the hayloft; a trapdoor opened, and three bundles of fodder came through—the goats were fed.

That was his way.

A bright idea; an inspiration, maybe, sent from God. The man had none to help him but himself. It served his need until late in the autumn; then came the first snow, then rain, then snow again, snowing all the time. And his machine went wrong; the bucket was filled from above, opening the trap too soon. He fixed a cover over, and all went well again for a time; then came winter, the drop of water froze to an icicle, and stopped the machine for good.

The goats must do as their master—learn to do without. Hard times—the man had need of help, and there was none, yet still he found a way. He worked and worked at his home; he made a window in the hut with two panes of real glass, and that was a bright and wonderful day in his life. No need of lighting fires to see; he could sit indoors and work at his wooden troughs by daylight. Better days, brighter days . . . eyah!

He read no books, but his thoughts were often with God; it was natural, coming of simplicity and awe. The stars in the sky, the wind in the trees, the solitude and the wide-spreading snow, the might of earth and over earth filled him many times a day with a deep earnestness. He was a sinner and feared God; on Sundays he washed himself out of reverence for the holy day, but worked none the less as through the week.

Spring came; he worked on his patch of ground, and planted potatoes. His livestock multiplied; the two she-goats had each had twins, making seven in all about the place. He made a bigger shed for them, ready for further increase, and put a couple of glass panes in there too. Aye, 'twas lighter and brighter now in every way.

And then at last came help; the woman he needed. She tacked about for a long time, this way and that across the hillside, before venturing near; it was evening before she could bring herself to come down. And then she came—a big, brown-eyed girl, full-built and coarse, with good, heavy hands, and rough hide brogues on her feet as if she had been a Lapp, and a calfskin bag slung from her shoulders. Not altogether young; speaking politely; somewhere nearing thirty.

There was nothing to fear; but she gave him greeting and said hastily: "I was going cross the hills, and took this way, that was all."

"Ho," said the man. He could barely take her meaning, for she spoke in a slovenly way; also, she kept her face turned aside.

"Aye," said she, " 'tis a long way to come."

"Aye, it's that," says the man. "Cross the hills, you said?"

"Yes."

"And what for?"

"I've my people there."

"Eh, so you've your people there? And what's your name?"

"Inger. And what's yours?"

"Isak."

"Isak? H'm. D'you live here yourself, maybe?"

"Aye, here, such as it is."

"Why, 'tis none so bad," said she to please him.

Now he had grown something clever to think out the way of things, and it struck him then she'd come for that very business and no other; had started out two days back just to come here. Maybe she had heard of his wanting a woman to help.

"Go inside a bit and rest your feet," said he.

They went into the hut and took a bit of the food she had brought, and some of his goats' milk to drink; then they made coffee, that she had brought with her in a bladder. Settled down comfortably over their coffee until bedtime. And in the night, he lay wanting her, and she was willing.

She did not go away next morning; all that day she did not go, but helped about the place; milked the goats, and scoured pots and things with fine sand, and got them clean. She did not go away at all. Inger was her name. And Isak was his name.

And now it was another life for the solitary man. True, this wife of his had a curious slovenly way of speech, and always turning her face aside, by reason of a harelip that she had, but that was no matter. Save that her mouth was disfigured, she would hardly have come to him at all; he might well be grateful for that she was marked with a harelip. And as to that, he himself was no beauty. Isak with the iron beard and rugged body, a grim and surly figure of a man; aye, as a man seen through a flaw in the window-pane. His look was not a gentle one; as if Barabbas might break loose at any minute. It was a wonder Inger herself did not run away.

She did not run away. When he had been out, and came home again, there was Inger at the hut; the two were one, the woman and the hut.

It was another mouth for him to feed, but no loss in that;

he had more freedom now, and could go and stay as he needed. And there were matters to be looked to away from home. There was the river; pleasant to look at, and deep and swift besides; a river not to be despised; it must come from some big water up in the hills. He got himself some fishing gear and went exploring; in the evening he came back with a basket of trout and char. This was a great thing to Inger, and a marvel; she was overwhelmed, being no way used to fine dishes. She clapped her hands and cried out: "Why! wherever . . ." And she was not slow to see how he was pleased at her surprise, and proud of it, for she said more in the same strain—oh, she had never seen the like, and how had he ever managed to find such things!

Inger was a blessing, too, in other ways. No clever head nor great in wit, maybe—but she had two lambing ewes with some of her kinfolk, and brought them down. It was the best they could have wished for at the hut; sheep with wool and lambs, four new head to their stock about the place; it was growing, getting bigger; a wonder and a marvel how their stock was grown. And Inger brought more; clothes, and little trifles of her own, a looking-glass, and a string of pretty glass beads, a spinning-wheel, and carding-combs. Why, if she went on that gait, the hut would soon be filled from floor to roof, and no room for more! Isak was astonished in his turn at all this wealth of goods, but being a silent man, and slow to speak, he said nothing, only shambled out to the door-slab and looked at the weather, and shambled in again. Aye, he had been lucky indeed; he felt himself more and more in love, or drawn towards her, or whatever it might be.

"You've no call to fetch along all such stuff," said he. " 'Tis more than's needed."

"I've more if I like to fetch it. And there's Uncle Sivert besides—you've heard of him?"

"No."

"Why, he's a rich man, and district treasurer besides."

Love makes a fool of the wise. Isak felt he must do something grand himself, and overdid it. "What I was going to say; you've no need to bother with hoeing potatoes. I'll do it myself the evening, when I come home."

And he took his ax and went off to the woods.

She heard him felling in the woods, not so far off; she could hear from the crash that he was felling big timber. She listened for a while, and then went out to the potato field and set to work hoeing. Love makes fools wise.

Isak came home in the evening, hauling a huge trunk by a rope. Oh, that simple and innocent Isak, he made all the noise he could with his tree-trunk, and coughed and hemmed, all for her to come out and wonder at him. And sure enough:

"Why, you're out of your senses," said Inger when she came out. "Is that work for a man single-handed?" He made no answer; wouldn't have said a word for anything. To do a little more than was work for a man single-handed was nothing to speak of—nothing at all. A stick of timber —huh! "And what are you going to do with it?" she asked.

"Oh, we'll see," he answered carelessly, as if scarcely heeding she was there.

But when he saw that she had hoed the potatoes after all he was not pleased. It was as if she had done almost as much as he; and that was not to his liking. He slipped the rope from the tree-trunk and went off with it once more.

"What, haven't you done yet?"

"No," said he gruffly.

And he came back with another stick like the last, only with no noise nor sign of being out of breath; hauled it up to the hut like an ox, and left it there.

That summer he felled a mass of timber, and brought it to the hut.

NGER packed up some food one day in her calfskin bag. "I'd thought of going across to see my people, just how they're faring."

"Aye," said Isak.

"I must have a bit of talk with them about things."

Isak did not go out at once to see her off, but waited quite a while. And when at last he shambled out, looking never the least bit anxious, never the least bit miserable and full of fear, Inger was all but vanished already through the fringe of the forest.

"Hem!" He cleared his throat, and called, "Will you be coming back maybe?" He had not meant to ask her that, but . . .

"Coming back? Why, what's in your mind? Of course I'll be coming back."

"H'm."

So he was left alone again—eyah, well . . . ! With his strength, and the love of work that was in him, he could not idle in and out about the hut doing nothing; he set to, clearing timber, felling straight, good sticks, and cutting them flat on two sides. He worked at this all through the day, then he milked the goats and went to bed.

Sadly bare and empty now in the hut; a heavy silence clung about the peat walls and the earthen floor; a deep and solemn loneliness. Spinning-wheel and carding-combs were in their place; the beads, too, were safe as they had been, stowed away in a bag under the roof. Inger had taken nothing of her belongings. But Isak, unthinkably simple as he was, grew afraid of the dark in the light summer nights, and saw Shapes and Things stealing past the window. He got up before dawn, about two o'clock by the light, and ate his breakfast, a mighty dish of porridge to last the day, and save the waste of time in cooking more. In the evening he turned up new ground, to make a bigger field for the potatoes.

Three days he worked with spade and ax by turns; Inger should be coming on the next. 'Twould be but reasonable to have a platter of fish for her when she came—but the straight road to the water lay by the way she would come, and it might seem . . . So he went a longer way; a new way, over the hills where he had never been before. Grey rock and brown, and strewed about with bits of heavy stone, heavy as copper or lead. There might be many things in those heavy stones; gold or silver, like as not—he had no knowledge of such things, and did not care. He came to the water; the fly was up, and the fish were biting well that night. He brought home a basket of fish that Inger would open her eyes to see! Going back in the morning by the way he had come, he picked up a couple of the heavy little stones among the hills; they were brown, with specks of dark blue here and there, and wondrous heavy in the hand.

Inger had not come, and did not come. This was the fourth day. He milked the goats as he had used to do when he lived alone with them and had no other to help; then he went up to a quarry near by and carried down stones; great piles of carefully chosen blocks and flakes, to build a wall. He was busy with no end of things.

On the fifth evening, he turned in to rest with a little fear at his heart—but there were the carding-combs and spinning-wheel, and the string of beads. Sadly empty and bare in the hut, and never a sound; the hours were long, and when at last he did hear something like a sound of footsteps outside, he told himself that it was fancy, nothing more. "Eyah, *Herregud!*" [1] he murmured, desolate in spirit. And Isak was not one to use words lightly. There was the tramping of feet again outside, and a moment after something gliding past the window; something with horns, something alive. He sprang up, over to the door, and lo, a vision! "God or the devil," muttered Isak, who did not use words lightly. He saw a cow; Inger and a cow, vanishing into the shed.

If he had not stood there himself and heard it—Inger talking softly to the cow in the shed—he would not have believed. But there he stood. And all at once a black misgiving came into his mind: a clever wife, aye, a manager of wonders—but, after all . . . No, it was too much, and that was the only word for it. A spinning-wheel and carding-combs at a pinch; even the beads perhaps, though they were over-fine to be come by in any way proper and natural. But a cow, picked up straying on the road, maybe, or in a field—it would be missed in no time, and have to be found.

Inger stepped out of the shed, and said with a proud little laugh:

"It's only me. I've brought my cow along."

"H'm," said Isak.

"It was that made me so long—I couldn't go but softly with her over the hills."

"And so you've brought a cow?" said he.

"Yes," said she, all ready to burst with greatness and riches on earth. "Don't you believe me, perhaps?"

Isak feared the worst, but made no sign, and only said:

"Come inside and get something to eat."

[1] Literally, "Lord God." The word is frequently used, as here, in a sense of resignation, as it were a sigh.

"Did you see her? Isn't she a pretty cow?"

"Aye, a fine cow," said Isak. And speaking as carelessly as he could, he asked: "Where d'you get her?"

"Her name's Goldenhorns. What's that wall to be for you've been building up here? You'll work yourself to death, you will. Oh, come and look at the cow, now, won't you?"

They went out to look, and Isak was in his underclothes, but that was no matter. They looked and looked the cow all over carefully, in every part, and noted all the markings, head and shoulders, buttocks and thighs, where it was red and white, and how it stood.

"How old d'you think she might be?" asked Isak cautiously.

"Think? Why, she's just exactly a tiny way on in her fourth year. I brought her up myself, and they all said it was the sweetest calf they'd ever seen. But will there be feed enough here, d'you think?"

Isak began to believe, as he was only too willing to do, that all was well. "As for the feed, why, there'll be feed enough, never fear."

Then they went indoors to eat and drink and make an evening together. They lay awake talking of Cow; of the great event. "And isn't she a dear cow, too? Her second's on the way. And her name's Goldenhorns. Are you asleep, Isak?"

"No."

"And what do you think, she knew me again; knew me at once, and followed me like a lamb. We lay up in the hills a bit last night."

"Ho?"

"But she'll have to be tied up through the summer, all the same, or she'll be running off. A cow's a cow."

"Where's she been before?" asked Isak at last.

"Why, with my people, where she belonged. And they

were quite sorry to lose her, I can tell you; and the little ones cried when I took her away."

Could she be making it all up, and coming out with it so pat? No, it wasn't thinkable. It must be true, the cow was hers. Ho, they were getting well-to-do, with this hut of theirs, this farm of theirs; why, 'twas good enough for anyone. Aye, they'd as good as all they could wish for already. Oh, that Inger; he loved her and she loved him again; they were frugal folk; they lived in primitive wise, and lacked for nothing. "Let's go to sleep!" And they went to sleep. And wakened in the morning to another day, with things to look at, matters to see to, once again; aye, toil and pleasure, ups and downs, the way of life.

As, for instance, with those timber balks—should he try to fit them up together? Isak had kept his eyes about him down in the village, with that very thing in mind, and seen how it was done; he could build with timber himself, why not? Moreover, it was a call upon him; it must be done. Hadn't they a farm with sheep, a farm with a cow already, goats that were many already and would be more? Their livestock alone was crowding them out of the turf hut; something must be done. And best get on with it at once, while the potatoes were still in flower, and before the hay-time began. Inger would have to lend a hand here and there.

Isak wakes in the night and gets up, Inger sleeping fine and sound after her long tramp, and out he goes to the cowshed. Now it must not be thought that he talked to Cow in any obsequious and disgustful flattery; no, he patted her decently, and looked her over once more in every part, to see if there should, by chance, be any sign, any mark of her belonging to strange owners. No mark, no sign, and Isak steals away relieved.

There lies the timber. He falls to, rolling the balks, then lifting them, setting them up against the wall in a framework; one big frame for a parlor, and a smaller one—there must be a room to sleep in. It was heavy work, hard-breathing work, and his mind being set on it, he forgot the time. There comes a smoke from the roof-hole of the hut, and Inger steps out and calls to breakfast.

"And what are you busy with now?" asked Inger.

"You're early about," says Isak, and that was all.

Ho, that Isak with his secrets and his lordly ways! But it pleased him, maybe, to have her asking and wondering, and curious about his doings. He ate a bit, and sat for a while in the hut before going out again. What could he be waiting for?

"H'm," says he at last, getting up. "This won't do. Can't sit here idling today. Work to be done."

"Seems like you're building," says Inger. "What?"

And he answered condescendingly, this great man who went about building with timber all by himself, he answered: "Why, you can see as much, I take it."

"Yes. . . . Yes, of course."

"Building—why, there's no help for it as I can see. Here's you come bringing a whole cow to the farm—that means a cowshed, I suppose?"

Poor Inger, not so eternally wise as he, as Isak, that lord of creation. And this was before she learned to know him, and reckon with his way of putting things. Says Inger:

"Why, it's never a cowshed you're building, surely?"

"Ho," says he.

"But you don't mean it? I—I thought you'd be building a house first."

"Think so?" asks Isak, putting up a face as if he'd never in life have thought of that himself.

"Why, yes. And put the beasts in the hut."

Isak thought for a bit. "Aye, maybe 'twould be best so."

"There," says Inger, all glad and triumphant. "You see I'm some good after all."

"Aye, that's true. And what'd you say to a house with two rooms in?"

"*Two* rooms? Oh . . . ! Why, 'twould be just like other folks. Do you think we could?"

They did. Isak he went about building, notching his balks and fitting up his framework; also he managed a hearth and fireplace of picked stones, though this last was troublesome, and Isak himself was not always pleased with his work. Haytime came, and he was forced to climb down from his building and go about the hillsides far and near, cutting grass and bearing home the hay in mighty loads. Then one rainy day he must go down to the village.

"What you want in the village?"

"Well, I can't say exactly as yet. . . ."

He set off, and stayed away two days, and came back with a cooking-stove—a barge of a man surging up through the forest with a whole iron stove on his back. " 'Tis more than a man can do," said Inger. "You'll kill yourself that gait." But Isak pulled down the stone hearth, that didn't look so well in the new house, and set up the cooking-stove in its place. " 'Tisn't everyone has a cooking-stove," said Inger. "Of all the wonders, how we're getting on! . . ."

Haymaking still; Isak bringing in loads and masses of hay, for woodland grass is not the same as meadow grass, more's the pity, but poorer by far. It was only on rainy days now that he could spare time for his building; 'twas a lengthy business, and even by August, when all the hay was in, safely stored under the shelter of the rock, the new house was still but halfway done. Then by September: "This won't do," said Isak. "You'd better run down to the village and get a man to help." Inger had been something poorly of late, and didn't run much now, but all the same she got herself ready to go.

But Isak had changed his mind again; had put on his lordly manner again, and said he would manage by himself.

"No call to bother with other folk," says he; "I can manage it alone."

" 'Tis more than one man's work," says Inger. "You'll wear yourself out."

"Just help me to hoist these up," says Isak, and that was all.

October came, and Inger had to give up. This was a hard blow, for the roof-beams must be got up at any cost, and the place covered in before the autumn rains; there was not a day to be lost. What could be wrong with Inger? Not going to be ill? She would make cheese now and then from the goats' milk, but beyond that she did little save shifting Goldenhorns a dozen times a day where she grazed.

"Bring up a good-sized basket, or a box," she had said, "next time you're down to the village."

"What d'you want that for?" asked Isak.

"I'll just be wanting it," said Inger.

Isak hauled up the roof-beams on a rope, Inger guiding them with one hand; it seemed a help just to have her about. Bit by bit the work went on; there was no great height to the roof, but the timber was huge and heavy for a little house.

The weather kept fine, more or less. Inger got the potatoes in by herself, and Isak had the roofing done before the rain came on in earnest. The goats were brought in of a night into the hut and all slept there together; they managed somehow, they managed everyway, and did not grumble.

Isak was getting ready for another journey down to the village. Said Inger very humbly:

"Do you think perhaps you could bring up a good-sized basket, or a box?"

"I've ordered some glass windows," said Isak. "And a couple of painted doors. I'll have to fetch them up," said he in his lordly way.

"Aye well, then. It's no great matter about the basket."

"What did you want with a basket? What's it for?"

"What's it for? . . . Oh, haven't you eyes in your head!"

Isak went off deep in thought. Two days later he came back, with a window and a door for the parlor, and a door for the bedroom; also he had hung round his neck in front a good-sized packing-case, and full of provisions to boot.

"You'll carry yourself to death one day," said Inger.

"Ho, indeed!" Isak was very far indeed from being dead; he took out a bottle of medicine from his pocket—naphtha it was—and gave it to Inger with orders to take it regularly and get well again. And there were the windows and the painted doors that he could fairly boast of; he set to work at once fitting them in. Oh, such little doors, and secondhand at that, but painted up all neat and fine again in red and white; 'twas almost as good as having pictures on the walls.

And now they moved into the new building, and the animals had the turf hut to themselves, only a lambing ewe was left with Cow, lest she should feel lonely.

They had done well, these builders in the waste; aye, 'twas a wonder and a marvel to themselves.

ℬSAK worked on the land until the frost set in; there were stones and roots to be dug up and cleared away, and the meadow to be leveled ready for next year. When the ground hardened, he left his field work and became a woodman, felling and cutting up great quantities of logs.

"What do you want with all these logs?" Inger would say.

"Oh, they'll be useful some way," said Isak offhandedly, as though he had no plan. But Isak had a plan, never fear. Here was virgin forest, a dense growth, right close up to the house, a barrier hedging in his fields where he wanted room. Moreover, there must be some way of getting the logs down to the village that winter; there were folk enough would be glad of wood for firing. It was sound enough, and Isak was in no doubt; he stuck to his work in the forest, felling trees and cutting them up into logs.

Inger came out often to watch him at work. He took no notice, but made as if her coming were no matter, and not at all a thing he wished for her to do; but she understood all the same that it pleased him to have her there. They had a strange way, too, of speaking to each other at times.

"Couldn't you find things to do but come out here and get stark frozen?" says Isak.

"I'm well enough for me," says Inger. "But I can't see there's any living sense in you working yourself to death like you do."

"Ho! You just pick up that coat of mine there and put it on you."

"Put on your coat? Likely, indeed. I've no time to sit here now, with Goldenhorns ready to calve and all."

"H'm. Calving, you say?"

"As if you didn't know! But what do you think now about that same calf? Let it stay and be weaned, maybe?"

"Do as you think; 'tis none of my business with calves and things."

"Well, 'twould be a pity to eat up Calf, seems to me. And leave us with but one cow on the place."

"Don't seem to me like you'd do that anyway," says Isak.

That was their way. Lonely folk, ugly to look at and overfull of growth, but a blessing for each other, for the beasts, and for the earth.

And Goldenhorns calved. A great day in the wilderness, a joy and a delight. They gave her flour-wash, and Isak himself saw to it there was no stint of flour, though he had carried it all the way himself, on his back. And there lay a pretty calf, a beauty, red-flanked like her mother, and comically bewildered at the miracle of coming into the world. In a couple of years she would be having calves of her own.

" 'Twill be a grand fine cow when she grows up," said Inger. "And what are we to call her, now? I can't think."

Inger was childish in her ways, and no clever wit for anything.

"Call her?" said Isak. "Why, Silverhorns, of course; what else?"

The first snow came. As soon as there was a passable road, Isak set out for the village, full of concealment and mystery as ever, when Inger asked his errand. And sure enough, he came back this time with a new and unthinkable surprise. A horse and sledge, nothing less.

"Here's foolishness," says Inger. "And you've not stolen it, I suppose?"

"Stolen it?"

"Well, found it, then?"

Now if only he could have said: " 'Tis my horse—our horse. . . ." But to tell the truth, he had only hired it, after all. Hired horse and sledge to cart his logs.

Isak drove down with his loads of firewood, and brought back food, herrings and flour. And one day he came up with a young bull on the sledge; bought it for next to nothing, by reason they were getting short of fodder down in the village. Shaggy and thin, no ways a beauty, but decently built for all that, and wanted no more than proper feed to set it right. And with a cow they had already . . .

"What'll you be bringing up next?" said Inger.

Isak brought up a host of things. Brought up planks and a saw he had got in exchange for timber; a grindstone, a wafer iron, tools—all in exchange for his logs. Inger was bursting with riches, and said each time: "What, more things! When we've cattle and all a body could think of!"

They had enough to meet their needs for no little time to come, and were well-to-do folk. What was Isak to start on again next spring? He had thought it all out, tramping down beside his loads of wood that winter; he would clear more ground over the hillside and level it off, cut up more logs to dry through the summer, and take down double loads when the snow came fit for sledging. It worked out beautifully.

But there was another matter Isak had thought of times out of number: that Goldenhorns, where had she come from, whose had she been? There was never a wife on earth like Inger. Ho! a wild thing she was, that let him do as he pleased with her, and was glad of it. But—suppose one day they were to come for the cow, and take it away—and worse, maybe, to come after? What was it Inger herself had said about the horse: "You haven't stolen it, I suppose, or found it?" That was her first thought, yes. That was

what she had said; who could say if she were to be trusted
—what should he do? He had thought of it all many a time.
And here he had brought up a mate himself for the cow—
for a stolen cow, maybe!

And there was the horse he would have to return again.
A pity—for 'twas a little friendly beast, and grown fond of
them already.

"Never mind," said Inger comfortingly. "Why, you've
done wonders already."

"Aye, but just now with the spring coming on—and I've
need of a horse. . . ."

Next morning he drove off quietly with the last load,
and was away two days. Coming back on foot the third day,
he stopped as he neared the house, and stood listening.
There was a curious noise inside. . . . A child crying—
eyah, *Herregud!* . . . Well, there it was; but a terrible
strange thing. And Inger had never said a word.

He stepped inside, and there first thing of all was the
packing-case—the famous packing-case that he had carried
home slung round his neck in front; there it was, hung up
by a string at each end from the ceiling, a cradle and a bed-
place for the child. Inger was up, pottering about half
dressed—she had milked the cow and the goats, as it might
have been just an ordinary day.

The child stopped crying. "You're through with it already?" said Isak.

"Aye, I'm through with it now."

"H'm."

"It came the first evening you were gone."

"H'm."

"I'd only to get my things off and hang up the cradle
there, but it was too much for me, like, and I had to lie
down."

"Why didn't you tell me before?"

"Why, I couldn't say to a minute when it'd be. 'Tis a boy."

"Ho, a boy."

"And I can't for the life of me think what we're to call him," said Inger.

Isak peeped at the little red face; well shaped it was, and no harelip, and a growth of hair all thick on the head. A fine little fellow for his rank and station in a packing-case; Isak felt himself curiously weak. The rugged man stood there with a miracle before him; a thing created first of all in a sacred mist, showing forth now in life with a little face like an allegory. Days and years, and the miracle would be a human being.

"Come and have your food," said Inger. . . .

Isak is a woodman, felling trees and sawing logs. He is better off now than before, having a saw. He works away, and mighty piles of wood grow up; he makes a street of them, a town, built up of stacks and piles of wood. Inger is more about the house now, and does not come out as before to watch him at his work; Isak must find a pretext now and then to slip off home for a moment instead. Queer to have a little fellow like that about the place! Isak, of course, would never dream of taking any notice—'twas but a bit of a thing in a packing-case. And as for being fond of it . . . But when it cried, well, it was only human nature to feel just a little something for a cry like that; a little tiny cry like that.

"Don't touch him!" says Inger. "With your hands all messed up with resin and all!"

"Resin, indeed!" says Isak. "Why, I haven't had resin on my hands since I built this house. Give me the boy, let me take him—there, he's as right as can be!"

• • •

Early in May came a visitor. A woman came over the hills to that lonely place where none ever came; she was of Inger's kinsfolk, though not near, and they made her welcome.

"I thought I'd just look in," she says, "and see how Goldenhorns gets on since she left us."

Inger looks at the child, and talks to it in a little pitying voice: "Ah, there's none asks how he's getting on, that's but a little tiny thing."

"Why, as for that, anyone can see how he's getting on. A fine little lad and all. And who'd have thought it a year gone, Inger, to find you here with house and husband and child and all manner of things."

" 'Tis no doing of mine to praise. But there's one sitting there that took me as I was and no more."

"And wedded? Not wedded yet, no, I see."

"We'll see about it, the time this little man's to be christened," says Inger. "We'd have been wedded before, but couldn't come by it, getting down to a church and all. What do you say, Isak?"

"Wedded?" says Isak. "Why, yes, of course."

"But if as you'd help us, Oline," says Inger. "Just to come up for a few days in the off time once, and look to the creatures here while we're away?"

Aye, Oline would do that.

"We'll see it's no loss to you after."

Why, as to that, she'd leave it to them. . . . "And you're building again, I see. Now what'll that be for? Isn't there built enough?"

Inger sees her chance and puts in here: "Why, you must ask him about that. I'm not to know."

"Building?" says Isak. "Oh, 'tis nothing to speak of. A bit of a shed, maybe, if we should need it. What's that you were saying about Goldenhorns? You'd like to see her?"

They go across to the cowshed, and there's cow and calf

to show, and an ox to boot. The visitor nods her head, looking at the beasts, and at the shed; all fine as could be, and
clean as couldn't be cleaner. "Trust Inger for looking after
creatures every way," says Oline.

Isak puts a question: "Goldenhorns was at your place
before?"

"Aye, from a calf. Not my place, though; at my son's.
But 'tis all the same. And we've her mother still."

Isak had not heard better news a long while; it was a
burden lighter. Goldenhorns was his and Inger's by honest
right. To tell the truth, he had half thought of getting rid
of his trouble in a sorry way; to kill off the cow that autumn, scrape the hide, bury the horns, and thus make away
with all trace of Cow Goldenhorns in this life. No need
for that now. And he grew mightily proud of Inger all at
once.

"Aye, Inger," says he. "She's one to manage things,
that's true. There's not her like nor equal to be found. 'Twas
a poor place here till I got a woman of my own, as you
might say."

"Why, 'tis but natural so," says Oline.

And so this woman from across the hills, a soft-spoken
creature with her wits about her, and by name Oline, she
stayed with them a couple of days, and had the little room
to sleep in. And, when she set out for home, she had a
bundle of wool that Inger had given her, from the sheep.
There was no call to hide that bundle of wool, but Oline
took care that Isak should not see it.

Then the child and Isak and his wife again; the same
world again, and the work of the day, with many little joys
and big. Goldenhorns was yielding well, the goats had
dropped their kids and were yielding well; Inger had a row
of red and white cheeses already, stored away to get ripe.
It was her plan to save up cheeses till there were enough
to buy a loom. Oh, that Inger; she knew how to weave.

And Isak built a shed—he too had a plan of his own, no doubt. He set up a new wing built out from the side of the turf hut, with double paneling-boards, made a doorway in it, and a neat little window with four panes; laid on a roof of outer boards, and made do with that till the ground thawed and he could get turf. All that was useful and necessary; no flooring, no smooth-planed walls, but Isak had fixed up a box partition, as for a horse, and a manger.

It was nearing the end of May. The sun had thawed the high ground; Isak roofed in his shed with turf and it was finished. Then one morning he ate a meal to last for the day, took some more food with him, shouldered pick and spade, and went down to the village.

"Bring up three yards of cotton print, if you can," Inger called after him.

"What do you want with that?" said Isak.

Isak was long away; it almost seemed as if he had gone for good. Inger looked at the weather every day, noting the way of the wind, as if she were expecting a sailing-ship; she went out at nighttime to listen; even thought of taking the child on her arm and going after him. Then at last he came back, with a horse and cart. "*Ptro!*" shouted Isak as he drew up; shouted so as to be heard. And the horse was well behaved, and stood as quiet as could be, nodding at the turf hut as if it knew the place again. Nevertheless, Isak must call out: "Hi, come and hold the horse a bit, can't you?"

Out goes Inger. "Where is it now? Oh, Isak, have you hired him again? Where have you been all this time? 'Tis six days gone."

"Where d'you think I'd be? Had to go all sorts of ways round to find a road for this cart of mine. Hold the horse a bit, can't you?"

"Cart of yours! You don't mean to say you've bought that cart?"

Isak dumb; Isak swelling with things unspoken. He lifts out a plow and a harrow he has brought; nails, provisions, a grindstone, a sack of grain. "And how's the child?" he asks.

"Child's all right. Have you bought that cart, that's what I want to know? For here have I been longing and longing for a loom," says she jestingly, in her gladness at having him back again.

Isak dumb once more, for a long space, busied with his own affairs, pondering, looking round for a place to put all his goods and implements; it was hard to find room for them all. But when Inger gave up asking, and began talking to the horse instead, he came out of his lofty silence at last.

"Ever see a farm *without* a horse and cart, and plow and harrows, and all the rest of it? And since you want to know, why, I've bought that horse and cart, and all that's in it," says he.

And Inger could only shake her head and murmur: "Well, I never did see such a man!"

Isak was no longer littleness and humility; he had paid, as it were, like a gentleman, for Goldenhorns. "Here you are," he could say. "I've brought along a horse; we can call it quits."

He stood there, upright and agile, against his wont; shifted the plow once more, picked it up and carried it with one hand and stood it up against the wall. Oh, he could manage an estate! He took up the other things: the harrow, the grindstone, a new fork he had bought, all the costly agricultural implements, treasures of the new home, a grand array. All requisite appliances—nothing was lacking.

"H'm. As for that loom, why, we'll manage that too, I dare say, as long as I've my health. And there's your cotton print; they'd none but blue, so I took that."

There was no end to the things he brought. A bottom-less well, rich in all manner of things, like a city store.

Says Inger: "I wish Oline could have seen all this when she was here."

Just like a woman! Sheer senseless vanity—as if that mattered! Isak sniffed contemptuously. Though perhaps he himself would not have been displeased if Oline had been there to see.

The child was crying.

"Go in and look after the boy," said Isak. "I'll look to the horse."

He takes out the horse and leads it into the stable: aye, here is Isak putting his horse into the stable! Feeds it and strokes it and treats it tenderly. And how much was owing now, on that horse and cart? Everything, the whole sum, a mighty debt; but it should all be paid that summer, never fear. He had stacks of cordwood to pay with, and some building-bark from last year's cut, not to speak of heavy timber. There was time enough. But later on, when the pride and glory had cooled off a little, there were bitter hours of fear and anxiety; all depended on the summer and the crops; how the year turned out.

The days now were occupied in field work and more field work; he cleared new bits of ground, getting out roots and stones; plowing, manuring, harrowing, working with pick and spade, breaking lumps of soil and crumbling them with hand and heel; a tiller of the ground always, laying out fields like velvet carpets. He waited a couple of days longer —there was a look of rain about—and then he sowed his grain.

For generations back, into forgotten time, his fathers before him had sowed grain; solemnly, on a still, calm evening, best with a gentle fall of warm and misty rain, soon after the grey-goose flight. Potatoes were a new thing, nothing mystic, nothing religious; women and children could plant them—earth-apples that came from foreign parts, like coffee; fine rich food, but much like turnips and beets. Grain was nothing less than bread; grain or no grain meant life or death.

Isak walked bareheaded, in Jesu name, a sower. Like a tree-stump with hands to look at, but in his heart like a child. Every cast was made with care, in a spirit of kindly resignation. Look! the tiny grains that are to take life and grow, shoot up into ears, and give more grain again; so it is throughout all the earth where grain is sown. Palestine, America, the valleys of Norway itself—a great wide world, and here is Isak, a tiny speck in the midst of it all, a sower. Little showers of grain flung out fanwise from his hand; a kindly clouded sky, with a promise of the faintest little misty rain.

CHAPTER IV

T was the slack time between the seasons, but the woman Oline did not come.

Isak was free of the soil now; he had two scythes and two rakes ready for the haymaking; he made long bottom boards for the cart for getting in the hay, and procured a couple of runners and some suitable wood to make a sledge for the winter. Many useful things he did. Even to shelves. He set up a pair of shelves inside the house, as an excellent place to keep various things, such as an almanac—he had bought one at last—and ladles and vessels not in use. Inger thought a deal of those two shelves.

Inger was easily pleased; she thought a great deal of everything. There was Goldenhorns, for instance, no fear of her running away now, with the calf and bull to play with; she ran about in the woods all day long. The goats too were thriving, their heavy udders almost dragging on the ground. Inger made a long robe of blue cotton print, and a little cap of the same stuff, as pretty as could be—and that was for the christening. The boy himself watched her at work many a time; a blessed wonder of a boy he was, and if she was so bent on calling him Eleseus, why, Isak supposed she must have her way. When the robe was finished, it had a long train to it, nigh on a yard and a half of cotton print, and every inch of it money spent; but what of that—the child was their first-born.

"What about those beads of yours?" said Isak. "If as they're ever to be used at all . . ."

Oh, but Inger had thought of them already, those beads of hers. Trust a mother for that. Inger said nothing, and was very proud. The beads were none so many; they would not make a necklace for the boy, but they would look pretty stitched on the front of his cap, and there they should be.

But Oline did not come.

If it had not been for the cattle, they could have gone off all three of them, and come back a few days later with the child properly christened. And if it had not been for that matter of getting wedded, Inger might have gone by herself.

"If we put off the wedding business for a bit?" said Isak. But Inger was loth to put it off; it would be ten or twelve years at least before Eleseus was old enough to stay behind and look to the milking while they went.

No, Isak must use his brains to find a way. The whole thing had come about somehow without their knowing; maybe the wedding business was just as important as the christening—how should he know? The weather looked like drought—a thoroughly wicked drought; if the rain did not come before long, their crops would be burnt up. But all was in the hand of God. Isak made ready to go down to the village and find some one to come up. All those miles again!

And all that fuss just to be wed and christened! Aye, out-lying folks had many troubles, great and small.

At last Oline did come. . . .

And now they were wedded and christened, everything decently in order; they had remembered to have the wedding first, so the child could be christened as of a wedded pair. But the drought kept on, and the tiny grainfields were parched, those velvet carpets parched—and why? 'Twas all in the hand of God. Isak mowed his bits of meadow; there was little grass on them for all he had manured them well that spring. He mowed and mowed on the hillsides, farther and farther out; mowing and turning and carting home loads of hay, as if he would never tire—for he had a horse already, and a well-stocked farm. But by mid-July he had to cut the grain for green fodder, there was no help for it. And now all depended on the potato crop.

What was that about potatoes? Were they just a thing from foreign parts, like coffee; a luxury, an extra? Oh, the potato is a lordly fruit; drought or downpour, it grows and grows all the same. It laughs at the weather, and will stand anything; only deal kindly with it, and it yields fifteen-fold again. Not the blood of a grape, but the flesh of a chestnut, to be boiled or roasted, used in every way. A man may lack grain to make bread, but give him potatoes and he will not starve. Roast them in the embers, and there is supper; boil them in water, and there's a breakfast ready. As for meat, it's little is needed beside. Potatoes can be served with what you please; a dish of milk, a herring, is enough. The rich eat them with butter; poor folk manage with a tiny pinch of salt. Isak could make a feast of them on Sundays, with a mess of cream from Goldenhorns's milk. Poor despised potato—a blessed thing!

But now—things look black even for the potato crop.

Isak looked at the sky unnumbered times in the day. And the sky was blue. Many an evening it looked as if a shower were coming. Isak would go in and say: "Like as not we'll be getting that rain after all." And a couple of hours later all would be as hopeless as before.

The drought had lasted seven weeks now, and the heat was serious; the potatoes stood all the time in flower; flowering marvelously, unnaturally. The grainfields looked from a distance as if under snow. Where was it all to end? The almanac said nothing—almanacs nowadays were not what they used to be; an almanac now was no good at all. Now it looked like rain again, and Isak went in to Inger: "We'll have rain this night, God willing."

"Is it looking that way?"

"Aye. And the horse is shivering a bit, like they will."

Inger glanced towards the door and said: "Aye, you see, 'twill come right enough."

A few drops fell. Hours passed, they had their supper, and when Isak went out in the night to look, the sky was blue.

"Well, well," said Inger; "anyway, 'twill give the last bit of lichen another day to dry," said she to comfort him all she could.

Isak had been getting lichen, as much as he could, and had a fine lot, all of the best. It was good fodder, and he treated it as he would hay, covering it over with bark in the woods. There was only a little still left out, and now, when Inger spoke of it, he answered despairingly, as if it were all one: "I'll not take it in if it is dry."

"Isak, you don't mean it!" said Inger.

And next day, sure enough, he did not take it in. He left it out and never touched it, just as he had said. Let it stay where it was, there'd be no rain anyway; let it stay where it was in God's name! He could take it in some time before Christmas, if so be as the sun hadn't burnt it all up to nothing.

Isak was deeply and thoroughly offended. It was no longer a pleasure and a delight to sit outside on the door-slab and look out over his lands and be the owner of it all. There was the potato field flowering madly, and drying up; let the lichen stay where it was—what did he care? That Isak! Who could say; perhaps he had a bit of a sly little thought in his mind for all his stolid simpleness; maybe he knew what he was doing after all, trying to tempt the blue sky now, at the change of the moon.

That evening it looked like rain once more. "You ought to have got that lichen in," said Inger.

"What for?" said Isak, looking all surprised.

"Aye, you with your nonsense—but it might be rain after all."

"There'll be no rain this year, you can see for yourself."

But for all that, it grew curiously dark in the night. They could see through the glass window that it was darker—aye, and as if something beat against the panes, something wet, whatever it might be. Inger woke up. " 'Tis rain! look at the windowpanes."

But Isak only sniffed. "Rain? Not a bit of it. Don't know what you're talking about."

"Ah, it's no good pretending," said Inger.

Isak was pretending—aye, that was it. Rain it was, sure enough, and a good heavy shower—but as soon as it had rained enough to spoil Isak's lichen, it stopped. The sky was blue. "What did I say," said Isak, stiffnecked and hard.

The shower made no difference to the potato crop, and days came and went; the sky was blue. Isak set to work on his timber sledge, worked hard at it, and bowed his heart, and planed away humbly at runners and shafts. Eyah, *Herregud!* Aye, the days came and went, and the child grew. Inger churned and made cheeses; there was no serious danger; folk that had their wits about them and could work need not die for the sake of one bad year. Moreover, after nine weeks, there came a regular blessing of rain, rain all one day and night, and sixteen hours of it pouring as hard as it could. If it had come but two weeks back, Isak would have said: "It's too late now!" As it was, he said to Inger, "You see, that'll save some of the potatoes."

"Aye," said Inger hopefully. "It'll save the lot, you'll see."

And now things were looking better. Rain every day;

good, thorough showers. Everything looking green again, as by a miracle. The potatoes were flowering still, worse than before, and with big berries growing out at the tops, which was not as it should be; but none could say what might be at the roots—Isak had not ventured to look. Then one day Inger went out and found over a score of little potatoes under one plant. "And they've five weeks more to grow in," said Inger. Oh, that Inger, always trying to comfort and speak hopefully through her harelip. It was not pretty to hear when she spoke, for a sort of hissing, like steam from a leaky valve, but a comfort all the same out in the wilds. And a happy and cheerful soul she was at all times.

"I wish you could manage to make another bed," she said to Isak one day.

"Ho!" said he.

"Why, there's no hurry, but still . . ."

They started getting in the potatoes, and finished by Michaelmas, as the custom is. It was a middling year—a good year; once again it was seen that potatoes didn't care so much about the weather, but grew up all the same, and could stand a deal. A middling year—a good year . . . well, not perhaps, if they worked it out exactly, but that they couldn't do this year. A Lapp had passed that way one day and said how fine their potatoes were up there; it was much worse, he said, down in the village.

And now Isak had a few weeks more to work the ground before the frost set in. The cattle were out, grazing where they pleased; it was good to work with them about, and hear the bells, though it did take some of his time now and again. There was the bull, mischievous beast, would take to butting at the lichen stacks; and as for the goats, they were high and low and everywhere, even to the roof of the hut.

Troubles great and small.

One day Isak heard a sudden shout; Inger stood on the door-slab with the child in her arms, pointing over to the bull and the pretty little cow Silverhorns—they were making love. Isak threw down his pick and raced over to the pair, but it was too late, by the look of it. The mischief was done. "Oh, the little rascal, she's all too young—half a year too soon, a child!" Isak got her into the hut, but it was too late.

"Well, well," says Inger, " 'tis none so bad after all, in a way; if she'd waited, we'd have had both of them bearing at the same time." Oh, that Inger; not so bright as some, maybe yet, for all that, she may well have known what she was about when she let the pair loose together that morning.

Winter came, Inger carding and spinning, Isak driving down with loads of wood; fine dry wood and good going; all his debts paid off and settled; horse and cart, plow and harrow his very own. He drove down with Inger's goats'-milk cheeses, and brought back woolen thread, a loom, shuttles and beam and all; brought back flour and provisions, more planks, and boards and nails; one day he brought home a lamp.

"As true as I'm here I won't believe it," says Inger. But she had long had in her mind about a lamp for all that. They lit it the same evening, and were in paradise; little Eleseus, he thought, no doubt, it was the sun. "Look how he stares all wondering like," said Isak. And now Inger could spin of an evening by lamplight.

He brought up linen for shirts, and new hide shoes for Inger. She had asked for some dye-stuffs, too, for the wool, and he brought them. Then one day he came back with a clock. With what? A clock. This was too much for Inger; she was overwhelmed and could not say a word. Isak hung it up on the wall, and set it at a guess, wound it up, and let it strike. The child turned its eyes at the sound and then looked at its mother. "Aye, you may wonder," said Inger, and took the child to her, not a little touched herself. Of all good things, here in a lonely place, there was nothing could be better than a clock to go all the dark winter through, and strike so prettily at the hours.

When the last load was carted down, Isak turned woodman once more, felling and stacking, building his streets, his town of woodpiles for next winter. He was getting farther and farther from the homestead now, there was a great broad stretch of hillside all ready for tillage. He would not cut close any more, but simply throw the biggest trees with dry tops.

He knew well enough, of course, what Inger had been thinking of when she asked for another bed; best to hurry up and get it ready. One dark evening he came home from the woods, and sure enough, Inger had got it over—another boy—and was lying down. That Inger! Only that very morning she had tried to get him to go down to the village again: " 'Tis time the horse had something to do," says she. "Eating his head off all day."

"I've no time for such-like nonsense," said Isak shortly, and went out. Now he understood; she had wanted to get him out of the way. And why? Surely 'twas as well to have him about the house.

"Why can't you ever tell a man what's coming?" said he.

"You make a bed for yourself and sleep in the little room," said Inger.

As for that, it was not only a bedstead to make; there must be bedclothes to spread. They had but one skin rug, and there would be no getting another till next autumn, when there were wethers to kill—and even then two skins would not make a blanket. Isak had a hard time, with cold at nights, for a while; he tried burying himself in the hay under the rock-shelter, tried to bed down for himself with the cows. Isak was homeless. Well for him that it was May; soon June would be in; July . . .

A wonderful deal they had managed, out there in the wilderness; house for themselves and housing for the cattle, and ground cleared and cultivated, all in three years. Isak was building again—what was he building now? A new shed, a lean-to, jutting out from the house. The whole place rang with the noise as he hammered in his eight-inch nails. Inger came out now and again and said it was trying for the little ones.

"Aye, the little ones—go in and talk to them then, sing a bit. Eleseus, he can have a bucket lid to hammer on himself. And it's only while I'm doing these big nails just here, at the crossbeams, that's got to bear the whole. Only planks after that, two-and-a-half-inch nails, as gentle as building dolls' houses."

Small wonder if Isak hammered and thumped. There stood a barrel of herrings, and the flour, and all kinds of foodstuffs in the stable; better than lying out in the open, maybe, but the pork tasted of it already; a shed they must have, and that was clear. As for the little ones, they'd get used to the noise in no time. Eleseus was inclined to be ailing somehow, but the other took nourishment sturdily, like a fat cherub, and when he wasn't crying he slept. A wonder of a child! Isak made no objection to his being called Sivert, though he himself would rather have preferred Jacob. Inger could hit on the right thing at times. Eleseus was named after the priest of her parish, and that was a fine name to be sure; but Sivert was called after his mother's uncle, the district treasurer, who was a well-to-do man, with neither wife nor child to come after him. They couldn't do better than name the boy after him.

Then came spring, and the new season's work; all was down in the earth before Whitsun. When there had been only Eleseus to look after, Inger could never find time to help her husband, being tied to her first-born; now, with two children in the house, it was different; she helped in the fields and managed a deal of odd work here and there; planting potatoes, sowing carrots and turnips. A wife like that is none so easy to find. And she had her loom besides; at all odd minutes she would slip into the little room and weave a couple of spools, making half-wool stuff for underclothes for the winter. Then when she had dyed her wools, it was red and blue dress material for herself and the little ones; at last she put in several colors, and made a bedspread for Isak all by herself. No fancy work from Inger's loom; useful and necessary things, and sound all through.

Oh, they were doing famously, these settlers in the wilds; they had got on so far, and if this year's crops turned out well they would be enviable folk, no less. What was lacking on the place at all? A hayloft, perhaps; a big barn with a threshing-floor inside—but that might come in time. Aye, it would come, never fear, only give them time. And now pretty Silverhorns had calved, the sheep had lambs, the goats had kids, the young stock fairly swarmed about the place. And what of the little household itself? Eleseus could walk already, walk by himself wherever he pleased, and little Sivert was christened. Inger? By all signs and tokens, making ready for another turn; she was not what you'd call niggardly at bearing. Another child—oh, a mere nothing to Inger! Though, to be sure, she was proud enough of them when they came. Fine little creatures, as anyone could see. 'Twas not all, by a long way, that the Lord had blessed with such fine big children. Inger was young, and making the most of it. She was no beauty, and had suffered all her girlhood by reason of the same, being set aside and looked down on. The young men never noticed her, though she could dance and work as well. They found nothing sweet in her, and turned elsewhere. But now her time had come; she was in full flower and constantly with child. Isak himself, her lord and master, was earnest and stolid as ever, but he had got on well, and was content. How he had managed to live till Inger came was a mystery; feeding, no doubt, on potatoes and goats' milk, or maybe venturesome dishes without a name; now, he had all that a man could think of in his place in the world.

There came another drought, a new bad year. Os-Anders the Lapp, coming by with his dog, brought news that folk in the village had cut their grain already, for fodder.

" 'Tis a poor lookout," said Inger, "when it comes to that."

"Aye. But they've the herring. A fine haul, 'tis said. Your Uncle Sivert, he's going to build a country house."

"Why, he was none so badly off before."

"That's true. And like to be the same with you, for all it seems."

"Why, as to that, thank God, we've enough for our little needs. What do they say at home about me up here?"

Os-Anders wags his head helplessly; there's no end to the great things they say; more than he can tell. A pleasant-spoken fellow, like all the Lapps.

"If as you'd care for a dish of milk now, you've only to say so," says Inger.

" 'Tis more than's worth your while. But if you've a sup for the dog here . . ."

Milk for Os-Anders, and food for the dog. Os-Anders lifts his head suddenly, at a kind of music inside the house.

"What's that?"

" 'Tis only our clock," says Inger. "It strikes the hours that way." Inger bursting with pride.

The Lapp wags his head again: "House and cattle and all manner of things. There's nothing a man could think of but you've that thing."

"Aye, we've much to be thankful for, 'tis true."

"I forgot to say, there's Oline was asking after you."

"Oline? How is it with her?"

"She's none so poorly. Where will your husband be now?"

"He'll be at work in the fields somewhere."

"They say he's not bought yet," says the Lapp carelessly.

"Bought? Who says so?"

"Why, 'tis what they say."

"But who's he to buy from? 'Tis common land."

"Aye, 'tis so."

"And sweat of his brow to every spade of it."

"Why, they say 'tis the State owns all the land."

Inger could make nothing of this. "Aye, maybe so. Was it Oline said so?"

"I don't remember," says the Lapp, and his shifty eyes looked all ways around.

Inger wondered why he did not beg for anything; Os-Anders always begged, as do all the Lapps. Os-Anders sits scraping at the bowl of his clay pipe, and lights up. What a pipe! He puffs and draws at it till his wrinkled old face looks like a wizard's runes.

"No need to ask if the little ones there are yours," says he, flattering again. "They're as like you as could be. The living image of yourself when you were small."

Now Inger was a monster and a deformity to look at; 'twas all wrong, of course, but she swelled with pride for all that. Even a Lapp can gladden a mother's heart.

"If it wasn't that your sack there's so full, I'd find you something to put in it," says Inger.

"Nay, 'tis more than's worth your while."

Inger goes inside with the child on her arm; Eleseus stays outside with the Lapp. The two make friends at once; the child sees something curious in the sack, something soft and fluffy, and wants to pat it. The dog stands alert, barking and whining. Inger comes out with a parcel of food; she gives a cry, and drops down on the door-slab.

"What's that you've got there? What is it?"

" 'Tis nothing. Only a hare."

"I saw it."

" 'Twas the boy wanted to look. Dog ran it down this morning and killed it, and I brought it along. . . ."

"Here's your food," said Inger.

CHAPTER V

ONE bad year never comes alone. Isak had grown patient, and took what fell to his lot. The grain was parched, and the hay was poor, but the potatoes looked like pulling through once more—bad enough, all things together, but not the worst. Isak had still a season's yield of cordwood and timber to sell in the village, and the herring fishery had been rich all round the coast, so there was plenty of money to buy wood. Indeed, it almost looked like a providence that the grain harvest had failed—for how could he have threshed it without a barn and threshing-floor? Call it providence; there's no harm in that sometimes.

There were other things not so easily put out of mind. What was it a certain Lapp had said to Inger that summer —something about not having bought? Buy, what should he buy for? The ground was there, the forest was there; he had cleared and tilled, built up a homestead in the midst of a natural wilderness, winning bread for himself and his, asking nothing of any man, but working, and working alone. He had often thought himself of asking the Lensmand [1] about the matter when he went down to the village, but had always put it off; the Lensmand was not a pleasant man to deal with, so people said, and Isak was not one to talk much. What could he say if he went—what had he come for?

One day that winter the Lensmand himself came driving up to the place. There was a man with him, and a lot of

[1] Sheriff's officer, in charge of a small district.

papers in a bag. Geissler himself, the Lensmand, no less.
He looked at the broad open hillside, cleared of timber,
smooth and unbroken under the snow; he thought perhaps
that it was all tilled land already, for he said:

"Why, this is a whole big farm you've got. You don't
expect to get all this for nothing?"

There it was! Isak was terror-stricken and said not a
word.

"You ought to have come to me at first, and bought the
land," said Geissler.

"Aye."

The Lensmand talked of valuations, of boundaries, taxes,
taxes to the State, and, when he had explained the matter
a little, Isak began to see that there was something reasonable in it after all. The Lensmand turned to his companion
teasingly. "Now then, you call yourself a surveyor, what's
the extent of cultivated ground here?" He did not wait for
the other to reply, but noted down himself, at a guess. Then
he asked Isak about the crops, how much hay, how many
bushels of potatoes. And then about boundaries. They
could not go round the place marking out waist-deep in
snow; and in summer no one could get up there at all.
What did Isak think himself about the extent of woodland
and pasturage? Isak had no idea at all; he had always
thought of the place as being his own as far as he could see.
The Lensmand said that the State required definite boundaries. "And the greater the extent, the more you will have
to pay."

"Aye."

"And they won't give you all you think you can swal-
low; they'll let you have what's reasonable for your needs."

"Aye."

Inger brought in some milk for the visitors; they drank
it, and she brought in some more. The Lensmand a surly
fellow? He stroked Eleseus's hair, and looked at something

the child was playing with. "Playing with stones, what? Let me see. H'm, heavy. Looks like some kind of ore."

"There's plenty such up in the hills," said Isak.

The Lensmand came back to business. "South and west from here's what you want most, I suppose? Shall we say a couple of furlongs to the southward?"

"Two furlongs!" exclaimed his assistant.

"*You* couldn't till two hundred yards," said his chief shortly.

"What will that cost?" asked Isak.

"Can't say. It all depends. But I'll put it as low as I can on my report; it's miles away from anywhere, and difficult to get at."

"But two furlongs!" said the assistant again.

The Lensmand entered duly, two furlongs to the southward, and asked: "What about the hills? How much do you want that way?"

"I'll need all up as far as the water. There's a big water up there," said Isak.

The Lensmand noted that. "And how far north?"

"Why, it's no great matter that way. 'Tis but moorland most, and little timber."

The Lensmand fixed the northward boundary at one furlong. "East?"

"That's no great matter either. 'Tis bare fjeld all from here into Sweden."

The Lensmand noted down again. He made a rapid calculation, and said: "It'll make a good-sized place, even at that. Anywhere near the village, of course, it'd be worth a lot of money; nobody could have bought it. I'll send in a report, and say a hundred daler would be fair. What do you think?" he asked his assistant.

"It's giving it away," said the other.

"A hundred daler?" said Inger. "Isak, you've no call to take so big a place."

"No-o," said Isak.

The assistant put in hurriedly: "That's just what I say. It's miles too big for you as it is. What will you do with it?"

"Cultivate it," said the Lensmand.

He had been sitting there writing and working in his head, with the children crying every now and then; he did not want to have the whole thing to do again. As it was, he would not be home till late that night, perhaps not before morning. He thrust the papers into the bag; the matter was settled.

"Put the horse in," he said to his companion. And turning to Isak: "As a matter of fact, they ought to give you the place for nothing, and pay you into the bargain, the way you've worked. I'll say as much when I send in the report. Then we'll see how much the State will ask for the title-deeds."

Isak—it was hard to say how he felt about it. Half as if he were not ill pleased after all to find his land valued at a big price, after the work he had done. As for the hundred daler, he could manage to pay that off, no doubt, in course of time. He made no further business about it; he could go on working as he had done hitherto, clearing and cultivating, fetching loads of timber from the untended woodlands. Isak was not a man to look about anxiously for what might come; he worked.

Inger thanked the Lensmand, and hoped he would put in a word for them with the State.

"Yes, yes. But I've no say in the matter myself. All I have to do is to say what I have seen, and what I think. How old is the youngest there?"

"Six months as near as can be."

"Boy or girl?"

"Boy."

The Lensmand was no tyrant, but shallow, and not over-conscientious. He ignored his assistant, Brede Olsen, who by virtue of his office should be an expert in such affairs; the matter was settled out of hand, by guesswork. Yet for Isak and his wife it was a serious matter enough—aye, and for who should come after them, maybe for generations. But he set it all down, as it pleased him, making a document of it on the spot. Withal a kindly man; he took a bright coin from his pocket and gave it to little Sivert; then he nodded to the others and went out to the sledge.

Suddenly he asked: "What do you call the place?"

"Call it?"

"Yes. What's its name? We must have a name for it."

No one had ever thought of that before. Inger and Isak looked at each other.

"Sellanraa?" said the Lensmand. He must have invented it out of his own head; maybe it was not a name at all. But he only nodded, and said again: "Sellanraa!" and drove off.

Settled again, at a guess; anything would do. The name, the price, the boundaries . . .

Some weeks later, when Isak was down in the village, he heard rumors of some business about Lensmand Geissler; there had been an inquiry about some moneys he could not account for, and the matter had been reported to his superior. Well, such things did happen; some folk were content to stumble through life anyhow, till they ran up against those that walked.

Then one day Isak went down with a load of wood, and coming back, who should drive with him on his sledge but Lensmand Geissler. He stepped out from the trees, on to the road, waved his hand, and simply said: "Take me along, will you?"

They drove for a while, neither speaking. Once the passenger took a flask from his pocket and drank; offered it to Isak, who declined. "I'm afraid this journey will upset my stomach," said the Lensmand.

He began at once to talk about Isak's deal in land. "I

sent off the report at once, with a strong recommendation on my own account. Sellanraa's a nice name. As a matter of fact, they ought to let you have the place for nothing, wouldn't do to say so, of course. If I had, they'd only have taken offense and put their own price on it. I suggested fifty daler."

"Ho. Fifty, you said? Not a hundred?"

The Lensmand puckered his brow and thought a moment. "As far as I recollect it was fifty. Yes. . . ."

"And where will you be going, now?" asked Isak.

"Over to Vesterbotten, to my wife's people."

" 'Tis none so easy that way at this time of year."

"I'll manage. Couldn't you go with me a bit?"

"Aye; you shan't go alone."

They came to the farm, and the Lensmand stayed the night, sleeping in the little room. In the morning he brought out his flask again, and remarked: "I'm sure this journey's going to upset my stomach." For the rest, he was much the same as last time, kindly, decisive, but fussy, and little concerned about his own affairs. Possibly it might not be so bad after all. Isak ventured to point out that the hillside was not all under cultivation yet, but only some small squares here and there. The Lensmand took the information in a curious fashion. "I knew that well enough, of course, last time I was here, when I made out the report. But Brede, the fellow who was with me, he didn't see it. Brede, he's no earthly good. But they work it out by table. With all the ground as I entered it, and only so few loads of hay, so few bushels of potatoes, they'll say at once that it must be poor soil, cheap soil, you understand. I did my best for you, and you take my word for it, that'll do the trick. It's two-and-thirty thousand fellows of your stamp the country wants."

The Lensmand nodded and turned to Inger. "How old's the youngest?"

"He's just three quarters of a year."

"And a boy, is he?"

"Yes."

"But you must see and get that business settled as soon as ever you can," said he to Isak again. "There's another man wants to purchase now, midway between here and the village, and as soon as he does, this'll be worth more. You buy now, get the place first, and let the price go up after—that way, you'll be getting some return for all the work you've put into it. It was you that started cultivating here at all. 'Twas all wilderness before."

They were grateful for his advice, and asked if it was not he himself that would arrange the matter. He answered that he had done all he could; everything now depended on the State. "I'm going across to Vesterbotten now, and I shan't be coming back," he told them straightforwardly.

He gave Inger an ort, and that was overmuch. "You can take a bit of meat down to my people in the village next time you're killing," said he. "My wife'll pay you. Take a cheese or so, too, any time you can. The children like it."

Isak went with him up over the hills; it was firm, good going on the higher ground, easier than below. Isak received a whole daler.

In that manner was it Lensmand Geissler left the place, and he did not come back. No great loss, folk said, he being looked on as a doubtful personage, an adventurer. Not that he hadn't the knowledge; he was a learned man, and had studied this and that, but he lived too freely, and spent other people's money. It came out later that he had left the place after a sharp reprimand from his superior, Amtmand Pleym; but nothing was done about his family officially, and they went on living there a good while after—his wife and three children. And it was not long before the money unaccounted for was sent from Sweden, so that Geissler's wife and children could not be said to be held as hostages, but stayed on simply because it pleased them.

Isak and Inger had no cause to complain of Geissler's dealings with them, not by a long way. And there was no saying what sort of man his successor would be—perhaps they would have to go over the whole business again!

The Amtmand [1] sent one of his clerks up to the village, to be the new Lensmand. He was a man about forty, son of a local magistrate, by name Heyerdahl. He had lacked the means to go to the university and enter the service that way; instead, he had been constrained to sit in an office, writing at a desk, for fifteen years. He was unmarried, having never been able to afford a wife. His chief, Amtmand Pleym, had inherited him from his predecessor, and paid him the same miserable wage that he had been given before; Heyerdahl took it, and went on writing at his desk as before.

Isak plucked up his courage, and went to see him.

"Documents in the Sellanraa case . . . ? Here they are, just returned from the Department. They want to know all sorts of things—the whole business is in a dreadful muddle, as Geissler left it," said the official. "The Department wishes to be informed as to whether any considerable crop of marketable berries is to be reckoned with on the estate. Whether there is any heavy timber. Whether possibly there may be ores or metals of value in the hills adjoining. Mention is made of water, but nothing stated as to any fishery in the same. This Geissler appears to have furnished certain information, but he's not to be trusted, and here have I to go through the whole affair again after him. I shall have to come up to Sellanraa and make a thorough inspection and valuation. How many miles is it up there? The Department, of course, requires that adequate bound-

[1] Governor of a county.

aries be drawn: yes, we shall have to beat the bounds in due order."

" 'Tis no light business setting up boundaries this time of year," said Isak. "Not till later on in the summer."

"Anyhow, it'll have to be done. The Department can't wait all through the summer for an answer. I'll come up myself as soon as I can get away. I shall have to be out that way in any case, there's another plot of land a man's inquiring about."

"Will that be him that's going to buy up between me and the village?"

"Can't say, I'm sure. Very likely. As a matter of fact, it's a man from the office here, my assistant in the office. He was here in Geissler's time. Asked Geissler about it, I understand, but Geissler put him off; said he couldn't cultivate a hundred yards of land. So he sent in an application to the Amtmand, and I'm instructed to see the matter through. More of Geissler's muddling!"

Lensmand Heyerdahl came up to the farm, and brought with him his assistant, Brede. They had got thoroughly wet crossing the moors, and wetter still they were before they'd finished tramping the boundary lines through melting snow and slush up and down the hills. The Lensmand set to work zealously the first day, but on the second he had had enough, and contented himself with standing still for the most part, pointing and shouting directions. There was no further talk about prospecting for ore in the "adjoining hills," and as for marketable berries—they would have a look at the moors on the way back, he said.

The Department requested information on quite a number of points—there were tables for all sorts of things, no doubt. The only thing that seemed reasonable was the question of timber. Certainly, there was some heavy timber, and that within the limits of Isak's proposed holding, but not enough to reckon with for sale; no more than would be required to keep up the place. Even if there had been timber in plenty, who was to carry it all the many miles to where it could be sold? Only Isak, trundling like a tub-wheel through the forest in wintertime carting some few heavy sticks down to the village, to bring back planks and boards for his building.

Geissler, the incomprehensible, had, it seemed, sent in a report which was not easily upset. Here was his successor going through the whole thing again, trying to find mistakes and blatant inaccuracies—but all in vain. It was noticeable that he consulted his assistant at every turn, and paid heed to what he said, which was not Geissler's way at all. That same assistant, moreover, must presumably have altered his own opinion, since he was now a would-be purchaser himself of lands from the common ground held by the State.

"What about the price?" asked the Lensmand.

"Fifty daler is the most they can fairly ask of any buyer," answered the expert.

Lensmand Heyerdahl drew up his report in elegant phrasing. Geissler had written: "The man will also have to pay land tax every year; he cannot afford to pay more for the place than fifty daler, in annual installments over ten years. The State can accept his offer, or take away his land and the fruits of his work." Heyerdahl wrote: "He now humbly begs to submit this application to the Department: that he be allowed to retain this land, upon which, albeit without right of possession, he has up to this present effected considerable improvements, for a purchase price of 50—fifty—speciedaler, the amount to be paid in annual installments as may seem fit to the Department to apportion the same."

Lensmand Heyerdahl promised Isak to do his best. "I hope to succeed in procuring you possession of the estate," he said.

HE BIG bull is to be sent away. It has grown to an enormous beast, and costs too much to feed; Isak is taking it down to the village, to bring up a suitable yearling in exchange.

It was Inger's idea. And Inger had no doubt her own reasons for getting Isak out of the place on that particular day.

"If you are going at all, you'd better go today," she said. "The bull's in fine condition; 'twill fetch a good price at this time of year. You take him down to the village, and they'll send him to be sold in town—townfolk pay anything for their meat."

"Aye," says Isak.

"If only the beast doesn't make trouble on the way down."

Isak made no answer.

"But he's been out and about now this last week, and getting used to things."

Isak was silent. He took a big knife, hung it in a sheath at his waist, and led out the bull.

A mighty beast it was, glossy-coated and terrible to look at, swaying at the buttocks as it walked. A trifle short in the leg; when it ran it crushed down the undergrowth with its chest; it was like a railway engine. Its neck was huge almost to deformity; there was the strength of an elephant in that neck.

"If only he doesn't get mad with you," said Inger.

Isak thought for a moment. "Why, if as he takes it that way, I'll just have to slaughter him halfway and carry down the meat."

Inger sat down on the door-slab. She was in pain; her face was aflame. She had kept her feet till Isak was gone; now he and the bull were out of sight, and she could give way to a groan without fear. Little Eleseus can talk a little already; he asks: "Mama hurt?"—"Yes, hurt." He mimics her, pressing his hands to his sides and groaning. Little Sivert is asleep.

Inger takes Eleseus inside the house, gives him some things to play with on the floor, and gets into bed herself. Her time was come. She is perfectly conscious all the while, keeps an eye on Eleseus, glances at the clock on the wall to see the time. Never a cry, hardly a movement; the struggle is in her vitals—a burden is loosened and glides from her. Almost at the same moment she hears a strange cry in the bed, a blessed little voice; poor thing, poor little thing . . . and now she cannot rest, but lifts herself up and looks down. What is it? Her face is grey and blank in a moment, without expression or intelligence; a groan is heard; unnatural, impossible—a choking gasp.

She slips back on the bed. A minute passes; she cannot rest, the little cry down there in the bed grows louder, she raises herself once more, and sees—O God, the direst of all! No mercy, no hope—and this a girl!

Isak could not have gone more than a couple of miles or so. It was hardly an hour since he had left. In less than ten minutes Inger had borne her child and killed it.

Isak came back on the third day, leading a half-starved yearling bull. The beast could hardly walk; it had been a long business getting up to the place at all.

"How did you get on?" asked Inger. She herself was ill and miserable enough.

Isak had managed very well. True, the big bull had been mad the last two miles or so, and he had to tie it up and fetch help from the village. Then, when he got back, it had broken loose and took a deal of time to find. But he had managed somehow, and had sold for a good price to a trader in the village, buying up for butchers in the town. "And here's the new one," said Isak. "Let the children come and look."

Any addition to the livestock was a great event. Inger looked at the bull and felt it over, asked what it had cost; little Sivert was allowed to sit on its back. "I shall miss the big one, though," said Inger. "So glossy and fine he was. I do hope they'll kill him nicely."

It was the busy season now, and there was work enough. The animals were let loose; in the empty shed were cases and bins of potatoes left to grow. Isak sowed more grain this year than last, and did all he could to get it nicely down. He made beds for carrots and turnips, and Inger sowed the seeds. All went on as before.

Inger went about for some time with a bag of hay under her dress, to hide any change in her figure, taking out a little from time to time, and finally discarding the bag altogether. At last, one day, Isak noticed something, and asked in surprise:

"Why, how's this? Hasn't anything happened? I thought. . . ."

"No. Not this time."

"Ho. Why, what was wrong?"

" 'Twas meant to be so, I suppose. Isak, how long d'you think it'll take you to work over all this land of ours?"

"Yes, but . . . you mean you had your trouble— didn't go as it should?"

"Aye, that was it—yes."

"But yourself—you're not hurt anyway after it?"

"No. Isak, I've been thinking, we ought to have a pig."

Isak was not quick to change the subject that way. He was silent a little, then at last he said: "Aye, a pig. I've thought of that myself each spring. But we'll need to have more potatoes first, and more of the small, and a bit of grain beside; we've not enough to feed a pig. We'll see how this year turns out."

"But it would be nice to have a pig."

"Aye."

Days pass, rain comes, fields and meadows are looking well—oh, the year will turn out well, never fear! Little happenings and big, all in their turn: food, sleep, and work; Sundays, with washing of faces and combing of hair, and Isak sitting about in a new red shirt of Inger's weaving and sewing. Then an event, a happening of note in the ordinary round: a sheep, roaming with her lamb, gets caught in a cleft among the rocks. The others come home in the evening. Inger at once sees there are two missing, and out goes Isak in search. Isak's first thought is to be thankful it is Sunday, so he is not called away from his work and losing time. He tramps off—there is an endless range of ground to be searched; and meanwhile the house is all anxiety. Mother hushes the children with brief words; there are two sheep missing, and they must be good. All share the feeling; what has happened is a matter for the whole little community. Even the cows know that something unusual is going on, and give tongue in their own fashion, for Inger goes out every now and then, calling aloud towards the woods, though it is near night. It is an event in the wilderness, a general misfortune. Now and again she gives a long-drawn hail to Isak, but there is no answer; he must be out of hearing.

Where are the sheep—what can have come to them? Is there a bear abroad? Or have the wolves come down over the hills from Sweden and Finland? Neither, as it turns out. Isak finds the ewe stuck fast in a cleft of rock, with a broken leg and lacerated udder. It must have been there some time, for despite its wounds, the poor thing has nibbled the grass down to the roots as far as it could reach. Isak lifts the sheep and sets it free; it falls to grazing at once. The lamb makes for its mother and sucks away—a blessed relief for the wounded udder to be emptied now.

Isak gathers stones and fills up the dangerous cleft; a wicked place; it shall break no more sheep's thighs! Isak wears leather braces; he takes them off now and fastens them round the sheep's middle, as a support for the udder. Then, lifting the animal on his shoulders, he sets off home, the lamb at his heels.

After that—splints and tar bandages. In a few days' time the patient begins twitching the foot of the wounded leg; it is the fracture aching as it grows together. Aye, all things getting well again—until next time something happens.

The daily round; little matters that are all important to the settler-folk themselves. Oh, they are not trifles after all, but things of fate, making for their happiness and comfort and well-being, or against them.

In the slack time between the seasons, Isak smooths down some new tree-trunks he has thrown; to be used for something or other, no doubt. Also he digs out a number of useful stones and gets them down to the house; as soon as there are stones enough, he builds a wall of them. A year or so back, Inger would have been curious, wondering what her man was after with all this—now, she seemed for the most part busied with her own work, and asked no questions. Inger is busy as ever, but she has taken to singing, which is something new, and she is teaching Eleseus an evening prayer; this also is something new. Isak misses her questioning; it was her curiosity and her praise of all he did that made him the contented man, the incomparable man he was. But now she goes by, saying nothing, or at most with a word or so that he is working himself to death. "She's troubled after that last time, for all she says," thinks Isak to himself.

Oline comes over to visit them once more. If all had been as before she would have been welcome, but now it is different. Inger greets her from the first with some ill will; be it what it may, there is something that makes Inger look on her as an enemy.

"I'd half a thought I'd be coming just at the right time again," says Oline, with delicate meaning.

"How d'you mean?"

"Why for the third one to be christened. How is it with you now?"

"Nay," says Inger. "For that matter you might have saved yourself the trouble."

"Ho."

Oline falls to praising the children, so fine and big they've grown; and Isak taking over more ground, and going to build again, by the look of things—there's no end to things with them; a wonderful place, and hard to find its like. "And what is he going to build this time?"

"Ask him yourself," says Inger. "I don't know."

"Nay," says Oline. " 'Tis no business of mine. I just looked along to see how things were with you here; it's a pleasure and delight for me to see. As for Goldenhorns, I'll not ask nor speak of her—she's fallen into proper ways, as anyone can see."

They talk for a while companionably; Inger is no longer harsh. The clock on the wall strikes with its sweet little note. Oline looks up with tears in her eyes; never in all her humble life did she hear such a thing—'tis like church and organ music, says Oline. Inger feels herself rich and generous-minded towards her poor relation, and says: "Come into the next room and see my loom."

Oline stays all day. She talks to Isak, and praises all his

doings. "And I hear you've bought up the land for miles on every side. Couldn't you have got it for nothing, then? There's none as I can see would take it from you."

Isak had been feeling the need of praise, and is the better for it now. Feels a man again. "I'm buying from the Government," says Isak.

"Aye, Government. But they've no call to be grasping in a deal, surely? What are you building now?"

"Why, I don't know. Nothing much, anyway."

"Aye, you're getting on; building and getting on you are. Painted doors to the house, and a clock on the wall—'tis a new grand house you're building, I suspect."

"You, with your foolish talk . . ." says Isak. But he is pleased all the same, and says to Inger: "Couldn't you make a bit of a dish of nice cream custard for one that comes a-visiting?"

"That I can't," says Inger, "for I've churned all there was."

" 'Tis no foolish talk," puts in Oline hurriedly; "I'm but a simple woman asking to know. And if it's not a new grand house, why, 'twill be a new big barn, I dare say; and why not? With all these fields and meadow lands, fine and full of growth; aye, and full of milk and honey, as the Bible says."

Isak asks: "How's things looking your way—crops and the like?"

"Why, 'tis there as it is till now. If only the Lord don't set fire to it all again this year, and burn up the lot— Heaven forgive me I should say the word. 'Tis all in His hand and almighty power. But we've nothing our parts that's any way like this place of yours to compare, and that's the solemn truth."

Inger asks after other relatives, her Uncle Sivert in particular. He is the great man of the family, and owns rich fisheries; 'tis almost a wonder how he can find a way to spend all he has. The women talk of Uncle Sivert, and Isak and his doings somehow drop out of sight; no one asks any more about his building now, so at last he says:

"Well, if you want to know, 'tis a bit of a barn with a threshing-floor I'm trying to get set up."

"Just as I thought," says Oline. "Folk with real sound sense in their heads, they do that way. Forethought and back-thought and all as it should be. There's not a pot nor pitcher in the place you haven't thought of. A threshing-floor, you said?"

Isak is a child. Oline's flattering words go to his head, and he answers something foolishly with fine words: "As to that new house of mine, there must be a threshing-floor in the same, necessarily. 'Tis my intention so."

"A threshing-floor?" says Oline, wagging her head.

"And where's the sense of growing grain on the place if we've nowhere to thresh it?"

"Aye, 'tis as I say, not a thing as could be but you have it all there in your head."

Inger is suddenly out of humor again. The talk between the other two somehow displeases her, and she breaks in:

"Cream custard indeed! And where's the cream to come from? Fish it up in the river, maybe?"

Oline hastens to make peace. "Inger, Lord bless you, child, don't speak of such a thing. Not a word of cream nor custard either—an old creature like me that does but idle about from house to neighbor . . . !"

Isak sits for a while, then up, and saying suddenly: "Here am I doing nothing middle of the day, and stones to fetch and carry for that wall of mine!"

"Aye, a wall like that'll need a mighty lot of stone, to be sure."

"Stone?" says Isak. " 'Tis like as if there'd never be enough."

When Isak is gone, the two womenfolk get on nicely together for a while; they sit for hours talking of this and
that. In the evening, Oline must go out and see how their
livestock has grown: cows, a bull, two calves, and a swarm
of sheep and goats. "I don't know where it'll ever end,"
says Oline, with her eyes turned heavenwards.

And Oline stays the night.

Next morning she goes off again. Once more she has a
bundle of something with her. Isak is working in the quarry,
and she goes another way round, so that he shall not see.

Two hours later, Oline comes back again, steps into the
house, and asks at once: "Where is Isak?"

Inger is washing up. Oline should have passed by the
quarry where Isak was at work, and the children with him;
Inger at once guesses something wrong.

"Isak? What d'you want with him?"

"Want with him? Why, nothing. Only I didn't see him
to say good-bye."

Silence. Oline sits down on a bench without being asked,
drops down as if her legs refuse to carry her. Her manner
is intended to show that something serious is the matter;
she is overcome.

Inger can control herself no longer. Her face is all terror
and fury as she says:

"I saw what you sent me by Os-Anders. Aye, 'twas a
nice thing to send!"

"Why . . . what . . . ?"

"That hare."

"What do you mean?" asks Oline in a strangely gentle
voice.

"Ah, don't deny it!" cries Inger, her eyes wild. "I'll
break your face in with this ladle here—see that!"

Struck her? Aye, she did so. Oline took the first blow
without falling, and only cried out: "Mind what you're do-

ing, woman! I know what I know about you and your do-ings!" Inger strikes again, gets Oline down to the floor, falls on her there, and thrusts her knees into her.

"D'you mean to murder me?" asks Oline. The terrible woman with the harelip was kneeling on her, a great strong creature armed with a huge wooden ladle, heavy as a club. Oline was bruised already, and bleeding, but still sullenly refusing to cry out. "So you're trying to murder me *too*!"

"Aye, kill you," says Inger, striking again. "There! I'll see you dead before I've done with you." She was certain of it now. Oline knew her secret; nothing mattered now. "I'll spoil your beastly face."

"Beastly face?" gasps Oline. "Huh! Look to your own. With the Lord His mark on it!"

Oline is hard, and will not give in; Inger is forced to give over the blows that are exhausting her own strength. But she threatens still—glares into the other's eyes and swears she has not finished with her yet. "There's more to come, aye, more, more. Wait till I get a knife. I'll show you!"

She gets on her feet again, and moves as if to look for a knife, a table knife. But now her fury is past its worst, and she falls back on curses and abuse. Oline heaves herself up to the bench again, her face all blue and yellow, swollen and bleeding; she wipes the hair from her forehead, straightens her kerchief, and spits; her mouth too is bruised and swollen. "You devil!" she says.

"You've been nosing about in the woods!" cries Inger. "That's what you've been doing. You've found that little bit of a grave there. Better if you'd dug one for yourself the same time."

"Aye, you wait," says Oline, her eyes glowing revenge-fully. "I'll say no more—but you wait—there'll be no fine two-roomed house for you, with musical clocks and all."

"You can't take it from me, anyway!"

"Aye, you wait. You'll see what Oline can do."

And so they keep on. Oline does not curse, and hardly raises her voice; there is something almost gentle in her cold cruelty, but she is bitterly dangerous. "Where's that bundle? I left it in the woods. But you shall have it back—I'll not own your wool."

"Ho, you think I've stolen it, maybe."

"Ah, you know best what you've done."

So back and forth again about the wool. Inger offers to show the very sheep it was cut from. Oline asks quietly, smoothly: "Aye, but who knows where you got the first sheep to start with?"

Inger names the place and people where her first sheep were out to keep with their lambs. "And you mind and care and look to what you're saying," says she threateningly. "Guard your mouth, or you'll be sorry."

"Ha ha ha!" laughs Oline softly. Oline is never at a loss, never to be silenced. "My mouth, eh? And what of your own, my dear?" She points to Inger's harelip, calling her a ghastly sight for God and man.

Inger answers furiously, and Oline being fat, she calls her a lump of blubber—"a lump of dog's blubber like you. You sent me a hare—I'll pay you for that."

"Hare again?" says Oline. "If I'd no more guilt in anything than I have about that hare. What was it like?"

"What was it like? Why, what's a hare always like?"

"Like you. The very image."

"Out with you—get out!" shrieks Inger. " 'Twas you sent Os-Anders with that hare. I'll have you punished; I'll have you put in prison for that."

"Prison—was it prison you said?"

"Oh, you're jealous and envious of all you see; you hate me for all the good things I've got," says Inger again. "You've lain awake with envy since I got Isak and all that's here. Heavens, woman, what have I ever done to you? Is it my fault that your children never got on in the world, and turned out badly, every one of them? You can't bear the sight of mine, because they're fine and strong, and better named than yours. Is it my fault they're prettier flesh and blood than yours ever were?"

If there was one thing could drive Oline to fury it was this. She had been a mother many times, and all she had was her children, such as they were; she made much of them, and boasted of them, told of great things they had never really done, and hid their faults.

"What's that you're saying?" answered Oline. "Oh that you don't sink in your grave for shame! My children! They were a bright host of angels compared with yours. You dare to speak of my children? Seven blessed gifts of God they were from they were little, and all grown up now every one. You dare to speak . . ."

"What about Lise, that was sent to prison?" asks Inger.

"For never a thing. She was as innocent as a flower," answers Oline. "And she's in Bergen now; lives in a town and wears a hat—but what about you?"

"What about Nils—what did they say of him?"

"Oh, I'll not lower myself. . . . But there's one of yours now lying buried out there in the woods—what did you do to it, eh?"

"Now . . . ! One-two-three—out you go!" shrieks Inger again, and makes a rush at Oline.

But Oline does not move, does not even rise to her feet. Her stolid indifference paralyzes Inger, who draws back, muttering: "Wait till I get that knife."

"Don't trouble," says Oline. "I'm going. But as for you, turning your own kin out of doors one-two-three . . . Nay, I'll say no more."

"Get out of this, that's all you need to do!"

But Oline is not gone yet. The two of them fall to again with words and abuse, a long bout of it again, and when the clock strikes half of the hour, Oline laughs scornfully,

making Inger wilder than ever. At last both calm down a
little, and Oline makes ready to go. "I've a long road before
me," says she, "and it's late enough to be starting. It
wouldn't ha' been amiss to have had a bite with me on the
way. . . ."

Inger makes no answer. She has come to her senses
again now, and pours out water in a basin for Oline to
wash. "There—if you want to tidy yourself," she says.
Oline too thinks it as well to make herself as decent as may
be, but cannot see where the blood is, and washes the
wrong places. Inger looks on for a while, and then points
with her finger.

"There—wash there too, over your eye. No, not that,
the other one; can't you see where I'm pointing?"

"How can I see which one you're pointing at?" answers
Oline.

"And there's more there, by your mouth. Are you afraid
of water? It won't bite you!"

In the end Inger washes the patient herself, and throws
her a towel.

"What I was going to say," says Oline, wiping herself,
and quite peaceable now. "About Isak and the children—
how will they get over this?"

"Does he know?" asks Inger.

"Know? He came and saw it."

"What did he say?"

"What could he say? He was speechless, same as me."
Silence.

"It's all your fault," wails Inger, beginning to cry.

"My fault? I wish I may never have more to answer
for!"

"I'll ask Os-Anders, anyhow, be sure of that."

"Aye, do."

They talk it all over quietly, and Oline seems less re-
vengeful now. An able politician, is Oline, and quick to

find expedients; she speaks now as if in sympathy—what a terrible thing it will be for Isak and the children when it is found out!

"Yes," says Inger, crying again. "I've thought and thought of that night and day." Oline thinks she might be able to help, and be a savior to them in distress. She could come and stay on the place to look after things, while Inger is in prison.

Inger stops crying; stops suddenly as if to listen and take thought. "No, you don't care for the children."

"Don't care for them, don't I? How could you say such a thing?"

"Ah, I know. . . ."

"Why, if there's one thing in the world I do feel and care for, 'tis children."

"Aye, for your own," says Inger. "But how would you be with mine? And when I think how you sent that hare for nothing else but to ruin me altogether—oh, you're no better than a heap of wickedness!"

"Am I?" says Oline. "Is it me you mean?"

"Yes, 'tis you I mean," says Inger, crying; "you've been a wicked wretch, you have, and I'll not trust you. And you'd steal all the wool, too, if you did come. And all the cheeses that'd go to your people instead of mine. . . ."

"Oh you wicked creature to think of such a thing!" answers Oline.

Inger cries, and wipes her eyes, saying a word or so between. Oline does not try to force her. If Inger does not care about the idea, 'tis all the same to her. She can go and stay with her son Nils, as she has always done. But now that Inger is to be sent away to prison, it will be a hard time for Isak and the innocent children; Oline could stay on the place and give an eye to things. "You can think it over," says Oline.

Inger has lost the day. She cries and shakes her head and

looks down. She goes out as if walking in her sleep, and makes up a parcel of food for Oline to take with her. " 'Tis more than's worth your while," says Oline.

"You can't go all that way without a bite to eat," says Inger.

When Oline has gone, Inger steals out, looks round, and listens. No, no sound from the quarry. She goes nearer, and hears the children playing with little stones. Isak is sitting down, holding the crowbar between his knees, and resting on it like a staff. There he sits.

Inger steals away into the edge of the wood. There was a spot where she had set a little cross in the ground; the cross is thrown down now, and where it stood the turf has been lifted, and the ground turned over. She stoops down and pats the earth together again with her hands. And there she sits.

She had come out of curiosity, to see how far the little grave had been disturbed by Oline; she stays there now because the cattle have not yet come in for the night. Sits there crying, shaking her head, and looking down.

CHAPTER VII

AND the days pass.

A blessed time for the soil, with sun and showers of rain; the crops are looking well. The haymaking is nearly over now, and they have got in a grand lot of hay; almost more than they can find room for. Some is stowed away under overhanging rocks, in the stable, under the flooring of the house itself; the shed at the side is emptied of everything to make room for more hay. Inger herself works early and late, a faithful helper and support. Isak takes advantage of every fall of rain to put in a spell of roofing on the new barn, and get the south wall at least fully done; once that is ready, they can stuff in as much hay as they please. The work is going forward; they will manage, never fear!

And their great sorrow and disaster—aye, it was there, the thing was done, and what it brought must come. Good things mostly leave no trace, but something always comes of evil. Isak took the matter sensibly from the first. He made no great words about it, but asked his wife simply: "How did you come to do it?" Inger made no answer to that. And a little after, he spoke again: "Strangled it—was that what you did?"

"Yes," said Inger.

"You shouldn't have done that."

"No," she agreed.

"And I can't make out how you ever could bring yourself to do it."

"She was all the same as myself," said Inger.

"How d'you mean?"

"Her mouth."

Isak thought over that for some time. "Aye, well," said he.

And nothing more was said about it at the time; the days went on, peacefully as ever; there was all the mass of hay to be got in, and a rare heavy crop all round, so that by degrees the thing slipped into the background of their minds. But it hung over them, and over the place, none the less. They could not hope that Oline would keep the secret; it was too much to expect. And even if Oline said nothing, others would speak; dumb witnesses would find a tongue; the walls of the house, the trees around the little grave in the wood. Os-Anders the Lapp would throw out hints; Inger herself would betray it, sleeping or waking. They were prepared for the worst.

Isak took the matter sensibly—what else was there to do? He knew now why Inger had always taken care to be left alone at every birth; to be alone with her fears of how the child might be, and face the danger with no one by. Three times she had done the same thing. Isak shook his head, touched with pity for her ill fate—poor Inger. He learned of the coming of the Lapp with the hare, and acquitted her. It led to a great love between them, a wild love; they drew closer to each other in their peril. Inger was full of a desperate sweetness towards him, and the great heavy fellow, lumbering carrier of burdens, felt a greed and an endless desire for her in himself. And Inger, for all that she wore hide shoes like a Lapp, was no withered little creature as the Lapland women are, but splendidly big. It was summer now, and she went about barefooted, with her naked legs showing almost to the knee—Isak could not keep his eyes from those bare legs.

All through the summer she went about singing bits of hymns, and she taught Eleseus to say prayers; but there grew up in her an un-Christian hate of all Lapps, and she spoke plainly enough to any that passed. Someone might have sent them again; like as not they had a hare in their bag as before; let them go on their way, and no more about it.

"A hare? What hare?"

"Ho, you haven't heard perhaps what Os-Anders he did that time?"

"No."

"Well, I don't care who knows it—he came up here with a hare, when I was with child."

"Dear, and that was a dreadful thing! And what happened?"

"Never you mind what happened, just get along with you, that's all. Here's a bite of food, and get along."

"You don't happen to have an odd bit of leather anywhere, I could mend my shoe with?"

"No! But I'll give you a bit of stick if you don't get out!"

Now a Lapp will beg as humbly as could be, but say no to him, and he turns bad, and threatens. A pair of Lapps with two children came past the place; the children were sent up to the house to beg, and came back and said there was no one to be seen about the place. The four of them stood there a while talking in their own tongue, then the man went up to see. He went inside, and stayed. Then his wife went up, and the children after; all of them stood inside the doorway, talking Lapp. The man puts his head in the doorway and peeps through into the room; no one there either. The clock strikes the hour, and the whole family stand listening in wonder.

Inger must have had some idea there were strangers about; she comes hurrying down the hillside, and seeing Lapps, strange Lapps into the bargain, asks them straight out what they are doing there. "What do you want in here? Couldn't you see there was no one at home?"

"H'm . . ." says the man.

"Get out with you," says Inger again, "and go on your way."

The Lapps move out slowly, unwillingly. "We were just listening to that clock of yours," says the man; " 'tis a wonder to hear, that it is."

"You haven't a bit of bread to spare?" says his wife.

"Where do you come from?" asks Inger.

"From the water over beyond. We've been walking all night."

"And where are you going to now?"

"Across the hills."

Inger makes up some food for them; when she comes out with it, the woman starts begging again: a bit of stuff for a cap, a tuft of wool, a stump of cheese—anything. Inger has no time to waste, Isak and the children are in the hayfield. "Be off with you now," she says.

The woman tries flattery. "We saw your place up here, and the cattle—a host of them, like the stars in the sky."

"Aye, a wonder," says the man. "You haven't a pair of old shoes to give away to needy folk?"

Inger shuts the door of the house and goes back to her work on the hillside. The man called after her—she pretended not to hear, and walked on unheeding. But she heard it well enough: "You don't want to buy any hares, maybe?"

There was no mistaking what he had said. The Lapp himself might have spoken innocently enough; someone had told him, perhaps. Or he might have meant it ill. Be that as it may, Inger took it as a warning—a message of what was to come. . . .

The days went on. The settlers were healthy folk; what was to come would come; they went about their work and waited. They lived close to each other like beasts of the forest; they slept and ate; already the year was so far advanced that they had tried the new potatoes, and found them large and floury. The blow that was to fall—why did it not come? It was late in August already, soon it would be September; were they to be spared through the winter? They lived in a constant watchfulness; every night they crept close together in their cave, thankful that the day had passed without event. And so the time went on until one day in October, when the Lensmand came up with a man and a bag. The Law stepped in through their doorway.

The investigation took some time. Inger was called up and examined privately; she denied nothing. The grave in the wood was opened, and its contents removed, the body being sent for examination. The little body—it was dressed in Eleseus's christening-robe, and a cap sewn over with beads.

Isak seemed to find speech again. "Aye," said he, "it's as bad as well can be with us now. I've said before—you ought never to have done it."

"No," said Inger.

"How did you do it?"

Inger made no answer.

"That you could find it in your heart . . ."

"She was just the same as myself to look at. And so I took and twisted her face round."

Isak shook his head slowly.

"And then she was dead," went on Inger, beginning to cry.

Isak was silent for a while. "Well, well, 'tis too late to be crying over it now," said he.

"She had brown hair," sobbed Inger, "there at the back of her head. . . ."

And again no more was said.

Time went on as before. Inger was not locked up; the Law was merciful. Lensmand Heyerdahl asked her questions just as he might have spoken to anyone, and only said: "It's a great pity such things should happen at all." Inger asked who had informed against her, but the Lensmand answered that it was no one in particular; many had spoken of the matter, and he had heard of it from several quarters. Had she not herself said something about it to some Lapps?

Inger—aye, she had told some Lapps about Os-Anders, how he came and brought a hare that summer, and gave her unborn child the harelip. And wasn't it Oline who had sent the hare?—The Lensmand knew nothing about that. But in any case, he could not think of putting down such ignorant superstition in his report.

"But my mother saw a hare just before I was born," said Inger. . . .

The barn was finished; a great big place it was, with hay-stalls on both sides and a threshing-floor in the middle. The shed and the other makeshift places were emptied now, and all the hay brought into the barn; the grain was reaped, dried in stacks, and carted in. Inger took up the carrots and turnips. All their crops were in now. And everything might have been well with them—they had all they needed. Isak had started on new ground again, before the frost came, to make a bigger grainfield; Isak was a tiller of the soil. But in November Inger said one day: "She would have been six months old now, and known us all."

" 'Tis no good talking of that now," said Isak.

When the winter came, Isak threshed his grain on the new threshing-floor, and Inger helped him often, with an arm as quick to the work as his own, while the children played in the hay-stalls at the side. It was fine plump grain. Early in the new year the roads were good, and Isak started carting down his loads of wood to the village; he had his regular customers now, and the summer-dried wood fetched a good price. One day he and Inger agreed that they should take the fine bull-calf from Goldenhorns and drive it down to Fru Geissler, with a cheese into the bargain. She was delighted, and asked how much it cost.

"Nothing," said Isak. "The Lensmand paid for it before."

"Heaven bless him, and did he?" said Fru Geissler, touched at the thought. She sent things up for Eleseus and Sivert in return—cakes and picturebooks and toys. When Isak came back and Inger saw the things, she turned away and cried.

"What is it?" asked Isak.

"Nothing," answered Inger. "Only—she'd have been just a year now, and able to see it all."

"Aye, but you know how it was with her," said Isak, for comfort's sake. "And after all, it may be we'll get off easier than we thought. I've found out where Geissler is now."

Inger looked up. "But how's that going to help us?"

"I don't know. . . ."

Then Isak carried his grain to the mill and had it ground, and brought back flour. Then he turned woodman again, cutting the wood to be ready for next winter. His life was spent in this work and that, according to the season; from the fields to the woods, and back to the fields again. He had worked on the place for six years now, and Inger five; all might have been well, if it were only allowed to last. But it was not. Inger worked at her loom and tended the animals; also, she was often to be heard singing hymns, but it was a pitiful singing; she was like a bell without a tongue.

As soon as the roads were passable, she was sent for down to the village to be examined. Isak had to stay behind. And being there all alone, it came into his mind to go across to Sweden and find out Geissler; the former Lensmand had been kind to them, and might perhaps still lend a helping hand some way to the folks at Sellanraa. But when Inger returned, she had asked about things herself, and learned something of what her sentence was likely to be. Strictly speaking, it was imprisonment for life, Paragraph 1. But . . . after all, she had stood up in the court itself and simply confessed. The two witnesses from the village had looked pityingly at her, and the judge had put his questions kindly; but for all that, she was no match for the bright intellects of the law. Lawyers are great men to simple folk; they can quote paragraph this and section that; they have learned such things by rote, ready to bring out at any moment. Oh, they are great men indeed. And apart from all this knowledge, they are not always devoid of sense; sometimes even not altogether heartless. Inger had no cause to complain of the court; she made no mention of the hare, but when she tearfully explained that she could not be so cruel to her poor deformed child as to let it live, the magistrate nodded, quietly and seriously.

"But," said he, "think of yourself; you have a harelip, and it has not spoilt your life."

"No, thanks be to God," was all she said. She could not tell them of all she had suffered in secret as a child, as a young girl.

But the magistrate must have understood something of what it meant; he himself had a clubfoot, and could not dance. "As to the sentence," he said, "I hardly know. Really, it should be imprisonment for life, but . . . I can't say, perhaps we might get it commuted, second or third degree, fifteen to twelve years, or twelve to nine. There's a commission sitting to reform the criminal code, make it more humane, but the final decision won't be ready yet. Anyhow, we must hope for the best," said he.

Inger came back in a state of dull resignation; they had not found it necessary to keep her in confinement meantime. Two months passed; then one evening, when Isak came back from fishing, the Lensmand and his new assistant had been to Sellanraa. Inger was cheerful and welcomed her husband kindly, praising his catch, though it was little he had brought home.

"What I was going to say—has anyone been here?" he asked.

"Anyone been? Why, who should there be?"

"There's fresh footmarks outside. Men with boots on."

"Why—there's been no one but the Lensmand and one other."

"What did they want?"

"You know that without asking."

"Did they come to fetch you?"

"Fetch me? No, 'twas only about the sentence. The Lord is kind, 'tis not so bad as I feared."

"Ah," said Isak eagerly. "Not so long, maybe?"

"No. Only a few years."

"How many years?"

"Why, you might think it a lot, maybe. But I'm thankful to God all the same."

Inger did not say how long it would be. Later that evening Isak asked when they would be coming to fetch her away, but this she could not or would not tell. She had grown thoughtful again, and talked of what was to come; how they would manage she could not think—but she supposed they would have to get Oline to come. And Isak had no better plan to offer.

What had become of Oline, by the way? She had not been up this year as she used to do. Was she going to stay away forever, now that she had upset everything for them? The working-season passed, but Oline did not come—did she expect them to go and fetch her? She would come loitering up of herself, no doubt, the great lump of blubber, the monster.

And at last one day she did. Extraordinary person—it was as nothing whatever had occurred to make ill-feeling between them; she was even knitting a pair of new stockings for Eleseus, she said.

"Just came up to see how you were getting on over here," said she. And it turned out that she had brought her clothes and things up in a sack, and left in the woods close by, ready to stay.

That evening Inger took her husband aside and said: "Didn't you say something about seeking out Geissler? 'Tis in the slack time now."

"Aye," said Isak. "Now that Oline is come, I can go off tomorrow morning, first thing."

Inger was grateful, and thanked him. "And take your money with you," she said "—all you have in the place."

"Why, can't you keep the money here?"

"No," said she.

Inger made up a big parcel of food at once, and Isak woke while it was yet night, and got ready to start. Inger went out on the door-slab to see him off; she did not cry or complain, but only said:

"They may be coming for me now any day."

"You don't know when?"

"No, I can't say. And I don't suppose it will be just yet, but anyhow . . . If only you could get hold of Geissler, perhaps he might be able to say something."

What could Geissler do to help them now? Nothing. But Isak went.

Inger—oh, she knew, no doubt, more than she had been willing to say. It might be, too, that she herself had sent for Oline. When Isak came from Sweden, Inger was gone and Oline was there with the two children.

It was dark news for a homecoming. Isak's voice was louder than usual as he asked: "Is she gone?"

"Aye," said Oline.

"What day was it?"

"The day after you left." And Isak knew now that Inger

had got him out of the way on purpose—that was why she had persuaded him to take the money with him. Oh, but she might have kept a little for herself, for that long journey!

But the children could think of nothing else but the little pig Isak had brought with him. It was all he had for his trouble; the address he had was out of date, and Geissler was no longer in Sweden, but had returned to Norway and was now in Trondhjem. As for the pig, Isak had carried it in his arms all the way, feeding it with milk from a bottle, and sleeping with it on his breast among the hills. He had been looking forward to Inger's delight when she saw it; now Eleseus and Sivert played with it, and it was a joy to them. And Isak, watching them, forgot his trouble for the moment. Moreover, Oline had a message from the Lensmand; the State had at last given its decision in the matter of the land at Sellanraa. Isak had only to go down to the office and pay the amount. This was good news, and served to keep him from the worst depth of despair. Tired and worn out as he was, he packed up some food in a bag and set off for the village at once. Maybe he had some little hope of seeing Inger once again before she left there.

But he was disappointed. Inger was gone—for eight years. Isak felt himself in a mist of darkness and emptiness; heard only a word here and there of all the Lensmand said —a pity such things should happen . . . hoped it might be a lesson to her . . . reform and be a better woman after, and not kill her children any more!

Lensmand Heyerdahl had married the year before. His wife had no intention of ever being a mother—no children for her, thank you! And she had none.

"And now," said the Lensmand, "this business about Sellanraa. At last I am in a position to settle it definitely. The Department is graciously pleased to approve the sale of the land, more or less according to the terms I suggested."

"H'm," said Isak.

"It has been a lengthy business, but I have the satisfaction of knowing that my endeavors have not been altogether fruitless. The terms I proposed have been agreed to almost without exception."

"Without exception," said Isak, and nodded.

"Here are the title-deeds. You can have the transfer registered at the first session."

"Aye," said Isak. "And how much is there to pay?"

"Ten daler a year. The Department has made a slight alteration here—ten daler per annum instead of five. You have no objection to that, I presume?"

"As long as I can manage to pay . . ." said Isak.

"And for ten years." Isak looked up, half frightened.

"Those are the terms—the Department insists. Even then, it's no price really for all that land, cleared and cultivated as it is now."

Isak had the ten daler for that year—it was the money he had got for his loads of wood, and for the cheeses Inger had laid by. He paid the amount, and had still a small sum left.

"It's a lucky thing for you the Department didn't get to hear about your wife," said the Lensmand. "Or they might have sold to someone else."

"Aye," said Isak. He asked about Inger. "Is it true that she's gone away for eight years?"

"That is so. And can't be altered—the law must take its course. As a matter of fact, the sentence is extraordinarily light. There's one thing you must do now—that is, to set up clear boundaries between your land and the State's. A straight, direct line, following the marks I set up on the spot, and entered in my register at the time. The timber cleared from the boundary line becomes your property. I will come up sometime and have a look at what you have done."

Isak trudged back to his home.

TIME flies? Aye, when a man is growing old. Isak was not old, he had not lost his vigor; the years seemed long to him. He worked on his land, and let his iron beard grow as it would.

Now and again the monotony of the wilderness was broken by the sight of a passing Lapp, or by something happening to one of the animals on the place, then all would be as before. Once there came a number of men at once; they rested at Sellanraa, and had some food and a dish of milk; they asked Isak and Oline about the path across the hills; they were marking out the telegraph line, they said. And once came Geissler—Geissler himself, and no other. There he came, free and easy as ever, walking up from the village, two men with him, carrying mining tools, pick and spade.

Oh, that Geissler! Unchanged, the same as ever; meeting and greeting as if nothing had happened, talked to the children, went into the house and came out again, looked over the ground, opened the doors of cowshed and hayloft and looked in. "Excellent!" said he. "Isak, have you still got those bits of stone?"

"Bits of stone?" said Isak, wondering.

"Little heavy lumps of stone I saw the boy playing with when I was here once before."

The stones were out in the larder, serving as weights for so many mousetraps; Isak brought them in. Geissler and the two men examined them, talking together, tapped them here and there, weighed them in the hand. "Copper," they said.

"Could you go up with us and show where you found them?" asked Geissler.

They all went up together; it was not far to the place where Isak had found the stones, but they stayed up in the hills for a couple of days, looking for veins of metal, and firing charges here and there. They came down to Sellanraa with two bags filled with heavy lumps of stone.

Isak had meanwhile had a talk with Geissler, and told him everything as to his own position: about the purchase of the land, which had come to a hundred daler instead of fifty.

"That's a trifle," said Geissler easily. "You've thousands, like as not, on your part of the hills."

"Ho!" said Isak.

"But you'd better get those title-deeds entered in the register as soon as ever you can."

"Aye."

"Then the State can't come any nonsense about it after, you understand."

Isak understood. " 'Tis worst about Inger," he said.

"Aye," said Geissler, and remained thoughtful longer than was usual with him. "Might get the case brought up again. Set out the whole thing properly; very likely get the sentence reduced a bit. Or we could put in an application for a pardon, and that would probably come to the same thing in the end."

"Why, if as that could be done . . ."

"But it wouldn't do to try for a pardon at once. Have to wait a bit. What was I going to say . . . you've been taking things down to my wife—meat and cheese and things—what?"

"Why, as to that, Lensmand paid for all that before."

"Did I, though?"

"And helped us kindly in many a way."

"Not a bit of it," said Geissler shortly. "Here—take this." And he took out some daler notes.

Geissler was not the man to take things for nothing, that was plain. And he seemed to have plenty of money about him, from the way his pocket bulged. Heaven only knew if he really had money or not.

"But she writes all's well and getting on," said Isak, coming back to his one thought.

"What? Oh, your wife!"

"Aye. And since the girl was born—she's had a girl-child, born while she was there. A fine little one."

"Excellent!"

"Aye, and now they're all as kind as can be, and help her every way, she says."

"Look here," said Geissler, "I'm going to send these bits of stone in to some mining experts, and find out what's in them. If there's a decent percentage of copper, you'll be a rich man."

"H'm," said Isak. "And how long do you think before we could apply for a pardon?"

"Well, not so very long, perhaps. I'll write the thing for you. I'll be back here again soon. What was it you said—your wife has had a child since she left here?"

"Yes."

"Then they took her away while she was expecting it. That's a thing they've no right to do."

"Ho!"

"Anyhow, it's one more reason for letting her out earlier."

"Aye, if that could be . . ." said Isak gratefully.

Isak knew nothing of the many lengthy writings backward and forward between the different authorities concerning the woman who was expecting a child. The local authorities had let her go free while the matter was pending, for two reasons: in the first place, they had no lock-up in the village where they could keep her, and, in the second place, they wished to be as lenient as possible. The consequence was something they could not have foreseen. Later, when they had sent to fetch her away, no one had inquired about her condition, and she herself had said nothing of it. Possibly she had concealed the matter on purpose, in order to have a child with her during the years of imprisonment; if she behaved well, she would no doubt be allowed to see it now and again. Or perhaps she had been merely indifferent, and had gone off carelessly, despite her state. . . .

Isak worked and toiled, dug ditches and broke new ground, set up his boundary lines between his land and the State's, and gained another season's stock of timber. But now that Inger was no longer there to wonder at his doings, he worked more from habit than for any joy in what he did. And he had let two sessions pass without having his title-deeds registered, caring little about it; at last, that autumn, he had pulled himself together and got it done. Things were not as they should be with Isak now. Quiet and patient as ever—yes, but now it was because he did not care. He got out hides because it had to be done—goatskins and calf-skins—steeped them in the river, laid them in bark, and tanned them after a fashion ready for shoes. In the winter —at the very first threshing—he set aside his seed grain for the next spring, in order to have it done; best to have things done and done with; he was a methodical man. But it was a grey and lonely life; eyah, *Herregud!* a man without a wife again, and all the rest. . . .

What pleasure was there now in sitting at home Sundays, cleanly washed, with a neat red shirt on, when there was no one to be clean and neat for! Sundays were the longest days of all, days when he was forced to idleness and weary thoughts; nothing to do but wander about over the place, counting up all that should have been done. He always took the children with him, always carried one on his arm. It was a distraction to hear their chatter, and answer their questions of everything.

He kept old Oline because there was no one else he could get. And Oline was, after all, of use in a way. Carding and spinning, knitting stockings and mittens, and making cheese—she could do all these things, but she lacked Inger's happy touch, and had no heart in her work; nothing of all she handled was her own. There was a thing Isak had bought once at the village store, a china pot with a dog's head on the lid. It was a sort of tobacco-box, really, and stood on a shelf. Oline took off the lid and dropped it on the floor. Inger had left behind some cuttings of fuchsia, under glass. Oline took the glass off and, putting it back, pressed it down hard and maliciously; next day, all the cuttings were dead. It was not so easy for Isak to bear with such things; he looked displeased, and showed it, and, as there was nothing swanlike and gentle about Isak, it may well be that he showed it plainly. Oline cared little for looks; soft-spoken as ever, she only said: "Now, could I help it?"

"That I can't say," answered Isak. "But you might have left the things alone."

"I'll not touch her flowers again," said Oline. But the flowers were already dead.

Again, how could it be that the Lapps came up to Sellanraa so frequently of late? Os-Anders, for instance, had no business there at all, he should have passed on his way. Twice in one summer he came across the hills, and Os-Anders, it should be remembered, had no reindeer to look to, but lived by begging and quartering himself on other Lapps. As soon as he came up to the place, Oline left her work and fell to chatting with him about people in the village, and, when he left, his sack was heavy with no end of things. Isak put up with it for two years, saying nothing.

Then Oline wanted new shoes again, and he could be silent no longer. It was in the autumn, and Oline wore shoes every day, instead of going in wooden pattens or rough hide.

"Looks like being fine today," said Isak. "H'm." That was how he began.

"Aye," said Oline.

"Those cheeses, Eleseus," went on Isak again, "wasn't it ten you counted on the shelf this morning?"

"Aye," said Eleseus.

"Well, there's but nine there now."

Eleseus counted again, and thought for a moment inside his little head; then he said: "Yes, but then Os-Anders had one to take away; that makes ten."

There was silence for quite a while after that. Then little Sivert must try to count as well, and says after his brother: "That makes ten."

Silence again. At last Oline felt she must say something.

"Aye, I did give him a tiny one, that's true. I didn't think that could do any harm. But the children, they're no sooner able to talk than they show what's in them. And who they take after's more than I can think or guess. For 'tis not your way, Isak, that I do know."

The hint was too plain to pass unchecked. "The children are well enough," said Isak shortly. "But I'd like to know what good Os-Anders has ever done to me and mine."

"What good?"

"Aye, that's what I said."

"What good Os-Anders . . . ?"

"Aye, since I'm to give him cheeses in return."

Oline has had time to think, and has her answer ready now.

"Well, now, I wouldn't have thought it of you, Isak, that I wouldn't. Was it me, pray, that first began with Os-Anders? I wish I may never move alive from this spot if I ever so much as spoke his name."

Brilliant success for Oline. Isak has to give in, as he has done many a time before.

But Oline had more to say. "And if you mean I'm to go here clean barefoot, with the winter coming on and all, and never own the like of a pair of shoes, why, you'll please to say so. I said a word of it three and four weeks gone, that I needed shoes, but never sign of a shoe to this day, and here I am."

Said Isak: "What's wrong with your pattens, then, that you can't use them?"

"What's wrong with them?" repeats Oline, all unprepared.

"Aye, that's what I'd like to know."

"With my pattens?"

"Aye."

"Well . . . and me carding and spinning, and tending cattle and sheep and all, looking after children here—have you nothing to say to that? I'd like to know; that wife of yours that's in prison for her deeds, did you let her go barefoot in the snow?"

"She wore her pattens," said Isak. "And for going to church and visiting and the like, why, rough hide was good enough for her."

"Aye, and all the finer for it, no doubt."

"Aye, that she was. And when she did wear her hide shoes in summer, she did but stuff a wisp of grass in them, and never no more. But you—you must wear stockings in your shoes all the year round."

Said Oline: "As for that, I'll wear out my pattens in time, no doubt. I'd no thought there was any such haste to wear out good pattens all at once." She spoke softly and gently, but with half-closed eyes, the same sly Oline as ever. "And as for Inger," said she, "the changeling, as we called her, she went about with children of mine and learned both this and that, for years she did. And this is what we get for it. Because I've a daughter that lives in Bergen and wears a hat, I suppose that's what Inger must be gone away south for; gone to Trondhjem to buy a hat, he he!"

Isak got up to leave the room. But Oline had opened her heart now, unlocked the store of blackness within; aye, she gave out rays of darkness, did Oline. Thank Heaven, none of her children had their faces slit like a fire-breathing dragon, so to speak; but they were none the worse for that, maybe. No, 'twasn't everyone was so quick and handy at getting rid of the young they bore—strangling them in a twinkling. . . .

"Mind what you're saying," shouted Isak. And to make his meaning perfectly clear, he added: "You cursed old hag!"

But Oline was not going to mind what she was saying; not in the least, he he! She turned up her eyes to heaven and hinted that a harelip might be this or that, but some folk seemed to carry it too far, he he!

Isak may well have been glad to get safely out of the house at last. And what could he do but get Oline the shoes? A tiller of earth in the wilds; no longer even something of a god, that he could say to his servant: "Go!" He was helpless without Oline; whatever she did or said, she had nothing to fear, and she knew it.

The nights are colder now, with a full moon; the marshlands harden till they can almost bear, but thawing again when the sun comes out, to an impassable swamp once more. Isak goes down to the village one cold night, to order shoes for Oline. He takes a couple of cheeses with him, for Fru Geissler.

Halfway down to the village a new settler has appeared. A well-to-do man, no doubt, since he had called in folk from the village to build his house, and hired men to plow up a patch of sandy moorland for potatoes; he himself did little or nothing. The new man was Brede Olsen, Lens-

mand's assistant, a man to go to when the doctor had to be
fetched, or a pig to be killed. He was not yet thirty, but had
four children to look after, not to speak of his wife, who
was as good as a child herself. Oh, Brede was not so well
off, perhaps, after all; 'twas no great money he could earn
running hither and thither on all odd businesses, and collecting taxes from people that would not pay. So now he
was trying a new venture on the soil. He had raised a loan
at the bank to start house in the wilds. Breidablik, he called
the place; and it was Lensmand Heyerdahl's lady that had
found that splendid name.

Isak hurries past the house, not wasting time on looking in, but he can see through the window that all the children are up already, early as it is. Isak has no time to lose,
if he is to be back as far as this on the homeward journey
next night, while the roads are hard. A man living in the
wilds has much to think of, to reckon out and fit in as best
can be. It is not the busiest time for him just now, but he
is anxious about the children, left all alone with Oline.

He thinks, as he walks, of the first time he had come
that way. Time has passed, the two last years had been
long; there had been much that was good at Sellanraa, and
a deal that was not—eyah, *Herregud!* And now here was
another man clearing ground in the wilds. Isak knew the
place well; it was one of the kindlier spots he had noted
himself on his way up, but he had gone on farther. It was
nearer the village, certainly, but the timber was not so
good; the ground was less hilly, but a poorer soil; easy to
work on the surface, but hard to deal with farther down.
That fellow Brede would find it took more than a mere
turning-over of the soil to make a field that would bear. And
why hadn't he built out a shed from the end of the hayloft
for carts and implements? Isak noticed that a cart had been
left standing out in the yard, uncovered, in the open.

He got through his business with the shoemaker, and,

Fru Geissler having left the place, he sold his cheeses to the man at the store. In the evening, he starts out for home. The frost is getting harder now, and it is good, firm going, but Isak trudges heavily for all that. Who could say when Geissler would be back, now that his wife had gone; maybe he would not be coming at all? Inger was far away, and time was getting on. . . .

He does not look in at Brede's on the way back; on the contrary, he goes a long way round, keeping away from the place. He does not care to stop and talk to folk, only trudge on. Brede's cart is still out in the open—does he mean to leave it there? Well, 'tis his own affair. Isak himself had a cart of his own now, and a shed to house it, but none the happier for that. His home is but half a thing; it had been a home once, but now only half a thing.

It is full day by the time he gets within sight of his own place up on the hillside, and it cheers him somewhat, weary and exhausted as he is after forty-eight hours on the road. The house and buildings, there they stand, smoke curling up from the chimney; both the little ones are out, and come down to meet him as he appears. He goes into the house, and finds a couple of Lapps sitting down. Oline starts up in surprise: "What, you back already!" She is making coffee on the stove. Coffee? *Coffee!*

Isak has noticed the same thing before. When Os-Anders or any of the other Lapps have been there, Oline makes coffee in Inger's little pot for a long time after. She does it while Isak is out in the woods or in the fields, and when he comes in unexpectedly and sees it, she says nothing. But he knows that he is the poorer by a cheese or a bundle of wool each time. And it is to his credit that he does not pick up Oline in his fingers and crush her to pieces for her meanness. Altogether, Isak is trying hard indeed to make himself a better man, better and better, whatever may be his idea, whether it be for the sake of peace in the house, or in some hope that the Lord may give him back his Inger the sooner. He is something given to superstition and a pondering upon things; even his rustic wariness is innocent in its way. Early that autumn he found the turf on the roof of the stable was beginning to slip down inside. Isak chewed at his beard for a while, then, smiling like a man who understands a jest, he laid some poles across to keep it up. Not a bitter word did he say. And another thing: the shed where he kept his store of provisions was simply built on high stone feet at the corners, with nothing between. After a while, little birds began to find their way in through the big gaps in the wall, and stayed fluttering about inside, unable to get out. Oline complained that they picked at the food and spoiled the meat, and made a nasty mess about the place. Isak said: "Aye, 'tis a pity small birds should come in and not be able to get out again." And in the thick of a busy season he turned stonemason and filled up the gaps in the wall.

Heaven knows what was in his mind that he took things so; whether maybe he fancied Inger might be given back to him the sooner for his gentleness.

CHAPTER IX

THE YEARS pass by.

Once more there came visitors to Sellanraa; an engineer, with a foreman and a couple of workmen, marking out telegraph lines again over the hills. By the route they were taking now, the line would be carried a little above the house, and a straight road cut through the forest. No harm in that. It would make the place less desolate, a glimpse of the world would make it brighter.

"This place," said the engineer, "will be just about midway between two lines through the valleys on either side. They'll very likely ask you to take on the job of linesman for both."

"Ho!" said Isak.

"It will be twenty-five daler a year in your pocket."

"H'm," said Isak. "And what am I to do for that?"

"Keep the line in repair, mend the wires when necessary, clear away forest growth on the route as it comes up. They'll set up a little machine thing in the house here, to hang on the wall, that'll tell you when you're wanted. And when it does, you must leave whatever you're doing and go."

Isak thought it over. "I could do it all right in winter," he said.

"That's no good. It would have to be for the whole year, summer and winter alike."

"Can't be done," said Isak. "Spring and summer and autumn I've my work on the land, and no time for other things."

The engineer looked at him for quite a while, and then put an astonishing question, as follows: "Can you make more money that way?"

"Make more money?" said Isak.

"Can you earn more money in a day by working on the land than you could by working for us?"

"Why, as to that, I can't say," answered Isak. "It's just this way, you see—'tis the land I'm here for. I've many souls and more beasts to keep alive—and 'tis the land that keeps us. 'Tis our living."

"If you won't, I can find someone else," said the engineer.

But Isak only seemed rather relieved at the threat. He did not like to disoblige the great man, and tried to explain. " 'Tis this way," he said. "I've a horse and five cows, besides the bull. I've twenty sheep and sixteen goats. The beasts, they give us food and wool and hide; we must give them food."

"Yes, yes, of course," said the other shortly.

"Well, and so I say, how am I to feed them when I've to run away all times in the busy season, to work on the telegraph line?"

"Say no more about it," said the engineer. "I'll get the man down below you, Brede Olsen; he'll be glad to take it." He turned to his men with a brief word: "Now, lads, we'll be getting on."

Now Oline had heard from the way Isak spoke that he was stiff-necked and unreasonable in his mind, and she would make the most of it.

"What was that you said, Isak? Sixteen goats? There's no more than fifteen," said she.

Isak looked at her, and Oline looked at him again, straight in the face.

"Not sixteen goats?" said he.

"No," said she, looking helplessly towards the strangers, as if to say how unreasonable he was.

"Ho!" said Isak softly. He drew a tuft of his beard between his teeth and stood chewing it.

The engineer and his men went on their way.

Now, if Isak had wanted to show his displeasure with Oline and maybe thrash her for her doings, here was his chance—a Heaven-sent chance to do that thing. They were alone in the house; the children had gone after the men when they went. Isak stood there in the middle of the room, and Oline was sitting by the stove. Isak cleared his throat once or twice, just to show that he was ready to say something if he pleased. But he said nothing. That was his strength of soul. What, did he not know the number of his goats as he knew the fingers on his hands—was the woman mad? Could one of the beasts be missing, when he knew every one of them personally and talked to them every day —his goats that were sixteen in number? Oline must have traded away one of them the day before, when the woman from Breidablik had come up to look at the place. "H'm," said Isak, and this time words were on the very tip of his tongue. What was it Oline had done? Not exactly murder, perhaps, but something not far from it. He could speak in deadly earnest of that sixteenth goat.

But he could not stand there forever, in the middle of the room, saying nothing. "H'm," he said. "Ho! So there's but fifteen goats there now, you say?"

"That's all I make it," answered Oline gently. "But you'd better count for yourself and see."

Now was his time—he could do it now: reach out with his hands and alter the shape of Oline considerably, with but one good grip. He could do it. He did not do it, but said boldly, making for the door: "I'll say no more just now." And he went out, as if plainly showing that, next time, he would have proper words to say, never fear.

"Eleseus!" he called out.

Where was Eleseus, where were the children? Their father had something to ask them; they were big fellows now, with their eyes about them. He found them under the floor of the barn; they had crept in as far as they could, hiding away invisibly, but betraying themselves by an anxious whispering. Out they crept now like two sinners.

The fact of the matter was that Eleseus had found a stump of colored pencil the engineer had left behind, and started to run after him to give it back, but the big men with their long strides were already far up in the forest. Eleseus stopped. The idea occurred to him that he might keep the pencil—if only he could! He hunted out little Sivert, so that they might at least be two to share the guilt, and the pair of them had crept in under the floor with their find. Oh, that stump of pencil—it was an event in their lives, a wonder! They found shavings and covered them all over with signs; the pencil, they discovered, made blue marks with one end and red with the other, and they took it in turns to use. When their father called out so loudly and insistently, Eleseus whispered: "They've come back for the pencil!" All their joy was dashed in a moment, swept out of their minds at a touch, and their little hearts began beating and thumping terribly. The brothers crept forth. Eleseus held out the pencil at arm's length; here it was, they had not broken it; only wished they had never seen the thing.

No engineer was to be seen. Their hearts settled to a quieter beat; it was heavenly to be rid of that dreadful tension.

"There was a woman here yesterday," said their father.

"Yes."

"The woman from the place down below. Did you see her go?"

"Yes."

"Had she a goat with her?"

"No," said the boys. "A goat?"

"Didn't she have a goat with her when she left?"

"No. What goat?"

Isak wondered and wondered. In the evening when the animals came home, he counted the goats once over—there were sixteen. He counted them once more, counted them five times. There were sixteen. None missing.

Isak breathed again. But what did it all mean? Oline, miserable creature, couldn't she count as far as sixteen? He asked her angrily: "What's all this nonsense? there *are* sixteen goats."

"Are there sixteen?" she asked innocently.

"Aye."

"Aye, well, then."

"A nice one to count, you are."

Oline answered quietly, in an injured tone: "Since all the goats are there, why, then, thank Heaven, you can't say Oline's been eating them up. And well for her, poor thing."

Oline had taken him in completely with her trickery; he was content, imagining all was well. It did not occur to him, for instance, to count the sheep. He did not trouble about further counting of the stock at all. After all, Oline was not as bad as she might have been; she kept house for him after a fashion, and looked to his cattle; she was merely a fool, and that was worst for herself. Let her stay, let her live—she was not worth troubling about. But it was a grey and joyless thing to be Isak, as life was now.

Years had passed. Grass had grown on the roof of the house, even the roof of the barn, which was some years younger, was green. The wild mouse, native of the woods, had long since found way into the storehouse. Tits and all

manner of little birds swarmed about the place; there were
more birds up on the hillside; even the crows had come.
And most wonderful of all, the summer before, seagulls
had appeared, seagulls coming all the way up from the coast
to settle on the fields there in the wilderness. Isak's farm
was known far and wide to all wild creatures. And what of
Eleseus and little Sivert when they saw the gulls? Oh,
'twas some strange birds from ever so far away; not so
many of them, just six white birds, all exactly alike, wad-
dling this way and that about the fields, and pecking at the
grass now and then.

"Father, what have they come for?" asked the boys.

"There's foul weather coming out at sea," said their father. Oh, a grand and mysterious thing to see those gulls!

And Isak taught his sons many other things good and
useful to know. They were of an age to go to school, but
the school was many miles away down in the village, out of
reach. Isak had himself taught the boys their ABC on Sundays, but 'twas not for him, not for this born tiller of the
soil, to give them any manner of higher education; the Cat-
echism and Bible history lay quietly on the shelf with the
cheeses. Isak apparently thought it better for men to grow
up without book-knowledge, from the way he dealt with
his boys. They were a joy and a blessing to him, the two;
many a time he thought of the days when they had been
tiny things, and their mother would not let him touch them
because his hands were sticky with resin. Ho, resin, the
cleanest thing in the world! Tar and goats' milk and mar-
row, for instance, all excellent things, but resin, clean gum
from the fir—not a word!

So the lads grew up in a paradise of dirt and ignorance,
but they were nice lads for all that when they were washed,
which happened now and again; little Sivert he was a splendid fellow, though Eleseus was something finer and deeper.

"How do the gulls know about the weather?" he asked.

"They're weather-sick," said his father. "But as for that they're no more so than the flies. How it may be with flies, I can't say, if they get the gout, or feel giddy, or what. But never hit out at a fly, for 'twill only make him worse—remember that, boys! The horsefly he's a different sort, he dies of himself. Turns up suddenly one day in summer, and there he is; then one day suddenly he's gone, and that's the end of him."

"But how does he die?" asked Eleseus.

"The fat inside him stiffens, and he lies there dead."

Every day they learned something new. Jumping down from high rocks, for instance, to keep your tongue in your mouth, and not get i⁺ between your teeth. When they grew bigger, and wanted to smell nice for going to church, the thing was to rub oneself with a little tansy that grew on the hillside. Father was full of wisdom. He taught the boys about stones, about flint, how that the white stone was harder than the grey; but when he had found a flint, he must also make tinder. Then he could strike fire with it. He taught them about the moon, how when you can grip in the hollow side with your left hand it is waxing; and grip in with the right, it's on the wane: remember that, boys! Now and again, Isak would go too far, and grow mysterious; one day he declared that it was harder for a camel to enter the kingdom of heaven than for a human being to thread the eye of a needle. Another time, telling them of the glory of the angels, he explained that angels had stars set in their heels instead of hobnails. Good and simple teaching, well fitted for settlers in the wilds; the schoolmaster in the village would have laughed at it all, but Isak's boys found good use for it in their inner life. They were trained and taught for their own little world, and what could be better? In the autumn, when animals were to be killed, the lads were greatly curious, and fearful, and heavy at heart for the ones that were to die. There was Isak holding with one hand, and the other ready to strike; Oline stirred the blood. The old goat was led out, bearded and wise; the boys stood peeping round the corner. "Filthy cold wind this time," said Eleseus, and turned away to wipe his eyes. Little Sivert cried more openly, could not help calling out: "Oh, poor old goat!" When the goat was killed, Isak came up to them and gave them this lesson: "Never stand around saying 'Poor thing' and being pitiful when things are being killed. It makes them tough and harder to kill. Remember that!"

So the years passed, and now it was nearing spring again.

Inger had written home to say she was well, and was learning a lot of things where she was. Her little girl was big, and was called Leopoldine, after the day she was born, the 15th November. She knew all sorts of things, and was a genius at hemstitch and crochet, wonderful fine work she could do on linen or canvas.

The curious thing about this letter was that Inger had written and spelt it all herself. Isak was not so learned but that he had to get it read for him down in the village, by the man at the store; but once he had got it into his head it stayed there; he knew it off by heart when he got home.

And now he sat down with great solemnity at the head of the table, spread out the letter, and read it aloud to the boys. He was willing enough that Oline also should see how easily he could read writing, but he did not speak so much as a word to her directly. When he had finished, he said: "There now, Eleseus, and you, Sivert, 'tis your mother herself has written that letter and learned all these things. Even that little tiny sister of yours, she knows more than all the rest of us here. Remember that!" The boys sat still, wondering in silence.

"Aye, 'tis a grand thing," said Oline.

And what did she mean by that? Was she doubting that

Inger told the truth? Or had she her suspicions as to Isak's reading? It was no easy matter to get at what Oline really thought, when she sat there with her simple face, saying dark things. Isak determined to take no notice.

"And when your mother comes home, boys, you shall learn to write too," said he to the lads.

Oline shifted some clothes that were hanging near the stove to dry; shifted a pot, shifted the clothes again, and busied herself generally. She was thinking all the time.

"So fine and grand as everything's getting here," she said at last. "I do think you might have bought a paper of coffee for the house."

"*Coffee?*" said Isak. It slipped out.

Oline answered quietly: "Up to now I've bought a little now and again out of my own money, but . . ."

Coffee was a thing of dreams and fairy tales for Isak, a rainbow. Oline was talking nonsense, of course. He was not angry with her, no; but, slow of thought as he was, he called to mind at last her bartering with the Lapps, and he said bitterly:

"Aye, I'll buy you coffee, that I will. A paper of coffee, was it? Why not a pound? A pound of coffee, while you're about it."

"No need to talk that way, Isak. My brother Nils, he gets coffee; down at Breidablik, too, they've coffee."

"Aye, for they've no milk. Not a drop of milk on the place, they've not."

"That's as it may be. But you that know such a lot, and read writing as pat as a cockroach running, you ought to know that coffee's a thing should be in everybody's house."

"You creature!" said Isak.

At that Oline sat down and was not to be silenced. "As for that Inger," said she, "if so be I may dare to say such a word . . ."

"Say what you will, 'tis all one to me."

"She'll be coming home, and learned everything of sorts. And beads and feathers in her hat, maybe?"

"Aye, that may be."

"Aye," said Oline; "and she can thank me a little for all the way she's grown so fine and grand."

"You?" asked Isak. It slipped out.

Oline answered humbly: "Aye, since 'twas my modest doing that she ever went away."

Isak was speechless at that; all his words were checked, he sat there staring. Had he heard aright? Oline sat there looking as if she had said nothing. No, in a battle of words Izak was altogether lost.

He swung out of the house, full of dark thoughts. Oline, that beast that throve in wickedness and grew fat on it— why had he not wrung her neck the first year? So he thought, trying to pull himself together. He could have done it—he? Couldn't he, though! No one better.

And then a ridiculous thing happened. Isak went into the shed and counted the goats. There they are with their kids, the full number. He counts the cows, the pig, fourteen hens, two calves. "I'd all but forgotten the sheep," he says to himself; he counts the sheep, and pretends to be all anxiety lest there should be any missing there. Isak knows very well that there is a sheep missing; he has known that a long time; why should he let it appear otherwise? It was this way. Oline had tricked him nicely once before, saying one of the goats was gone, though all the goats were there as they should be; he had made a great fuss about it at the time, but to no purpose. It was always the same when he came into conflict with Oline. Then, in the autumn, at slaughtering time, he had seen at once that there was one ewe short, but he had not found courage to call her to account for it at the time. And he had not found that courage since.

But today he is stern; Isak is stern. Oline has made him thoroughly angry this time. He counts the sheep over again, putting his forefinger on each and counting aloud—Oline may hear it if she likes, if she should happen to be outside. And he says many hard things about Oline—says them out loud; how that she uses a new method of her own in feeding sheep, a method that simply makes them vanish— here's a ewe simply vanished. She is a thieving baggage, nothing less, and she may know it! Oh, he would just have liked Oline to be standing outside and hear it, and be thoroughly frightened for once.

He strides out from the shed, goes to the stable and counts the horse; from there he will go in—will go into the house and speak his mind. He walks so fast that his shirt stands out like a very angry shirt behind him. But Oline as like as not has noticed something, looking out through the glass window; she appears in the doorway, quietly and steadily, with buckets in her hands, on her way to the cow-shed.

"What have you done with that ewe with the flat ears?" he asks.

"Ewe?" she asks.

"Aye. If she'd been here she'd have had two lambs by now. What have you done with them? She always had two. You've done me out of three together, do you understand?"

Oline is altogether overwhelmed, altogether annihilated by the accusation; she wags her head, and her legs seem to melt away under her—she might fall and hurt herself. Her head is busy all the time; her ready wit had always helped her, always served her well; it must not fail her now.

"I steal goats and I steal the sheep," she says quietly. "And what do I do with them, I should like to know? I don't eat them up all by myself, I suppose?"

"You know best what you do with them."

"Ho! As if I didn't have enough and to spare of meat and food and all, with what you give me, Isak, that I should have to steal more? But I'll say that, anyway, I've never needed so much, all these years."

"Well, what have you done with the sheep? Has Os-Anders had it?"

"Os-Anders?" Oline has to set down the buckets and fold her hands. "May I never have more guilt to answer for! What's all this about a ewe and lambs you're talking of? Is it the goat you mean, with the flat ears?"

"You creature!" said Isak, turning away.

"Well, if you're not a miracle, Isak, I will say. . . . Here you've all you could wish for every sort, and a heavenly host of sheep and goats and all in your own shed, and you've not enough. How should I know what sheep, and what two lambs, you're trying to get out of me now? You should be thanking the Lord for His mercies from generation to generation, that you should. 'Tis but this summer and a bit of a way to next winter, and you've the lambing season once more, and three times as many again."

Oh, that woman Oline!

Isak went off grumbling like a bear. "Fool I was not to murder her the first day!" he thought, calling himself all manner of names. "Idiot, lump of rubbish that I was! But it's not too late yet; just wait, let her go to the cowshed if she likes. It wouldn't be wise to do anything tonight, but tomorrow . . . aye, tomorrow morning's the time. Three sheep lost and gone! And coffee, did she say!"

CHAPTER X

NEXT day was fated to bring a great event. There came a visitor to the farm—Geissler came. It was not yet summer on the moors, but Geissler paid no heed to the state of the ground; he came on foot, in rich high boots with broad, shiny tops; yellow gloves, too, he wore, and was elegant to see; a man from the village carried his things.

He had come, as a matter of fact, to buy a piece of Isak's land, up in the hills—a copper mine. And what about the price? Also, by the way, he had a message from Inger— good girl, everyone liked her; he had been in Trondhjem, and seen her. "Isak, you've put in some work here."

"Aye, I dare say. And you've seen Inger?"

"What's that you've got over there? Built a mill of your own, have you? grind your own corn? Excellent. And you've turned up a good bit of ground since I was here last."

"Is she well?"

"Eh? Oh, your wife!—yes, she's well and fit. Let's go in the next room. I'll tell you all about it."

" 'Tis not in order," put in Oline. Oline had her own reasons for not wishing them to go in.

They went into the little room nevertheless, and closed the door. Oline stood in the kitchen and could hear nothing.

Geissler sat down, slapped his knee with a powerful hand, and there he was—master of Isak's fate.

"You haven't sold that copper tract yet?" he asked.

"No."

"Good. I'll buy it myself. Yes, I've seen Inger and some other people too. She'll be out before long, if I'm not greatly mistaken—the case has been submitted to the King."

"The King?"

"The King, yes. I went in to have a talk with your wife—they managed it for me, of course, no difficulty about that—and we had a long talk. 'Well, Inger, how are you getting on? Nicely, what?' 'Why, I've no cause to complain.' 'Like to be home again?' 'Aye, I'll not say no.' 'And so you shall before very long,' said I. And I'll tell you this much, Isak, she's a good girl, is Inger. No blubbering, not so much as a tear, but smiling and laughing . . . they've fixed up that trouble with her mouth, by the way—operation—sewed it up again. 'Good-bye, then,' said I. 'You won't be here very long, I'll promise you that.'

"Then I went to the Governor—he saw me, of course, no difficulty about that. 'You've a woman here,' said I, 'that ought to be out of the place, and back in her home—Inger Sellanraa.' 'Inger?' said he; 'why, yes. She's a good sort—I wish we could keep her for twenty years,' said he. 'Well, you won't,' said I. 'She's been here too long already.' 'Too long?' says he. 'Do you know what she's in for?' 'I know all about it,' says I, 'being Lensmand in the district.' 'Oh,' says he, 'won't you sit down?' Quite the proper thing to say, of course. 'Why,' says the Governor then, 'we do what we can for her here, and her little girl too. So she's from your part of the country is she? We've helped her to get a sewing-machine of her own; she's gone through the workshops right to the top, and we've taught her a deal—weaving, household work, dyeing, cutting out. Been here too long, you say?' Well, I'd got my answer ready for that all right, but it could wait, so I only said her case had been badly muddled, and had to be taken up again; now, after the revision of the criminal code, she'd probably have been acquitted altogether. And I told him about the hare. 'A hare?' says the Governor. 'A hare,' says I. 'And the child was born with a harelip.' 'Oh,' says he, smiling, 'I see. And you think they ought to have made more allowance for that?' 'They didn't make any at all,' said I, 'for it wasn't mentioned.' 'Well, I dare say it's not so bad, after all.' 'Bad enough for her, anyway.' 'Do you believe a hare can work miracles, then?' says he. 'As to that,' said I, 'whether a hare can work miracles or not's a matter I won't discuss just now. The question is, what effect the *sight* of a hare might have on a woman with her disfigurement, in her condition.' Well, he thought over that for a bit. 'H'm,' says he at last. 'Maybe, maybe. Anyhow, we're not concerned with that here. All we have to do is to take over the people they send us; not to revise their sentences. And according to her sentence, Inger's not yet finished her time.'

"Well, then, I started on what I wanted to say all along. 'There was a serious oversight made in bringing her here to begin with,' says I. 'An oversight?' 'Yes. In the first place, she ought never to have been sent across the country at all in the state she was in.' He looks at me stiffly. 'No, that's perfectly true,' says he. 'But it's nothing to do with us here, you know.' 'And in the second place,' said I, 'she ought certainly not to have been in the prison for full two months without any notice taken of her condition by the authorities here.' That put him out, I could see; he said nothing for quite a while. 'Are you instructed to act on her behalf?' says he at last. 'Yes, I am,' said I. Well, then, he started on about how pleased they had been with her, and telling me over again all they'd taught her and done for her there— taught her to write too, he said. And the little girl had been put out to nurse with decent people, and so on. Then I told him how things were at home, with Inger away. Two youngsters left behind, and only a hired woman to look after them, and all the rest. 'I've a statement from her husband,' said I, 'that I can submit whether the case be taken up for thorough revision, or an application be made for a pardon.' 'I'd like to see that statement,' says the Governor. 'Right,' said I. 'I'll bring it along tomorrow in visiting hours.' "

Isak sat listening—it was thrilling to hear, a wonderful tale from foreign parts. He followed Geissler's mouth with slavish eyes.

Geissler went on: "I went straight back to the hotel and wrote out a statement; did the whole thing myself, you understand, and signed it 'Isak Sellanraa.' Don't imagine, though, I said a word against the way they'd managed things in the prison. Not a word. Next day I went along with the paper. 'Won't you sit down?' says the Governor, the moment I got inside the door. He read through what I'd written, nodded here and there, and at last he says: 'Very good, very good indeed. It'd hardly do, perhaps, to have the case brought up again for revision, but . . .' 'Wait a bit,' said I. 'I've another document that I think will make it right.' Had him there again, you see. 'Well,' he says, all of a hurry, 'I've been thinking over the matter since yesterday, and I consider there's good and sufficient grounds to apply for a pardon.' 'And the application would have the Governor's support?' I asked. 'Certainly; yes, I'll give it my best recommendation.' Then I bowed and said: 'In that case, there will be no difficulty about the pardon, of course. I thank you, sir, on behalf of a suffering woman and a stricken home.' Then says he: 'I don't think there should be any need of further declarations—from the district, I mean—about her case. You know the woman yourself—that should be quite enough.' I knew well enough, of course, why he wanted the thing settled quietly as possible, so I just agreed: said it would only delay the proceedings to collect further material. . . .

"And there you are, Isak, that's the whole story." Geissler looked at his watch. "And now let's get to business. Can you go with me up to the ground again?"

Isak was a stony creature, a stump of a man; he did not find it easy to change the subject all at once; he was all preoccupied with thoughts and wondering, and began asking questions of this and that. He learned that the application had been sent up to the King, and might be decided in one of the first State Councils. " 'Tis all a miracle," said he.

Then they went up into the hills; Geissler, his man, and Isak, and were out for some hours. In a very short time Geissler had followed the lie of the copper vein over a wide stretch of land and marked out the limits of the tract he wanted. Here, there, and everywhere he was. But no fool, for all his hasty movements; quick to judge, but sound enough for all that.

When they came back to the farm once more with a sack full of samples of ore—he got out writing-materials and sat down to write. He did not bury himself completely in his writing, though, but talked now and again. "Well, Isak, it won't be such a big sum this time, for the land, but I can give you a couple of hundred daler anyway, on the spot." Then he wrote again. "Remind me before I go, I want to see that mill of yours," said he. Then he caught sight of some blue and red marks on the frame of the loom, and asked, "Who drew that?" Now that was Eleseus, had drawn a horse and a goat; he used his colored pencil on the loom and woodwork anywhere, having no paper. "Not at all bad," said Geissler, and gave Eleseus a coin.

Geissler went on writing for a bit, and then looked up. "You'll be having other people taking up land hereabouts before long."

At this the man with him spoke: "There's some started already."

"Ho! And who might that be?"

"Well, first, there's the folk at Breidablik, as they call it
—man Brede, at Breidablik."

"Him—puh!" sniffed Geissler contemptuously.

"Then there's one or two others besides, have bought."

"Doubt if they're any good, any of them," said Geissler.
And noticing at the same moment that there were two boys
in the room, he caught hold of little Sivert and gave him
a coin. A remarkable man was Geissler. His eyes, by the
way, had begun to look soreish; there was a kind of redness
at the edges. Might have been sleeplessness; the same
thing comes at times from drinking of strong waters. But
he did not look dejected at all; and for all his talking of this
and that between times, he was thinking no doubt of his
document all the while, for suddenly he picked up the pen
and wrote a piece more.

At last he seemed to have finished.

He turned to Isak: "Well, as I said, it won't make you a
rich man all at once, this deal. But there may be more to
come. We'll fix it up so that you get more later on. Anyhow, I can give you two hundred now."

Isak understood but little of the whole thing, but two
hundred daler was at any rate another miracle, and an unreasonable sum. He would get it on paper, of course, not
paid in cash, but let that be. Isak had other things in his
head just now.

"And you think she'll be pardoned?" he asked.

"Eh? Oh, your wife! Well, if there'd been a telegraph
office in the village, I'd have wired to Trondhjem and asked
if she hadn't been set free already."

Isak had heard men speak of the telegraph; a wonderful
thing, a string hung up on big poles, something altogether
above the common earth. The mention of it now seemed to
shake his faith in Geissler's big words, and he put in anxiously: "But suppose the King says no?"

Said Geissler: "In that case, I send in my supplementary

material, a full account of the whole affair. And then they *must* set her free. There's not a shadow of doubt."

Then he read over what he had written; the contract for purchase of the land. Two hundred daler cash down, and later, a nice high percentage of receipts from working, or ultimate disposal by further sale, of the copper tract. "Sign your name here," said Geissler.

Isak would have signed readily enough, but he was no scholar; in all his life he had got no farther than cutting initials in wood. But there was that hateful creature Oline looking on; he took up the pen—a beastly thing, too light to handle anyway—turned it right end down, and *wrote*—wrote his name. Whereupon Geissler added something, presumably an explanation, and the man he had brought with him signed as a witness.

Settled.

But Oline was still there, standing immovable—it was indeed but now she had turned so stiff. What was to happen?

"Dinner on the table, Oline," said Isak, possibly with a touch of dignity, after having signed his name in writing on a paper. "Such as we can offer," he added to Geissler.

"Smells good enough," said Geissler. "Sound meat and drink. Here, Isak, here's your money!" Geissler took out his pocketbook—thick and fat it was, too—drew from it two bundles of notes and laid them down. "Count it over yourself."

Not a movement, not a sound.

"Isak," said Geissler again.

"Aye. Yes," answered Isak, and murmured, overwhelmed, " 'Tis not that I've asked for it, nor would—after all you've done."

"Ten tens in that—should be, and twenty fives here," said Geissler shortly. "And I hope there'll be more than that by a long way for your share soon."

And then it was that Oline recovered from her trance. The wonder had happened after all. She set the food on the table.

Next morning Geissler went out to the river to look at the mill. It was small enough, and roughly built; aye, a mill for dwarfs, for trollfolk, but strong and useful for a man's work. Isak led his guest a little farther up the river, and showed him another fall he had been working on a bit; it was to turn a saw, if so be God gave him health. "The only thing," he said, "it's a heavy long way from school: I'll have to get the lads to stay down in the village." But Geissler, always so quick to find a way, saw nothing to worry about here. "There are more people buying and settling here now," said he. "It won't be long before there's enough to start a school."

"Aye, maybe, but not before my boys are grown."

"Well, why not let them live on a farm down in the village? You could drive in with the boys and some food, and bring them up again three weeks—six weeks after; it would be easy enough for you, surely?"

"Aye, maybe," said Isak.

Aye, all things would be easy enough, if Inger came home. House and land and food and grand things enough, and a big sum of money too he had, and his strength; he was hard as nails. Health and strength—aye, full and unspoiled, unworn, in every way, the health and strength of a man.

When Geissler had gone, Isak began thinking of many presumptuous things. Aye, for had not Geissler, that blessing to them all, said at parting that he would send a message very soon—would send a telegram as soon as ever he could. "You can call in at the post office in a fortnight's time," he had said. And that in itself was a wonderful thing enough. Isak set to work making a seat for the cart. A seat, of course, that could be taken off when using the cart for manure, but to be put in again when anyone wanted to drive. And when he had got the seat made, it looked so white and new that it had to be painted darker. As for that, there were things enough that had to be done! The whole place wanted painting, to begin with. And he had been thinking for years past of building a proper barn with a bridge, to house in the crop. He had thought, too, of getting that saw set up and finished; of fencing in all his cultivated ground; of building a boat on the lake up in the hills. Many things he had thought of doing. But hard as he worked, unreasonably hard—what did it help against time? Time—it was the time that was too short. It was Sunday before he knew, and then directly after, lo, it was Sunday again!

Paint he would, in any case; that was decided and emphatic. The buildings stood there grey and bare—stood there like houses in their shirt sleeves. There was time yet before the busy season; the spring was hardly begun yet; the young things were out, but there was frost in the ground still.

Isak goes down to the village, taking with him a few score of eggs for sale, and brings back paint. There was enough for one building, for the barn, and it was painted red. He fetches up more paint, yellow ocher this time, for the house itself. "Aye, 'tis as I said, here's going to be fine and grand," grumbles Oline every day. Aye, Oline could guess, no doubt, that her time at Sellanraa would soon be up; she was tough and strong enough to bear it, though not without bitterness. Isak, on his part, no longer sought to settle up old scores with her now, though she pilfered and put away things lavishly enough towards the end. He made her a present of a young wether; after all, she had been with him a long time, and worked for little pay. And Oline had not been so bad with the children; she was not stern and strictly righteous and that sort of thing, but had a knack of dealing with children: listened to what they said, and let them do more or less as they pleased. If they came round while she was making cheese, she would give them a bit to taste; if they begged to be let off washing their faces one Sunday, she would let them off.

When Isak had given his walls a first coat, he went down to the village again and brought up all the paint he could carry. Three coats he put on in all, and white on the window-frames and corners. To come back now and look at his home there on the hillside, it was like looking at a fairy palace. The wilderness was inhabited and unrecognizable, a blessing had come upon it, life had arisen there from a long dream, human creatures lived there, children played about the houses. And the forest stretched away, big and kindly, right up to the blue heights.

But the last time Isak went down for paint, the storekeeper gave him a blue envelope with a crest on, and five skilling to pay. It was a telegram which had been forwarded by post, and was from Lensmand Geissler. A blessing on that man Geissler, wonderful man that he was! He telegraphed these few words, that Inger was free: "Home soonest possible: Geissler." And at this the store took to whirling curiously round and round; the counter and the people in the shop were suddenly far away. Isak felt rather than heard himself saying: "*Herregud!*" and "Praise and thanks to God."

"She might be here no later than tomorrow the day," said the storekeeper, "if so be she's left Trondhjem in time."

"Ho!" said Isak.

He waited till the next day. The carrier came up with letters, from the landing-stage where the steamer put in, but no Inger. "Then she won't be here now till next week," the storekeeper said.

Almost as well, after all, that there was time to wait—

Isak has many things to do. Should he forget himself altogether, and neglect his land? He sets off home again and begins carting out manure. It is soon done. He sticks a crowbar into the earth, noting how the frost disappears from day to day. The sun is big and strong now, the snow is gone, green showing everywhere; the cattle are out to graze. Isak plows one day, and a few days later he is sowing grain, planting potatoes. Ho, the youngsters too, planting potatoes like angels; blessed little hands they have, and what can their father do but watch?

Then Isak washes out the cart down by the river, and puts the seat in. Talks to the lads about a little journey; he must have a little journey down to the village.

"But aren't you going to walk?"

"Not today. I've took into my head to go down with horse and cart today."

"Can't we come too?"

"You've got to be good boys, and stay at home this time. Your own mother'll be coming very soon, and she'll learn you a many things."

Eleseus is all for learning things; he asks: "Father, when you did that writing on the paper—what does it feel like?"

"Why, 'tis hardly to feel at all; just like a bit of nothing in the hand."

"But doesn't it slip, like on the ice?"

"What slip?"

"The pen thing, that you write with?"

"Aye, there's the pen. But you have to learn to steer it, you'll see."

But little Sivert he was of another mind, and said nothing about pens; he wanted to ride in the cart; just to sit up on the seat before the horse was put in, and drive like that, driving ever so fast in a cart without a horse. And it was all his doing that father let them both sit up and ride with him a long way down the road.

ᴵsᴀᴋ drives on till he comes to a tarn, a bit of a pool on the moor, and there he pulls up. A pool on the moors, black, deep down, and the little surface of the water perfectly still; Isak knew what that was good for; he had hardly used any other mirror in his life than such a bit of water on the moors. Look how nice and neat he is today, with a red shirt; he takes out a pair of scissors now, and trims his beard. Vain barge of a man; is he going to make himself handsome all at once, and cut away five years' growth of iron beard? He cuts and cuts away, looking at himself in his glass. He might have done all this at home, of course, but was shy of doing it before Oline; it was quite enough to stand there right in front of her nose and put on a red shirt. He cuts and cuts away, a certain amount of beard falls into his patent mirror. The horse grows impatient at last and is moving on; Isak is fain to be content with himself as he is, and gets up again. And indeed he feels somehow younger already—devil knows what it could be, but somehow slighter of build. Isak drives down to the village.

Next day the mail boat comes in. Isak climbs up on a rock by the storekeeper's wharf, looking out, but still no Inger to be seen. Passengers there were, grown-up folk and children with them—*Herregud!*—but no Inger. He had kept in the background, sitting on his rock, but there was no need to stay behind any longer; he gets down and goes to the steamer. Barrels and cases trundling ashore, people and mailbags, but still Isak lacked what he had come for. There was something there—a woman with a little girl, up at the entrance to the landing-stage already; but the woman was prettier to look at than Inger—though Inger was good enough. What—why—but it was Inger! "H'm," said Isak, and trundled up to meet them. Greetings: "*God-dag*," said Inger, and held out her hand; a little cold, a little pale after the voyage, and being ill on the way. Isak, he just stood there; at last he said:

"H'm. 'Tis a fine day and all."

"I saw you down there all along," said Inger. "But I didn't want to come crowding ashore with the rest. So you're down in the village today?"

"Aye, yes. H'm."

"And all's well at home, everything all right?"

"Aye, thank you kindly."

"This is Leopoldine; she's stood the voyage much better than I did. This is your papa, Leopoldine; come and shake hands nicely."

"H'm," said Isak, feeling very strange—aye, he was like a stranger with them all at once.

Said Inger: "If you find a sewing-machine down by the boat, it'll be mine. And there's a chest as well."

Off goes Isak, goes off more than willingly, after the chest; the men on board showed him which it was. The sewing-machine was another matter; Inger had to go down and find that herself. It was a handsome box, of curious shape, with a round cover over, and a handle to carry it by—a sewing-machine in these parts! Isak hoisted the chest and the sewing-machine on to his shoulders, and turned to his wife and child:

"I'll have these up in no time, and come back for her after."

"Come back for who?" asked Inger, with a smile. "Did you think she couldn't walk by herself, a big girl like that?"

They walked up to where Isak had left the horse and cart.

"New horse, you've got?" said Inger. "And what's that you've got—a cart with a seat in?"

" 'Tis but natural," said Isak. "What I was going to say: Wouldn't you care for a little bit of something to eat? I've brought things all ready."

"Wait till we get a bit on the way," said she. "Leopoldine, can you sit up by yourself?"

But her father won't have it; she might fall down under the wheels. "You sit up with her and drive yourself."

So they drove off, Isak walking behind.

He looked at the two in the cart as he walked. There was Inger, all strangely dressed and strange and fine to look at, with no harelip now, but only a tiny scar on the upper lip. No hissing when she talked; she spoke all clearly, and that was the wonder of it all. A grey-and-red woolen wrap with a fringe looked grand on her dark hair. She turned round in her seat on the cart, and called to him:

"It's a pity you didn't bring a skin rug with you; it'll be cold, I doubt, for the child towards night."

"She can have my jacket," said Isak. "And when we get up in the woods, I've left a rug there on the way."

"Oh, have you a rug up in the woods?"

"Aye. I wouldn't bring it down all the way, for if you didn't come today."

"H'm. What was it you said before—the boys are well and all?"

"Aye, thank you kindly."

"They'll be big lads now, I doubt?"

"Aye, that's true. They've just been planting potatoes."

"Oh!" said the mother, smiling, and shaking her head. "Can they plant potatoes already?"

"Why, Eleseus, he gives a hand with this, and little Sivert helps with that," said Isak proudly.

Little Leopoldine was asking for something to eat. Oh, the pretty little creature; a ladybird up on a cart! She talked with a sing in her voice, with a strange accent, as she had learned in Trondhjem. Inger had to translate now and again. She had her brothers' features, the brown eyes and oval cheeks that all had got from their mother; aye, they were their mother's children, and well that they were so! Isak was something shy of his little girl, shy of her tiny shoes and long, thin, woolen stockings and short frock; when she had come to meet her strange papa she had curtseyed and offered him a tiny hand.

They got up into the woods and halted for a rest and a meal all round. The horse had his fodder; Leopoldine ran about in the heather, eating as she went.

"You've not changed much," said Inger, looking at her husband.

Isak glanced aside, and said: "No, you think not? But you've grown so grand and all."

"Ha ha! Nay, I'm an old woman now," said she jestingly.

It was no use trying to hide the fact: Isak was not a bit sure of himself now. He could find no self-possession, but still kept aloof, shy, as if ashamed of himself. How old could his wife be now? She couldn't be less than thirty—that is to say, she couldn't be more, of course. And Isak, for all that he was eating already, must pull up a twig of heather and fall to biting that.

"What—are you eating heather?" cried Inger laughingly.

Isak threw down the twig, took a mouthful of food, and going over to the road, took the horse by its forelegs and heaved up its forepart till the animal stood on its hind legs. Inger looked on with astonishment.

"What are you doing that for?" she asked.

"Oh, he's so playful," said Isak, and set the horse down again.

Now what *had* he done that for? A sudden impulse to do just that thing; perhaps he had done it to hide his embarrassment.

They started off again, and all three of them walked a bit of the way. They came to a new farm.

"What's that there?" asked Inger.

" 'Tis Brede's place, that he's bought."

"Brede?"

"Breidablik, he calls it. There's wide moorland, but the timber's poor."

They talked of the new place as they passed on. Isak noticed that Brede's cart was still left out in the open.

The child was growing sleepy now, and Isak took her gently in his arms and carried her. They walked and walked. Leopoldine was soon fast asleep, and Inger said:

"We'll wrap her up in the rug, and she can lie down in the cart and sleep as long as she likes."

" 'Twill shake her all to pieces," said Isak, and carries her on. They cross the moors and get into the woods again.

"*Ptro!*" says Inger, and the horse stops. She takes the child from Isak, gets him to shift the chest and the sewing-machine, making a place for Leopoldine in the bottom of the cart. "Shaken? not a bit of it!"

Isak fixes things to rights, tucks his little daughter up in the rug, and lays his jacket folded under her head. Then off again.

Man and wife gossiping of this and that. The sun is up till late in the evening, and the weather warm.

"Oline," says Inger, "—where does she sleep?"

"In the little room."

"Ho! And the boys?"

"They've their own bed in the big room. There's two beds there, just as when you went away."

"Looking at you now," said Inger, "I can see you're just as you were before. And those shoulders of yours, they've carried some burdens up along this way, but they've not grown the weaker by it, seems."

"H'm. Maybe. What I was going to say: How it was like with you all the years there? Bearable like?" Oh, Isak was soft at heart now; he asked her that, and wondered in his mind.

And Inger said: "Aye, 'twas nothing to complain of."

They talked more feelingly together, and Isak asked if she wasn't tired of walking, and would get up in the cart a bit of way. "No, thanks all the same," said she. "But I don't know what's the matter with me today; after being ill on the boat, I feel hungry all the time."

"Why, did you want something, then?"

"Yes, if you don't mind stopping so long."

Oh, that Inger, maybe 'twas not for herself at all, but for Isak's sake. She would have him eat again; he had spoiled his last meal chewing twigs of heather.

And the evening was light and warm, and they had but a few miles more to go; they sat down to eat again.

Inger took a parcel from her box, and said:

"I've a few things I brought along for the boys. Let's go over there in the bushes, it's warmer there."

They went across to the bushes, and she showed him the things; neat braces with buckles for the boys to wear, copybooks with copies at the top of the page, a pencil for each, a pocketknife for each. And there was an excellent book for herself, she had. "Look, with my name in and all. A prayerbook." It was a present from the Governor, by way of remembrance.

Isak admired each thing in silence. She took out a bundle

of little collars—Leopoldine's, they were. And gave Isak a black neckerchief for himself, shiny as silk.

"Is that for me?" said he.

"Yes, it's for you."

He took it carefully in his hands, and stroked it.

"Do you think it's nice?"

"Nice—why I could go round the world in such."

But Isak's fingers were rough; they stuck in the curious silky stuff.

Now Inger had no more things to show. But when she had packed them all up again, she sat there still; and the way she sat, he could see her legs, could see her red-bordered stockings.

"H'm," said he. "Those'll be town-made things, I doubt?"

" 'Tis wool was bought in the town, but I knitted them myself. They're ever so long—right up above the knee—look. . . ."

A little while after she heard herself whispering: "Oh, you . . . you're the same—the same as ever!"

And after that halt they drove on again, and Inger sat up, holding the reins. "I've brought a paper of coffee too," she said. "But you can't have any this evening, for it's not roasted yet."

" 'Tis more than's needed this evening and all," said he.

An hour later the sun goes down, and it grows colder. Inger gets down to walk. Together they tuck the rug closer about Leopoldine, and smile to see how soundly she can sleep. Man and wife talk together again on their way. A pleasure it is to hear Inger's voice; none could speak clearer than Inger now.

"Wasn't it four cows we had?" she asks.

" 'Tis more than that," says he proudly. "We've eight."

"Eight cows!"

"That is to say, counting the bull."

"Have you sold any butter?"

"Aye, and eggs."

"What, have we chickens now?"

"Aye, of course we have. And a pig."

Inger is so astonished at all this that she forgets herself altogether, and stops for a moment—"*Ptro!*" And Isak is proud and keeps on, trying to overwhelm her completely.

"That Geissler," he says, "you remember him? He came up a little while back."

"Oh?"

"I've sold him a copper mine."

"Ho! What's that—a copper mine?"

"Copper, yes. Up in the hills, all along the north side of the water."

"You—you don't mean he paid you money for it?"

"Aye, that he did. Geissler he wouldn't buy things and not pay for them."

"What did you get, then?"

"H'm. Well, you might not believe it—but it was two hundred daler."

"You got two hundred daler!" shouts Inger, stopping again with a "*Ptro!*"

"I did—yes. And I've paid for my land a long while back," said Isak.

"Well—you are a wonder, you are!"

Truly, it was a pleasure to see Inger all surprised, and make her a rich wife. Isak did not forget to add that he had no debts nor owings at the store or anywhere else. And he had not only Geissler's two hundred untouched, but more than that—a hundred and sixty daler more. Aye, they might well be thankful to God!

They spoke of Geissler again; Inger was able to tell how he had helped to get her set free. It had not been an easy matter for him, after all, it seemed; he had been a long time getting the matter through, and had called on the Governor ever so many times. Geissler had also written to some of the State Councillors, or some other high authorities; but this he had done behind the Governor's back, and when the Governor heard of it he was furious, which was not surprising. But Geissler was not to be frightened; he demanded a revision of the case, new trial, new examination, and everything. And after that the King had to sign.

Ex-Lensmand Geissler had always been a good friend to them both, and they had often wondered why; he got nothing out of it but their poor thanks—it was more than they could understand. Inger had spoken with him in Trondhjem, and could not make him out. "He doesn't seem to care a bit about any in the village but us," she explained.

"Did he say so?"

"Yes. He's furious with the village here. He'd show them, he said."

"Ho!"

"And they'd find out one day, and be sorry they'd lost him, he said."

They reached the fringe of the wood, and came in sight of their home. There were more buildings there than before, and all nicely painted. Inger hardly knew the place again, and stopped dead.

"You—you don't say that's our place—all that?" she exclaimed.

Little Leopoldine woke at last and sat up, thoroughly rested now; they lifted her out and let her walk.

"Are we there now?" she asked.

"Yes. Isn't it a pretty place?"

There were small figures moving, over by the house; it was Eleseus and Sivert, keeping watch. Now they came running up. Inger was seized with a sudden cold—a dreadful cold in the head, with sniffing and coughing—even her eyes were all red and watering too. It always gives one a dreadful cold on board ship—makes one's eyes wet and all!

But when the boys came nearer they stopped running all of a sudden and stared. They had forgotten what their mother looked like, and little sister they had never seen. But father—they didn't know him at all till he came quite close. He had cut off his heavy beard.

CHAPTER XII

ALL is well now.

Isak sows his oats, harrows, and rolls it in. Little Leopoldine comes and wants to sit on the roller. Sit on a roller? Nay, she's all too little and unknowing for that yet. Her brothers know better. There's no seat on Father's roller.

But Father thinks it fine and a pleasure to see little Leopoldine coming up so trustingly to him already; he talks to her, and shows her how to walk nicely over the fields, and not get her shoes full of earth.

"And what's that—why, if you haven't a blue frock on today—come, let me see; aye, 'tis blue, so it is. And a belt round and all. Remember when you came on the big ship? And the engines—did you see them? That's right—and now run home to the boys again, they'll find you something to play with."

Oline is gone, and Inger has taken up her old work once more, in house and yard. She overdoes it a little, maybe, in cleanliness and order, just by way of showing that she was going to have things differently now. And indeed it was wonderful to see what a change was made; even the glass windows in the old turf hut were cleaned, and the boxes swept out.

But it was only the first days, the first week; after that she began to be less eager about the work. There was really no need to take all that trouble about cowsheds and things; she could make better use of her time now. Inger had

learned a deal among the townfolk, and it would be a pity
not to turn it to account. She took to her spinning-wheel
and loom again—true enough, she was even quicker and
neater than before—a trifle too quick—*hui!*—especially
when Isak was looking on; he couldn't make out how anyone could learn to use their fingers that way—the fine long
fingers she had to her big hands. But Inger had a way of
dropping one piece of work to take up another, all in a moment. Well, well, there were more things to be looked to
now than before, and maybe she was not altogether so patient as she had been; a trifle of unrest had managed to
creep in.

First of all there were the flowers she had brought with
her—bulbs and cuttings; little lives these too, that must be
thought of. The glass window was too small, the ledge too
narrow to set flowerpots on; and besides, she had no flowerpots. Isak must make some tiny boxes for begonias, fuch-
sias, and roses. Also, one window was not enough—fancy
a room with only one window!

And: "Oh, by the way," said Inger, "I want an iron, you
know. There isn't one in the place. I could use a flatiron
for pressing when I'm sewing dresses and things, but you
can't do proper work without an iron of some sort."

Isak promised to get the blacksmith down at the village
to make a first-rate pressing-iron. Oh, Isak was ready to do
anything, do all that she asked in every way; for he could
see well enough that Inger had learned a heap of things
now, and matchless clever she was grown. She spoke, too,
in a different way, a little finer, using elegant words. She
never shouted out to him now as she used to: "Come and
get your food!" but would say instead: "Dinner's ready, if
you please." Everything was different now. In the old days
he would answer simply: "Aye," or say nothing at all, and
go on working for a bit before he came. Now, he said:
"Thanks," and went in at once. Love makes the wise a

fool; now and then Isak would say: "Thanks, thanks." Aye, all was different now—maybe a trifle too fine in some ways. When Isak spoke of dung, and was rough in his speech, as peasants are, Inger would call it manure, "for the sake of the children, you know."

She was careful with the children, and taught them everything, educated them. Let tiny Leopoldine go on quickly with her crochet work, and the boys with writing and schooling; they would not be altogether behindhand when the time came for them to go to school in the village. Eleseus in particular was grown a clever one, but little Sivert was nothing much, if the truth must be told—a madcap, a jackanapes. He even ventured to screw a little at Mother's sewing-machine, and had already hacked off splinters from table and chairs with his new pocketknife. Inger had threatened to take it away altogether.

The children, of course, had all the animals about the place, and Eleseus had still his colored pencil besides. He used it very carefully, and rarely lent it to his brother, but for all that the walls were covered with blue and red drawings as time went on, and the pencil got smaller and smaller. At last Eleseus was simply forced to put Sivert on rations with it, lending him the pencil on Sunday only, for one drawing. Sivert was not pleased with the arrangement, but Eleseus was a fellow who would stand no nonsense. Not so much as being the stronger, but he had longer arms, and could manage better when it came to a quarrel.

But that Sivert! Now and again he would come across a bird's nest in the woods; once he talked about a mouse-hole he had found, and made a lot of that; another time it was a great fish as big as a man, he had seen in the river. But it was all evidently his own invention; he was somewhat inclined to make black into white, was Sivert, but a good sort for all that. When the cat had kittens, it was he who brought her milk, because she hissed too much for Eleseus. Sivert was never tired of standing looking at the box full of movement, a nest of tumbling furry paws.

The chickens, too, he noticed every day: the cock with his lordly carriage and fine feathers, the hens tripping about chattering low, and pecking at the sand, or screaming out as if terribly hurt every time they had laid an egg.

And there was the big wether. Little Sivert had read a good deal to what he knew before, but he could not say of the wether that the beast had a fine Roman nose, begad! That he could not say. But he could do better than that. He knew the wether from the day when it had been a lamb, he understood it and was one with it—a kinsman, a fellow-creature. Once, a strange primitive impression flickered through his senses: it was a moment he never forgot. The wether was grazing quietly in the field; suddenly it threw up its head, stopped munching, simply stood there looking out. Sivert looked involuntarily in the same direction. No —nothing remarkable. But Sivert himself felt something strange within him: " 'Tis most as if he stood looking into the garden of Eden," he thought.

There were the cows,—the children had each a couple —great sailing creatures, so friendly and tame that they let themselves be caught whenever you liked; let human children pat them. There was the pig, white and particular about its person when decently looked after, listening to every sound, a comical fellow, always eager for food, and ticklish and fidgety as a girl. And there was the billy-goat; there was always one old billy-goat at Sellanraa, for as soon as one died another was ready to take his place. And was there ever anything so solemnly ridiculous to look at? Just now he had a whole lot of goats to look after, but at times he would get sick and tired of them all, and lie down, a bearded, thoughtful spectacle, a veritable Father Abraham. And then in a moment, up again and off after the flock. He always left a trail of sourish air behind him.

The daily round of the farm goes on. Now and again a traveler comes by on his way up to the hills and asks: "And how's all with ye here?"

And Isak answers: "Aye, thank ye kindly."

Isak works and works, consulting the almanac for all that he does, notes the changes of the moon, pays heed to the signs of the weather, and works on. He has beaten out so much of a track down to the village that he can drive in now with horse and cart, but for the most part, he carries his load himself; carries loads of cheese or hides, and bark and resin, and butter and eggs; all things he can sell, to bring back other wares instead. No, in the summer he does not often drive down—for one thing, because the road down from Breidablik, the last part of the way, is so badly kept. He has asked Brede Olsen to help with the upkeep of the road, and do his share. Brede Olsen promises, but does not hold to his word. And Isak will not ask him again. Rather carry a load on his back himself. And Inger says: "I can't understand how you ever manage it all." Oh, but he could manage anything. He had a pair of boots, so unimaginably heavy and thick, with great slabs of iron on the soles, even the straps were fastened with copper nails—it was a marvel that one man could walk in such boots at all.

On one of his journeys down, he came upon several gangs of men at work on the moors; putting down stone sockets and fixing telegraph poles. Some of them are from the village, Brede Olsen is there too, for all that he has taken up land of his own and ought to be working on that. Isak wonders that Brede can find time.

The foreman asks if Isak can sell them telegraph poles. Isak says no. Not if he's well paid for them?—No.—Oh, Isak was grown a thought quicker in his dealings now, he could say no. If he sold them a few poles, to be sure it would be money in his pockets, so many daler more; but he had no timber to spare, there was nothing gained by that. The engineer in charge comes up himself to ask, but Isak refuses.

"We've poles enough," says the engineer, "but it would be easier to take them from your ground up there, and save transport."

"I've no timber to spare myself," says Isak. "I want to get up a bit of a saw and do some cutting; there's some more buildings I'll need to have ready soon."

Here Brede Olsen put in a word, and says: "If I was you, Isak, I'd sell them poles."

For all his patience, Isak gave Brede a look and said: "Aye, I dare say you would."

"Well—what?" asks Brede.

"Only that I'm not you," said Isak.

Some of the workmen chuckled a little at this.

Aye, Isak had reason enough just then to put his neighbor down; that very day he had seen three sheep in the fields at Breidablik, and one of them he knew—the one with the flat ears that Oline had bartered away. He may keep it, thought Isak, as he went on his way; Brede and his woman may get all the sheep they want, for me!

That business of the saw was always in his thoughts; it was as he had said. Last winter, when the roads were hard, he had carted up the big circular blade and the fittings, ordered from Trondhjem through the village store. The parts were lying in one of the sheds now, well smeared with oil to keep off the rust. He had brought up some of the beams too, for the framework; he could begin building when he pleased, but he put it off. What could it be? Was he beginning to grow slack, was he wearing out? He could not understand it himself. It would have been no surprise to others, perhaps, but Isak could not believe it.

Was his head going? He had never been afraid of taking up a piece of work before; he must have changed somehow, since the time when he had built his mill across a river just as big. He could get in help from the village, but he would try again alone; he would start in a day or so—and Inger could lend him a hand.

He spoke to Inger about it.

"H'm. I don't know if you could find time one of these days to lend a hand with that sawmill?"

Inger thought for a moment. "Ye-s, if I can manage it. So you're going to set up a sawmill?"

"Aye, 'tis my intention so. I've worked it all out in my head."

"Will that be harder than the mill was?"

"Much harder, ten times as hard. Why, it's all got to be as close and exact—down to the tiniest line, and the saw itself exactly midways."

"If only you can manage it," said Inger thoughtlessly.

Isak was offended, and answered: "As to that, we shall see."

"Couldn't you get a man to help you, someone that knows the work?"

"No."

"Well, then, you won't be able to manage it," said she again.

Isak put up his hand to his hair—it was like a bear lifting his paw.

" 'Twas just that I've been fearing," said he. "That I might not manage it. And that's why I wanted you that's learned so much to help me."

That was one to the bear. But nothing gained after all. Inger tossed her head and turned aside unkindly, and would have nothing to do with his saw.

"Well, then—" said Isak.

"Why, do you want me to stand getting drenched in the

river and have me laid up? And who's to do all the sewing, and look to the animals and keep house, and all the rest?"

"No, that's true," said Isak.

Oh, but it was only the four corner posts and the middle ones for the two long sides he wanted help with, that was all. Inger—was she really grown so different in her heart through living among folk from the towns?

The fact was that Inger had changed a good deal; she thought now less of their common good than of herself. She had taken loom and wheel into use again, but the sewing-machine was more to her taste; and when the pressing-iron came up from the blacksmith's, she was ready to set up as a fully trained dressmaker. She had a profession now. She began by making a couple of little frocks for Leo-poldine. Isak thought them pretty, and praised them, maybe, a thought too much; Inger hinted that it was noth-ing to what she could do when she tried.

"But they're too short," said Isak.

"They're worn that way in town," said Inger. "You know nothing about it."

Isak saw he had gone too far, and, to make up for it, said something about getting some material for Inger herself, for something or other.

"For a cloak?" said Inger.

"Aye, or what you'd like."

Inger agreed to have something for a cloak, and described the sort of stuff she wanted.

But when she had made the cloak, she had to find some-one to show it to; accordingly, when the boys went down to the village to be put to school, Inger herself went with them. And that journey might have seemed a little thing, but it left its mark.

They came first of all to Breidablik, and the Breidablik woman and her children came out to see who it was going by. There sat Inger and the two boys, driving down lordly-wise—the boys on their way to school, nothing less, and Inger wearing a cloak. The Breidablik woman felt a sting at the sight; the cloak she could have done without—thank Heaven, *she* set no store by such foolishness—but . . . she had children of her own: Barbro, a great girl already, Helge, the next, and Katrine, all of an age for school. The two eldest had been to school before, when they lived down in the village, but after moving up to Breidablik, to an out-of-the-way place up on the moors, they had been forced to give it up, and let the children run heathen again.

"You'll be wanting a bite for the boys, maybe," said the woman.

"Food? Do you see this chest here? It's my traveling-trunk, that I brought home with me—I've that full of food."

"And what'll be in it of sorts?"

"What sorts? I've meat and pork in plenty, and bread and butter and cheese besides."

"Aye, you've no lack up at Sellanraa," said the other; and her poor, sallow-faced children listened with eyes and ears to this talk of rich things to eat. "And where will they be staying?" asked the mother.

"At the blacksmith's," said Inger.

"Ho!" said the other. "Aye, mine'll be going to school again soon. They'll stay with the Lensmand."

"Ho!" said Inger.

"Aye, or at the doctor's, maybe, or at the parsonage. Brede he's in with the great folks there, of course."

Inger fumbled with her cloak, and managed to turn it so that a bit of black silk fringe appeared to advantage.

"Where did you get the cloak?" asked the woman. "One you had with you, maybe?"

"I made it myself."

"Aye, aye, 'tis as I said: wealth and riches full and running over. . . ."

Inger drove on, feeling all set up and pleased with herself, and, coming into the village, she may have been a trifle overproud in her bearing. Lensmand Heyerdahl's lady was not pleased at the sight of that cloak; the Sellanraa woman was forgetting her place—forgetting where it was she had come from after five years' absence. But Inger had at least a chance of showing off her cloak, and the storekeeper's wife and the blacksmith's wife and the schoolmaster's wife all thought of getting one like it for themselves—but it could wait a bit.

And now it was not long before Inger began to have visitors. One or two women came across from the other side of the hills, out of curiosity. Oline had perhaps chanced to say something against her will, to this one or that. Those who came now brought news from Inger's own birthplace; what more natural than that Inger should give them a cup of coffee, and let them look at her sewing-machine! Young girls came up in pairs from the coast, from the village, to ask Inger's advice; it was autumn now, and they had been saving up for a new dress, and wanted her to help them. Inger, of course, would know all about the latest fashions after being out in the world, and now and again she would do a little cutting out. Inger herself brightened up at these visits, and was glad; kindly and helpful she was too, and clever at the work, besides; she could cut out material without a pattern. Sometimes she would even hem a whole length on her machine, and all for nothing, and give the stuff back to the girls with a delightful jest: "There —now you can sew the buttons on yourself!"

Later in the year Inger was sent for down to the village, to do dressmaking for some of the great folks there. Inger could not go; she had a household to look after, and animals besides, all the work of the home, and she had no servant.

Had no what? Servant!

She spoke to Isak one day.

"If only I had someone to help me, I could put in more time sewing."

Isak did not understand. "Help?"

"Yes, help in the house—a servant-girl."

Isak must have been taken aback at this; he laughed a little in his iron beard, and took it as a jest. "Aye, we should have a servant-girl," said he.

"Housewives in the towns always have a servant," said Inger.

"Ho!" said Isak.

Well, Isak was not perhaps in the best of humor just then, not exactly gentle and content, no, for he had started work on that sawmill, and it was a slow and toilsome business; he couldn't hold the balks with one hand, and a level in the other, and fix ends at the same time. But when the boys came back from school again it was easier; the lads were useful and a help, bless them! Sivert especially had a genius for knocking in nails, but Eleseus was better at handling a plumbline. By the end of a week, Isak and the boys had actually got the foundation posts in, and soundly fixed with stretcher pieces as thick as the beams themselves.

It worked out all right—everything worked out all right somehow. But Isak was beginning to feel tired in the evenings now—whatever it could be. It was not only building a sawmill and getting that done—there was everything else besides. The hay was in, but the grain was standing yet, soon it would have to be cut and stacked: there were the potatoes too, they would have to be taken up before long. But the boys were a wonderful help. He did not thank them; 'twas not the way among folk of their sort, but he was mightily pleased with them for all that. Now and again they would sit down in the middle of their work and talk together, the father almost asking his sons' advice as to what they should do next. Those were proud moments for the lads, they learned also to think well before they spoke, lest they should be in the wrong.

" 'Twould be a pity not to have the saw roofed in before the autumn rains," said their father.

If only Inger had been as in the old days! But Inger was not so strong as she had been, it seemed, and that was natural enough after her long spell within walls. That her mind, too, seemed changed was another matter. Strange, how little thought, how little care, she seemed to take now; shallow and heedless—was this Inger?

One day she spoke of the child she had killed.

"And a fool I was to do it," she said. "We might have had her mouth sewed up too, and then I needn't have throttled her." And she never stole off now to a tiny grave in the forest, where once she had patted the earth with her hands and set up a little cross.

But Inger was not altogether heartless yet; she cared for her other children, kept them clean and made new clothes for them; she would sit up late at night mending their things. It was her ambition to see them get on in the world.

The grain was stacked, and the potatoes were taken up. Then came the winter. No, the sawmill did not get roofed in that autumn, but that could not be helped—after all, 'twas not a matter of life or death. Next summer would be time and means enough.

CHAPTER XIII

THE WINTER round of work was as before; carting wood, mending tools and implements. Inger kept house, and did sewing in her spare time. The boys were down in the village again for the long term at school. For several winters past they had had a pair of skis between them; they managed well enough that way as long as they were at home, one waiting while the other took his turn, or one standing on behind the other. Aye, they managed finely with but one pair, it was the finest thing they knew, and they were innocent and glad. But down in the village things were different. The school was full of skis; even the children at Breidablik, it seemed, had each a pair. And the end of it was that Isak had to make a new pair for Eleseus, Sivert keeping the old pair for his own.

Isak did more; he had the boys well clad, and gave them everlasting boots. But when that was done, Isak went to the storekeeper and asked for a ring.

"A ring?" said the man.

"A finger-ring. Aye, I've grown that high and mighty now I must give my wife a ring."

"Do you want a silver one, or gold, or just a brass ring dipped to look like gold?"

"Let's say a silver ring."

The storekeeper thought for a while.

"Look you, Isak," he said. "If you want to do the proper

thing, and give your wife a ring she needn't be ashamed to wear, you'd better make it a gold ring."

"What!" said Isak aloud. Though maybe in his inmost heart he had been thinking of a gold ring all the time.

They talked the matter over seriously, and agreed about getting a measurement of some sort for the ring. Isak was thoughtful, and shook his head and reckoned it was a big thing to do, but the storekeeper refused to order anything but a gold ring. Isak went home again, secretly pleased with his decision, but somewhat anxious, for all that, at the extravagant lengths he had gone to, all for being in love with his wife.

There was a good average snowfall that winter, and early in the year, when the roads were passable, folk from the village began carting up telegraph poles over the moors, dropping their loads at regular intervals. They drove big teams, and came up past Breidablik, past Sellanraa farm, and met new teams beyond, coming down with poles from the other side of the hills—the line was complete.

So life went on day by day, without any great event. What was there to happen, anyway? Spring came, and the work of setting up the poles began. Brede Olsen was there again, with the gangs, though he should have been working on his own land at that season. " 'Tis a wonder he's the time," thought Isak.

Isak himself had barely time to eat and sleep; it was a close thing to get through the season's work now, with all the land he had brought under tillage.

Then, between seasons, he got his sawmill roofed in, and could set to work putting up the machine parts. And look you, 'twas no marvel of fine woodwork he had set up, but strong it was, as a giant of the hills, and stood there to good use. The saw could work, and cut as a sawmill should; Isak had kept his eyes about him down in the village, and used them well. It was hearty and small, this sawmill he had built, but he was pleased with it; he carved the date above the doorway, and put his mark.

And that summer, something more than usual did come about after all at Sellanraa.

The telegraph workers had now reached so far up over the moors that the foremost gang came to the farm one evening and asked to be lodged for the night. They were given shelter in the big barn. As the days went on, the other gangs came along, and all were housed at Sellanraa. The work went on ahead, passing the farm, but the men still came back to sleep in the barn. One Saturday evening came the engineer in charge, to pay the men.

At sight of the engineer Eleseus felt his heart jump, and stole out of the house lest he should be asked about that colored pencil. Oh, there would be trouble now—and Sivert nowhere to be seen; he would have to face it alone. Eleseus slipped round the corner of the house, like a pale ghost, found his mother, and begged her to tell Sivert to come. There was no help for it now.

Sivert took the matter less to heart—but then, he was not the chief culprit. The two brothers went a little way off and sat down, and Eleseus said: "If you'd say it was you, now!"

"Me?" said Sivert.

"You're younger, he wouldn't do anything to you."

Sivert thought over it, and saw that his brother was in distress; also it flattered him to feel that the other needed his help.

"Why, I might help you out of it, perhaps," said he in a grown-up voice.

"Aye, if you would!" said Eleseus, and quite simply gave his brother the bit of pencil that was left. "You can have it for keeps," he said.

They were going in again together, but Eleseus recol-

lected he had something he must do over at the sawmill, or
rather, at the grain mill; something he must look to, and it
would take some time—he wouldn't be finished just yet.
Sivert went in alone.

There sat the engineer, paying out notes and silver, and
when he had finished, Inger gave him milk to drink, a jug
and a glass, and he thanked her. Then he talked to little
Leopoldine, and then, noticing the drawings on the walls,
asked straight out who had done that. "Was it you?" he
asked, turning to Sivert. The man felt, perhaps, he owed
something for Inger's hospitality, and praised the drawings
just to please her. Inger, on her part, explained the matter
as it was: it was her boys had made the drawings—both of
them. They had no paper till she came home and looked to
things, so they had marked all about the walls. But she
hadn't the heart to wash it off again.

"Why, leave it as it is," said the engineer. "Paper, did
you say?" And he took out a heap of big sheets. "There,
draw away on that till I come round again. And how are
you off for pencils?"

Sivert stepped forward simply with the stump he had,
and showed how small it was. And behold, the man gave
him a new colored pencil, not even sharpened. "There, now
you can start afresh. But I'd make the horses red if I were
you, and do the goats with blue. Never seen a blue horse,
have you?"

And the engineer went on his way.

That same evening, a man came up from the village with
a basket—he handed out some bottles to the workmen, and
went off again. But after he had gone, it was no longer so
quiet about the place; someone played an accordion, the
men talked loudly, and there was singing, and even dancing, at Sellanraa. One of the men asked Inger out to dance,
and Inger—who would have thought it of her?—she

laughed a little laugh and actually danced a few turns round. After that, some of the others asked her, and she danced not a little in the end.

Inger—who could say what was in her mind? Here she was dancing gaily, maybe for the first time in her life; sought after, riotously pursued by thirty men, and she alone, the only one to choose from, no one to cut her out. And those burly telegraph men—how they lifted her! Why not dance? Eleseus and Sivert were fast asleep in the little chamber, undisturbed by all the noise outside; little Leopoldine was up, looking on wonderingly at her mother as she danced.

Isak was out in the fields all the time; he had gone off directly after supper, and when he came home to go to bed, someone offered him a bottle. He drank a little, and sat watching the dancing, with Leopoldine on his lap.

" 'Tis a gay time you're having," said he kindly to Inger "—footing it properly tonight!"

After a while the music stopped, and the dance was over. The workmen got ready to leave—they were going down to the village for the rest of the evening, and would be there all next day, coming back on Monday morning. Soon all was quiet again at Sellanraa; a couple of the older men stayed behind, and turned in to sleep in the barn.

Isak woke up in the night—Inger was not there. Could she be gone to see to the cows? He got up and went across to the cowshed. "Inger!" he called. No answer. The cows turned their heads and looked at him; all was still. Unthinkingly, from ancient habit, he counted heads, counted the sheep also; there was one of the ewes had a bad habit of staying out at night—and out it was now. "Inger!" he called again. Still no answer. Surely she couldn't have gone with them down to the village?

The summer night was light and warm. Isak stayed a while sitting on the door-slab, then he went out into the woods to look for the ewe. And he found Inger. Inger and one other. They sat in the heather, she twirling his peaked cap on one finger, both talking together—they were after her again, it seemed.

Isak trundled slowly over towards them. Inger turned and saw him, and bowed forward where she sat; all the life went out of her, she hung like a rag.

"H'm. Did you know that ewe's out again?" asked Isak. "But no, you wouldn't know," said he.

The young telegraph hand picked up his cap and began sidling away. "I'll be getting along after the others," he said. "Good night to ye." No one answered.

"So you're sitting here," said Isak. "Going to stay out a bit, maybe?" And he turned towards home. Inger rose to her knees, got on her feet and followed after, and so they went, man in front and wife behind, tandem-wise. They went home.

Inger must have found time to think. Oh, she found a way. " 'Twas the ewe I was after," said she. "I saw it was out again. Then one of the men came up and helped me look. We'd not been sitting a moment when you came. Where are you going now?"

"I? Seems I'd better look for the creature myself."

"No, no, go and lie down. If anyone's to go, let me. Go and lie down, you'll be needing rest. And as for that, the ewe can stay out where she is—'twon't be the first time."

"And be eaten up by some beast or other," said Isak, and went off.

Inger ran after him. "Don't, don't, it's not worth it," she said. "You need rest. Let me go."

Isak gave in. But he would not hear of Inger going out to search by herself. And they went indoors together.

Inger turned at once to look for the children; went into the little chamber to see to the boys, as if she had been out on some perfectly natural errand; it almost seemed, indeed, as if she were trying to make up to Isak—as if she expected him to be more in love with her than ever that evening—after she had explained it all so neatly. But no, Isak was not so easy to turn; he would rather have seen her thoroughly distressed and beside herself with contrition. Aye, that would have been better. What matter that she had collapsed for a moment when he came on her in the woods; the little moment of shame—what was the good of that when it all passed off so soon?

He was far from gentle, too, the next day, and that a Sunday; went off and looked to the sawmill, looked to the grain mill, looked over the fields, with the children or by himself. Inger tried once to join him, but Isak turned away: "I'm going up to the river," he said. "Something up there . . ." There was trouble in his mind, like enough, but he bore it silently, and made no scene. Oh, there was something great about Isak; as it might be Israel, promised and ever deceived, but still believing.

By Monday the tension was less marked, and as the days went on, the impression of that unhappy Saturday evening grew fainter. Time can mend a deal of things; a spit and a shake, a meal and a good night's rest, and it will heal the sorriest of wounds. Isak's trouble was not so bad as it might have been; after all, he was not certain that he had been wronged, and apart from that, he had other things to think of; the harvesting was at hand. And last, not least, the telegraph line was all but finished now; in a little while they would be left in peace. A broad light road, a king's highway, had been cut through the dark of the forest; there were poles and wires running right up over the hills.

Next Saturday paytime, the last there was to be, Isak managed to be away from home—he wished it so. He went down into the village with cheese and butter, and came back on Sunday night. The men were all gone from the barn; nearly all, that is; the last man stumbled out of the yard with his pack on his shoulder—all but the last, that is. That it was not altogether safe as yet Isak could see, for there was a bundle left on the floor of the barn. Where the owner was he could not say, and did not care to know, but there was a peaked cap on top of the bundle—an offense to the eye.

Isak heaved the bundle out into the yard, flung the cap out after it, and closed the door. Then he went into the stable and looked out through the window. And thought, belike: "Let the bundle stay there, and let the cap lie there, 'tis all one whose they may be. A bit of dirt he is, and not worth my while"—so he might have thought. But when the fellow comes for his bundle, never doubt but that Isak will be there to take him by the arm and make that arm a trifle blue. And as for kicking him off the place in a way he'd remember—why, Isak would give him that too!

Whereupon Isak left his window in the stable and went back to the cowshed and looked out from there, and could not rest. The bundle was tied up with string; the poor fellow had no lock to his bag, and the string had come undone—Isak could not feel sure he had not dealt over-hardly with that bundle. Whatever it might be—he was not sure he had acted rightly. Only just now he had been in the village, and seen his new harrow, a brand-new harrow he had ordered—oh, a wonderful machine, an idol to worship, and it had just come. A thing like that must carry a blessing with it. And the powers above, that guide the footsteps of men, might be watching him now at this moment, to see if he deserved a blessing or not. Isak gave much thought to the powers above; aye, he had seen God with his own eyes, one night in harvest-time, in the woods; it was rather a curious sight.

Isak went out into the yard and stood over the bundle. He was still in doubt; he thrust his hat back and scratched his head, which gave him a devil-may-care appearance for the moment; something lordly and careless, as it might have been a Spaniard. But then he must have thought something like this: "Nay, here am I, and far from being in any way splendid or excellent; a very dog." And then he tied up the bundle neatly once more, picked up the cap, and carried all back into the barn again. And that was done.

As he went out from the barn and over to the mill, away from the yard, away from everything, there was no Inger to be seen in the window of the house. Nay, then, let her be where she pleased—no doubt she was in bed—where else should she be? But in the old days, in those first innocent years, Inger could never rest, but sat up at nights waiting for him when he had been down to the village. It was different now, different in every way. As, for instance, when he had given her that ring. Could anything have been more utterly a failure? Isak had been gloriously modest, and far from venturing to call it a gold ring. " 'Tis nothing grand, but you might put it on your finger just to try."

"Is it gold?" she asked.

"Aye, but 'tis none so thick," said he.

And here she was to have answered: "Aye, but indeed it is." But instead she had said: "No, 'tis not very thick, but still . . ."

"Nay, 'tis worth no more than a bit of grass, belike," said he at last, and gave up hope.

But Inger had indeed been glad of the ring, and wore it on her right hand, looking fine there when she was sewing; now and again she would let the village girls try it on, and sit with it on their finger for a bit when they came up to ask of this or that. Foolish Isak—not to understand that she was proud of it beyond measure! . . .

It was a profitless business sitting there alone in the mill, listening to the fall the whole night through. Isak had done no wrong; he had no cause to hide himself away. He left the mill, went up over the fields, and home—into the house.

And then in truth it was a shamefaced Isak, shamefaced and glad. Brede Olsen sat there, his neighbor and no other; sat there drinking coffee. Aye, Inger was up, the two of them sat there simply and quietly, talking and drinking coffee.

"Here's Isak," said Inger pleasantly as could be, and got up and poured out a cup for him. "Evening," said Brede, and was just as pleasant too.

Isak could see that Brede had been spending the evening with the telegraph gangs, the last night before they went; he was somewhat the worse for it, maybe, but friendly and good-humored enough. He boasted a little, as was his way: hadn't the time really to bother with this telegraphic work, the farm took all of a man's day—but he couldn't very well say no when the engineer was so anxious to have him. And so it had come about, too, that Brede had had to take over the job of line inspector. Not for the sake of the money, of course, he could earn many times that down in the village, but he hadn't liked to refuse. And they'd given him a neat little machine set up on the wall, a curious little thing, a sort of telegraph in itself.

Aye, Brede was a wastrel and a boaster, but for all that Isak could bear him no grudge; he himself was too relieved at finding his neighbor in the house that evening instead of a stranger. Isak had the peasant's coolness of mind, his few feelings, stability, stubbornness; he chatted with Brede and nodded at his shallowness. "Another cup for Brede," said he. And Inger poured it out.

Inger talked of the engineer; a kindly man he was beyond measure; had looked at the boys' drawings and writings, and even said something about taking Eleseus to work under him.

"To work with him?" said Isak.

"Aye, to the town. To do writing and things, be a clerk in the office—all for he was so pleased with the boy's writing and drawing."

"Ho!" said Isak.

"Well, and what do you say? He was going to have him confirmed too. That was a great thing, to my mind."

"Aye, a great thing indeed," said Brede. "And when the engineer says he'll do a thing, he'll do it. I know him, and you can take my word for that."

"We've no Eleseus to spare on this farm as I know of," said Isak.

There was something like a painful silence after that. Isak was not an easy man to talk to.

"But when the boy himself wants to get on," said Inger at last, "and has it in him, too." Silence again.

Then said Brede with a laugh: "I wish he'd ask for one of mine, anyway. I've enough of them and to spare. But Barbro's the eldest, and she's a girl."

"And a good girl enough," said Inger, for politeness's sake.

"Aye, I'll not say no," said Brede. "Barbro's well enough, and clever at this and that—she's going to help at the Lensmand's now."

"Going to the Lensmand's?"

"Well, I had to let her go—his wife was so set on it, I couldn't say no."

It was well on towards morning now, and Brede rose to go.

"I've a bundle and a cap I left in your barn," he said. "That is if the men haven't run off with it," he added jestingly.

ᴀɴᴅ time went on.

Yes, Eleseus was sent to town after all; Inger managed that. He was there for a year, then he was confirmed, and after that had a regular place in the engineer's office, and grew more and more clever at writing and things. To see the letters he sent home—sometimes with red and black ink, like pictures almost. And the talk of them, the words he used. Now and again he asked for money, something towards his expenses. A watch and chain, for instance, he must have, so as not to oversleep himself in the morning and be late at the office; money for a pipe and tobacco also, such as the other young clerks in the town always had. And for something he called pocket-money, and something he called evening classes, where he learned drawing and gymnastics and other matters proper to his rank and position. Altogether, it was no light matter to keep Eleseus going in a berth in town.

"Pocket-money?" said Isak. "Is that money to keep in your pocket, maybe?"

"That must be it, no doubt," said Inger. "So as not to be altogether without. And it's not much; only a daler now and then."

"Aye, that's just it," said Isak harshly. "A daler now and a daler then . . ." But his harshness was all because he missed Eleseus himself, and wanted him home. "It makes too many daler in the long run," said he. "I can't keep on like this; you must write and tell him he can have no more."

"Ho, very well then!" said Inger in an offended tone.

"There's Sivert—what does he get by way of pocket-money?"

Inger answered: "You've never been in a town, and so you don't know these things. Sivert's no need of pocket-money. And talking of money, Sivert ought to be none so badly off when his Uncle Sivert dies."

"You don't know."

"Aye, but I do know."

And this was right enough in a way; Uncle Sivert had said something about making little Sivert his heir. Uncle Sivert had heard of Eleseus and his grand doings in town, and the story did not please him; he nodded and bit his lips, and muttered that a nephew called up as his name-sake—named after Uncle Sivert—should not come tó want. But what was this fortune Uncle Sivert was supposed to possess? Had he really, besides his neglected farm and his fishery, the heap of money and means folk generally thought? No one could say for certain. And apart from that, Uncle Sivert himself was an obstinate man; he insisted that little Sivert should come to stay with him. It was a point of honor with him, this last; he should take little Sivert and look after him, as the engineer had done with Eleseus.

But how could it be done? Send little Sivert away from home? It was out of the question. He was all the help left to Isak now. Moreover, the lad himself had no great wish to go and stay with his famous uncle; he had tried it once, but had come home again. He was confirmed, shot up in stature, and grew; the down showed on his cheek, his hands were big, a pair of willing slaves. And he worked like a man.

Isak could hardly have managed to get the new barn built

at all without Sivert's help—but there it stood now, with
bridgeway and air-holes and all, as big as they had at the
parsonage itself. True, it was only a half-timbered building
covered with boarding, but extra stout built, with iron
clinches at the corners, and covered with one-inch plank
from Isak's own sawmill. And Sivert had hammered in
more than one nail at the work, and lifted the heavy beams
for the framework till he was near fainting. Sivert got on
well with his father, and worked steadily at his side; he
was made of the same stuff. And yet he was not above
such simple ways as going up the hillside for tansy to rub
with so as to smell nice in church. 'Twas Leopoldine was
the one for getting fancies in her head, which was natural
enough, she being a girl, and the only daughter. That summer, if you please, she had discovered that she could not
eat her porridge at supper without treacle—simply couldn't.
And she was no great use at any kind of work either.

Inger had not yet given up her idea of keeping a servant;
she brought up the question every spring, and every time
Isak opposed it stubbornly. All the cutting out and sewing
and fine weaving she could do, not to speak of making embroidered slippers, if she had but the time to herself! And
of late, Isak had been something less firm in his refusal,
though he grumbled still. Ho, the first time! He had made
a whole long speech about it; not as a matter of right and
reason, nor yet from pride, but, alas! from weakness, from
anger at the idea. But now, he seemed to be giving way,
as if ashamed.

"If ever I'm to have help in the house, now's the time,"
said Inger. "A few years more, and Leopoldine'll be big
enough to do this and that."

"Help?" said Isak. "What do you want help with, anyway?"

"Want with it, indeed? Haven't you help yourself?
Haven't you Sivert all the time?"

What could Isak say to a meaningless argument like that? He answered: "Aye, well; when you get a girl up here, I doubt you'll be able to plow and sow and reap and manage all by yourselves. And then Sivert and I can go our ways."

"That's as may be," said Inger. "But I'll just say this: that I could get Barbro to come now; she's written home about it."

"What Barbro?" said Isak. "Is it that Brede's girl you mean?"

"Yes. She's in Bergen now."

"I'll not have that Brede's girl Barbro up here," said he. "Whoever you get, I'll have none of her."

That was better than nothing; Isak refused to have Barbro; he no longer said they would have no servant at all.

Barbro from Breidablik was not the sort of girl Isak approved of; she was shallow and unsettled like her father—maybe like her mother too—a careless creature, no steady character at all. She had not stayed long at the Lensmand's; only a year. After her confirmation, she went to help at the storekeeper's, and was there another year. Here she turned pious and got religion, and when the Salvation Army came to the village she joined it, and went about with a red band on her sleeve and carried a guitar. She went to Bergen in that costume, on the storekeeper's boat—that was last year. And she had just sent home a photograph of herself to her people at Breidablik. Isak had seen it; a strange young lady with her hair curled up and a long watch-chain hanging down over her breast. Her parents were proud of little Barbro, and showed the photograph about to all who came; 'twas grand to see how she had learned town ways and got on in the world. As for the red band and the guitar, she had given them up, it seemed.

"I took the picture along and showed it to the Lensmand's lady," said Brede. "She didn't know her again."

"Is she going to stay in Bergen?" said Isak suspiciously.

"Why, unless she goes on to Christiania, perhaps," said Brede. "What's there for her to do here? She's got a new place now, as housekeeper, for two young clerks. They've no wives nor womenfolk of their own, and they pay her well."

"How much?" said Isak.

"She doesn't say exactly in the letter. But it must be something altogether different from what folk pay down here, that's plain. Why, she gets Christmas presents, and presents other times as well, and not counted off her wages at all."

"Ho!" said Isak.

"You wouldn't like to have her up at your place?" asked Brede.

"I?" said Isak, all taken aback.

"No, of course, he he! It was only a way of speaking. Barbro's well enough where she is. What was I going to say? You didn't notice anything wrong with the line coming down—the telegraph, what?"

"With the telegraph? No."

"No, no . . . There's not much wrong with it now since I took over. And then I've my own machine here on the wall to give a warning if anything happens. I'll have to take a walk up along the line one of these days and see how things are. I've too much to manage and look after, 'tis more than one man's work. But as long as I'm Inspector here, and hold an offical position, of course I can't neglect my duties. If I hadn't the telegraph, of course . . . and it may not be for long. . . ."

"Why?" said Isak. "You thinking of giving it up, maybe?"

"Well, I can't say exactly," said Brede. "I haven't quite decided. They want me to move down into the village again."

"Who is it wants you?" asked Isak.

"Oh all of them. The Lensmand wants me to go and be assistant there again, and the doctor wants me to drive for him, and the parson's wife said more than once she misses me to lend a hand, if it wasn't such a long way to go. How was it with that strip of hill, Isak—the bit you sold? Did you get as much for it as they say?"

"Aye, 'tis no lie," answered Isak.

"But what did Geissler want with it, anyway? It lies there still—curious thing! Year after year and nothing done."

It was a curious thing; Isak had often wondered about it himself; he had spoken to the Lensmand about it, and asked for Geissler's address, thinking to write to him. . . . Aye, it was a mystery.

" 'Tis more than I can say," said Isak.

Brede made no secret of his interest in this matter of the sale. "They say there's more of the same sort up there," he said, "besides yours. Maybe there's more in it than we know. 'Tis a pity that we should sit here like dumb beasts and know nothing of it all. I've thought of going up one day myself to have a look."

"But do you know anything about metals and such-like?" asked Isak.

"Why, I know a bit. And I've asked one or two others. Anyhow, I'll have to find something; I can't live and keep us all here on this bit of a farm. It's sheer impossible. 'Twas another matter with you that's got all that timber and good soil below. 'Tis naught but moorland here."

"Moorland's good soil enough," said Isak shortly. "I've the same myself."

"But there's no draining it," said Brede. . . . "It can't be done."

But it could be done. Coming down the road that day Isak noticed other clearings; two of them were lower down,

nearer the village, but there was one far up above, between
Breidablik and Sellanraa—aye, men were beginning to
work on the land now; in the old days when Isak first came
up, it had lain waste, all of it. And these three new settlers
were folks from another district; men with some sense in
their heads, by the look of things. They didn't begin by
borrowing money to build a house; no, they came up one
year and did their spadework and went away again; vanished as if they were dead. That was the proper way;
ditching first, then plow and sow. Axel Ström was nearest
to Isak's land now, his next-door neighbor. A clever fellow,
unmarried, he came from Helgeland. He had borrowed
Isak's new harrow to break up his soil, and not till the
second year had he set up a hayshed and a turf hut for
himself and a couple of animals. He had called his place
Maaneland, because it looked nice in the moonlight. He
had no womenfolk himself, and found it difficult to get help
in the summer, lying so far out, but he managed things the
right way, no doubt about that. Not as Brede Olsen did,
building a house first, and then coming up with a big
family and little ones and all, with neither soil nor stock to
feed them. What did Brede Olsen know of draining moorland and breaking new soil?

He knew how to waste his time idling, did Brede. He
came by Sellanraa one day, going up to the hills—simply to
look for precious metals. He came back the same evening;
had not found anything definite, he said, but certain signs
—and he nodded. He would come up again soon, and go
over the hills thoroughly, over towards Sweden.

And sure enough, Brede came up again. He had taken
a fancy to the work, no doubt; but he called it telegraph
business this time—must go up and look over the whole
of the line. Meanwhile his wife and children at home
looked after the farm, or left it to look after itself. Isak was
sick and tired of Brede's visits, and went out of the room

when he came; then Inger and Brede would sit talking heartily together. What could they have to talk about? Brede often went down to the village, and had always some news to tell of the great folk there; Inger, on the other hand, could always draw upon her famous journey to Trondhjem and her stay there. She had grown talkative in the years she had been away, and was always ready to gossip with anyone. No, she was no longer the same straightforward, simple Inger of the old days.

Girls and women came up continually to Sellanraa to have a piece of work cut out, or a long hem put through the machine in a moment, and Inger entertained them well. Oline too came again, couldn't help it, belike; came both spring and autumn; fair-spoken, soft as butter, and thoroughly false. "Just looked along to see how things are with you," she said each time. "And I've been longing so for a sight of the lads, I'm that fond of them, the little angels they were. Aye, they're big fellows now, but it's strange . . . I can't forget the time when they were small and I had them in my care. And here's you building and building again, and making a whole town of the place. Going to have a bell to ring, maybe, at the roof of the barn, same as at the parsonage?"

Once Oline came and brought another woman with her, and the pair of them and Inger had a nice day together. The more Inger had sitting round her, the better she worked at her sewing and cutting out, making a show of it, waving her scissors and swinging the iron. It reminded her of the place where she had learned it all—there was always many of them in the workrooms there. Inger made no secret of where she had got her knowledge and all her art from; it was from Trondhjem. It almost appeared as if she had not been in prison at all, in the ordinary way, but at school, in an institute, where one could learn to sew and weave and write, and do dressing and dyeing—all that she had learned in Trondhjem. She spoke of the place as of a home; there were so many people she knew there, superintendents and forewomen and attendants, it had been dull and empty to come back here again, and hard to find herself altogether cut off from the life and society she had been accustomed to. She even made some show of having a cold—couldn't stand the keen air there; for years after her return she had been too poorly to work out of doors in all seasons. It was for the outside work she really ought to have a servant.

"Aye, Heaven save us," said Oline, "and why shouldn't you have a servant indeed, when you've means and learning and a great fine house and all!"

It was pleasant to meet with sympathy, and Inger did not deny it. She worked away at her machine till the place shook, and the ring on her finger shone.

"There, you can see for yourself," said Oline to the woman with her. "It's true what I said, Inger she wears a gold ring on her finger."

"Would you like to see it?" asked Inger, taking it off.

Oline seemed still to have her doubts; she turned it in her fingers as a monkey with a nut, looked at the mark. "Aye, 'tis as I say; Inger with all her means and riches."

The other woman took the ring with veneration, and smiled humbly. "You can put it on for a bit if you like," said Inger. "Don't be afraid, it won't break."

And Inger was amiable and kind. She told them about the cathedral at Trondhjem, and began like this: "You haven't seen the cathedral at Trondhjem, maybe? No, you haven't been there!" And it might have been her own cathedral, from the way she praised it, boasted of it, told them height and breadth; it was a marvel! Seven priests could stand there preaching all at once and never hear one another. "And then I suppose you've never seen St. Olaf's Well? Right in the middle of the cathedral itself, it is, on one side, and it's a bottomless well. When we went there, we took each a little stone with us, and dropped it in, but it never reached the bottom."

"Never reached the bottom?" whispered the two women, shaking their heads.

"And there's a thousand other things besides in that cathedral," exclaimed Inger delightedly. "There's the silver chest to begin with. It's Holy St. Olaf his own silver chest that he had. But the Marble Church—that was a little church all of pure marble—the Danes took that from us in the war. . . ."

It was time for the women to go. Oline took Inger aside, led her out into the larder where she knew all the cheeses were stored, and closed the door. "What is it?" asked Inger.

Oline whispered: "Os-Anders, he doesn't dare come here any more. I've told him."

"Ho!" said Inger.

"I told him if he only dared, after what he'd done to you."

"Aye," said Inger. "But he's been here many a time since for all that. And he can come if he likes, I'm not afraid."

"No, that's so," said Oline. "But I know what I know, and if you like, I'll lay a charge against him."

"Ho!" said Inger. "No, you've no call to do that. 'Tis not worth it."

But she was not ill pleased to have Oline on her side; it cost her a cheese, to be sure, but Oline thanked her so fulsomely: " 'Tis as I say, 'tis as I've always said: Inger, she gives with both hands; nothing grudging, nothing sparing about her! No, maybe you're not afraid of Os-Anders, but I've forbid him to come here all the same. 'Twas the least I could do for you."

Said Inger then: "What harm could it do if he did come, anyway? He can't hurt me any more."

Oline pricked up her ears: "Ho, you've learned a way yourself, maybe?"

"I shan't have any more children," said Inger.

And now they were quits, each holding as good a trump as the other: for Oline stood there knowing all the time that Os-Anders the Lapp had died the day before. . . .

Why should Inger say that about having no more children? She was not on bad terms with her husband, 'twas no cat-and-dog life between them—far from it. They had each their own little ways, but it was rarely they quarreled, and never for long at a time; it was soon made up. And many a time Inger would suddenly be just as she had been in the old days, working hard in the cowshed or in the field; as if she had had a relapse into health again. And at such times Isak would look at his wife with grateful eyes; if he had been the sort of man to speak his mind at once, he might have said: "H'm. What does this mean, heh?" or something of the sort, just to show he appreciated it. But he waited too long, and his praise came too late. So Inger, no doubt, found it not worth while, and did not care to keep it up.

She might have had children till past fifty; as it was, she was perhaps hardly forty now. She had learned all sorts of things at the institution—had she also learned to play tricks with herself? She had come back so thoroughly trained and educated after her long association with the other murderesses; maybe the men had taught her something too—the jailers, the doctors. She told Isak one day what one young medical man had said of her little crime: "Why should it be a criminal offense to kill children—aye, even healthy children?" They were nothing but lumps of flesh after all.

Isak asked: "Wasn't he terribly cruel himself, then?"

"Him!" exclaimed Inger, and told how kind he had been

to her herself; it was he who had got another doctor to operate on her mouth and make a human being of her. Now there was only a scar to be seen.

Only a scar, yes. And a fine woman she was in her way, tall and not over-stout, dark, with rich hair; in summer she went barefooted mostly and with her skirt kilted high; Inger was not afraid of letting her calves be seen. Isak saw them—as who did not!

They did not quarrel, no. Isak had no talent for quarreling, and his wife had grown readier-witted to answer back. A thorough good quarrel took a long time to grow with Isak, heavy stub of a man as he was; he found himself all entangled in her words, and could say next to nothing himself; and besides, he was fond of her—powerfully in love was Isak. And it was not often he had any need to answer. Inger did not complain; he was an excellent husband in many ways, and she let him alone. What had she to complain of at all? Isak was not a man to be despised; she might have married a worse. Worn out, was he? True, he showed signs of being tired now at times, but nothing serious. He was full of old health and unwasted strength, like herself, and in this autumn of their married life he fulfilled his part at least as affectionately as she did.

But nothing particularly beautiful nor grand about him? No. And here came her superiority. Inger might well think to herself at times how she had seen finer men; handsome gentlemen with walking-sticks and handkerchiefs and starched collars to wear—oh, those gentlemen of the town! And so she kept Isak in his place, treated him, as it were, no better than he deserved. He was only a peasant, a clodhopper of the wilds; if her mouth had been as it was now from the start she would never have taken him; be sure of that. No, she could have done better than that! The home he had given her, the life he offered her, were poor enough;

she might at least have married someone from her own village, and lived among neighbors, with a circle of friends, instead of here like an outcast in the wilds. It was not the place for her now; she had learned to look differently at life.

Strange, how one could come to look differently at things! Inger found no pleasure now in admiring a new calf; she did not clap her hands in surprise when Isak came down from the hills with a big basket of fish; no, she had lived for six years among greater things. And of late she had even ceased to be heavenly and sweet when she called him in to dinner. "Your food's ready, aren't you coming in?" was all she said now. And it didn't sound nice. Isak wondered a little at first; it was a curious way to speak; a nasty, uncaring, take-it-or-leave-it way to speak. And he answered: "Why, I didn't know 'twas ready." But when Inger pointed out that he ought to have known, or might have guessed it, anyway, by the sun, he said no more, and let the matter drop.

Ah, but once he got a hold on her and used it—that was when she tried to steal his money from him. Not that Isak was a miser in that way, but the money was clearly his. Ho, it was nearly being ruin and disaster for her that time! But even then it was not exactly thoroughgoing, out-and-out wickedness on Inger's part; she wanted the money for Eleseus—for her blessed boy Eleseus in town, who was asking for his daler again. Was he to go there among all the fine folk and with empty pockets? After all, she had a mother's heart. She asked his father for the money first, and, finding it was no good, had taken it herself. Whether Isak had had some suspicion beforehand, or had found it out by accident—anyhow, it was found out. And suddenly Inger found herself gripped by both arms, felt herself lifted from the floor, and thumped down on the floor again. It was something strange and terrible—a sort of avalanche. Isak's hands were not weak, not worn out now. Inger gave a groan, her head fell back, she shivered, and gave up the money.

Even then Isak said little though Inger made no attempt to hinder him from speaking. What he did say was uttered, as it were, in one hard breath: "Huttch! You—you're not fit to have in the place!"

She hardly knew him again. Oh, but it must have been long-stored bitterness that would not be repressed.

A miserable day, and a long night, and a day beyond. Isak went out of the house and lay outside, for all that there was hay to be got in; Sivert was with his father. Inger had little Leopoldine and the animals to keep her company; but lonely she was for all that, crying nearly all the time and shaking her head at herself. Only once in all her life before had she felt so moved, and this day called it to mind; it was when she had lain in her bed and throttled a newborn child.

Where were Isak and his son? They had not been idle; no, they had stolen a day and a night or thereabouts from the haymaking, and had built a boat up on the lake. Oh, a rough and poor-looking vessel enough, but strong and sound as their work had always been; they had a boat now, and could go fishing with nets.

When they came home the hay was dry as ever. They had cheated providence by trusting it, and suffered no loss; they had gained by it. And then Sivert flung out an arm, and said: "Ho! Mother's been haymaking!" Isak looked down over the fields and said "H'm." Isak had noticed already that some of the hay had been shifted; Inger ought to be home now for her midday meal. It was well done indeed of her to get in the hay, after he had scolded her the day before and said "Huttch!" And it was no light hay to move; she must have worked hard, and all the cows and goats to milk besides. . . . "Go in and get something to eat," he said to Sivert.

"Aren't you coming, then?"

"No."

A little while after, Inger came out and stood humbly on the door-slab and said:

"If you'd think of yourself a little—and come in and have a bite to eat."

Isak grumbled at that and said: "H'm." But it was so strange a thing of late for Inger to be humble in any way, that his stubbornness was shaken.

"If you could manage to set a couple of teeth in my rake, I could get on again with the hay," said she. Aye, she came to her husband, the master of the place, to ask for something, and was grateful that he did not turn scornfully away.

"You've worked enough," said he, "raking and carting and all."

"No, 'tis not enough."

"I've no time, anyway, to mend rakes now. You can see there's rain coming soon."

And Isak went off to his work.

It was all meant to save her, no doubt; for the couple of minutes it would have taken to mend the rake would have been more then tenfold repaid by letting Inger work on. Anyhow, Inger came out with her rake as it was, and fell to haymaking with a will; Sivert came up with the horse and haycart, and all went at it, sweating at the work, and the hay was got in. It was a good stroke of work, and Isak fell to thinking once more of the powers above that guide all our ways—from stealing a daler to getting a crop of hay. Moreover, there lay the boat; after half a generation of thinking it over, the boat was finished; it was there, up on the lake.

"Eyah, *Herregud!*" said Isak.

CHAPTER XV

It was a strange evening altogether: a turning-point. Inger had been running off the line for a long time now; and one lift up from the floor had set her in her place again. Neither spoke of what had happened. Isak had felt ashamed of himself after—all for the sake of a daler, a trifle of money, that he would have had to give her after all, because he himself would gladly have let the boy have it. And then again—was not the money as much Inger's as his own? There came a time when Isak found it his turn to be humble.

There came many sorts of times. Inger must have changed her mind again, it seemed; once more she was different, gradually forgetting her fine ways and turning earnest anew: a settler's wife, earnest and thoughtful as she had been before. To think that a man's hard grip could work such wonders! But it was right; here was a strong and healthy woman, sensible enough, but spoiled and warped by long confinement in an artificial air—and she had butted into a man who stood firmly on his feet. Never for a moment had he left his natural place on the earth, on the soil. Nothing could move him.

Many sorts of times. Next year came the drought again, killing the growth off slowly, and wearing down human courage. The grain stood there and shriveled up; the potatoes—the wonderful potatoes—they did not shrivel up, but flowered and flowered. The meadows turned grey, but the potatoes flowered. The powers above guided all things, no doubt, but the meadows were turning grey.

Then one day came Geissler—ex-Lensmand Geissler came again at last. It was good to find that he was not dead, but had turned up again. And what had he come for now?

Geissler had no grand surprises with him this time, by the look of it; no purchases of mining rights and documents and such-like. Geissler was poorly dressed, his hair and beard turned greyer, and his eyes redder at the edges than before. He had no man, either, to carry his things, but had his papers in a pocket, and not even a bag.

"*Goddag*," said Geissler.

"*Goddag*," answered Isak and Inger. "Here's the like of visitors to see this way!"

Geissler nodded.

"And thanks for all you did that time—in Trondhjem," said Inger all by herself.

And Isak nodded at that, and said: "Aye, 'tis two of us owe you thanks for that."

But Geissler—it was not his way to be all feelings and sentiments; he said: "Yes, I'm just going across to Sweden."

For all their trouble of mind over the drought, Sellanraa's folk were glad to see Geissler again; they gave him the best they had, and were heartily glad to do what they could for him after all he had done.

Geissler himself had no troubles that could be seen; he grew talkative at once, looked out over the fields and nodded. He carried himself upright as ever, and looked as if he had several hundreds of daler in his pockets. It livened them up and brightened everything to have him there; not that he made any boisterous fun, but a lively talker, that he was.

"Fine place, Sellanraa, splendid place," he said. "And now there's others coming up one after another, since you've started, Isak. I counted five myself. Are there any more?"

"Seven in all. There's two that can't be seen from the road."

"Seven holdings; say fifty souls. Why, it'll be a densely populated neighborhood before long. And you've a school already, so I hear?"

"Aye, we have."

"There—what did I say? A school all to yourselves, down by Brede's place, being more in the middle. Fancy Brede as a farmer in the wilds!" and Geissler laughed at the thought. "Aye, I've heard all about you, Isak; you're the best man here. And I'm glad of it. Sawmill, too, you've got?"

"Aye, such as it is. But it serves me well enough. And I've sawed a bit now and again for them down below."

"Bravo! That's the way!"

"I'd be glad to hear what you think of it, Lensmand, if so be you'd care to look at that sawmill for yourself."

Geissler nodded, with the air of an expert; yes, he would look at it, examine it thoroughly. Then he asked: "You had two boys, hadn't you—what's become of the other? In town? Clerk in an office? H'm," said Geissler. "But this one here looks a sturdy sort—what was your name, now?"

"Sivert."

"And the other one?"

"Eleseus."

"And he's in an engineer's office—what's he reckon to learn there? A starvation business. Much better have come to me," said Geissler.

"Aye," said Isak, for politeness's sake. He felt a sort of pity for Geissler at the moment. Oh, that good man did not look as if he could afford to keep clerks; had to work hard enough by himself, belike. That jacket—it was worn to fringes at the wrists.

"Won't you have some dry hose to put on?" said Inger, and brought out a pair of her own. They were from her best days; fine and thin, with a border.

"No, thanks," said Geissler shortly, though he must have been wet through. "Much better have come to me," he said again, speaking of Eleseus. "I want him badly." He took a small silver tobacco-box from his pocket and sat playing with it in his fingers. It was perhaps the only thing of value left him now.

But Geissler was restless, changing from one thing to another. He slipped the thing back into his pocket again and started a new theme. "But—what's that? Why, the meadow that's all grey. I thought it was the shadow. The ground is simply parched. Come along with me, Sivert."

He rose from the table suddenly, thinking no more of food, turned in the doorway to say "Thank you" to Inger for the meal, and disappeared, Sivert following.

They went across to the river, Geissler peering keenly about all the time. "Here!" he cried, and stopped. And then he explained: "Where's the sense of letting your land dry up to nothing when you've a river there big enough to drown it in a minute? We'll have that meadow green by tomorrow!"

Sivert, all astonishment, said: "Yes."

"Dig down obliquely from here, see?—on a slope. The ground's level; have to make some sort of a channel. You've a sawmill there—I suppose you can find some long planks from somewhere? Good! Run and fetch a pick and spade, and start here; I'll go back and mark out a proper line."

He ran up to the house again, his boots squelching, for they were wet through. He set Isak to work making pipes, a whole lot of them, to be laid down where the ground could not well be cut with ditches. Isak tried to object that the water might not get so far; the dry ground would soak it up before it reached the parched fields. Geissler explained that it would take some time; the earth must drink a little first, but then gradually the water would go on—"field and meadow green by this time tomorrow."

"Ho!" said Isak, and fell to boxing up long planks as hard as he could.

Off hurries Geissler to Sivert once more: "That's right—keep at it—didn't I say he was a sturdy sort? Follow these stakes, you understand, where I've marked out. If you come up against heavy boulders, or rock, then turn aside and go round, but keep the level—the same depth; you see what I mean?"

Then back to Isak again: "That's one finished—good! But we shall want more—half a dozen, perhaps. Keep at it, Isak; you see, we'll have it all green by tomorrow—we've saved your crops!" And Geissler sat down on the ground, slapped his knees with both hands and was delighted, chattered away, thought in flashes of lightning. "Any pitch, any oakum, or anything about the place? That's splendid—got everything. These things'll leak at the edges you see, to begin with, but the wood'll swell after a while, and they'll be as taut as a bottle. Oakum and pitch—fancy you having it too! What? Built a boat, you say? Where is the boat? Up in the lake? Good! I must have a look at that too."

Oh, Geissler was all promises. Light come, light go—and he seemed more given to fussing about than before. He worked at things by fits and starts, but at a furious rate when he did work. There was a certain superiority about him after all. True, he exaggerated a bit—it was impossible, of course, to get all green by this time tomorrow, as he had said, but for all that, Geissler was a sharp fellow, quick to see and take a decision; aye, a strange man was Geissler. And it was he and no other that saved the crops that year at Sellanraa.

"How many have you got done? Not enough. The more

wood you can lay, the quicker it'll flow. Make them twenty feet long or twenty-five, if you can. Any planks that length on the place? Good; fetch them along—you'll find it'll pay you at harvest-time!"

Restless again—up and off to Sivert once more. "That's the way, Sivert man; getting on finely. Your father's turning out culverts like a poet, there'll be more than I ever thought. Run across and get some now, and we'll make a start."

All that afternoon was one hurrying spell; Sivert had never seen such a furious piece of work; he was not accustomed to see things done at that pace. They hardly gave themselves time to eat. But the water was flowing already! Here and there they had to dig deeper, a culvert had to be raised or lowered, but it flowed. The three men were at it till late that night, touching up their work, and keenly on the lookout for any fault. But when the water began to trickle out over the driest spots, there was joy and delight at Sellanraa. "I forgot to bring my watch," said Geissler. "What's the time, I wonder? Aye, she'll be green by this time tomorrow!" said he.

Sivert got up in the middle of the night to see how things were going, and found his father out already on the same errand. Oh, but it was a thrilling time—a day of great events!

But next day, Geissler stayed in bed till nearly noon, worn out now that the fit had passed. He did not trouble to go up and look at the boat on the lake; and but for what he had said the day before, he would never have bothered to look at the sawmill. Even the irrigation works interested him less than at first—and when he saw that neither field nor meadow had turned green in the course of the night, he lost heart, never thinking of how the water flowed, and flowed all the time, and spread out farther and farther over the ground. He backed down a little, and said now: "It may

take time—you won't see any change perhaps before tomorrow again. But it'll be all right, never fear."

Later in the day Brede Olsen came lounging in; he had
brought some samples of rock he wanted Geissler to see.
"And something out of the common, this time, to my
mind," said Brede.

Geissler would not look at the things. "That the way you
manage a farm," he asked scornfully, "pottering about up
in the hills looking for a fortune?"

Brede apparently did not fancy being taken to task now
by his former chief; he answered sharply, without any form
of respect, treating the ex-Lensmand as an equal: "If you
think I care what you say . . ."

"You've no more sense than you had before," said Geissler. "Fooling away your time."

"What about yourself?" said Brede. "What about you,
I'd like to know? You've got a mine of your own up here,
and what have you done with it? Huh! Lies there doing
nothing. Aye, you're the sort to have a mine, aren't you?
He he!"

"Get out of this," said Geissler. And Brede did not stay
long, but shouldered his load of samples and went down
to his own ménage, without saying good-bye.

Geissler sat down and began to look over some papers
with a thoughtful air. He seemed to have caught a touch
of the fever himself, and wanted now to look over that business of the copper mine, the contract, the analyses. It was
fine ore, almost pure copper; he must do something with it,
and not let everything slide.

"What I really came up for was to get the whole thing
settled," he said to Isak. "I've been thinking of making a
start here, and that very soon. Get a lot of men to work, and
run the thing properly. What do you think?"

Isak felt sorry for the man, and would not say anything
against it.

"It's a matter that concerns you as well, you know. There'll be a lot of bother, of course; a lot of men about the place, and a bit rowdy at times, perhaps. And blasting up in the hills—I don't know how you'll like that. On the other hand, there'll be more life in the district where we begin, and you'll have a good market close at hand for farm produce and that sort of thing. Fix your own price, too."

"Aye," said Isak.

"Besides your share in the mine—you'll get a high percentage of earnings, you know. Big money, Isak."

Said Isak: "You've paid me fairly already, and more than enough. . . ."

Next morning Geissler left, hurrying off eastward, over toward Sweden. "No, thanks," he said shortly, when Isak offered to go with him. It was almost painful to see him start off in that poor fashion, on foot and all alone. Inger had put up a fine parcel of food for him to take, all as nice as she could make it, and made some wafers specially to put in. Even that was not enough; she would have given him a can of cream and a whole lot of eggs, but he wouldn't carry them, and Inger was disappointed.

Geissler himself must have found it hard to leave Sellanraa without paying as he generally did for his keep; so he pretended that he had paid; made as if he had laid down a big note in payment, and said to little Leopoldine: "Here, child, here's something for you as well." And with that he gave her the silver box, his tobacco-box. "You can rinse it out and use it to keep pins and things in," he said. "It's not the sort of thing for a present really. If I were at home I could have found her something else; I've a heap of things. . . ."

But Geissler's waterwork remained after Geissler had gone; there it was, working wonders day and night, week after week; the fields turned green, the potatoes ceased to flower, the corn shot up. . . .

The settlers from the holdings farther down began to come up, all anxious to see the marvel for themselves. Axel Ström—the neighbor from Maaneland, the man who had no wife, and no woman to help him, but managed for himself—he came too. He was in a good humor that day; he told them how he had just got a promise of a girl to help through the summer—and that was a weight off his mind. He did not say who the girl was, and Isak did not ask, but it was Brede's girl Barbro who was to come. It would cost the price of a telegram to Bergen to fetch her; but Axel paid the money, though he was not one of your extravagant sort, but rather something of a miser.

It was the waterwork business that had enticed him up today; he had looked it over from one end to the other, and was highly interested. There was no big river on his land, but he had a bit of a stream; he had no planks, either, to make culverts with, but he would dig his channels in the earth; it could be done. Up to now, things were not absolutely at their worst on his land, which lay lower down the slopes; but if the drought continued, he, too, would have to irrigate. When he had seen what he wanted, he took his leave and went back at once. No, he would not come in, hadn't the time; he was going to start ditching that same evening. And off he went.

This was something different from Brede's way.

Oh, Brede, he could run about the moorland farms now telling news: miraculous waterworks at Sellanraa! "It doesn't pay to work your soil overmuch," he had said. "Look at Isak up there; he's dug and dug about so long that at last he's had to water the whole ground."

Isak was patient, but he wished many a time that he could get rid of the fellow, hanging about Sellanraa with his boastful ways. Brede put it all down to the telegraph; as long as he was a public official, it was his duty to keep the line in order. But the telegraph company had already had occasion several times to reprimand him for neglect, and had again offered the post to Isak. No, it was not the telegraph that was in Brede's mind all the time, but the ore up in the hills; it was his one idea now, a mania.

He took to dropping in often now at Sellanraa, confident that he had found the treasure; he would nod his head and say: "I can't tell you all about it yet, but I don't mind saying I've struck something remarkable this time." Wasting hours and energy all for nothing. And when he came back in the evening to his little house, he would fling down a little sack of samples on the floor, and puff and blow after his day's work, as if no man could have toiled harder for his daily bread. He grew a few potatoes on sour, peaty soil, and cut the tufts of grass that grew by themselves on the ground about the house—that was Brede's farming. He was never made for a farmer, and there could be but one end to it all. His turf roof was falling to pieces already, and the steps to the kitchen were rotten with damp; a grindstone lay on the ground, and the cart was still left uncovered in the open.

Brede was fortunate perhaps in that such little matters never troubled him. When the children rolled his grindstone about for play, he was kind and indulgent, and would even help them to roll it himself. An easy-going, idle nature, never serious, but also never downhearted, a weak, irresponsible character; but he managed to find food, such as it was, and kept himself and his alive from day to day; managed to keep them somehow. But it was not to be expected that the storekeeper could go on feeding Brede and his family forever; he had said so more than once to Brede himself, and he said it now in earnest. Brede admitted he was right, and promised to turn over a new leaf—he would sell his place, and very likely make a good thing out of it—and pay what he owed at the store!

Oh, but Brede would sell out anyhow, even at a loss;

what was the good of a farm for him? He was homesick for the village again, the easy gossiping life there, and the little shop—it suited him better than settling down here to work, and trying to forget the world outside. Could he ever forget the Christmas trees and parties, or the national feastings on Constitution Day, or the bazaars held in the meeting-rooms? He loved to talk with his kind, to exchange news and views, but who was there to talk with here? Inger up at Sellanraa had seemed to be one of his sort for a while, but then she had changed—there was no getting a word out of her now. And besides, she had been in prison; and for a man in his position—no, it would never do.

No, he had made a mistake in ever leaving the village; it was throwing himself away. He noted with envy that the Lensmand had got another assistant, and the doctor another man to drive for him; he had run away from the people who needed him, and now that he was no longer there, they managed without him. But the men who had taken his place—they were no earthly good, of course. Properly speaking, he, Brede, ought to be fetched back to the village in triumph!

Then there was Barbro—why had he backed up the idea of getting her to go as help to Sellanraa? Well, that was after talking over things with his wife. If all went well, it might mean a good future for the girl, perhaps a future of a sort for all of them. All very well to be housekeeper for two young clerks in Bergen, but who could say what she would get out of that in the long run? Barbro was a pretty girl, and liked to look well; there might be a better chance for her here, after all. For there were two sons at Sellanraa.

But when Brede saw that this plan would never come to anything, he hit on another. After all, there was no great catch in marrying into Inger's lot—Inger who had been in prison. And there were other lads to be thought of besides

those two Sellanraa boys—there was Axel Ström, for instance. He had a farm and a hut of his own, he was a man
who scraped and saved and little by little managed to get
hold of a bit of livestock and such-like, but with no wife,
and no woman to help him. "Well, I don't mind telling you,
if you take Barbro, she'll be all the help you'll need," said
Brede to him. "Look, here's her picture; you can see."

And after a week or so, came Barbro. Axel was in the
midst of his haymaking, and had to do his mowing by day
and haymaking by night, and all by himself—and then
came Barbro! It was a godsend. Barbro soon showed she
was not afraid of work; she washed clothes and cleaned
things, cooked and milked and helped in the hayfield—
helped to carry in the hay, she did. Axel determined to give
her good wages, and not lose by it.

She was not merely a photograph of a fine lady here.
Barbro was straight and thin, spoke somewhat hoarsely,
showed sense and experience in various ways—she was not
a child. Axel wondered what made her so thin and haggard
in the face. "I'd know you by your looks," he said; "but
you're not like the photograph."

"That's only the journey," she said, "and living in town
air all that time."

And indeed, she very soon grew plump and well-looking
again. "Take my word for it," said Barbro, "it pulls you
down a bit, a journey like that, and living in town like that."
She hinted also at the temptations of life in Bergen—one
had to be careful there. But while they sat talking, she
begged him to take in a paper—a Bergen newspaper—so
that she could read a bit and see the news of the world. She
had got accustomed to reading, and theaters and music,
and it was so dull in a place like this.

Axel was pleased with the results of his summer help,
and took in a paper. He also bore with the frequent visits
of the Brede family, who were constantly dropping in at his

place and eating and drinking. He was anxious to show that he appreciated this servant-girl of his. And what could be nicer and homelier than when Barbro sat there of a Sunday evening twanging the strings of a guitar and singing a little with her hoarse voice? Axel was touched by it all, by the pretty, strange songs, by the mere fact that someone really sat there singing on his poor half-baked farm.

True, in the course of the summer he learned to know other sides of Barbro's character, but on the whole, he was content. She had her fancies, and could answer hastily at times; was somewhat over-quick to answer back. That Saturday evening, for instance, when Axel himself had to go down to the village to get some things, it was wrong of Barbro to run away from the hut and the animals and leave the place to itself. They had a few words over that. And where had she been? Only to her home, to Breidablik, but still . . . When Axel came back to the hut that night, Barbro was not there; he looked to the animals, got himself something to eat, and turned in. Towards morning Barbro came. "I only wanted to see what it was like to step on a wooden floor again," she said, somewhat scornfully. And Axel could find nothing much to say to that, seeing that he had as yet but a turf hut with a floor of beaten earth. He did say, however, that if it came to that, he could get a few planks himself, and no doubt but he'd have a house with a wooden floor himself in time! Barbro seemed penitent at that; she was not altogether unkindly. And for all it was Sunday, she went off at once to the woods and gathered fresh juniper twigs to spread on the earthen floor.

And then, seeing she was so fine-hearted and behaved so splendidly, what could Axel do but bring out the kerchief he had bought for her the evening before, though he had really thought of keeping it by a while, and getting something respectable out of her in return. And there! she was pleased with it, and tried it on at once—aye, she turned to him and asked if she didn't look nice in it. And yes, indeed she did; and she might put on his old fur cap if she liked, and she'd look nice in that! Barbro laughed at this and tried to say something really nice in return; she said: "I'd far rather go to church and communion in this kerchief than wear a hat. In Bergen, of course, we always wore hats—all except common servant-girls from the country."

Friends again, as nice as could be.

And when Axel brought out the newspaper he had fetched from the post office, Barbro sat down to read news of the world: of a burglary at a jeweler's shop in one Bergen street, and a quarrel between two gypsies in another; of a horrible find in the harbor—the dead body of a newborn child sewed up in an old shirt with the sleeves cut off. "I wonder who can have done it?" said Barbro. And she read the list of marketing prices too, as she always did.

So the summer passed.

CHAPTER XVI

GREAT changes at Sellanraa.

There was no knowing the place again, after what it had been at first: sawmill, grain mill, buildings of all sorts and kinds—the wilderness was peopled country now. And there was more to come. But Inger was perhaps the strangest of all; so altered she was, and good and clever again.

The great event of last year, when things had come to a head, was hardly enough in itself, perhaps, to change her careless ways; there was backsliding now and then, as when she found herself beginning to talk of the "Institute" again, and the cathedral at Trondhjem. Oh, innocent things enough; and she took off her ring, and let down that bold skirt of hers some inches. She was grown thoughtful, there was more quiet about the place, and visits were less frequent; the girls and women from the village came but rarely now, for Inger no longer cared to see them. No one can live in the depth of the wilds and have time for such foolishness. Happiness and nonsense are two different things.

In the wilds, each season has its wonders, but always, unchangingly, there is that immense heavy sound of heaven and earth, the sense of being surrounded on all sides, the darkness of the forest, the kindliness of the trees. All is heavy and soft, no thought is impossible there. North of Sellanraa there was a little tarn, a mere puddle, no bigger than an aquarium. There lived some tiny baby fish that never grew bigger, lived and died there and were no use at all—*Herregud!* no use on earth. One evening Inger stood there listening for the cowbells; all was dead about her, she heard nothing, and then came a song from the tarn. A little, little song, hardly there at all, almost lost. It was the tiny fishes' song.

They had this good fortune at Sellanraa, that every spring and autumn they could see the grey geese sailing in fleets above that wilderness, and hear their chatter up in the air—delirious talk it was. And as if the world stood still for a moment, till the train of them had passed. And the human souls beneath, did they not feel a weakness gliding through them now? They went to their work again, but drawing breath first; something had spoken to them, something from beyond.

Great marvels were about them at all times; in the winter were the stars; in winter often, too, the northern lights, a firmament of wings, a conflagration in the mansions of God. Now and then, not often; not commonly, but now and then, they heard the thunder. It came mostly in the autumn, and a dark and solemn thing it was for man and beast; the animals grazing near home would bunch together and stand waiting. Bowing their heads—what for? Waiting for the end? And man, what of man standing in the wilds with bowed head, waiting, when the thunder came? Waiting for what?

The spring—aye, with its haste and joy and madcap delight; but the autumn! It called up a fear of darkness, drove one to an evening prayer; there were visions about, and warnings on the air. Folks might go out one day in autumn seeking for something—the man for a piece of timber to his work, the woman after cattle that ran wild now after mushroom growths: they would come home with many secrets in their mind. Did they tread unexpectedly upon an ant, crushing its hind part fast to the path, so the fore part could not free itself again? Or step too near a white-grouse nest, putting up a fluttering hissing mother to dash against them? Even the big cow-mushrooms are not altogether meaningless; not a mere white emptiness in the eye. The big mushroom does not flower, it does not move, but there is something overturning in the look of it; it is a monster, a thing like a lung standing there alive and naked—a lung without a body.

Inger grew despondent at last, the wilds oppressed her, she turned religious. How could she help it? No one can help it in the wilds; life there is not all earthly toil and worldliness; there is piety and the fear of death and rich superstition. Inger, maybe, felt that she had more reason than others to fear the judgment of Heaven, and it would not pass her by; she knew how God walked about in the evening-time looking out over all His wilderness with fabulous eyes; aye, He would find her. There was not so much in her daily life wherein she could improve; true, she might bury her gold ring deep in the bottom of a clothes chest, and she could write to Eleseus and tell him to be converted too; after that, there was nothing more she could find beyond doing her work well and not sparing herself. Aye, one thing more; she could dress in humble things, only fastening a blue ribbon at her neck of Sundays. False, unnecessary poverty—but it was the expression of a kind of philosophy, self-humiliation, stoicism. The blue ribbon was not new; it had been cut from a cap little Leopoldine had grown out of; it was faded here and there, and, to tell the truth, a little dirty—Inger wore it now as a piece of modest finery on holy days. Aye, it may be that she went beyond reason, feigning to be poor, striving falsely to imitate the wretched who live in hovels; but even so—would her desert have been greater if that sorry finery had been her best? Leave her in peace; she has a right to peace!

She overdid things finely, and worked harder than she ought. There were two men on the place, but Inger took the chance when both were away at once, and set to work herself sawing wood; and where was the good of torturing and mortifying the flesh that way? She was so insignificant a creature, so little worth, her powers of so common a sort; her death or life would not be noticed in the land, in the State, only here in the wilds. Here, she was almost great—at any rate, the greatest; and she may well have thought herself worth all the chastening she ordered and endured. Her husband said:

"Sivert and I, we've been talking about this; we're not going to have you sawing wood, and wearing yourself out."

"I do it for conscience's sake," she answered.

Conscience! The word made Isak thoughtful once more. He was getting on in years, slow to think, but weighty when he did come to anything. Conscience must be something pretty strong if it could turn Inger all upside down like that. And however it might be, Inger's conversion made a change in him also; he caught it from her, grew tame, and given to pondering. Life was all heavy-like and stern that winter; he sought for loneliness, for a hiding-place. To save his own trees he had bought up a piece of the State forest near by, with some good timber, over toward the Swedish side, and he did the felling now alone, refusing all help. Sivert was ordered to stay at home, and see that his mother did not work too much.

And so, in those short winter days, Isak went out to his work in the dark, and came home in the dark; it was not always there was a moon, or any stars, and at times his own track of the morning would be covered with snow by nightfall, so he was hard put to it to find his way. And one evening something happened.

He was nearing home; in the fine moonlight he could see Sellanraa there on the hillside, neat and clear of the forest,

but small, undergroundish to look at, by reason of the snow
banked high against the walls. He had more timber now,
and it was to be a grand surprise for Inger and the children when they heard what use he would make of it—the
wonderful building he had in mind. He sat down in the
snow to rest a bit, not to seem worn out when he came
home.

All is quiet around him, and God's blessing on this quiet
and thoughtfulness, for it is nothing but good! Isak is a
man at work on a clearing in the forest, and he looks out
over the ground, reckoning what is to be cleared next turn;
heaving aside great stones in his mind—Isak had a real
talent for that work. There, he knows now, is a deep, bare
patch on his ground; it is full of ore; there is always a
metallic film over every puddle of water there—and now
he will dig it out. He marks out squares with his eye, making his plans for all, speculating over all; they are to be
made green and fruitful. Oh, but a piece of tilled soil was
a great and good thing; it was like right and order to his
mind, and a delight beyond . . .

He got up, and felt suddenly confused. H'm. What had
happened now? Nothing, only that he had been sitting
down a bit. Now there is something standing there before
him, a Being, a spirit; grey silk—no, it was nothing. He
felt strange—took one short, uncertain step forward, and
walked straight into a look, a great look, a pair of eyes. At
the same moment the aspens close by began rustling. Now
anyone knows that an aspen can have a horrible eerie way
of rustling at times; anyhow, Isak had never before heard
such an utterly horrible rustling as this, and he shuddered.
Also he put out one hand in front of him, and it was
perhaps the most helpless movement that hand had ever
made.

But what was this thing before him? Was it ghost-work
or reality? Isak would all his days have been ready to swear

that this was a higher power, and once indeed he had seen it, but the thing he saw now did not look like God. Possibly the Holy Ghost? If so, what was it standing there for anyway, in the midst of nowhere; two eyes, a look, and nothing more? If it had come to him, to fetch away his soul, why, so it would have to be; it would happen one day, after all, and then he would go to heaven and be among the blessed.

Isak was eager to see what would come next; he was shivering still; a coldness seemed to radiate from the figure before him—it must be the Evil One! And here Isak was no longer sure of his ground, so to speak. It might be the Evil One—but what did he want here? What had he, Isak, been doing? Nothing but sitting still and tilling the ground, as it were, in his thoughts—there could surely be no harm in that? There was no other guilt he could call to mind just then; he was only coming back from his work in the forest, a tired and hungry woodman, going home to Sellanraa—he means no harm. . . .

He took a step forward again, but it was only a little one, and, to tell the truth, he stepped back again immediately. The vision would not give way. Isak knitted his brows, as if beginning to suspect something. If it were the Evil One, why, let it be; the Evil One was not all-powerful—there was Luther, for instance, who had nearly killed the fiend himself, not to speak of many who had put him to flight by the sign of the cross and Jesu name. Not that Isak meant to defy the peril before him; it was not in his mind to sit down and laugh in its face, but he certainly gave up his first idea of dying and the next world. He took two steps forward straight at the vision, crossed himself, and cried out: "In Jesu name!"

H'm. At the sound of his own voice he came, as it were, to himself again, and saw Sellanraa over on the hillside once more. The two eyes in the air had gone.

He lost no time in getting home, and took no steps to challenge the specter further. But when he found himself once more safely on his own door-slab, he cleared his throat with a sense of power and security; he walked into the house with lofty mien, like a man—aye, a man of the world.

Inger started at the sight of him, and asked what made him so pale.

And at that he did not deny having met the Evil One himself.

"Where?" she asked.

"Over there. Right up towards our place."

Inger evinced no jealousy on her part. She did not praise him for it, true, but there was nothing in her manner suggestive of a hard word or a contemptuous kick. Inger herself, you see, had grown somewhat lighter of heart and kindlier of late, whatever the cause; and now she merely asked:

"The Evil One himself?"

Isak nodded: as far as he could see it was himself and no other.

"And how did you get rid of him?"

"I went for him in Jesu name," said Isak.

Inger wagged her head, altogether overwhelmed, and it was some time before she could get his supper on the table.

"Anyhow," said she at last, "we'll have no more of you going out alone in the woods by yourself."

She was anxious about him—and it did him good to know it. He made out to be as bold as ever, and altogether careless whether he went alone or in company; but this was only to quiet Inger's mind, not to frighten her more than necessary with the awful thing that had happened to himself. It was his place to protect her and them all; he was the Man, the Leader.

But Inger saw through it also, and said: "Oh, I know

you don't want to frighten me. But you must take Sivert
with you all the same."

Isak only sniffed.

"You might be taken poorly of a sudden, taken ill out in
the woods—you've not been over-well lately."

Isak sniffed again. Ill? Tired, perhaps, and worn out a
bit, but ill? No need for Inger to start worrying and making
a fool of him; he was sound and well enough; ate, slept, and
worked; his health was simply terrific, it was incurable!
Once, felling a tree, the thing had come down on top of
him, and broken his ear; but he made light of it. He set the
ear in place again, and kept it there by wearing his cap
drawn over it night and day, and it grew together again
that way. For internal complaints he dosed himself with
treak boiled in milk to make him sweat—liquorice it was,
bought at the store, an old and tried remedy, the *teriak* of
the ancients. If he chanced to cut his hand, he treated the
wound with an ever-present fluid containing salts, and it
healed up in a few days. No doctor was ever sent for to
Sellanraa.

No, Isak was not ill. A meeting with the Evil One might
happen even to the healthiest man. And he felt none the
worse for his adventure afterwards; on the contrary, it
seemed to have strengthened him. And as the winter drew
on, and it was not such a dreadful time to wait till the
spring, he, the Man and the Leader, began to feel himself
almost a hero: he understood these things; only trust to him
and all would be well. In case of need, he could exorcise the
Evil One himself!

Altogether, the days were longer and lighter now; Easter
was past, Isak had hauled up all his timber, everything
looked bright, human beings could breathe again after another winter gone.

Inger was again the first to brighten up; she had been
more cheerful now for a long time. What could it be? Ho,

'twas for a very simple reason; Inger was heavy again; expecting a child again. Everything worked out easily in her life, no hitch anywhere. But what a mercy, after the way she had sinned! It was more than she had any right to expect. Aye, she was fortunate, fortunate. Isak himself actually noticed something one day, and asked her straight out: "Looks to me as if you're on the way again; what do you say yourself?"

"Aye, Lord be thanked, 'tis surely so," she answered.

They were both equally astonished. Not that Inger was past the age, of course; to Isak's mind, she was not too old in any way. But still, another child . . . well, well. . . . And little Leopoldine going to school several times a year down at Breidablik—that left them with no little ones about the place now—besides which, Leopoldine herself was grown up now.

Some days passed, and Isak resolutely threw away a whole weekend—from Saturday evening till Monday morning—on a trip down to the village. He would not say what he was going for when he set out, but on his return, he brought with him a girl. "This is Jensine," he said. "Come to help."

" 'Tis all your nonsense," said Inger. "I've no need of help at all."

Isak answered that she did need a help—just now.

Need or not—it was a kind and generous thought of his; Inger was abashed and grateful. The new girl was a daughter of the blacksmith, and she was to stay with them for the present; through the summer, anyhow, and then they would see.

"And I've sent a telegram," said Isak, "After him Eleseus."

This fairly startled Inger; startled the mother. A telegram? Did he mean to upset her completely with his thoughtfulness? It had been her great sorrow of late that boy Eleseus was away in town—in the evil-minded town; she had written to him about God, and likewise explained to him how his father here was beginning to sink under the work, and the place getting bigger all the time; little Sivert couldn't manage it all by himself, and besides, he was to have money after his uncle one day—all this she had written, and sent him the money for his journey once for all. But Eleseus was a man-about-town now, and had no sort of longing for a peasant's life; he answered something about what was he to do anyway if he did come home? Work on a farm and throw away all the knowledge and learning he had gained? "In point of fact"—that was how he put it—"I've no desire to come back now. And if you could send me some stuff for underclothes, it would save me getting the things on credit." So he wrote. And yes, his mother sent him stuff—sent him remarkable quantities of stuff from time to time for underclothes. But when she was converted, and got religion, the scales fell from her eyes, and she understood that Eleseus was selling the stuff and spending the money on other things.

His father saw it too. He never spoke of it; he knew that Eleseus was his mother's darling, and how she cried over him and shook her head; but one piece of finely woven stuff went after another the same way, and he knew it was more than any living man could use for underclothes. Altogether, it came to this: Isak must be Man and Leader again —head of the house, and step in and interfere. It had cost a terrible lot of money, to be sure, getting the storekeeper to send a telegram; but in the first place, a telegram could not fail to make an impression on the boy, and also—it was something unusually fine for Isak himself to come home and tell Inger. He carried the servant-girl's box on his back as he strode home; but for all that, he was proud and full of weighty secrets as he had been the day he came home with that gold ring. . . .

It was a grand time after that. For a long while, Inger could not do enough in the way of showing her husband how good and useful she could be. She would say to him now, as in the old days: "You're working yourself to death!" Or again: " 'Tis more than any man can stand." Or again: "Now, you're not to work any more; come in and have dinner—I've made some wafers for you!" And to please him, she said: "I should just like to know, now, what you've got in your mind with all that wood, and what you're going to build, now, next?"

"Why, I can't say as yet," said Isak, making a mystery of it.

Aye, just as in the old days. And after the child was born —and it was a little girl—a great big girl, fine-looking and sturdy and sound—after that, Isak must have been a stone and a miserable creature if he had not thanked God. But what was he going to build? It would be more news for Oline to go gadding about with—a new building again at Sellanraa. A new wing of the house—a new house it was to be. And there were so many now at Sellanraa—they had a servant-girl; and Eleseus, he was coming home; and a brand-new little girl-child of their own, just come—the old house would be just an extra room now, nothing more.

And, of course, he had to tell Inger about it one day; she was so curious to know, and though maybe Inger knew it all beforehand, from Sivert—they two were often whispering together—she was all surprised as anyone could be, and let her arms fall, and said: " 'Tis all your nonsense— you don't mean it?"

And Isak, brimming over with greatness inside, he answered her: "Why, with you bringing I don't know how many more children on the place, 'tis the least I can do, it seems."

The two menfolk were out now every day getting stone for the walls of the new house. They worked their utmost together each in his own way: the one young, and with his young body firmly set, quick to see his way, to mark out the stones that would suit; the other ageing—tough, with long arms, and a mighty weight to bear down on a crow bar. When they had managed some specially difficult feat, they would hold a breathing-space, and talk together in a curious, reserved fashion of their own.

"Brede, he talks of selling out," said the father.

"Aye," said the son. "Wonder what he'll be asking for the place?"

"Aye, I wonder."

"You've not heard anything?"

"No."

"I've heard two hundred."

The father thought for a while, and said: "What d'you think, 'll this be a good stone?"

"All depends if we can get this shell off him," said Sivert, and was on his feet in a moment, giving the setting-hammer to his father, and taking the sledge himself. He grew red and hot, stood up to his full height and let the sledge-hammer fall; rose again and let it fall; twenty strokes alike —twenty thunderstrokes. He spared neither tool nor strength; it was heavy work; his shirt rucked up from his trousers at the waist, leaving him bare in front; he lifted on his toes each time to give the sledge a better swing. Twenty strokes.

"Now! Let's look!" cried his father.

The son stops, and asks: "Marked him any?"

And they lay down together to look at the stone; look at the beast, the devil of a thing; no, not marked any as yet.

"I've a mind to try with the sledge alone," said the father, and stood up. Still harder work this, sheer force alone, the hammer grew hot, the steel crushed, the pen grew blunt.

"She'll be slipping the head," he said and stopped. "And I'm no hand at this any more," he said.

Oh, but he never meant it; it was not his thought, that he was no hand at the work any more!

This father, this barge of a man, simple, full of patience and goodness, he would let his son strike the last few blows and cleave the stone. And there it lay, split in two.

"Aye, you've the trick of it," said the father. "H'm, yes . . . Breidablik . . . might make something out of that place."

"Aye, should think so," said the son.

"Only the land was fairly ditched and turned."

"The house'd have to be done up."

"Aye, that of course. Place all done up—'twould mean a lot of work at first, but . . . What I was going to say, d'you know if your mother was going to church come Sunday?"

"Aye, she said something like it."

"Ho! . . . H'm. Keep your eyes open now and look out for a good big door-slab for the new house. You haven't seen a bit would do?"

"No," said Sivert.

And they fell to work again.

A couple of days later both agreed they had enough stone now for the walls. It was Friday evening; they sat taking a breathing-space, and talking together the while.

"H'm—what d'you say?" said the father. "Should we think it over, maybe, about Breidablik?"

"How d'you mean?" asked the son. "What to do with it?"

"Why, I don't know. There's the school there, and it's midway down this tract now."

"And what then?" asked the son. "I don't know what we'd do with it, though; it's not worth much as it is."

"That's what you've been thinking of?"

"No, not that way. . . . Unless Eleseus he'd like to have the place to work on."

"Eleseus? Well, no, I don't know—"

Long pause, the two men thinking hard. The father begins gathering tools together, packing up to go home.

"Aye, unless . . ." said Sivert. "You might ask him what he says."

The father made an end of the matter thus: "Well, there's another day, and we haven't found that door-slab yet, either."

Next day was Saturday, and they had to be off early to get across the hills with the child. Jensine, the servant-girl, was to go with them; that was one godmother, the rest they would have to find from among Inger's folk on the other side.

Inger looked nice; she had made herself a dainty cotton dress, with white at the neck and wrists. The child was all in white, with a new blue silk ribbon drawn through the lower edge of its dress; but then she was a wonder of a child, to be sure, that could smile and chatter already, and lay and listened when the clock struck on the wall. Her father had chosen her name. It was his right; he was determined to have his say—only trust to him! He had hesitated between Jacobine and Rebecca, as being both sort of related to Isak; and at last he went to Inger and asked timidly: "What d'you think, now, of Rebecca?"

"Why, yes," said Inger.

And when Isak heard that, he grew suddenly independent and master in his own house. "If she's to have a name at all," he said sharply, "it shall be Rebecca! I'll see to that."

And of course he was going with the party to church, partly to carry, and partly for propriety's sake. It would never do to let Rebecca go to be christened without a decent following! Isak trimmed his beard and put on a red shirt, as in his younger days; it was in the worst of the hot weather, but he had a nice new winter suit, that looked well on him, and he wore it. But for all that, Isak was not the man to make a duty of finery and show; as now, for instance, he put on a pair of fabulously heavy boots for the march.

Sivert and Leopoldine stayed behind to look after the place.

Then they rowed in a boat across the lake, and that was a deal easier than before, when they had had to walk round all the way. But halfway across, as Inger unfastened her dress to nurse the child, Isak noticed something bright hung in a string round her neck; whatever it might be. And in the church he noticed that she wore that gold ring on her finger. Oh, Inger—it had been too much for her after all!

CHAPTER XVII

ELESEUS came home.

He had been away now for some years, and had grown taller than his father, with long white hands and a little dark growth on his upper lip. He did not give himself airs, but seemed anxious to appear natural and kindly; his mother was surprised and pleased. He shared the small bedroom with Sivert; the two brothers got on well together, and were constantly playing tricks on each other by way of amusement. But, naturally, Eleseus had to take his share of the work in building the house; and tired and miserable it made him, all unused as he was to bodily fatigue of any kind. It was worse still when Sivert had to go off and leave it all to the other two; Eleseus then was almost more of a hindrance than a help.

And where had Sivert gone off to? Why, 'twas Oline had come over the hills one day with word from Uncle Sivert that he was dying; and, of course, young Sivert had to go. A nice state of things all at once—it couldn't have happened worse than to have Sivert running off just now. But there was no help for it.

Said Oline: "I'd no time to go running errands, and that's the truth; but for all that . . . I've taken a fancy to the children here, all of them, and little Sivert, and if as I could help him to his legacy . . ."

"But was Uncle Sivert very bad, then?"

"Bad? Heaven bless us, he's falling away day by day."

"Was he in bed, then?"

"In bed? How can you talk so light and flighty of death before God's judgment-seat? Nay, he'll neither hop nor run again in this world, will your Uncle Sivert."

All this seemed to mean that Uncle Sivert had not long to live, and Inger insisted that little Sivert should set off at once.

But Uncle Sivert, incorrigible old knave, was not on his deathbed; was not even confined to bed at all. When young Sivert came, he found the little place in terrible muddle and disorder; they had not finished the spring season's work properly yet—had not even carted out all the winter manure; but as for approaching death, there was no sign of it that he could see. Uncle Sivert was an old man now, over seventy; he was something of an invalid, and pottered about half dressed in the house, and often kept his bed for a time. He needed help on the place in many ways, as, for instance, with the herring nets that hung rotting in the sheds. Oh, but for all that he was by no means at his last gasp; he could still eat sour fish and smoke his pipe.

When Sivert had been there half an hour and seen how things were, he was for going back home again.

"Home?" said the old man.

"We're building a house, and father's none to help him properly."

"Ho!" said his uncle. "Isn't Eleseus come home, then?"

"Aye, but he's not used to the work."

"Then why did you come at all?"

Sivert told him about Oline and her message, how she had said that Uncle Sivert was on the point of death.

"Point of death?" cried the old man. "Said I was on the point of death, did she? A cursed old fool!"

"Ha ha ha!" said Sivert.

The old man looked sternly at him. "Eh? Laugh at a dying man, do you, and you called after me and all!"

But Sivert was too young to put on a graveyard face for that; he had never cared much for his uncle. And now he wanted to get back home again.

"Ho, so you thought so, too?" said the old man again. "Thought I was at my last gasp, and that fetched you, did it?"

" 'Twas Oline said so," answered Sivert.

His uncle was silent for a while, then spoke again:

"Look you here. If you'll mend that net of mine and put it right, I'll show you something."

"H'm," said Sivert. "What is it?"

"Well, never you mind," said the old man sullenly, and went to bed again.

It was going to be a long business, evidently. Sivert writhed uncomfortably. He went out and took a look round the place; everything was shamefully neglected and uncared for; it was hopeless to begin work here. When he came in after a while, his uncle was sitting up, warming himself at the stove.

"See that?" He pointed to an oak chest on the floor at his feet. It was his money chest. As a matter of fact, it was a lined case made to hold bottles, such as visiting justices and other great folk used to carry with them when traveling about the country in the old days, but there were no bottles in it now; the old man had used it for his documents and papers as district treasurer; he kept his accounts and his money in it now. The story ran that it was full of uncounted riches; the village folk would shake their heads and say: "Ah! if I'd only as much as lies in old Sivert his chest!"

Uncle Sivert took out a paper from the box and said solemnly: "You can read writing, I suppose?"

Little Sivert was not by any means a great hand at that, it is true, but he made out so much as told him he was to inherit all that his uncle might leave at his death.

"There," said the old man. "And now you can do as you please." And he laid the paper back in the chest.

Sivert was not greatly impressed; after all, the paper told him no more than he had known before; ever since he was a child he heard say that he was to have what Uncle Sivert left one day. A sight of the treasure would be another matter.

"There's some fine things in that chest, I doubt," said he.

"There's more than you think," said the old man shortly.

He was angry and disappointed with his nephew; he locked up the box and went to bed again. There he lay, delivering jets of information. "I've been district treasurer and warden of the public moneys in this village over thirty year; *I've* no need to beg and pray for a helping hand from any man! Who told Oline, I'd like to know, that I was on my deathbed? I can send three men, carriage, and cart to fetch a doctor if I want one. Don't try your games with me, young man! Can't even wait till I'm gone, it seems. I've shown you the document and you've seen it, and it's there in the chest—that's all I've got to say. But if you go running off and leave me now, you can just carry word to Eleseus and tell *him* to come. He's not named after me and called by my earthly name—let *him* come."

But for all the threatening tone, Sivert only thought a moment, and said: "Aye, I'll tell Eleseus to come."

Oline was still at Sellanraa when Sivert got back. She had found time to pay a visit lower down, to Axel Ström and Barbro on their place, and came back full of mysteries and whisperings. "That girl Barbro's filling out a deal of late—Lord knows what it may mean. But not a word that I've said so! And here's Sivert back again? No need to ask what news, I suppose? Your Uncle Sivert's passed away?

Aye, well, an old man he was and an aged one, on the brink
of the grave. What—not dead? Well, well, we've much to
be thankful for, and that's a solemn word! Me talking nonsense, you say? Oh, if I'd never more to answer for! How
was I to know your uncle he was lying there a sham and a
false pretender before the Lord? Not long to live, that's
what I said. And I'll hold by it, when the time comes, before the Throne. What's that you say? Well, and wasn't he
lying there his very self in his bed, and folding his hands
on his breast and saying 'twould soon be over?"

There was no arguing with Oline, she bewildered her
adversaries with talk and cast them down. When she
learned that Uncle Sivert had sent for Eleseus, she grasped
at that too, and made her own advantage of it: "There you
are, and see if I was talking nonsense. Here's old Sivert
calling up his kinsfolk and longing for a sight of his own
flesh and blood; aye, he's nearing his end! You can't refuse
him, Eleseus; off with you at once this minute and see your
uncle while there's life in him. I'm going that way too, we'll
go together."

Oline did not leave Sellanraa without taking Inger aside
for more whisperings of Barbro. "Not a word I've said—
but I could see the signs of it! And now I suppose she'll be
wife and all on the farm there. Aye, there's some folk are
born to great things, for all they may be small as the sands
of the sea in their beginnings. And who'd have ever
thought it of that girl Barbro! Axel, yes, never doubt but
he's a toiling sort and getting on, and great fine lands and
means and all like you've got here—'tis more than we know
of over on our side the hills, as you know's a true word,
Inger, being born and come of the place yourself. Barbro,
she'd a trifle of wool in a chest; 'twas naught but winter
wool, and I wasn't asking and she never offered me. We
said but '*Goddag*' and '*Farvel*,' for all that I'd known her
from she was a toddling child all that time I was here at

Sellanraa by reason of you being away and learning knowledge at the Institute. . . ."

"There's Rebecca crying," said Inger, breaking in on Oline. But she gave her a handful of wool.

Then a great thanksgiving speech from Oline: aye, wasn't it just as she had said to Barbro herself of Inger, and how there was not her like to be found for giving to folk; aye, she'd give till she was bare, and give her fingers to the bone, and never complain. Aye, go in and see to the sweet angel, and never was there a child in the world so like her mother as Rebecca—no. Did Inger remember how she'd said one day as she'd never have children again? Ah, now she could see! No, better give ear to them as were grown old and had borne children of their own, for who should fathom the Lord His ways, said Oline.

And with that she padded off after Eleseus up through the forest, shrunken with age, grey and abject, and forever nosing after things, imperishable. Going to old Sivert now, to let him know how she, Oline, had managed to persuade Eleseus to come.

But Eleseus had needed no persuading, there was no difficulty there. For, look you, Eleseus had turned out better, after all, than he'd begun; a decent lad in his way, kindly and easy-going from a child, only nothing great in the way of bodily strength. It was not without reason he had been unwilling to come home this time; he knew well enough that his mother had been in prison for child-murder; he had never heard a word about it there in the town, but at home in the village everyone would remember. And it was not for nothing he had been living with companions of another sort. He had grown to be more sensitive and finer feeling than ever before. He knew that a fork was really just as necessary as a knife. As a man of business, he used the terms of the new coinage, whereas, out in the wilds, men still counted money by the ancient daler. Aye, he was not unwilling to walk across the hills to other parts; here, at home, he was constantly forced to keep down his own superiority. He tried his best to adapt himself to the others, and he managed well; but it was always having to be on his guard. As, for instance, when he had first come back to Sellanraa a couple of weeks go, he had brought with him his light spring overcoat, though it was midsummer; and when he hung it up on a nail, he might just as well have turned it so as to show the silver plate inside with his initials, but he didn't. And the same with his stick—his walking-stick. True, it was only an umbrella stick really, that he had dismantled and taken the framework off; but here he had not used it as he did in town, swinging it about— only carried it hidden against his thigh.

No, it was not surprising that Eleseus went across the hills. He was no good at building houses; he was good at writing with letters, a thing not everyone could do, but here at home there was no one in all the place that set any store by the art of it save perhaps his mother. He set off gaily through the woods, far ahead of Oline; he could wait for her farther up. He ran like a calf; he hurried. Eleseus had in a way stolen off from the farm; he was afraid of being seen. For, to tell the truth, he had taken with him both spring coat and walking-stick for the journey. Over on the other side there might be a chance of seeing people, and being seen himself; he might even be able to go to church. And so he sweated happily under the weight of an unnecessary spring coat in the heat of the sun.

They did not miss him at the building, far from it. Isak had Sivert back again, and Sivert was worth a host of his brother at that work; he could keep at it from morning to night. It did not take them long to get the framework up; it was only three walls, as they were building out from the other. And they had less trouble with the timber; they could cut their planks at the sawmill, which gave them the out-

side pieces for roofing at the same time. And one fine day
there was the house all finished, before their eyes, roofed,
floored, and with the windows in. They had no time for
more than this between the seasons; the boarding and painting would have to wait.

And now came Geissler with a great following across
the hills from Sweden. And the men with him rode on
horseback with glossy-coated horses and yellow saddles;
rich travelers they must be no doubt; stout, heavy men; the
horses bowed under their weight. And among all these
great personages came Geissler on foot. Four gentlemen
and Geissler made up the party, and then there were a
couple of servants, each leading a packhorse.

The riders dismounted outside the farm, and Geissler
said: "Here's Isak—here's the Margrave of the place himself. *Goddag*, Isak! I've come back again, you see, as I said
I would."

Geissler was the same as ever. For all that he came on
foot, his manner showed no consciousness of inferiority to
the rest; aye, his threadbare coat hung long and wretched-
looking down over his shrunken back, but he put on a
grand enough air for all that. He even said: "We're going
up into the hills a bit, these gentlemen and myself—it'll do
them good to get their weight down a bit."

The gentlemen themselves were nice and pleasant
enough; they smiled at Geissler's words, and hoped Isak
would excuse their coming rioting over his land like this.
They had brought their own provisions, and did not pro-
pose to eat him out of house and home, but they would be
glad of a roof over their heads for the night. Perhaps he
could put them up in the new building there?

When they had rested a while, and Geissler had been inside with Inger and the children, the whole party went up
into the hills and stayed out till evening. Now and again in

the course of the afternoon, the folks at Sellanraa could hear an unusually heavy report from the distance, and the train of them came down with new bags of samples. "Blue copper," they said, nodding at the ore. They talked long and learnedly, and consulting a sort of map they had drawn; there was an engineer among them, and a mining expert; one appeared to be a big landowner or manager of works. They talked of aerial railways and cable traction. Geissler threw in a word here and there, and each time as if advising them; they paid great attention to what he said.

"Who owns the land south of the lake?" one of them asked Isak.

"The State," answered Geissler quickly. He was wide awake and sharp, and held in his hand the document Isak had once signed with his mark. "I told you before—the State," he said. "No need to ask again. If you don't believe me, you can find out for yourself if you please."

Later in the evening, Geissler took Isak aside and said: "Look here, shall we sell that copper mine?"

Said Isak: "Why, as to that, 'twas so that Lensmand bought it of me once, and paid for it."

"True," said Geissler. "I bought the ground. But then there was a provision that you were to have a percentage of receipts from working or sale; are you willing to dispose of your share?"

This was more than Isak could understand, and Geissler had to explain. Isak could not work a mine, being a farmer and a clearer of forest land; Geissler himself couldn't run a mine either. Money, capital? Ho, as much as he wanted, never fear! But he hadn't the time, too many things to do, always running about the country, attending to his property in the south, his property in the north. And now Geissler was thinking of selling out to these Swedish gentlemen here; they were relatives of his wife, all of them, and rich men. "Do you see what I mean?"

"I'll do it what way you please," said Isak.

A strange thing—this complete confidence seemed to comfort Geissler wonderfully in his threadbareness. "Well, I'm not sure it's the best thing you could do," he said thoughtfully. Then suddenly he was certain, and went on: "But if you'll give me a free hand to act on my discretion, I can do better for you at any rate than you could by yourself."

"H'm," began Isak. "You've always been a good man to us all here. . . ."

But Geissler frowned at that, and cut him short: "All right, then."

Next morning the gentlemen sat down to write. It was a serious business; there was first of all a contract for forty thousand kroner for the sale of the mine, then a document whereby Geissler made over the whole of the money to his wife and children. Isak and Sivert were called in to witness the signatures to these. When it was done, the gentlemen wanted to buy over Isak's percentage for a ridiculous sum— five hundred kroner. Geissler put a stop to that, however. "Jesting apart," he said.

Isak himself understood but little of the whole affair; he had sold the place once, and got his money. But in any case, he did not care much about kroner—it was not real money like daler. Sivert, on the other hand, followed the business with more understanding. There was something peculiar, he thought, about the tone of these negotiations; it looked very much like a family affair between the parties. One of the strangers would say: "My dear Geissler, you ought not to have such red eyes, you know." Whereto Geissler answered sharply, if evasively: "No, I ought not, I know. But we don't all get what we ought to in this world!"

It looked very much as if Fru Geissler's brothers and kinsmen were trying to buy off her husband, secure themselves against his visits for the future, and get quit of a

troublesome relation. As to the mine, it was worth something in itself, no doubt, no one denied it; but it lay far out
of the way, and the buyers themselves said they were only
taking it over in order to sell it again to someone better in
a position to work it. There was nothing unreasonable in
that. They declared too, quite frankly, that they had no idea
what they would be able to get for it as it stood; if it were
taken up and worked, then the forty thousand might turn
out to be only a fraction of what it was worth; if it were
allowed to lie there as it was, the money was simply thrown
away. But in any case, they wanted to have a clear title,
without encumbrance, and therefore they offered Isak five
hundred kroner for his share.

"I'm acting on his behalf," said Geissler, "and I'm not
going to sell out his share for less than ten per cent of the
purchase-money."

"Four thousand!" said the others.

"Four thousand," said Geissler. "The land was his, and
his share comes to four thousand. It wasn't mine, and I get
forty thousand. Kindly turn that over in your minds, if you
please."

"Yes, but—four thousand kroner!"

Geissler rose from his place, and said: "That, or no sale."

They thought it over, whispered about it, went out into
the yard, talking as long as they could. "Get the horses
ready," they called to the servants. One of the gentlemen
went in to Inger and paid royally for coffee, a few eggs, and
their lodging. Geissler walked about with a careless air, but
he was wide awake all the same.

"How did that irrigation work turn out last year?" he
asked Sivert.

"It saved the whole crop."

"You've cut away that mound there since I was here last,
what?"

"Aye."

"You must have another horse on the farm," said Geissler. He noticed everything.

One of the strangers came up. "Now then, let's get this matter settled and have done with it," he said.

They all went into the new building again, and Isak's four thousand kroner were counted out. Geissler was given a paper, which he thrust into his pocket as if it were of no value at all. "Keep that carefully," they told him, "and in a few days your wife shall have the bankbook sent."

Geissler puckered his forehead and said shortly: "Very good."

But they were not finished with Geissler yet. Not that he opened his mouth to ask for anything; he simply stood there, and they saw how he stood there: maybe he had stipulated beforehand for a trifle on his own account. The leader gave him a bundle of notes, and Geissler simply nodded again, and said: "Very good."

"And now I think we ought to drink a glass with Geissler," said the other.

They drank, and that was done. And then they took leave of Geissler.

Just at that moment came Brede Olsen walking up. Now what did he want? Brede had doubtless heard the reports of the blasting-charges the day before, and understood that there was something on foot in the way of mines. And now he came up ready to sell something too. He walked straight past Geissler, and addressed himself to the gentlemen; he had found some remarkable specimens of rock hereabouts, quite extraordinary, some bloodlike, others like silver; he knew every cranny and corner in the hills around and could go straight to every spot; he knew of long veins of some heavy metal—whatever it might be.

"Have you any samples?" asked the mining expert.

Yes, Brede had samples. But couldn't they just as well go up and look at the places at once? It wasn't far. Samples

—oh, sacks of them, whole packing-cases full. No, he had not brought them with him, they were at home—he could run down and fetch them. But it would be quicker just to run up into the hills and fetch some more, if they would only wait.

The men shook their heads and went on their way.

Brede looked after them with an injured air. If he had felt a glimmer of hope for the moment, it was gone now; fate was against him, nothing ever went right. Well for Brede that he was not easily cast down; he looked after the men as they rode away, and said at last: "Wish you a pleasant journey!" And that was all.

But now he was humble again in his manner towards Geissler, his former chief, and no longer treated him as an equal, but used forms of respect. Geissler had taken out his pocketbook on some pretext or other, and anyone could see that it was stuffed full of notes.

"If only Lensmand could help me a bit," said Brede.

"Go back home and work your land properly," said Geissler, and helped him not a bit.

"I might easily have brought up a whole barrowload of samples, but wouldn't it have been easier to go up and look at the place itself while they were here?"

Geissler took no notice of him, and turned to Isak: "Did you see what I did with that document? It was a most important thing—a matter of several thousand kroner. Oh, here it is, in among a bundle of notes."

"Who were those people?" asked Brede. "Just out for a ride, or what?"

Geissler had been having an anxious time, no doubt, and now he cooled down. But he had still something of life and eagerness in him, enough to do a little more; he went up into the hills with Sivert, and took a big sheet of paper with him, and drew a map of the ground south of the lake— Heaven knows what he had in mind. When he came down to the farm some hours later, Brede was still there, but Geissler took no notice of his questions; Geissler was tired, and waved him aside.

He slept like a stone till next morning early, then he rose with the sun, and was himself again. "Sellanraa," said he, standing outside and looking all round.

"All that money," said Isak; "does it mean I'm to have it all?"

"All?" said Geissler. "Heavens, man, can't you see it ought to have been ever so much more? And it was my business really to pay you, according to our contract; but you saw how things were—it was the only way to manage it. What did you get? Only a thousand daler, according to the old reckoning. I've been thinking, you'll need another horse on the place now."

"Aye."

"Well, I know of one. That fellow Heyerdahl's assistant, he's letting his place go to rack and ruin; takes more interest in running about selling folk up. He's sold a deal of his stock already, and he'll be willing to sell the horse."

"I'll see him about it," said Isak.

Geissler waved his hand broadly around, and said: "Margrave, landowner—that's you! House and stock and cultivated land—they can't starve you out if they try!"

"No," said Isak. "We've all we could wish for that the Lord ever made."

Geissler went fussing about the place, and suddenly slipped in to Inger. "Could you manage a bit of food for me to take along again?" he asked. "Just a few wafers—no butter and cheese; there's good things enough in them already. No, do as I say; I can't carry more."

Out again. Geissler was restless, he went into the new building and sat down to write. He had thought it all out beforehand, and it did not take long now to get it down. Sending in an application to the State, he explained loftily to Isak—"to the Ministry of the Interior, you understand. Yes, I've no end of things to look after all at once."

When he had got his parcel of food and had taken leave, he seemed to remember something all of a sudden: "Oh, by the way, I'm afraid I owe you something from last time— I took out a note from my pocketbook on purpose, and then stuck it in my waistcoat pocket—I found it there after- wards. Too many things to think about all at once. . . ." He put something into Inger's hand and off he went.

Aye, off went Geissler, bravely enough to all seeming. Nothing downcast nor anyway nearing his end; he came to Sellanraa again after, and it was long years before he died. Each time he went away the Sellanraa folk missed him as a friend. Isak had been thinking of asking him about Breidablik, getting his advice, but nothing came of it. And maybe Geissler would have dissuaded him there; have thought it a risky thing to buy up land for cultivation and give it to Eleseus; to a clerk.

CHAPTER XVIII

Uncle Sivert died after all. Eleseus spent three weeks looking after him, and then the old man died. Eleseus arranged the funeral, and managed things very well; got hold of a fuchsia or so from the cottages round, and borrowed a flag to hoist at half-mast, and bought some black stuff from the store for lowered blinds. Isak and Inger were sent for, and came to the burial. Eleseus acted as host, and served out refreshments to the guests; aye, and when the body was carried out, and they had sung a hymn, Eleseus actually said a few suitable words over the coffin, and his mother was so proud and touched that she had to use her handkerchief. Everything went off splendidly.

Then on the way home with his father, Eleseus had to carry that spring coat of his openly, though he managed to hide the stick in one of the sleeves. All went well till they had to cross the water in a boat; then his father sat down unexpectedly on the coat, and there was a crack. "What was that?" asked Isak.

"Oh, nothing," said Eleseus.

But he did not throw the broken stick away; as soon as they got home, he set about looking for a bit of tube or something to mend it with. "We'll fix it all right," said Sivert, the incorrigible. "Look here, get a good stout splint of wood on either side, and lash all fast with waxed thread. . . ."

"I'll lash you with waxed thread," said Eleseus.

"Ha ha ha! Well, perhaps you'd rather tie it up neatly with a red garter?"

"Ha ha ha," said Eleseus himself at that; but he went in to his mother, and got her to give him an old thimble, filed off the end, and made quite a fine ferrule. Oh, Eleseus was not so helpless after all, with his long, white hands.

The brothers teased each other as much as ever. "Am I to have what Uncle Sivert's left?" asked Eleseus.

"You have it? How much is it?" asked Sivert.

"Ha ha ha, you want to know how much it is first, you old miser!"

"Well, you can have it, anyway," said Sivert.

"It's between five and ten thousand."

"Daler?" cried Sivert; he couldn't help it.

Now Eleseus never reckoned in daler, but he didn't like to say no at the time, so he just nodded, and left it at that till next day.

Then he took up the matter again. "Aren't you sorry you gave me all that yesterday?" he said.

"Woodenhead! Of course not," said Sivert. That was what he said, but—well, five thousand daler was five thousand daler, and no little sum; if his brother were anything but a lousy Indian savage, he ought to give back half.

"Well, to tell the truth," explained Eleseus, "I don't reckon to get fat on that legacy, after all."

Sivert looked at him in astonishment. "Ho, don't you?"

"No, nothing special, that is to say. Not what you might call *par excellence*."

Eleseus had some notions of accounts of course, and Uncle Sivert's money-chest, the famous bottle-case, had been opened and examined while he was there; he had had to go through all the accounts and make up a balance sheet. Uncle Sivert had not set this nephew to work on the fields or mending of herring nets; he had initiated him into a complex muddle of figures, the weirdest bookkeeping ever seen. If a man had paid his taxes some years back in kind, with a goat, say, or a load of dried cod, there was neither flesh nor fish to show for it now; but old Sivert searched his memory and said: "He's paid!"

"Right, then we'll cross him out," said Eleseus.

Eleseus was the man for this sort of work; he was bright and quick, and encouraged the invalid by assuring him that things were all right; the two had got on well together, even to jesting at times. Eleseus was a bit of a fool, perhaps, in some things, but so was his uncle; and the two of them sat there drawing up elaborate documents in favor not only of little Sivert but also to benefit the village, the commune which the old man had served for thirty years. Oh, they were grand days! "I couldn't have got a better man to help with all this than you, Eleseus boy," said Uncle Sivert. He sent out and bought mutton, in the middle of the summer; fish was brought up fresh from the sea, Eleseus being ordered to pay cash from the chest. They lived well enough. They got hold of Oline—they couldn't have found a better person to invite to a feast, nor one more sure to spread abroad the news of Uncle Sivert's greatness to the end. And the satisfaction was mutual. "We must do something for Oline, too," said Uncle Sivert, "she being a widow and not well off. There'll be enough for little Sivert, anyhow." Eleseus managed it with a few strokes of the pen; a mere codicil to the last will and testament, and lo, Oline was also a sharer in the inheritance.

"I'll look after you," said Uncle Sivert to her. "If so be I shouldn't get better this time and get about again on earth I'll take care you're not left out." Oline declared that she was speechless, but speechless she was not; she wept and was touched to the heart and grateful; there was none to compare with Oline for finding the immediate connection between a worldly gift and being "repaid a thousandfold eternally in the world to come." No, speechless she was not.

But Eleseus? At first, perhaps, he may have taken a bright enough view of his uncle's affairs, but after a while he began to think things over and talk as well. He tried at first with a slight hint: "The accounts aren't exactly as they should be," he said.

"Well, never mind that," said the old man. "There'll be enough and to spare when I'm gone."

"You've money outstanding besides, maybe?" said Eleseus. "In a bank, or so?" For so report had said.

"H'm," said the old man. "That's as it may be. But, anyhow, with the fishery, the farm and buildings and stock, red cows and white cows and all—don't you worry about that, Eleseus, my boy."

Eleseus had no idea what the fishery business might be worth, but he had seen the livestock; it consisted of one cow, partly red and partly white. Uncle Sivert must have been delirious. Some of the accounts, too, were difficult to make out at all; they were a muddle, a bare jumble of figures, especially from the date when the coinage was changed; the district treasurer had frequently reckoned the small kroner as if they were full daler! No wonder he fancied himself rich! But when everything was reduced to something like order, Eleseus feared there would not be much left over. Perhaps not enough to settle at all.

Aye, Sivert might easily promise him all that came to him from his uncle!

The two brothers jested about it. Sivert was not upset over the matter, not at all; perhaps, indeed, it might have irked him something more if he really had thrown away five thousand daler. He knew well enough that it had been a mere speculation, naming him after his uncle; he had no claim to anything there. And now he pressed Eleseus to take what there was. "It's to be yours, of course," said he. "Come along, let's get it set down in writing. I'd like to see you a rich man. Don't be too proud to take it!"

Aye, they had many a laugh together. Sivert, indeed, was the one that helped most to keep Eleseus at home; it would have been much harder but for him.

As a matter of fact, Eleseus was getting rather spoiled again; the three weeks' idling on the other side of the hills had not done him any good. He had also been to church there, and made a show; aye, he had even met some girls there. Here at Sellanraa there was nothing of that sort; Jensine, the servant-maid, was a mere nothing, a worker and no more, rather suited to Sivert.

"I've a fancy to see how that girl Barbro from Breidablik turned out now she's grown up," said Eleseus one day.

"Well, go down to Axel Ström's place and see," said Sivert.

Eleseus went down one Sunday. Aye, he had been away, gained confidence and high spirits once more; he had tasted excitement of a sort, and he made things livelier at Axel's little place. Barbro herself was by no means to be despised; at any rate she was the only one anywhere near. She played the guitar and talked readily; moreover, she did not smell of tansy, but of real scent, the sort you buy in shops. Eleseus, on his part, let it be understood that he was only home for a holiday, and would soon be called back to the office again. But it was not so bad being at home after all, in the old place, and, of course, he had the little bedroom to live in. But it was not like being in town!

"Nay, that's a true word," said Barbro. "Town's very different from this."

Axel himself was altogether out of it with these two townfolk; he found it dull with them, and preferred to go out and look over his land. The pair of them were left to do as they liked, and Eleseus managed things grandly. He told how he had been over to the neighboring village to bury his uncle, and did not forget to mention the speech he had made over the coffin.

When he took his leave, he asked Barbro to go part of the way home with him. But Barbro, thank you, was not inclined that way.

"Is that the way they do things where you've been," she asked "—for the ladies to escort the gentlemen home?"

That was a nasty hit for Eleseus; he turned red, and understood he had offended her.

Nevertheless, he went down to Maaneland again next Sunday, and this time he took his stick. They talked as before, and Axel was out of it altogether, as before. " 'Tis a big place your father's got," said he. "And building again, now, it seems."

"Aye, it's all very well for him," said Eleseus, anxious to show off a little. "He can afford it. It's another matter with poor folk like ourselves."

"How d'you mean?"

"Oh, haven't you heard? There's been some Swedish millionaires came down the other day and bought a mine of him, a copper mine."

"Why, you don't say? And he'll have got a heap of money for it, then?"

"Enormous. Well, I don't want to boast, but it was at any rate ever so many thousands. What was I going to say? Build? You've a deal of timber lying about here yourself. When are you going to start?"

Barbro put in her word here: "Never!"

Now that was pure exaggeration and impertinence. Axel had got his stones the autumn before, and carted them home that winter; now, between seasons, he had got the foundation walls done, and cellar and all else—all that remained was to build the timbered part above. He was hoping to get part of it roofed in this autumn, and had thought of asking Sivert to lend him a hand for a few days—what did Eleseus think of that?

Eleseus thought like as not. "But why not ask me?" he said, smiling.

"You?" said Axel, and he spoke with sudden respect at the idea. "You've talents for other things than that, I take it."

Oh, but it was pleasant to find oneself appreciated here in the wilds! "Why, I'm afraid my hands aren't much good at that sort of work," said Eleseus delicately.

"Let me look," said Barbro, and took his hand.

Axel dropped out of the conversation again, and went out, leaving the two of them alone. They were of an age, had been to school together, and played and kissed each other and raced about; and now, with a fine disdainful carelessness, they talked of old times—exchanging reminiscences—and Barbro, perhaps, was inclined to show off a little before her companion. True, this Eleseus was not like the really fine young men in offices, that wore glasses and gold watches and so on, but he could pass for a gentleman here in the wilds, there was no denying that. And she took out her photograph now and showed him—that's what she looked like then—"all different now, of course." And Barbro sighed.

"Why, what's the matter with you now?" he asked.

"Don't you think I've changed for the worse since then?"

"Changed for the worse, indeed! Well, I don't mind telling you you're ever so much prettier now," said he, "filled out all round. For the worse? Ho! That's a fine idea!"

"But it's a nice dress, don't you think? Cut open just a bit front and back. And then I had that silver chain you see there, and it cost a heap of money, too; it was a present from one of the young clerks I was with then. But I lost it. Not exactly lost it, you know, but I wanted money to come home."

Eleseus asked: "Can I have the photo to keep?"

"To keep? H'm. What'll you give me for it?"

Oh, Eleseus knew well enough what he wanted to say, but he dared not. "I'll have mine taken when I go back to town," he said instead, "and send it you."

Barbro put away the photograph. "No, it's the only one I've left."

That was a stroke of darkness to his young heart, and he stretched out his hand towards the picture.

"Well, give me something for it, now," she said, laughing. And at that he up and kissed her properly.

After that it was easier all round; Eleseus brightened up, and got on finely. They flirted and joked and laughed, and were excellent friends. "When you took my hand just now it was like a bit of swan's down—yours, I mean."

"Oh, you'll be going back to town again, and never come back here, I'll be bound," said Barbro.

"Do you think I'm that sort?" said Eleseus.

"Ah, I dare say there's a somebody there you're fond of."

"No, there isn't. Between you and me, I'm not engaged at all," said he.

"Oh yes, you are; I know."

"No, solemn fact, I'm not."

They carried on like this quite a while; Eleseus was plainly in love. "I'll write to you," said he. "May I?"

"Yes," said she.

"For I wouldn't be mean enough if you didn't care about it, you know." And suddenly he was jealous, and asked: "I've heard say you're promised to Axel here; is it true?"

"Axel?" she said scornfully, and he brightened up again. "I'll see him farther!" But then she turned penitent, and added: "Axel, he's good enough for me, though. . . . And he takes in a paper all for me to read, and gives me things now and again—lots of things. I will say that."

"Oh, of course," Eleseus agreed. "He may be an excellent fellow in his way, but that's not everything. . . ."

But the thought of Axel seemed to have made Barbro anxious; she got up, and said to Eleseus: "You'll have to go now; I must see to the animals."

Next Sunday Eleseus went down a good deal later than usual, and carried the letter himself. It was a letter! A whole week of excitement, all the trouble it had cost him to write, but here it was at last; he had managed to produce a letter: "To Fröken Barbro Bredesen. It is two or three times now I have had the inexpressible delight of seeing you again. . . ."

Coming so late as he did now, Barbro must at any rate have finished seeing to the animals, and might perhaps have gone to bed already. That wouldn't matter—quite the reverse, indeed.

But Barbro was up, sitting in the hut. She looked now as if she had suddenly lost all idea of being nice to him and making love—Eleseus fancied Axel had perhaps got hold of her and warned her.

"Here's the letter I promised you," he said.

"Thank you," said she, and opened it, and read it through without seeming much moved. "I wish I could write as nice a hand as that," she said.

Eleseus was disappointed. What had he done—what was the matter with her? And where was Axel? He was not there. Beginning to get tired of these foolish Sunday visits, perhaps, and preferred to stay away; or he might have had some business to keep him over, when he went down to the village the day before. Anyhow, he was not there.

"What d'you want to sit here in this stuffy old place for

on a lovely evening?" asked Eleseus. "Come out for a walk."

"I'm waiting for Axel," she answered.

"Axel? Can't you live without Axel, then?"

"Yes. But he'll want something to eat when he comes back."

Time went, time dribbled away, they came no nearer each other; Barbro was as cross and contrary as ever. He tried telling her again of his visit across the hills, and did not forget about the speech he had made: " 'Twasn't much I had to say, but all the same it brought out the tears from some of them."

"Did it?" said she.

"And then one Sunday I went to church."

"What news there?"

"News? Oh, nothing. Only to have a look round. Not much of a priest, as far as I know anything about it; no sort of manner, he had."

Time went.

"What d'you think Axel'd say if he found you here this evening again?" said Barbro suddenly.

There was a thing to say! It was as if she had struck him. Had she forgotten all about last time? Hadn't they agreed that he was to come this evening? Eleseus was deeply hurt, and murmured: "I can go, if you like. What have I done?" he asked then, his lips trembling. He was in distress, in trouble, that was plain to see.

"Done? Oh, you haven't done anything."

"Well, what's the matter with you, anyway, this evening?"

"With me? Ha ha ha! But come to think of it, 'tis no wonder Axel should be angry."

"I'll go, then," said Eleseus again. But she was still indifferent, not in the least afraid, caring nothing that he sat there struggling with his feelings. Fool of a woman!

And now he began to grow angry; he hinted his displeasure at first delicately: to the effect that she was a nice sort indeed, and a credit to her sex, huh! But when that produced no effect—oh, he would have done better to endure it patiently, and say nothing. But he grew no better for that; he said: "If I'd known you were going to be like this, I'd never have come this evening at all."

"Well, what if you hadn't?" said she. "You'd have lost a chance of airing that cane of yours that you're so fond of."

Oh, Barbro, she had lived in Bergen, she knew how to jeer at a man; she had seen real walking-sticks, and could ask now what he wanted to go swinging a patched-up umbrella handle like that for. But he let her go on.

"I suppose now you'll be wanting that photograph back you gave me," he said. And if that didn't move her, surely nothing would, for among folks in the wilds, there was nothing counted so mean as to take back a gift.

"That's as it may be," she answered evasively.

"Oh, you shall have it all right," he answered bravely. "I'll send it back at once, never fear. And now perhaps you'll give me back my letter." Eleseus rose to his feet.

Very well; she gave him back the letter. But now the tears came into her eyes as she did so; this servant-girl was touched; her friend was forsaking her—good-bye forever!

"You've no need to go," she said. "I don't care for what Axel says."

But Eleseus had the upper hand now, and must use it; he thanked her and said good-bye. "When a lady carries on that way," he said, "there's nothing else to be done."

He left the house, quietly, and walked up homeward, whistling, swinging his stick, and playing the man. Huh! A little while after came Barbro walking up; she called to him once or twice. Very well; he stopped, so he did, but was a wounded lion. She sat down in the heather looking penitent; she fidgeted with a sprig, and a little after he too softened, and asked for a kiss, the last time, just to say good-bye, he said. No, she would not. "Be nice and be a dear like you were last time," he begged, and moved round her on all sides, stepping quickly, if he could see his chance. But she would not be a dear; she got up. And there she stood. And at that he simply nodded and went.

When he was out of sight, Axel appeared suddenly from behind some bushes. Barbro started, all taken aback, and asked: "What's that—where have you been? Up that way?"

"No; I've been down that way," he answered. "But I saw you two going up here."

"Ho, did you? And a lot of good it did you, I dare say," she cried, suddenly furious. She was certainly not easier to deal with now. "What are you poking and sniffing about after, I'd like to know? What's it to do with you?"

Axel was not in the best of temper himself. "H'm. So he's been here again today?"

"Well, what if he has? What do you want with him?"

"I want with him? It's what you want with him, I'd like to ask. You ought to be ashamed."

"Ashamed? Huh! The least said about that, if you ask me," said Barbro. "I'm here to sit in the house like a statue, I suppose? What have I got to be ashamed of, anyway? If you like to go and get someone else to look after the place, I'm ready to go. You hold your tongue, that's all I've got to say, if it's not too much to ask. I'm going back now to get your supper and make the coffee, and after that I can do as I please."

They came home with the quarrel at its height.

No, they were not always the best of friends, Axel and Barbro; there was trouble now and again. She had been with him now for a couple of years, and they had had words before; mostly when Barbro talked of finding another place. He wanted her to stay there forever, to settle down there and share the house and life with him; he knew how hard it would be for him if he were left without help again. And she had promised several times—aye, in her more affectionate moments she would not think of going away at all. But the moment they quarreled about anything, she invariably threatened to go. If for nothing else, she must go to have her teeth seen to in town. Go, go away . . . Axel felt he must find a means to keep her.

Keep her? A lot Barbro cared for his trying to keep her if she didn't want to stay.

"Ho, so you want to go away again?" said he.

"Well, and if I do?"

"*Can* you, d'you think?"

"Well, and why not? If you think I'm afraid because the winter's coming on . . . But I can get a place in Bergen any day I like."

Then said Axel steadily enough: "It'll be some time before you can do that, anyway. As long as you're with child."

"With child? What are you talking about?"

Axel stared. Was the girl mad?

True, he himself should have been more patient. Now that he had the means of keeping her, he had grown too confident, and that was a mistake; there was no need to be sharp with her and make her wild; he need not have ordered her in so many words to help him with the potatoes that spring—he might have planted them by himself. There would be plenty of time for him to assert his authority after they were married; until then he ought to have had sense enough to give way.

But—it *was* too bad, this business with Eleseus, this clerk, who came swaggering about with his walking-stick and all his fine talk. For a girl to carry on like that when she was promised to another man—and in her condition!

It was beyond understanding. Up to then, Axel had had
no rival to compete with—now, it was different.

"Here's a new paper for you," he said. "And here's a
bit of a thing I got you. Don't know if you'll care about it."

Barbro was cold. They were sitting there together,
drinking scalding hot coffee from the bowl, but for all that
she answered icy cold:

"I suppose that's the gold ring you've been promising me
this twelvemonth and more."

This, however, was beyond the mark, for it *was* the ring
after all. But a gold ring it was not, and that he had never
promised her—'twas an invention of her own; silver it
was, with gilt hands clasped, real silver, with the mark on
and all. But ah, that unlucky voyage of hers to Bergen!
Barbro had seen real engagement rings—no use telling her!

"That ring! Huh! You can keep it yourself."

"What's wrong with it, then?"

"Wrong with it? There's nothing wrong with it that I
know," she answered, and got up to clear the table.

"Why, you'll needs make do with it for now," he said.
"Maybe I'll manage another some day."

Barbro made no answer.

A thankless creature was Barbro this evening. A new
silver ring—she might at least have thanked him nicely
for it. It must be that clerk with the town ways that had
turned her head. Axel could not help saying: "I'd like to
know what that fellow Eleseus keeps coming here for, anyway. What does he want with you?"

"With me?"

"Aye. Is he such a greenhorn and can't see how 'tis with
you now? Hasn't he eyes in his head?"

Barbro turned on him straight at that: "Oh, so you
think you've got a hold on me because of *that*? You'll find
out you're wrong, that's all."

"Ho!" said Axel.

"Aye, and I'll not stay here, neither."

But Axel only smiled a little at this; not broadly and laughing in her face, no; for he did not mean to cross her. And then he spoke soothingly, as to a child: "Be a good girl now, Barbro. 'Tis you and me, you know."

And of course in the end Barbro gave in and was good, and even went to sleep with the silver ring on her finger.

It would all come right in time, never fear.

For the two in the hut, yes. But what about Eleseus? 'Twas worse with him; he found it hard to get over the shameful way Barbro had treated him. He knew nothing of hysterics, and took it as all pure cruelty on her part; that girl Barbro from Breidablik thought a deal too much of herself, even though she *had* been in Bergen. . . .

He sent her back the photograph in a way of his own—took it down himself one night and stuck it through the door to her in the hayloft, where she slept. 'Twas not done in any rough unmannerly way, not at all; he had fidgeted with the door a long time so as to wake her, and when she rose up on her elbow and asked, "What's the matter; can't you find your way in this evening?" he understood the question was meant for someone else, and it went through him like a needle; like a saber.

He walked back home—no walking-stick, no whistling. He did not care about playing the man any longer. A stab at the heart is no light matter.

And was that the last of it?

One Sunday he went down just to look; to peep and spy. With a sickly and unnatural patience he lay in hiding among the bushes, staring over at the hut. And when at last there came a sign of life and movement it was enough to make an end of him altogether: Axel and Barbro came out together and went across to the cowshed. They were loving and affectionate now, aye, they had a blessed hour;

they walked with their arms round each other, and he was going to help her with the animals. Ho, yes!

Eleseus watched the pair with a look as if he had lost all; as a ruined man. And his thought, maybe, was like this: There she goes arm in arm with Axel Ström. How she could ever do it I can't think; there was a time when she put her arms round me! And there they disappeared into the shed.

Well, let them! Huh! Was he to lie here in the bushes and forget himself? A nice thing for him—to lie there flat on his belly and forget himself. Who was she, after all? But he was the man he was. Huh! again.

He sprang to his feet and stood up. Brushed the twigs and dust from his clothes and drew himself up and stood upright again. His rage and desperation came out in a curious fashion now: he threw all care to the winds, and began singing a ballad of highly frivolous import. And there was an earnest expression on his face as he took care to sing the worst parts loudest of all.

CHAPTER XIX

SAK came back from the village with a horse.

Aye, it had come to that; he had bought the horse from the Lensmand's assistant; the animal was for sale, as Geissler had said, but it cost two hundred and forty kroner —that was sixty daler. The price of horseflesh had gone up beyond all bounds: when Isak was a boy the best horse could be bought for fifty daler.

But why had he never raised a horse himself? He had thought of it, had imagined a nice little foal—that he had been waiting for these two years past. That was a business for folk who could spare the time from their land, could leave waste patches lying waste till they got a horse to carry home the crop. The Lensmand's assistant had said: "I don't care about paying for a horse's keep myself; I've no more hay than my womenfolk can get it in by themselves while I'm away on duty."

The new horse was an old idea of Isak's, he had been thinking of it for years; it was not Geissler who had put him up to it. And he had also made preparations such as he could; a new stall, a new rope for tethering it in the summer; as for carts, he had some already, he must make some more for the autumn. Most important of all was the fodder, and he had not forgotten that, of course; or why should he have thought it so important to get that last patch broken up last year if it hadn't been to save getting rid of one of the cows, and yet have enough keep for a new horse? It was sown for green fodder now; that was for the calving cows.

Aye, he had thought it all out. Well might Inger be astonished again, and clap her hands just as in the old days.

Isak brought news from the village; Breidablik was to be sold, there was a notice outside the church. The bit of crop, such as it was—hay and potatoes—to go with the rest. Perhaps the livestock too; a few beasts only, nothing big.

"Is he going to sell up the home altogether and leave nothing?" cried Inger. "And where's he going to live?"

"In the village."

It was true enough. Brede was going back to the village. But he had first tried to get Axel Ström to let him live there with Barbro. He didn't succeed. Brede would never dream of interfering with the relations between his daughter and Axel, so he was careful not to make himself a nuisance, though to be sure it was a hard setback, with all the rest. Axel was going to get his new house built that autumn; well, then, when he and Barbro moved in there, why couldn't Brede and his family have a hut? No! 'Twas so with Brede, he didn't look at things like a farmer and a settler on new land; he didn't understand that Axel had to move out because he wanted the hut for his growing stock; the hut was to be a new cowshed. And even when this was explained to him, he failed to see the point of view; surely human beings should come before animals, he said. No, a settler's way was different; animals first; a man could always find himself a shelter for the winter. But Barbro put in a word herself now: "Ho, so you put the animals first and us after? 'Tis just as well I know it!" So Axel had made enemies of a whole family because he hadn't room to house them. But he would not give way. He was no good-natured fool, was Axel, but on the contrary he had grown more and more careful; he knew well that a crowd like that moving in would give him so many more mouths to fill. Brede bade his daughter be quiet, and tried to make out that he himself would rather move down to the village again; couldn't endure life in the wilderness, he said—'twas only for that reason he was selling the place.

Oh, but to tell the truth it was not so much Brede was selling the place; 'twas the Bank and the storekeeper were selling up Breidablik, though for the sake of appearances they let it be done in Brede's name. That way, he thought he was saved from disgrace. And Brede was not altogether dejected when Isak met him; he consoled himself with the thought that he was still Inspector on the telegraph line; that was a regular income, anyway, and in time he would be able to work up to his old position in the place as the Lensmand's companion and this and that. He was something affected at the change, of course; 'twas not so easy to say good-bye to a place where one had lived and toiled and moiled so many years, and come to care for. But Brede, good man, was never long cast down. 'Twas his best point, the charm of him. He had once in his life taken it into his head to be a tiller of the soil, 'twas an inspiration had come to him. True, he had not made a success of it, but he had taken up other plans in the same airy way and got on better; and who could say—perhaps his samples of ore might after all turn out something wonderful in time! And then look at Barbro, he had got her fixed up there at Maaneland, and she'd not be leaving Axel Ström now, that he could swear —'twas plain indeed for anyone to see.

No, there was nothing to fear as long as he had his health and could work for himself and those that looked to him, said Brede Olsen. And the children were just growing up, and big enough now to go out and make their own way in the world, said he. Helge was gone to the herring fisheries already, and Katrine was going to help at the doctor's. That left only the two youngest—well, well, there was a third on the way, true, but, anyhow . . .

Isak had more news from the village: the Lensmand's lady had had a baby. Inger suddenly interested at this: "Boy or girl?"

"Why, I didn't hear which," said Isak.

But the Lensmand's lady had had a child after all—after all the way she'd spoken at the women's club about the increasing birth-rate among the poor; better give women the franchise and let them have some say in their own affairs, she said. And now she was caught. Yes, the parson's wife had said: "She's had some say in lots of things—but her own affairs are none the better for it, ha ha ha!" And that was a clever saying that went the round of the village, and there were many that understood what was meant—Inger no doubt as well; it was only Isak who did not understand.

Isak understood his work, his calling. He was a rich man now, with a big farm, but the heavy cash payments that had come to him by a lucky chance he used but poorly; he put the money aside. The land saved him. If he had lived down in the village, maybe the great world would have affected even him; so much gaiety, so many elegant manners and ways; he would have been buying useless trifles, and wearing a red Sunday shirt on weekdays. Here in the wilds he was sheltered from all immoderation; he lived in clean air, washed himself on Sunday mornings, and took a bath when he went up to the lake. Those thousand daler—well, 'twas a gift from Heaven, to be kept intact. What else should he do? His ordinary outgoings were more than covered by the produce of his fields and stock.

Eleseus, of course, knew better; he had advised his father to put the money in the Bank. Well, perhaps that was the best, but Isak had put off doing it for the present—perhaps it would never be done at all. Not that Isak was above taking advice from his son; Eleseus was no fool, as he showed later on. Now, in the haymaking season, he had tried his hand with the scythe—but he was no master hand at that, no. He kept close to Sivert, and had to get him to use the whetstone every time. But Eleseus had long arms and could pick up hay in first-rate fashion. And he and Sivert and Leopoldine, and Jensine the servant-maid, they were all busy now in the fields with the first lot of hay that year. Eleseus did not spare himself either, but raked away till his hands were blistered and had to be wrapped in rags. He had lost his appetite for a week or so, but worked none the worse for it now. Something had come over the boy; it looked perhaps as if a certain unhappy love affair or something of the sort, a touch of never-to-be-forgotten sorrow and distress, had done him a world of good. And, look you, he had by now smoked the last of the tobacco he had brought with him from town; ordinarily, that would have been enough to make a clerk go about banging doors and expressing himself emphatically upon many points; but no, Eleseus only grew the steadier for it; firmer and more upright; a man indeed. Even Sivert, the jester, could not put him out of countenance. Today the pair of them were lying out on boulders in the river to drink, and Sivert imprudently offered to get some extra fine moss and dry it for tobacco—"unless you'd rather smoke it raw?" he said.

"I'll give you tobacco," said Eleseus, and reaching out, ducked Sivert head and shoulders in the water. Ho, one for him! Sivert came back with his hair still dripping.

"Looks like Eleseus he's turning out for the good," thought Isak to himself, watching his son at work. And to Inger he said: "H'm—wonder if Eleseus he'll be staying home now for good?"

And she just as queerly cautious again: " 'Tis more than I can say. No, I doubt if he will."

"Ho! Have you said a word of it to himself?"

"No—well, yes, I've talked a bit with him, maybe. But that's the way I think."

"Like to know, now—suppose he'd a bit of land of his own . . ."

"How do you mean?"

"If he'd work on a place of his own?"

"No."

"Well, have you said anything?"

"Said anything? Can't you see for yourself? No, I don't see anything in him Eleseus, that way."

"Don't sit there talking ill of him," said Isak impartially. "All I can see is, he's doing a good day's work down there."

"Aye, maybe," said Inger submissively.

"And I can't see what you've got to find fault with the lad," cried Isak, evidently displeased. "He does his work better and better every day, and what can you ask more?"

Inger murmured: "Aye, but he's not like he used to be. You try talking to him about waistcoats."

"About waistcoats? What d'you mean?"

"How he used to wear white waistcoats in summer when he was in town, so he says."

Isak pondered this a while; it was beyond him. "Well, can't he have a white waistcoat?" he said. Isak was out of his depth here; of course it was only women's nonsense; to his mind, the boy had a perfect right to a white waistcoat, if it pleased him; anyhow, he couldn't see what there was to make a fuss about, and was inclined to put the matter aside and go on.

"Well, what do you think, if he had Brede's bit of land to work on?"

"Who?" said Inger.

"Him Eleseus."

"Breidablik? Nay, 'tis more than's worth your while."

The fact was, she had already been talking over that very plan with Eleseus, she had heard it from Sivert, who could not keep the secret. And indeed, why should Sivert keep the matter secret when his father had surely told him of it

on purpose to feel his way? It was not the first time he had
used Sivert as a go-between. Well, but what had Eleseus
answered? Just as before, as in his letters from town, that
no, he would not throw away all he had learned, and be an
insignificant nothing again. That was what he had said.
Well, and then his mother had brought out all her good reasons, but Eleseus had said no to them all; he had other
plans for his life. Young hearts have their unfathomable
depths, and after what had happened, likely enough he
did not care about staying on with Barbro as a neighbor.
Who could say? He had put it loftily enough in talking to
his mother; he could get a better position in town than the
one he had; could go as clerk to one of the higher officials.
He must get on, he must rise in the world. In a few years,
perhaps, he might be a Lensmand, or perhaps a lighthouse
keeper, or get into the Customs. There were so many roads
open to a man with learning.

However it might be, his mother came round, was
drawn over to his point of view. Oh, she was so little sure
of herself yet; the world had not quite lost its hold on her.
Last winter she had gone so far as to read occasionally a
certain excellent devotional work which she had brought
from Trondhjem, from the Institute; but now, Eleseus
might be a Lensmand one day!

"And why not?" said Eleseus. "What's Heyerdahl himself but a former clerk in the same department?"

Splendid prospects. His mother herself advised him not
to give up his career and throw himself away. What was a
man like that to do in the wilds?

But why should Eleseus then trouble to work hard and
steadily as he was doing now on his father's land? Heaven
knows, he had some reason, maybe. Something of inborn
pride in him still, perhaps; he would not be outdone by
others; and besides, it would do him no harm to be in his

father's good books the day he went away. To tell the truth, he had a number of little debts in town, and it would be a good thing to be able to settle them at once—improve his credit a lot. And it was not a question now of a mere hundred kroner, but something worth considering.

Eleseus was far from stupid, but on the contrary, a sly fellow in his way. He had seen his father come home, and knew well enough he was sitting there in the window at that moment, looking out. No harm in putting his back into it then for a bit, working a little harder for the moment—it would hurt no one, and might do himself good.

Eleseus was somehow changed; whatever it might be, something in him had been warped, and quietly spoiled; he was not bad, but something blemished. Had he lacked a guiding hand those last few years? What could his mother do to help him now? Only stand by him and agree. She could let herself be dazzled by her son's bright prospects for the future, and stand between him and his father, to take his part—she could do that.

But Isak grew impatient at last over her opposition; to his mind, the idea about Breidablik was by no means a bad one. Only that very day, coming up, he had stopped the horse almost without thinking, to look out with a critical eye over the ill-tended land; aye, it could be made a fine place in proper hands.

"Why not worth while?" he asked Inger now. "I've that much feeling for Eleseus, anyway, that I'd help him to it."

"If you've any feeling for him, then say never a word of Breidablik again," she answered.

"Ho!"

"Aye, for he's greater thoughts in his head than the like of us."

Isak, too, is hardly sure of himself here, and it weakens him; but he is by no means pleased at having shown his hand, and spoken straight out about his plan. He is unwilling to give it up now.

"He shall do as I say," declares Isak suddenly. And he raises his voice threateningly, in case Inger by any chance should be hard of hearing. "Aye, you may look; I'll say no more. It's midway up, with a schoolhouse by, and everything; what's the greater thoughts he's got beyond that, I'd like to know? With a son like that I might starve to death —is that any better, d'you think? And can you tell me why my own flesh and blood should turn and go contrary to— to my own flesh and blood?"

Isak stopped; he realized that the more he talked the worse it would be. He was on the point of changing his clothes, getting out of his best things he had put on to go down to the village in; but no, he altered his mind, he would stay as he was—whatever he meant by that. "You'd better say a word of it to Eleseus," he says then.

And Inger answers: "Best if you'd say it yourself. He won't do as I say."

Very well, then, Isak is head of the house, so he should think; now see if Eleseus dares to murmur! But, whether it were because he feared defeat, Isak draws back now, and says: "Aye, 'tis true, I might say a word of it myself. But by reason of having so many things to do, and busy with this and that, I've something else to think of."

"Well . . . ?" said Inger in surprise.

And Isak goes off again—not very far, only to the farther fields, but still, he goes off. He is full of mysteries, and must hide himself out of the way. The fact is this: he had brought back a third piece of news from the village today, and that was something more than the rest, something enormous; and he had hidden it at the edge of the wood. There it stands, wrapped up in sacking and paper; he uncovers it, and lo, a huge machine. Look! red and blue, wonderful to see, with a heap of teeth and a heap of knives, with joints and arms and screws and wheels—a mowing-machine. No, Isak would not have gone down today for the new horse if it hadn't been for that machine.

He stands with a marvelously keen expression, going over in his mind from beginning to end the instructions for use that the storekeeper had read out; he sets a spring here, and shifts a bolt there, then he oils every hole and every crevice, then he looks over the whole thing once more. Isak had never known such an hour in his life. To pick up a pen and write one's mark on a paper, a document—aye, 'twas a perilous great thing that, no doubt. Likewise in the matter of a new harrow he had once brought up—there were many curiously twisted parts in that to be considered. Not to speak of the great circular saw that had to be set in its course to the nicety of a pencil line, never swaying east nor west, lest it should fly asunder. But this—this mowing-machine of his—'twas a crawling nest of steel springs and hooks and apparatus, and hundreds of screws—Inger's sewing-machine was a bookmarker compared with this!

Isak harnessed himself to the shafts and tried the thing. Here was the wonderful moment. And that was why he kept out of sight and was his own horse.

For—what if the machine had been wrongly put together and did not do its work, but went to pieces with a crash! No such calamity happened, however, the machine could cut grass. And so indeed it ought, after Isak had stood there, deep in study, for hours. The sun had gone down. Again he harnesses himself and tries it; aye, the thing cuts grass. And so indeed it ought!

When the dew began to fall close after the heat of the day, and the boys came out, each with his scythe to mow in readiness for next day, Isak came in sight close to the house and said:

"Put away scythes for tonight. Get out the new horse, you can, and bring him down to the edge of the wood."

And on that, instead of going indoors to his supper as the others had done already, he turned where he stood and went back the way he had come.

"D'you want the cart, then?" Sivert called after him.

"No," said his father, and walked on.

Swelling with mystery, full of pride; with a little lift and throw from the knee at every step, so emphatically did he walk. So a brave man might walk to death and destruction, carrying no weapon in his hand.

The boys came up with the horse, saw the machine, and stopped dead. It was the first mowing-machine in the wilds, the first in the village—red and blue, a thing of splendor to man's eyes. And the father, head of them all, called out, oh, in a careless tone, as if it were nothing uncommon: "Harness up to this machine here."

And they drove it; the father drove. *Brrr!* said the thing, and felled the grass in swaths. The boys walked behind, nothing in their hands, doing no work, smiling. The father stopped and looked back. H'm, not as clear as it might be. He screws up a nut here and there to bring the knives closer to the ground, and tries again. No, not right yet, all uneven; the frame with the cutters seems to be hopping a little. Father and sons discuss what it can be. Eleseus has found the instructions and is reading them. "Here, it says to sit up on the seat when you drive—then it runs steadier," he says.

"Ho!" says his father. "Aye, 'tis so, I know," he answers. "I've studied it all through." He gets up into the seat and starts off again; it goes steadily now. Suddenly the machine stops working—the knives are not cutting at all. "*Ptro!* What's wrong now?" Father down from his seat, no longer swelling with pride, but bending an anxious, questioning face down over the machine. Father and sons all stare at it; something must be wrong. Eleseus stands holding the instructions.

"Here's a bolt or something," says Sivert, picking up a thing from the grass.

"Ho, that's all right, then," says his father, as if that was all that was needed to set everything in order. "I was just looking for that bolt." But now they could not find the hole for it to fit in—where in the name of wonder could the hole be, now?

And it was now that Eleseus could begin to feel himself a person of importance; he was the man to make out a printed paper of instructions. What would they do without him? He pointed unnecessarily long to the hole and explained: "According to the illustration, the bolt should fit in there."

"Aye, that's where she goes," said his father. " 'Twas there I had it before." And, by way of regaining lost prestige, he ordered Sivert to set about looking for more bolts in the grass. "There ought to be another," he said, looking very important, as if he carried the whole thing in his head. "Can't you find another? Well, well, it'll be in its hole then, all right."

Father starts off again.

"Wait a minute—this is wrong," cried Eleseus. Ho, Eleseus standing there with the drawing in his hand, with the Law in his hand; no getting away from him! "That spring there goes outside," he says to his father.

"Aye, what then?"

"Why, you've got it in under, you've set it wrong. It's a steel spring, and you have to fix it outside, else the bolt jars out again and stops the knives. You can see in the picture here."

"I've left my spectacles behind, and can't see it quite," says his father, something meekly. "You can see better—you set it as it should go. I don't want to go up to the house for my spectacles now."

All in order now, and Isak gets up. Eleseus calls after

him: "You must drive pretty fast, it cuts better that way—
it says so here."

Isak drives and drives, and everything goes well, and
Brrr! says the machine. There is a broad track of cut grass
in his wake, neatly in line, ready to take up. Now they can
see him from the house, and all the womenfolk come out;
Inger carries little Rebecca on her arm, though little Rebecca has learned to walk by herself long since. But there
they come—four womenfolk, big and small—hurrying
with straining eyes down towards the miracle, flocking
down to see. Oh, but now is Isak's hour. Now he is truly
proud, a mighty man, sitting high aloft dressed in holiday
clothes, in all his finery; in jacket and hat, though the sweat
is pouring off him. He swings round in four big angles, goes
over a good bit of ground, swings round, drives, cuts grass,
passes along by where the women are standing; they are
dumbfounded, it is all beyond them, and *Brrr!* says the machine.

Then Isak stops and gets down. Longing, no doubt, to
hear what these folk on earth down there will say; what
they will find to say about it all. He hears smothered cries;
they fear to disturb him, these beings on earth, in his lordly
work, but they turn to one another with awed question-
ings, and he hears what they say. And now, that he may
be a kind and fatherly lord and ruler to them all, to encourage them, he says: "There, I'll just do this bit, and you can
spread it tomorrow."

"Haven't you time to come in and have a bite of food?"
says Inger, all overwhelmed.

"Nay, I've other things to do," he answers.

Then he oils the machine again; gives them to understand that he is occupied with scientific work. Drives off
again, cutting more grass. And, at long last, the womenfolk go back home.

Happy Isak—happy folk at Sellanraa!

Very soon the neighbors from below will be coming up. Axel Ström is interested in things, he may be up tomorrow. But Brede from Breidablik, he might be here that very evening. Isak would not be loth to show them his machine, explain it to them, tell them how it works, and all about it. He can point out how that no man with a scythe could ever cut so fine and clean. But it costs money, of course—oh, a red-and-blue machine like that is a terribly costly thing!

Happy Isak!

But as he stops for oil the third time, there! his spectacles fall from his pocket. And, worst of all, the two boys saw it. Was there a higher power behind that little happening—a warning against overweening pride? He had put on those spectacles time and again that day to study the instructions, without making out a word; Eleseus had to help him with that. Eyah, *Herregud*, 'twas a good thing, no doubt, to be book-learned. And, by way of humbling himself, Isak determines to give up his plan of making Eleseus a tiller of soil in the wilds; he will never say a word of it again.

Not that the boys made any great business about that matter of the spectacles; far from it. Sivert, the jester, had to say something, of course; it was too much for him. He plucked Eleseus by the sleeve and said: "Here, come along, we'll go back home and throw those scythes on the fire. Father's going to do all the mowing now with his machine!" And that was a jest indeed.

BOOK TWO

ELLANRAA is no longer a desolate spot in the waste; human beings live here—seven of them, counting great and small. But in the little time the haymaking lasted there came a stranger or so, folk wanting to see the mowing-machine. Brede Olsen was first, of course, but Axel Ström came, too, and other neighbors from lower down— aye, from right down in the village. And from across the hills came Oline, the imperishable Oline.

This time, too, she brought news with her from her own village; 'twas not Oline's way to come empty of gossip. Old Sivert's affairs had been gone into, his accounts reckoned up, and the fortune remaining after him came to nothing. Nothing!

Here Oline pressed her lips together and looked from one to another. Well, was there not a sigh—would not the roof fall down? Eleseus was the first to smile.

"Let's see—you're called after your Uncle Sivert, aren't you?" he asked softly.

And little Sivert answered as softly again:

"That's so. But I made you a present of all that might come to me after him."

"And how much was it?"

"Between five and ten thousand."

"Daler?" cried Eleseus suddenly, mimicking his brother.

Oline, no doubt, thought this ill-timed jesting. Oh, she had herself been cheated of her due; for all that she had managed to squeeze out something like real tears over old Sivert's grave. Eleseus should know best what he himself had written—so-and-so much to Oline, to be a comfort and support in her declining years. And where was that support? Oh, a broken reed!

Poor Oline, they might have left her something—single golden gleam in her life! Oline was not over-blessed with this world's goods. Practiced in evil—aye, well used to edging her way by tricks and little meannesses from day to day; strong only as a scandalmonger, as one whose tongue was to be feared; aye, so. But nothing could have made her worse than before; least of all a pittance left her by the dead. She had toiled all her life, had borne children, and taught them her own few arts; begged for them, maybe stolen for them, but always managing for them somehow— a mother in her poor way. Her powers were not less than those of other politicians; she acted for herself and those belonging to her, set her speech according to the moment, and gained her end, earning a cheese or a handful of wool each time; she also could live and die in commonplace insincerity and readiness of wit. Oline—maybe old Sivert had for a moment thought of her as young, pretty, and rosy-cheeked, but now she is old, deformed, a picture of decay; she ought to have been dead. Where is she to be buried? She has no family vault of her own; nay, she will be lowered down in a graveyard to lie among the bones of strangers and unknown; aye, to that she comes at last— Oline, born and died. She had been young once. A pittance left to her now, at the eleventh hour? Aye, a single golden gleam, and this slave-woman's hands would have been folded for a moment. Justice would have overtaken her with its late reward; for that she had begged for her children, maybe stolen for them, but always managed for them some way. A moment—and the darkness would reign in her as before; her eyes glower, her fingers feel out graspingly. "How much?" she would say. "What, no more?" she would say. She would be right again. A mother many times, realizing life—it was worthy of a great reward.

But all went otherwise. Old Sivert's accounts had appeared more or less in order after Eleseus had been through them; but the farm and the cow, the fishery and nets, were barely enough to cover the deficit. And it was due in some measure to Oline that things had turned out no worse; so earnest was she in trying to secure a small remainder for herself that she dragged to light forgotten items that she, as gossip and newsmonger for years, remembered still, or matters outstanding which others would have passed over on purpose, to avoid causing unpleasantness to respectable fellow-citizens. Oh, that Oline! And she did not even say a word against old Sivert now; he had made his will in kindness of heart, and there could have been a plenty after him, but that the two men sent by the Department to arrange things had cheated her. But one day all would come to the ears of the Almighty, said Oline threateningly.

Strange, she found nothing ridiculous in the fact that she was mentioned in the will; after all, it was an honor of a sort; none of her likes were named there with her!

The Sellanraa folk took the blow with patience; they were not altogether unprepared. True, Inger could not understand it—Uncle Sivert that had always been so rich. . . .

"He might have stood forth an upright man and a wealthy before the Lamb and before the Throne," said Oline, "if they hadn't robbed him."

Isak was standing ready to go out to his fields, and Oline said: "Pity you've got to go now, Isak; then I shan't see the new machine, after all. You've got a new machine, they say?"

"Aye."

"Aye, there's talk of it about, and how it cuts quicker

than a hundred scythes. And what haven't you got, Isak, with all your means and riches! Priest, our way, he's got a new plow with two handles; but what's he, compared with you, and I'd tell him so to his face."

"Sivert here'll show you the machine; he's better at working her than his father," said Isak, and went out.

Isak went out. There is an auction to be held at Breidablik that noon, and he is going; there's but just time to get there now. Not that Isak any longer thinks of buying the place, but the auction—it is the first auction held there in the wilds, and it would be strange not to go.

He gets down as far as Maaneland and sees Barbro, and would pass by with only a greeting, but Barbro calls to him and asks if he is going down. "Aye," said Isak, making to go on again. It is her home that is being sold, and that is why he answers shortly.

"You going to the sale?" she asks.

"To the sale? Well, I was only going down a bit. What you've done with Axel?"

"Axel? Nay, I don't know. He's gone down to sale. Doubt he'll be seeing his chance to pick up something for nothing, like the rest."

Heavy to look at was Barbro now—aye, and sharp and bitter-tongued!

The auction has begun; Isak hears the Lensmand calling out, and sees a crowd of people. Coming nearer, he does not know them all; there are some from other villages, but Brede is fussing about, in his best finery, and chattering in his old way. "*Goddag*, Isak. So you're doing me the honor to come and see my auction sale. Thanks, thanks. Aye, we've been neighbors and friends these many years now, and never an ill word between us." Brede grows pathetic: "Aye, 'tis strange to think of leaving a place where you've lived and toiled and grown fond of. But what's a man to do when it's fated so to be?"

"Maybe 'twill be better for you after," says Isak comfortingly.

"Why," says Brede, grasping at it himself, "to tell the truth, I think it will. I'm not regretting it, not a bit. I won't say I've made a fortune on the place here, but that's to come, maybe; and the young ones getting older and leaving the nest—aye, 'tis true the wife's got another on the way; but for all that . . ." And suddenly Brede tells his news straight out: "I've given up the telegraph business."

"What?" asks Isak.

"I've given up that telegraph."

"Given up the telegraph?"

"Aye, from new year to be. What was the good of it, anyway? And supposing I was out on business, or driving for the Lensmand or the doctor, then to have to look after the telegraph first of all—no, there's no sense nor meaning in it that way. Well enough for them that's time to spare. But running over hill and dale after a telegraph wire for next to nothing wages, 'tis no job that for Brede. And then, besides, I've had words with the people from the telegraph office about it—they've been making a fuss again."

The Lensmand keeps repeating the bids for the farm; they have got up to the few hundred kroner the place is judged to be worth, and the bidding goes slowly, now, with but five or ten kroner more each time.

"Why, surely—'tis Axel there's bidding," cries Brede suddenly, and hurries eagerly across. "What, you going to take over my place too? Haven't you enough to look after?"

"I'm bidding for another man," says Axel evasively.

"Well, well, 'tis no harm to me, 'twasn't that I meant."

The Lensmand raises his hammer, a new bid is made, a whole hundred kroner at once; no one bids higher, the Lensmand repeats the figure again and again, waits for a moment with his hammer raised, and then strikes.

Whose bid?

Axel Ström—on behalf of another.

The Lensmand notes it down: Axel Ström as agent.

"Who's that you buying for?" asks Brede. "Not that it's any business of mine, of course, but . . ."

But now some men at the Lensmand's table are putting their heads together; there is a representative from the Bank, the storekeeper has sent his assistant; there is something the matter; the creditors are not satisfied. Brede is called up, and Brede, careless and lighthearted, only nods and is agreed—"but who'd ever have thought it didn't come up to more?" says he. And suddenly he raises his voice and declares to all present:

"Seeing as we've an auction holding anyhow, and I've troubled the Lensmand all this way, I'm willing to sell what I've got here on the place: the cart, livestock, a pitchfork, a grindstone. I've no use for the things now; we'll sell the lot!"

Small bidding now. Brede's wife, careless and lighthearted as himself, for all the fullness of her in front, has begun selling coffee at a table. She finds it amusing to play at shop, and smiles; and when Brede himself comes up for some coffee, she tells him jestingly that he must pay for it like the rest. And Brede actually takes out his lean purse and pays. "There's a wife for you," he says to the others. "Thrifty, what?"

The cart is not worth much—it has stood too long uncovered in the open; but Axel bids a full five kroner more at last, and gets the cart as well. After that Axel buys no more, but all are astonished to see that cautious man buying so much as he has.

Then came the animals. They had been kept in their shed today, so as to be there in readiness. What did Brede want with livestock when he had no farm to keep them on? He had no cows; he had started farming with two goats, and had now four. Besides these, there were six sheep. No horse.

Isak bought a certain sheep with flat ears. When Brede's children led it out from the shed, he started bidding at once, and people looked at him. Isak from Sellanraa was a rich man, in a good position, with no need of more sheep than he had. Brede's wife stops selling coffee for a moment, and says: "Aye, you may buy her, Isak; she's old, 'tis true, but she's two and three lambs every blessed year, and that's the truth."

"I know it," said Isak, looking straight at her. "I've seen that sheep before."

He walks up with Axel Ström on the way back, leading his sheep on a string. Axel is taciturn, seemingly anxious about something, whatever it might be. There's nothing he need be troubled about that one can see, thinks Isak; his crops are looking well, most of his fodder is housed already, and he has begun timbering his house. All as it should be with Axel Ström; a thought slowly, but sure in the end. And now he had got a horse.

"So you've bought Brede's place?" said Isak. "Going to work it yourself?"

"No, not for myself. I bought it for another man."

"Ho!"

"What d'you think; was it too much I gave for it?"

"Why, no. 'Tis good land for a man that'll work it as it should."

"I bought it for a brother of mine up in Helgeland."

"Ho!"

"Then I thought perhaps I'd half a mind to change with him, too."

"Change with him—would you?"

"And perhaps how Barbro she'd like it better that way."

"Aye, maybe," said Isak.

They walk on for a good way in silence. Then says Axel:

"They've been after me to take over that telegraph business."

"The telegraph? H'm. Aye, I heard that Brede he's given it up."

"H'm," says Axel, smiling. " 'Tis not so much that way of it, but Brede that's been turned off."

"Aye, so," says Isak, and trying to find some excuse for Brede. "It takes a deal of time to look after, no doubt."

"They gave him notice to the new year, if he didn't do better."

"H'm."

"You don't think it'd be worth my while to take it?"

Isak thought for a long while, and answered: "Aye, there's the money, true, but still . . ."

"They've offered me more."

"How much?"

"Double."

"Double? Why, then, I'd say you should think it over."

"But they've made the line a bit longer now. No, I don't know what's best to do—there's not so much timber to sell here as you've got on yours, and I've need to buy more things for the work that I've got now. And buying things needs money in cash, and I've not so much out of the land and stock that there's much over to sell. Seems to me I'll have to try a year at the telegraph to begin with. . . ."

It did not occur to either of them that Brede might "do better" and keep the post himself.

When they reached Maaneland, Oline was there already, on her way down. Aye, a strange creature, Oline, crawling about fat and round as a maggot, and over seventy years and all, but still getting about. She sits drinking coffee in the hut, but seeing the men come up, all must give way to that, and she comes out.

"*Goddag*, Axel, and welcome back from the sale. You'll

not mind me looking in to see how you and Barbro's getting
on? And you're getting on finely, to see, and building a new
house and getting richer and richer! And you been buying
sheep, Isak?"

"Aye," said Isak. "You know her, maybe?"

"If I know her ? Nay . . ."

"With these flat ears, you can see."

"Flat ears? How d'you mean now? And what then?
What I was going to say: Who bought Brede's place, after
all? I was just saying to Barbro here, who'd be your neighbors that way now? said I. And Barbro, poor thing, she
sits crying, as natural enough, to be sure; but the Almighty
that's decreed her a new home here at Maaneland . . .
Flat ears? I've seen a deal of sheep in my day with flat ears
and all. And I'll tell you, Isak, that machine of yours, 'twas
almost more than my old eyes could see nor understand.
And what she'll have cost you I won't even ask, for I never
could count so far. Axel, if you've seen it, you know what I
mean; 'twas all as it might be Elijah and his chariot of
fire, and Heaven forgive me that I say it. . . ."

When the hay was all in, Eleseus began making preparations for his return to town. He had written to the engineer to say he was coming, but received the extraordinary
reply that times were bad, and they would have to econo-
mize; the office would have to dispense with Eleseus's
services, and the chief would do the work himself.

The deuce and all! But after all, what did a district surveyor want with an office staff? When he had taken Eleseus
on as a youngster, he had done so, no doubt, only to show
himself as a great man to these folks in the wilds; and if he
had given him clothes and board till his confirmation, he
had got some return for it in the way of writing-work, that
was true. Now the boy was grown up, and that made all
the difference.

"But," said the engineer, "if you do come back I will

do all I can to get you a place somewhere else, though it may be a difficult matter, as there are more young men than are wanted looking out for the same thing. With kind regards. . . ."

Eleseus would go back to town, of course, there could be no question about that. Was he to throw himself away? He wanted to get on in the world. And he said nothing to those at home as to the altered state of affairs; it would be no use, and, to tell the truth, he felt a little out of humor with the whole thing.

Anyhow, he said nothing. The life at Sellanraa was having its effect on him again; it was an inglorious, commonplace life, but quiet and dulling to the sense, a dreamy life; there was nothing for him to show off about, a lookingglass was a thing he had no use for. His town life had wrought a schism in himself, and made him finer than the others, made him weaker; he began indeed to feel that he must be homeless anywhere. He had come to like the smell of tansy again—let that pass. But there was no sense at all in a peasant lad's standing listening in the morning to the girls milking the cows and thinking thus: they're milking, listen now; 'tis almost by way of something wonderful to hear, a kind of song in nothing but little streams, different from the brass bands in the town and the Salvation Army and the steamer sirens. Music streaming into a pail. . . .

It was not the way at Sellanraa to show one's feelings overmuch, and Eleseus dreaded the moment when he would have to say good-bye. He was well equipped now; again his mother had given him a stock of woven stuff for underclothes, and his father had commissioned someone to hand him money as he went out of the door. Money—could Isak really spare such a thing as money? But it was so, and no otherwise. Inger hinted that it would doubtless be the last time; for was not Eleseus going to get on and rise in the world by himself?

"H'm," said Isak.

There was an atmosphere of solemnity, of stillness in the home; they had each had a boiled egg at the last meal, and Sivert stood outside all ready to go down with his brother and carry his things. It was for Eleseus to begin.

He began with Leopoldine. Well and good, she said good-bye in return, and managed it very well. Likewise Jensine the servant-maid, she sat carding wool and answered good-bye—but both girls stared at him, confound them! and all because he might perhaps be the least bit red about the eyes. He shook hands with his mother, and she cried of course quite openly, never caring to remember how he hated crying. "Goo-ood-bye and bl-bless you!" she sobbed out. It was worst with his father; worst of all with him. Oh, in every way; he was so toil-worn and so utterly faithful; he had carried the children in his arms, had told them of the seagulls and other birds and beasts, and the wonders of the field; it was not so long ago, a few years. . . . Father stands by the glass window, then suddenly he turns round, grasps his son's hand, and says quickly and peevishly: "Well, good-bye. There's the new horse getting loose," and he swings out of the door and hurries away. Oh, but he had himself taken care to let the new horse loose a while ago, and Sivert, the rascal, knew it too, as he stood outside watching his father, and smiling to himself. And, anyway, the horse was only in the rowens.

Eleseus had got it over at last.

And then his mother must needs come out on the door-slab and hiccup again and say: "God bless you!" and give him something. "Take this—and you're not to thank him, he says you're not to. And don't forget to write; write often."

Two hundred kroner.

Eleseus looked down the field: his father was furiously at work driving a tethering-peg into the ground; he seemed to find it a difficult matter, for all that the ground was soft enough.

The brothers set off down the road; they came to Maaneland, and there stood Barbro in the doorway and called to them to come up.

"You going away again, Eleseus? Nay, then, you must come in and take a cup of coffee at least."

They go into the hut, and Eleseus is no longer a prey to the pangs of love, nor wishful to jump out of windows and take poison; nay, he spreads his light spring overcoat across his knees, taking care to lay it so the silver plate is to be seen; then he wipes his hair with his handkerchief, and observes delicately: "Beautiful day, isn't it—simply classic!"

Barbro too is self-possessed enough; she plays with a silver ring on one hand and a gold ring on the other—aye, true enough, if she hasn't got a gold ring too—and she wears an apron reaching from neck to feet, as if to say she is not spoiled as to her figure, whoever else may be that way. And when the coffee is ready and her guests are drinking, she sews a little to begin with on a white cloth, and then does a little crochet-work with a collar of some sort, and so with all manner of maidenly tasks. Barbro is not put out by their visit, and all the better; they can talk naturally, and Eleseus can be all on the surface again, young and witty as he pleases.

"What have you done with Axel?" asks Sivert.

"Oh, he's about the place somewhere," she answers, pulling herself up. "And so we'll not be seeing you this way any more, I doubt?" she asks Eleseus.

"It's hardly probable," says he.

"Aye, 'tis no place for one as is used to the town. I only wish I could go along with you."

"You don't mean that, I know."

"Don't mean it? Oh, I've known what it is to live in

town, and what it's like here; and I've been in a bigger town than you, for that matter—and shouldn't I miss it?"

"I didn't mean that way," says Eleseus hastily. "After you being in Bergen itself and all." Strange, how impatient she was, after all!

"I only know that if it wasn't for having the papers to read, I'd not stay here another day," says she.

"But what about Axel, then, and all the rest?—'twas that I was thinking."

"As for Axel, 'tis no business of mine. And what about yourself—I doubt there'll be someone waiting for you in town?"

And at that, Eleseus couldn't help showing off a little and closing his eyes and turning over the morsel on his tongue: perhaps true enough there was someone waiting for him in town. Oh, but he could have managed this ever so differently, snapped at the chance, if it hadn't been for Sivert sitting there! As it was, he could only say: "Don't talk such nonsense!"

"Ho," said she—and indeed she was shamefully ill-humored today—"nonsense, indeed! Well, what can you expect of folk at Maaneland? We're not so great and fine as you—no."

Oh, she could go to the devil, what did Eleseus care; her face was visibly dirty, and her condition plain enough now even to his innocent eyes.

"Can't you play a bit on the guitar?" he asked.

"No," answered Barbro shortly. "What I was going to say: Sivert, couldn't you come and help Axel a bit with the new house a day or so? If you could begin tomorrow, say, when you come back from the village?"

Sivert thought for a moment. "Aye, maybe. But I've no clothes."

"I could run up and fetch your working-clothes this evening, so they'll be here when you get back."

"Aye," said Sivert, "if you could."

And Barbro unnecessarily eager now: "Oh, if only you would come! Here's summer nearly gone already, and the house that should be up and roofed before the autumn rains. Axel, he's been going to ask you a many times before, but he couldn't, somehow. Oh, you'd be helping us no end!"

"I'll help as well as I can," said Sivert.

And that was settled.

But now it was Eleseus's turn to be offended. He can see well enough that it's clever of Barbro and all that, to look out and manage to her own advantage and Axel's too, and get help for the building and save the house, but the whole thing is a little too plain; after all, she is not mistress of the place as yet, and it's not so long since he himself had kissed her—the creature! Was there never an atom of shame in her at all?

"Aye," said Eleseus, then suddenly: "I'll come back again in time and be a godfather when you're ready."

She sent him a glance, and answered in great offense: "Godfather, indeed! And who's talking nonsense now, I'd like to know? 'Twill be time enough for you when I send word I'm looking out for godfathers." And what could Eleseus do then but laugh foolishly and wish himself out of the place!

"Here's thanks!" says Sivert, and gets up from his seat to go.

"Here's thanks!" says Eleseus also; but he did not rise nor bow as a man should do in saying thanks for a cup of coffee; not he, indeed—he would see her at the devil for a bitter-tongued lump of ugliness.

"Let me look," said Barbro. "Oh yes; the young men I stayed with in town, they had silver plates on their overcoats too, much bigger than this," said she. "Well, then, you'll come in on your way back, Sivert, and stay the night? I'll get your clothes all right."

And that was good-bye to Barbro.

The brothers went on again. Eleseus was not distressed in any way in the matter of Barbro; she could go to the devil—and, besides, he had two big banknotes in his pocket! The brothers took care not to touch on any mournful things, such as the strange way Father had said good-bye, or how Mother had cried. They went a long way round to avoid being stopped at Breidablik, and made a jest of that little ruse. But when they came down in sight of the village, and it was time for Sivert to turn homeward again, they both behaved in somewhat unmanly fashion. Sivert, for instance, was weak enough to say: "I doubt it'll be a bit lonely, maybe, when you're gone."

And at that Eleseus must fall to whistling, and looking to his shoes, and finding a splinter in his finger, and searching after something in his pockets; some papers, he said, couldn't make out. . . . Oh, 'twould have gone ill with them if Sivert had not saved things at the last. "Touch!" he cried suddenly, and touched his brother on the shoulder and sprang away. It was better after that; they shouted a word of farewell or so from a distance, and went each on his own way.

Fate or chance—whatever it might be. Eleseus went back, after all, to the town, to a post that was no longer open for him, but that same occasion led to Axel Ström's getting a man to work for him. They began work on the house the 21st of August, and ten days later the place was roofed in. Oh, 'twas no great house to see, and nothing much in the way of height; the best that could be said of it was that it was a wooden house and no turf hut. But, at least, it meant that the animals would have a splendid shelter for the winter in what had been a house for human beings up to then.

CHAPTER II

On the 3rd of September Barbro was not to be found. 'Twas not that she was altogether lost, but she was not up at the house.

Axel was doing carpenter's work the best he could; he was trying hard to get a glass window and a door set in the new house, and it was taking all his time to do it. But being long past noon, and no word said about coming in to dinner, he went in himself into the hut. No one there. He got himself some food, and looked about while he was eating. All Barbro's clothes were hanging there; she must be out somewhere, that was all. He went back to his work on the new building, and kept at it for a while, then he looked in at the hut again—no, nobody there. She must be lying down somewhere. He sets out to find her.

"Barbro!" he calls. No. He looks all round the houses, goes across to some bushes on the edge of his land, searches about a long while, maybe an hour, calls out—no. He comes on her a long way off, lying on the ground, hidden by some bushes; the stream flows by at her feet, she is barefoot and bareheaded, and wet all up the back as well.

"You lying here?" says he. "Why didn't you answer?"

"I couldn't," she answers, and her voice so hoarse he can scarcely hear.

"What—you been in the water?"

"Yes. Slipped down—oh!"

"Is it hurting you now?"

"Aye—it's over now."

"Is it over?" says he.

"Yes. Help me to get home."

"Where's . . . ?"

"What?"

"Wasn't it—the child?"

"No. 'Twas dead."

"Was it dead?"

"Yes."

Axel is slow of mind, and slow to act. He stands there still. "Where is it, then?" he asks.

"You've no call to know," says she. "Help me back home. 'Twas dead. I can walk if you hold my arm a bit."

Axel carries her back home and sets her in a chair, the water dripping off her. "Was it dead?" he asks.

"I told you 'twas so," she answers.

"What have you done with it, then?"

"D'you want to smell it? D'you get anything to eat while I was away?"

"But what did you want down by the water?"

"By the water? I was looking for juniper twigs."

"Juniper twigs? What for?"

"For cleaning the buckets."

"There's none that way," says he.

"You get on with your work," says she hoarsely, and all impatient. "What was I doing by the water? I wanted twigs for a broom. Have you had anything to eat, d'you hear?"

"Eat?" says he. "How d'you feel now?"

" 'Tis well enough."

"I doubt I'd better fetch the doctor up."

"You'd better try!" says she, getting up and looking about for dry clothes to put on. "As if you'd no better to do with your money!"

Axel goes back to his work, and 'tis but little he gets done, but makes a bit of noise with planing and hammering, so she can hear. At last he gets the window wedged in, and stops the frame all round with moss.

That evening Barbro seems not to care for her food, but goes about, all the same, busy with this and that—goes to the cowshed at milking-time, only stepping a thought more carefully over the doorsill. She went to bed in the hayshed as usual. Axel went in twice to look at her, and she was sleeping soundly. She had a good night.

Next morning she was almost as usual, only so hoarse she could hardly speak at all, and with a long stocking wound round her throat. They could not talk together. Days passed, and the matter was no longer new; other things cropped up, and it slipped aside. The new house ought by rights to have been left a while for the timber to work together and make it tight and sound, but there was no time for that now; they had to get it into use at once, and the new cowshed ready. When it was done, and they had moved in, they took up the potatoes, and after that there was the grain to get in. Life was the same as ever.

But there were signs enough, great or small, that things were different now at Maaneland. Barbro felt herself no more at home there now than any other serving-maid; no more bound to the place. Axel could see that his hold on her had loosened with the death of the child. He had thought to himself so confidently: wait till the child comes! But the child had come and gone. And at last Barbro even took off the rings from her fingers, and wore neither.

"What's that mean?" he asked.

"What's it mean?" she said, tossing her head.

But it could hardly mean anything else than faithlessness and desertion on her part.

And he had found the little body by the stream. Not that he had made any search for it, to speak of; he knew pretty closely where it must be, but he had left the matter idly as it was. Then chance willed it so that he should not forget it altogether; birds began to hover above the spot, shrieking grouse and crows, and then, later on, a pair of eagles at a giddy height above. To begin with, only a single bird had seen something buried there, and, being unable to keep a secret like a human being, had shouted it abroad. Then Axel roused himself from his apathy, and waited for an opportunity to steal out to the spot. He found the thing under a heap of moss and twigs, kept down by flat stones, and wrapped in a cloth, in a piece of rag. With a feeling of curiosity and horror he drew the cloth a little aside—eyes closed, dark hair, a boy, and the legs crossed—that was all he saw. The cloth had been wet, but was drying now; the whole thing looked like a half-wrung bundle of washing.

He could not leave it there in the light of day, and in his heart, perhaps, he feared some ill to himself or to the place. He ran home for a spade and dug the grave deeper; but, being so near the stream, the water came in, and he had to shift it farther up the bank. As he worked, his fear lest Barbro should come and find him disappeared; he grew defiant and thoroughly bitter. Let her come, and he would make her wrap up the body neatly and decently after her, stillborn or no! He saw well enough all he had lost by the death of the child; how he was faced now with the prospect of being left without help again on the place—and that, moreover, with three times the stock to care for he had had at first. Let her come—he did not care! But Barbro—it might be she had some inkling of what he was at; anyway, she did not come, and Axel had to wrap up the body himself as best he could and move it to the new grave. He laid down the turf again on top, just as before, hiding it all. When he had done, there was nothing to be seen but a little green mound among the bushes.

He found Barbro outside the house as he came home.

"Where you been?" she asked.

The bitterness must have left him, for he only said: "Nowhere. Where've you been?"

Oh, but the look on his face must have warned her; she said no more, but went into the house.

He followed her.

"Look here," he said, and asked her straight out, "What d'you mean by taking off those rings?"

Barbro, maybe, found it best to give way a little; she laughed, and answered: "Well, you are serious today—I can't help laughing! But if you want me to put on the rings and wear them out weekdays, why, I will!" And she got out the rings and put them on.

But seeing him look all foolish and content at that, she grew bolder. "Is there anything else I've done, I'd like to know?"

"I'm not complaining," answered he. "And you've only to be as you were before, all the time before, when you first came. That's all I mean."

'Tis not so easy to be always together and always agree.

Axel went on: "When I bought that place after your father, 'twas thinking maybe you'd like better to be there, and so we could shift. What d'you think?"

Ho, there he gave himself away; he was afraid of losing her and being left without help, with none to look to the place and the animals again—she knew! "Aye, you've said that before," she answered coldly.

"Aye, so I have; but I've got no answer."

"Answer?" said she. "Oh, I'm sick of hearing it."

Axel might fairly consider he had been lenient; he had let Brede and his family stay on at Breidablik, and for all that he had bought the good crop with the place, he had carted home no more than a few loads of hay, and left the potatoes to them. It was all unreasonable of Barbro to be contrary now; but she paid no heed to that, and asked indignantly:

"So you'd have us move down to Breidablik now, and turn out a whole family to be homeless?"

Had he heard aright? He sat for a moment staring and gaping, cleared his throat as if to answer thoroughly, but it came to nothing; he only asked: "Aren't they going to the village, then?"

"Don't ask me," said Barbro. "Or perhaps you've got a place for them to be there?"

Axel was still loth to quarrel with her, but he could not help letting her see he was surprised at her, just a little surprised. "You're getting more and more cross and hard," said he, "though you don't mean any harm, belike."

"I mean every word I say," she answered. "And why couldn't you have let my folks come up here? Answer me that! Then I'd have had Mother to help me a bit. But you think, perhaps, I've so little to do, I've no need of help?"

There was some sense in this, of course, but also much that was unreasonable altogether. If Bredes had come, they would have had to live in the hut, and Axel would have had no place for his beasts—as badly off as before. What was the woman getting at? Had she neither sense nor wit in her head?

"Look here," said he, "you'd better have a servant-girl to help."

"Now—with the winter coming on and less to do than ever? No, you should have thought of that when I needed it."

Here, again, she was right in a way; when she had been heavy and ailing—that was the time to talk of help. But then Barbro herself had done her work all the time as if nothing were the matter; she had been quick and clever as usual, did all that had to be done, and had never spoken a word about getting help.

"Well, I can't make it out, anyway," said he hopelessly. Silence.

Barbro asked: "What's this about you taking over the telegraph after father?"

"What? Who said a word about that?"

"Well, they say it's to be."

"Why," said Axel, "it may come to something; I'll not say no."

"Ho!"

"But why d'you ask?"

"Nothing," said Barbro; "only that you've turned my father out of house and home, and now you're taking the bread out of his mouth."

Silence.

Oh, but that was the end of Axel's patience. "I'll tell you this," he cried, "you're not worth all I've done for you and yours!"

"Ho!" said Barbro.

"No!" said he, striking his fist on the table. And then he got up.

"You can't frighten me, so don't think," whimpered Barbro, and moved over nearer the wall.

"Frighten you?" he said again, and sniffed scornfully. "I'm going to speak out now in earnest. What about that child? Did you drown it?"

"Drown it?"

"Aye. It's been in the water."

"Ho, so you've seen it? You've been—" "sniffing at it," she was going to say, but dared not; Axel was not to be played with just then, by his looks. "You've been and found it?"

"I saw it had been in the water."

"Aye," said she, "and well it might. 'Twas born in the water; I slipped in and couldn't get up again."

"Slipped, did you?"

"Yes, and the child came before I could get out."

"H'm," said he. "But you took the bit of wrapping with

you before you went out—was that in case you should happen to fall in?"

"Wrapping?" said she again.

"A bit of white rag—one of my shirts you'd cut half across."

"Aye," said Barbro, " 'twas a bit of rag I took with me to carry back juniper twigs in."

"Juniper twigs?"

"Yes. Didn't I tell you that was what I'd been for?"

"Aye, so you said. Or else it was twigs for a broom."

"Well, no matter what it was . . ."

It was an open quarrel between them this time. But even that died away after a time, and all was well again. That is to say, not well exactly—no, but passable. Barbro was careful and more submissive; she knew there was danger. But that way, life at Maaneland grew even more forced and intolerable—no frankness, no joy between them, always on guard. It could not last long, but as long as it lasted at all, Axel was forced to be content. He had got this girl on the place, and had wanted her for himself and had her, tied his life to her; it was not an easy matter to alter all that. Barbro knew everything about the place: where pots and vessels stood, when cows and goats were to bear, if the winter feed would be short or plenty, how much milk was for cheese and how much for food—a stranger would know nothing of it all, and even so, a stranger was perhaps not to be had.

Oh, but Axel had thought many a time of getting rid of Barbro and taking another girl to help; she was a wicked thing at times, and he was almost afraid of her. Even when he had the misfortune to get on well with her he drew back at times in fear of her strange cruelty and brutal ways; but she was pretty to look at, and could be sweet at times, and bury him deep in her arms. So it had been—but that was over now. No, thank you—Barbro was not going to have all that miserable business over again. But it was not so easy to change. . . . "Let's get married at once, then," said Axel, urging her.

"At once?" said she. "Nay; I must go into town first about my teeth, they're all but gone as it is."

So there was nothing to do but go on as before. And Barbro had no real wages now, but far beyond what her wages would have been; and every time she asked for money and he gave it, she thanked him as for a gift. But for all that Axel could not make out where the money went —what could she want money for out in the wilds? Was she hoarding for herself? But what on earth was there to save and save for, all the year round?

There was much that Axel could not make out. Hadn't he given her a ring—aye, a real gold ring? And they had got on well together, too, after that last gift; but it could not last forever, far from it; and he could not go on buying rings to give her. In a word—did she mean to throw him over? Women were strange creatures! Was there a man with a good farm and a well-stocked place of his own waiting for her somewhere else? Axel could at times go so far as to strike his fist on the table in his impatience with women and their foolish humors.

A strange thing, Barbro seemed to have nothing really in her head but the thought of Bergen and town life. Well and good. But if so, why had she come back at all, confound her! A telegram from her father would never have moved her a step in itself; she must have had some other reason. And now here she was, eternally discontented from morning to night, year after year. All these wooden buckets, instead of proper iron pails; cooking-pots instead of saucepans; the everlasting milking instead of a little walk round to the dairy; heavy boots, yellow soap, a pillow stuffed with hay; no military bands, no people. Living like this . . .

They had many little bouts after the one big quarrel. Ho, time and again they were at it! "You say no more about it, if you're wise," said Barbro. "And not to speak of what you've done about Father and all."

Said Axel: "Well, what have I done?"

"Oh, you know well enough," said she. "But for all that you'll not be Inspector, anyway."

"Ho!"

"No, that you won't. I'll believe it when I see it."

"Meaning I'm not good enough, perhaps?"

"Oh, good enough and good enough . . . Anyway, you can't read nor write, and never so much as take a newspaper to look at."

"As to that," said he, "I can read and write all I've any need for. But as for you, with all your gabble and talk . . . I'm sick of it."

"Well, then, here's that to begin with," said she, and threw down the silver ring on the table.

"Ho!" said he, after a while. "And what about the other?"

"Oh, if you want your rings back that you gave me, you can have them," said she, trying to pull off the gold one.

"You can be as nasty as you please," said he. "If you think I care . . ." And he went out.

And naturally enough, soon after, Barbro was wearing both her rings again.

In time, too, she ceased to care at all for what he said about the death of the child. She simply sniffed and tossed her head. Not that she ever confessed anything, but only said: "Well, and suppose I had drowned it? You live here in the wilds and what do you know of things elsewhere?" Once when they were talking of this, she seemed to be trying to get him to see he was taking it all too seriously; she herself thought no more of getting rid of a child than the matter was worth. She knew two girls in Bergen who had done it; but one of them had got two months' imprisonment because she had been a fool and hadn't killed it, but only left it out to freeze to death; and the other had been acquitted. "No," said Barbro, "the law's not so cruel hard now as it used to be. And besides, it's not always it gets found out." There was a girl in Bergen at the hotel who had killed two children; she was from Christiania, and wore a hat—a hat with feathers in. They had given her three months for the second one, but the first was never discovered, said Barbro.

Axel listened to all this and grew more than ever afraid of her. He tried to understand, to make out things a little in the darkness, but she was right after all; he took these things too seriously in his way. With all her vulgar depravity, Barbro was not worth a single earnest thought. Infanticide meant nothing to her, there was nothing extraordinary in the killing of a child; she thought of it only with the looseness and moral nastiness that was to be expected of a servant-girl. It was plain, too, in the days that followed; never an hour did she give herself up to thought; she was easy and natural as ever, unalterably shallow and foolish, unalterably a servant-girl. "I must go and have my teeth seen to," she said. "And I want one of those new cloaks." There was a new kind of half-length coat that had been fashionable for some years past, and Barbro must have one.

And when she took it all so naturally, what could Axel do but give way? And it was not always that he had any real suspicion of her; she herself had never confessed, had indeed denied time and again, but without indignation, without insistence, as a trifle, as a servant-girl would have denied having broken a dish, whether she had done so or not. But after a couple of weeks, Axel could stand it no longer; he stopped dead one day in the middle of the room and saw it all as by a revelation. Great Heaven! Everyone must have seen how it was with her, heavy with child and plain to see—and now with her figure as before—but where was the child? Suppose others came to look for it? They would be asking about it sooner or later. And if there had been nothing wrong, it would have been far better to have had the child buried decently in the churchyard. Not there in the bushes, there on his land . . .

"No. 'Twould only have made a fuss," said Barbro. "They'd have cut it open and had an inquest, and all that. I didn't want to be bothered."

"If only it mayn't come to worse later on," said he.

Barbro asked easily: "What's there to worry about? Let it lie where it is." Aye, she smiled, and asked: "Are you afraid it'll come after you? Leave all that nonsense, and say no more about it."

"Aye, well . . ."

"Did I drown the child? I've told you it drowned itself in the water when I slipped in. I never heard such things as you get in your head. And, anyway, it would never be found out," said she.

" 'Twas found out all the same with Inger at Sellanraa," said Axel.

Barbro thought for a moment. "Well, I don't care," said she. "The law's all different now, and if you read the papers you'd know. There's heaps that have done it, and don't get anything to speak of." Barbro sets out to explain it, to teach him, as it were—getting him to take a broad view of things. It was not for nothing she herself had been out in the world and seen and heard and learned so much; now she could sit here and be more than a match for him. She had three main arguments which she was continually advancing: In the first place, she had not done it. In the second, it was not such a terrible thing, after all, if she had done it. But in the third place, it would never be found out.

"Everything gets found out, seems to me," he objected.

"Not by a long way," she answered. And whether to astonish him or to encourage him, or perhaps from sheer vanity and as something to boast of, all of a sudden she threw a bombshell. Thus: "I've done something myself that never got found out."

"You?" said he, all unbelieving. "What have you done?"

"What have I done? Killed something."

She had not meant, perhaps, to go so far, but she had to go on now; there he was, staring at her. Oh, and it was not grand, indomitable boldness even; it was mere bravado, vulgar showing-off; she wanted to look big herself, and silence him. "You don't believe me?" she cried. "D'you remember that in the paper about the body of a child found in the harbor? 'Twas me that did it."

"What?" said he.

"Body of a child. You never remember anything. We read about it in the paper you brought up."

After a moment he burst out: "You must be out of your senses!"

But his confusion seemed to incite her more, to give her a sort of artificial strength; she could even give the details. "I had it in my box—it was dead then, of course—I did that as soon as it was born. And when we got out into the harbor, I threw it overboard."

Axel sat dark and silent, but she went on. It was a long time back now, many years, the time she had first come to Maaneland. So, there, he could see 'twas not everything was found out, not by a long way! What would things be like if everything folk did got out? What about all the married people in the towns and the things they did? They killed their children before they were born—there were doctors who managed that. They didn't want more than one, or at most two children, and so they'd get in a doctor to get rid of it before it come. Ho, Axel need not think that was such a great affair out in the world!

"Ho!" said Axel. "Then I suppose you did get rid of the last one too, that way?"

"No, I didn't," she answered carelessly as could be, "for I dropped it," she said. But even then she must go on again about it being nothing so terrible if she had. She was plainly accustomed to think of the thing as natural and easy; it did not affect her now. The first time, perhaps, it might have been a little uncomfortable, something of an awkward feeling about it, to kill the child; but the second? She could think of it now with a sort of historic sense: as a thing that had been done, and could be done.

Axel went out of the house heavy in mind. He was not so much concerned over the fact that Barbro had killed her first child—that was nothing to do with himself. That she had had a child at all before she came to him was nothing much either; she was no innocent, and had never pretended to be so, far from it. She had made no secret of her knowledge, and had taught him many things in the dark. Well and good. But this last child—he would not willingly have lost it; a tiny boy, a little white creature wrapped up in a rag. If she were guilty of that child's death, then she had injured him, Axel—broken a tie that he prized, and that could not be replaced. But it might be that he wronged her, after all: that she *had* slipped in the water by accident. But then the wrapping—the bit of shirt she had taken with her . . .

Meantime, the hours passed; dinner-time came, and evening. And when Axel had gone to bed, and had lain staring into the dark long enough, he fell asleep at last, and slept till morning. And then came a new day, and after that day other days. . . .

Barbro was the same as ever. She knew so much of the world, and could take lightly many little trifles that were terrible and serious things for folk in the wilds. It was well in a way; she was clever enough for both of them, careless enough for both. And she did not go about like a terrible creature herself. Barbro a monster? Not in the least. She was a pretty girl, with blue eyes, a slightly turned-up nose, and quick-handed at her work. She was utterly sick and tired of the farm and the wooden vessels, that took such a lot of cleaning; sick and tired, perhaps, of Axel and all, of the out-of-the-way life she led. But she never killed any of the cattle, and Axel never found her standing over him with uplifted knife in the middle of the night.

Only once it happened that they came to talk again of the body in the wood. Axel still insisted that it ought to have been buried in the churchyard, in consecrated ground; but she maintained as before that her way was good enough. And then she said something which showed that she was reasoned after her fashion—ho, was sharp enough, could see beyond the tip of her nose; could think, with the pitiful little brain of a savage.

"If it gets found out I'll go and talk to the Lensmand; I've been in service with him. And Fru Heyerdahl, she'll put in a word for me, I know. It's not everyone that can get folk to help them like that, and they get off all the same. And then, besides, there's Father, that knows all the great folks, and been assistant himself, and all the rest."

But Axel only shook his head.

"Well, what's wrong with that?"

"D'you think your father'd ever be able to do anything?"

"A lot you know about it!" she cried angrily. "After you've ruined him and all, taking his farm and the bread out of his mouth."

She seemed to have a sort of idea herself that her father's reputation had suffered of late, and that she might lose by it. And what could Axel say to that? Nothing. He was a man of peace, a worker.

HAT winter, Axel was left to himself again at Maaneland. Barbro was gone. Aye, that was the end of it.

Her journey to town would not take long, she said; 'twas not like going to Bergen; but she wasn't going to stay on here losing one tooth after another, till she'd a mouth like a calf. "What'll it cost?" said Axel.

"How do I know?" said she. "But, anyway, it won't cost you anything. I'll earn the money myself."

She had explained, too, why it was best for her to go just then; there were but two cows to milk, and in the spring there would be two more, besides all the goats with kids, and the busy season, and work enough right on till June.

"Do as you please," said Axel.

It was not going to cost him anything, not at all. But she must have some money to start with, just a little; there was the journey, and the dentist to pay, and besides, she must have one of the new cloaks and some other little things. But, of course, if he didn't care to . . .

"You've had money enough up to now," said he.

"H'm," said she. "Anyway, it's all gone."

"Haven't you put by anything?"

"Put by anything? You can look in my box if you like. I never put by anything in Bergen, and I got more wages then."

"I've no money to give you," said he.

He had but little faith in her ever coming back at all, and she had plagued him so much with her humors this way and that; he had grown indifferent at last. And though he gave her money in the end, it was nothing to speak of; but he took no notice when she packed away an enormous hoard of food to take with her, and he drove her down himself, with her box, to the village to meet the steamer.

And that was done.

He could have managed alone on the place, he had learned to do so before, but it was awkward with the cattle; if ever he had to leave home, there was none to look to them. The storekeeper in the village had urged him to get Oline to come for the winter, she had been at Sellanraa for years before; she was old now, of course, but fit and able to work. And Axel did send for Oline, but she had not come, and sent no word.

Meantime, he worked in the forest, threshed out his little crop of grain, and tended his cattle. It was a quiet and lonely life. Now and again Sivert from Sellanraa would drive past on his way to and from the village, taking down loads of wood, or hides, or farm produce, but rarely bringing anything up home; there was little they needed to buy now at Sellanraa.

Now and again, too, Brede Olsen would come trudging along, more frequently of late—whatever he might be after. It looked as if he were trying to make himself indispensable to the telegraph people in the little time that remained, so as to keep his job. He never came in to see Axel now that Barbro was gone, but went straight by—a piece of high-and-mightiness ill fitted to his state, seeing that he was still living on at Breidablik and had not moved. One day, when he was passing without so much as a word of greeting, Axel stopped him, and asked when he had thought of getting out of the place.

"What about Barbro, and the way she left you?" asked Brede in return. And one word led to another: "You sent her off with neither help nor means, 'twas a near thing but she never got to Bergen at all."

"Ho! So she's in Bergen, is she?"

"Aye, got there at last, so she writes, but little thanks to you."

"I'll have you out of Breidablik, and that sharp," said Axel.

"Aye, if you'd be so kind," said the other, with a sneer. "But we'll be going of ourselves at the new year," he said, and went on his way.

So Barbro was gone to Bergen—aye, 'twas as Axel had thought. He did not take it to heart. Take it to heart? No, indeed; he was well rid of her. But for all that, he had hoped a little until then that she might come back. 'Twas all unreasonable, but somehow he had come to care over-much for the girl—aye, for that devil of a girl. She had her sweet moments, unforgettable moments, and it was on purpose to hinder her from running off to Bergen that he had given her so little money for the journey. And now she had gone there after all. A few of her clothes still hung in the house, and there was a straw hat with birds' wings on, wrapped up in a paper, in the loft, but she did not come to fetch them. Eyah, maybe he took it to heart a little, only a little. And as if to jeer at him, as a mighty jest in his trouble, came the paper he had ordered for her every week, and it would not stop now till the new year.

Well, well, there were other things to think about. He must be a man.

Next spring he would have to put up a shed against the north wall of the house; the timber would have to be felled that winter, and the planks cut. Axel had no timber to speak of, not growing close, but there were some heavy firs scattered about here and there on the outskirts of his land,

and he marked out those on the side toward Sellanraa, to have the shortest way to cart his timber up to the sawmill.

And so one morning he gives the beasts an extra feed, to last them till the evening, shuts all doors behind him, and goes out felling trees. Besides his ax and a basket of food, he carried a rake to clear the snow away. The weather was mild, there had been a heavy snowstorm the day before, but now it had stopped. He follows the telegraph line all the way to the spot, then pulls off his jacket and falls to work. As the trees are felled, he strips off the branches, leaving the clean trunks, and piles up the small wood in heaps.

Brede Olsen comes by on his way up—trouble on the line, no doubt, after yesterday's storm. Or maybe Brede was out on no particular errand, but simply from pure zeal —ho, he was mighty keen on his duty of late, was Brede! The two men did not speak, did not so much as lift a hand in greeting.

The weather is changing again, the wind is getting up. Axel marks it, but goes on with his work. It is long past noon, and he has not yet eaten. Then, felling a big fir, he manages to get in the way of its fall, and is thrown to the ground. He hardly knew how it happened—but here it was. A big fir swaying from the root: a man will have it fall one way, the storm says another—and the storm it is that wins. He might have got clear after all, but the lie of the ground was hidden by snow. Axel made a false step, lost his footing, and came down in a cleft of rock, astride of a boulder, pinned down by the weight of a tree.

Well, and what then? He might still have got clear, but, as it chanced, he had fallen awkwardly as could be—no bones broken, as far as he could tell, but twisted somehow, and unable to drag himself out. After a while he gets one hand free, supporting himself on the other, but the ax is beyond his reach. He looks round, takes thought, as any other beast in a trap would do; looks round and takes thought and tries to work his way out from under the tree. Brede must be coming by on his way down before long, he thinks to himself, and gives himself a breathing-space.

He does not let it trouble him much at first, it was only annoying to lose time at his work; there is no thought in his mind of being in danger, let alone in peril of his life. True, he can feel the hand that supports him growing numbed and dead, his foot in the cleft growing cold and helpless too; but no matter, Brede must be here soon.

Brede did not come.

The storm increased. Axel felt the snow driving full in his face. Ho, 'tis coming down in earnest now, says he to himself, still never troubling much about it all—aye, 'tis as if he blinks at himself through the snow, to look out, for now things are beginning in earnest! After a long while he gives a single shout. The sound would hardly carry far in the gale, but it would be upward along the line, towards Brede. Axel lies there with all sorts of vain and useless thoughts in his head: if only he could reach the ax, and perhaps cut his way out! If he could only get his hand up —it was pressing against something sharp, an edge of stone, and the stone was eating its way quietly and politely into the back of his hand. Anyhow, if only that infernal stone itself had not been there—but no one has ever yet heard tell of such a touching act of kindness on the part of a stone.

Getting late now, getting later, the snow drifting thick; Axel is getting snowed up himself. The snow packs all innocently, all unknowing, about his face, melting at first, till the flesh grows cold, and then it melts no longer. Aye, now 'tis beginning in earnest!

He gives two great shouts and listens.

His ax is getting snowed up now; he can see but a bit of the haft. Over there is his basket of food, hung on a tree—

if he could but have reached it, and had a feed—oh, huge big mouthfuls! And then he goes one step farther in his demands, and asks yet more: if he only had his coat on—it is getting cold. He gives another swinging shout. . . .

And there is Brede. Stopped in his tracks, standing still, looking toward the man as he calls; he stands there but for a moment, glancing that way, as if to see what is amiss.

"Reach me the ax here, will you?" calls Axel, a trifle weakly.

Brede looks away hurriedly, fully aware now of what is the matter; he glances up at the telegraph wires and seems to be whistling. What can he mean by that?

"Here, reach me the ax, can't you?" cries Axel louder. "I'm pinned here under a tree."

But Brede is strangely full of zeal in his duty now, he keeps on looking at the telegraph wires, and whistling all the time. Note, also, that he seems to be whistling gaily, as it were vengefully.

"Ho, so you're going to murder me—won't even reach me the ax?" cries Axel. And at that it seems as if there is trouble farther down the line, which Brede must see to without delay. He moves off, and is lost to sight in the driving snow.

Ho—well and good! But after that, well, it would just serve things generally right if Axel were to manage by himself after all, and get at the ax without help from anyone. He strains all the muscles of his chest to lift the huge weight that bears him down; the tree moves, he can feel it shake, but all he gains by that is a shower of snow. And after a few more tries, he gives up.

Growing dark now. Brede is gone—but how far can he have got? Axel shouts again, and lets off a few straightforward words into the bargain. "Leave me here to die, would you, like a murderer?" he cries. "Have ye no soul nor thought of what's to come? And the worth of a cow, no less, to lend a helping hand. But 'tis a dog you are and ever were, Brede, and leaving a man to die. Ho, but there's more shall know of this, never fear, and true as I'm lying here. And won't even come and reach me that ax . . ."

Silence. Axel strains away at the tree once more, lifts it a little, and brings down a new shower of snow. Gives it up again and sighs; he is worn out now, and getting sleepy. There's the cattle at home, they'll be standing in the hut and bellowing for food, not a bite nor a drop since the morning; no Barbro to look to them now—no. Barbro's gone, run off and gone, and taken both her rings, gold and silver, taken them with her. Getting dark now, aye, evening, night; well, well . . . But there's the cold to reckon with too; his beard is freezing; soon his eyes will freeze too as well; aye, if he had but his jacket from the tree there . . . and now his leg—surely, it can't be that—but all the same one leg feels dead now up to the hip. "All in God's hands," he says to himself—seems like he can talk all godly and pious when he will. Getting dark, aye; but a man can die without the light of a lamp. He feels all soft and good now, and of sheer humility he smiles, foolishly and kindly, at the snowstorm round; 'tis God's own snow, an innocent thing! Aye, he might even forgive Brede, and never say a word. . . .

He is very quiet now, and growing ever more sleepy, aye, as if some poison were numbing him all over. And there is too much whiteness to look at every way; woods and lands, great wings, white veils, white sails; white, white . . . what can it be? Nonsense, man! And he knows well enough it is but snow; he is lying out in the snow; 'tis no fancy that he is lying there, pinned down beneath a tree.

He shouts again at hazard, throws out a roar; there in the snow a man's great hairy chest swelling to a roar, bellowing so it could be heard right down at the hut, again and again. "Aye, and a swine and a monster," he cries after Brede again; "never a thought of how you're leaving me to lie and be perished. And couldn't even reach me the ax, that was all I asked; and call yourself a man, or a beast of the field? Aye, well then, go your way, and good luck to you if that's your will and thought to go. . . ."

He must have slept; he is all stiff and lifeless now, but his eyes are open; set in ice, but open, he cannot wink nor blink—has he been sleeping with open eyes? Dropped off for a second maybe, or for an hour, God knows, but here's Oline standing before him. He can hear her asking: "In Jesu name, say if there's life in you!" And asking him if it is him lying there, and if he's lost his wits or no.

Always something of a jackal about Oline; sniffing and scenting out, always on the spot where there was trouble; aye, she would nose it out. And how could she ever have managed through life at all if it hadn't been that same way? Axel's word had reached her, and for all her seventy years she had crossed the fjeld to come. Snowed up at Sellanraa in the storm of the day before, and then on again to Maaneland; not a soul on the place; fed the cattle, stood in the doorway listening, milked the cows at milking-time, listening again; what could it be? . . .

And then a cry comes down, and she nods; Axel, maybe, or maybe the hillfolk, devils—anyway, something to sniff and scent and find—to worm out the meaning of it all, the wisdom of the Almighty with the dark and the forest in the hollow of His hand—and He would never harm Oline, that was not worthy to unloose the latchet of His shoes. . . .

And there she stands.

The ax? Oline digs down and down in the snow, and finds no ax. Manage without, then—and she strains at the tree to lift it where it lies, but with no more strength than a child; she can but shake the branches here and there. Tries for the ax again—it is all dark, but she digs with hands and feet. Axel cannot move a hand to point, only tell where it lay before, but 'tis not there now. "If it hadn't been so far to Sellanraa," says Axel.

Then Oline falls to searching her own ways, and Axel calls to her that there's no ax there. "Aye, well," says Oline, "I was but looking a bit. And what's this, maybe?" says she.

"You've found it?" says he.

"Aye, by the grace of the Lord Almighty," answers Oline, with high-sounding words.

But there's little pride in Axel now, no more than he'll give in that he was wrong after all, and maybe not all clear in his head. And what's he to do with the ax now 'tis there? He cannot stir, and Oline has to cut him free herself. Oh, Oline has wielded an ax before that day; had axed off many a load of firing in her life.

Axel cannot walk, one leg is dead to the hip, and something wrong with his back; shooting pains that make him groan curiously—aye, he feels but a part of himself, as if something were left behind there under the tree. "Don't know," says he "—don't know what it can be. . . ." But Oline knows, and tells him now with solemn words; aye, for she has saved a human creature from death, and she knows it; 'tis the Almighty has seen fit to lay on her this charge, where He might have sent legions of angels. Let Axel consider the grace and infinite wisdom of the Almighty even in this! And if so be as it had been His pleasure to send a worm out of the earth instead, all things were possible to Him.

"Aye, I know," said Axel. "But I can't make out how 'tis with me—feels strange. . . ."

Feels strange, does it? Oh, but only wait, wait just a little. 'Twas but to move and stretch the least bit at a time, till the life came back. And get his jacket on and get warm again. But never in all her days would she forget how the

Angel of the Lord had called her out to the doorway that last time, that she might hear a voice—the voice of one crying in the forest. Aye, 'twas as in the days of Paradise, when trumpets blew and compassed round the walls of Jericho. . . .

Aye, strange. But while she talked, Axel was taking his time, learning the use of his limbs again, getting to walk.

They get along slowly towards home, Oline still playing savior and supporting him. They manage somehow. A little farther down they come upon Brede. "What's here?" says Brede. "Hurt yourself? Let me help a bit."

Axel takes no heed. He had given a promise to God not to be vengeful, not to tell of what Brede had done, but beyond that he was free. And what was Brede going up that way again for now? Had he seen that Oline was at Maaneland, and guessed that she would hear?

"And it's you here, Oline, is it?" goes on Brede easily. "Where d'you find him? Under a tree? Well, now, 'tis a curious thing," says he. "I was up that way just now on duty, along the line, and seems like I heard someone shouting. Turns round and listens quick as a flash—Brede's the man to lend a hand if there's need. And so 'twas Axel, was it, lying under a tree, d'you say?"

"Aye," says Axel. "And well you knew that saw and heard as well. But never helping hand . . ."

"Good Lord, deliver us!" cries Oline, aghast. "As I'm a sinner . . ."

Brede explains. "Saw? Why, yes, I saw you right enough. But why didn't you call out? You might have called out if there was anything wrong. I saw you right enough, aye, but never thought but you were lying down a bit to rest."

"You'd better say no more," says Axel warningly. "You know well enough you left me there and hoping I'd never rise again."

Oline sees her way now; Brede must not be allowed to interfere. She must be indispensable, nothing can come between her and Axel that could make him less completely indebted to herself. She had saved him, she alone. And she waves Brede aside; will not even let him carry the ax or the basket of food. Oh, for the moment she is all on Axel's side—but next time she comes to Brede and sits talking to him over a cup of coffee, she will be on his.

"Let me carry the ax and things, anyway," says Brede.

"Nay," says Oline, speaking for Axel. "He'll take them himself."

And Brede goes on again: "You might have called to me, anyway; we're not so deadly enemies that you couldn't say a word to a man? You did call? Well, you might have shouted then, so a man could hear. Blowing a gale and all. . . . Leastways, you might have waved a hand."

"I'd no hand to wave," answers Axel. "You saw how 'twas with me, shut down and locked in all ways."

"Nay, that I'll swear I didn't. Well, I never heard. Here, let me carry those things."

Oline puts in: "Leave him alone. He's hurt and poorly."

But Axel's mind is getting to work again now. He has heard of Oline before, and understands it will be a costly thing for him, and a plague besides, if she can claim to have saved his life all by herself. Better to share between them as far as may be. And he lets Brede take the basket and the tools; aye, he lets it be understood that this is a relief, that it eases him to get rid of it. But Oline will not have it, she snatches away the basket, she and no other will carry what's to be carried there. Sly simplicity at war on every side. Axel is left for a moment without support, and Brede has to drop the basket and hold him, though Axel can stand by himself now, it seems.

Then they go on a bit that way, Brede holding Axel's arm, and Oline carrying the things. Carrying, carrying, full

of bitterness and flashing fire; a miserable part indeed, to
carry a basket instead of leading a helpless man. What did
Brede want coming that way at all—devil of a man!

"Brede," says she, "what's it they're saying, you've sold
your place and all?"

"And who's it wants to know?" says Brede boldly.

"Why, as to that, I'd never thought 'twas any secret not
to be known."

"Why didn't you come to the sale, then, and bid with
the rest?"

"Me—aye, 'tis like you to make a jest of poor folk."

"Well, and I thought 'twas you had grown rich and
grand. Wasn't it you had left you old Sivert's chest and all
his money in? He he he!"

Oline was not pleased, not softened at being minded of
that legacy. "Aye, old Sivert, he'd a kindly thought for me,
and I'll not say otherwise. But once he was dead and gone,
'twas little they left after him in worldly goods. And you
know yourself how 'tis to be stripped of all, and live under
other man's roof; but old Sivert he's in palaces and mansions now, and the likes of you and me are left on earth to
be spurned underfoot."

"Ho, you and your talk!" says Brede scornfully, and
turns to Axel: "Well, I'm glad I came in time—help you
back home. Not going too fast, eh?"

"No."

Talk to Oline, stand up and argue with Oline! Was
never a man could do it but to his cost. Never in life would
she give in, and never her match for turning and twisting
heaven and earth to a medley of seeming kindness and
malice, poison and senseless words. This to her face now:
Brede making as if 'twas himself was bringing Axel home!

"What I was going to say," she begins: "The gentlemen came up to Sellanraa that time; did you ever get to
show them all those sacks of stone you'd got, eh, Brede?"

"Axel," says Brede, "let me hoist you on my shoulders, and I'll carry you down rest of the way."

"Nay," says Axel. "For all it's good of you to ask."

So they go on; not far now to go. Oline must make the best of her time on the way. "Better if you'd saved him at the point of death," says she. "And how was it, Brede, you coming by and seeing him in deadly peril and heard his cry and never stopped to help?"

"You hold your tongue," says Brede.

And it might have been easier for her if she had, wading deep in snow and out of breath, and a heavy burden and all, but 'twas not Oline's way to hold her tongue. She'd a bit in reserve, a dainty morsel. Ho, 'twas a dangerous thing to talk of, but she dared it.

"There's Barbro now," says she. "And how's it with her? Not run off and away, perhaps?"

"Ay, she has," answers Brede carelessly. "And left a place for you for the winter by the same."

But here was a first-rate opening for Oline again; she could let it be seen now what a personage she was; how none could manage long without Oline—Oline, that had to be sent for near or far. She might have been two places, aye, three, for that matter. There was the parsonage—they'd have been glad to have her there, too. And here was another thing—aye, let Axel hear it too, 'twould do no harm —they'd offered her so-and-so much for the winter, not to speak of a new pair of shoes and a sheepskin into the bargain. But she knew what she was doing, coming to Maaneland, coming to a man that was lordly to give and would pay her over and above what other folk did—and so she'd come. No, 'twas no need for Brede to trouble himself that gait—when her Heavenly Father had watched over her all those years, and opened this door and that before her feet, and bidden her in. Aye, and it seemed like God Himself had known what He was doing, sending her up to

Maaneland that day, to save the life of one of His creatures on earth. . . .

Axel was getting wearied again by now; his legs could hardly bear him, and seemed like giving up. Strange, he had been getting better by degrees, able to walk, as the life and warmth came back into his body. But now—he must lean on Brede for support! It seemed to begin when Oline started talking about her wages; and then, when she was saving his life again, it was worse than ever. Was he trying to lessen her triumph once more? Heaven knows—but his mind seemed to be working again. As they neared the house, he stopped, and said: "Looks like I'll never get there, after all."

Brede hoists him up without a word, and carries him. So they go on like that, Oline all venom, Axel up full length on Brede's back.

"What I was going to say," gets out Oline—"about Barbro—wasn't she far gone with child?"

"Child?" groans Brede, under the weight. Oh, 'tis a strange procession; but Axel lets himself be carried all the way till he's set down at his own door.

Brede puffs and blows, mightily out of breath.

"Aye, or how—was it ever born, after all?" asks Oline.

Axel cuts in quickly with a word to Brede: "I don't know how I'd ever have got home this night but for you." And he does not forget Oline: "And you, Oline, that was the first to find me. I've to thank you both for it all."

That was how Axel was saved. . . .

The next few days Oline would talk of nothing but the great event; Axel was hard put to it to keep her within bounds. Oline can point out the very spot where she was standing in the room when an angel of the Lord called her out to the door to hear a cry for help—Axel goes back to his work in the woods, and when he has felled enough, begins carting it up to the sawmill at Sellanraa.

Good, regular winter work, as long as it lasts; carting up rough timber and bringing back sawn planks. The great thing is to hurry and get through with it before the new year, when the frost sets in in earnest, and the saw cannot work. Things are going on nicely, everything as well as could be wished. If Sivert happens to come up from the village with an empty sledge, he stops and takes a stick of timber on the way, to help his neighbor. And the pair of them talk over things together, and each is glad of a talk with the other.

"What's the news down village?" asks Axel.

"Why, nothing much," says Sivert. "There's a new man coming to take up land, so they say."

A new man—nothing in that; 'twas only Sivert's way of putting it. New men came now every year or so, to take up land; there were five new holdings now below Breidablik. Higher up, things went more slowly, for all that the soil was richer that way. The one who had ventured farthest was Isak, when he settled down at Sellanraa; he was the boldest and the wisest of them all. Later, Axel Ström had come—and now there was a new man besides. The new man was to have a big patch of arable land and forest down below Maaneland—there was land enough.

"Heard what sort of a man it is?" asked Axel.

"Nay," said Sivert. "But he's bringing up houses all ready-made, to fix up in no time."

"Ho! A rich man, then?"

"Aye, seems like. And a wife and three children with him; and horse and cattle."

"Why, then, 'twill be a rich man enough. Any more about him?"

"No. He's three-and-thirty."

"And what's his name?"

"Aron, they say. Calls his place Storborg."

"Storborg? H'm. 'Tis no little place, then." [1]

"He's come up from the coast. Had a fishery there, so they say."

"H'm—fishery. Wonder if he knows much about farming?" says Axel. "That all you heard? Nothing more?"

"No. He paid all down in cash for the title-deeds. That's all I heard. Must have made a heap of money with his fishery, they say. And now he's going to start here with a store."

"Ho! A store?"

"Aye, so they say."

"H'm. So he's going to start a store?"

This was the one really important piece of news, and the two neighbors talked it over every way as they drove up. It was a big piece of news—the greatest event, perhaps, in all the history of the place; aye, there was much to say of that. Who was he going to trade with, this new man? The eight of them that had settled on the common lands? Or did he reckon on getting custom from the village as well? Anyway, the store would mean a lot to them; like as not, it would bring up more settlers again. The holdings might rise in value—who could say?

They talked it over as if they would never tire. Aye, here were two men with their own interests and aims, as great to them as other men's. The settlement was their world; work, seasons, crops were the adventures of their life. Was not that interest and excitement enough? Ho, enough indeed! Many a time they had need to sleep but lightly, to work on long past mealtimes; but they stood it, they endured it and were none the worse; a matter of seven hours lying pinned down beneath a tree was not a thing to spoil them for life as long as their limbs were whole. A narrow world, a life with no great prospects? Ho, indeed! What of

[1] *Stor* means "great."

this new Storborg, a shop and a store here in the wilds—was not that prospect enough?

They talked it over until Christmas came. . . .

Axel had got a letter, a big envelope with a lion on it; it was from the State. He was to fetch supplies of wire, a telegraph apparatus, tools and implements, from Brede Olsen, and take over inspection of the line from New Year's Day.

EAMS of horses driving up over the moors, carting up houses for the new man come to settle in the wilds; load after load, for days on end. Dump the things down on a spot that is to be called Storborg; 'twill answer to its name, no doubt, in time. There are four men already at work up in the hills, getting out stone for a wall and two cellars.

Carting loads, carting new loads. The sides of the house are built and ready beforehand, 'tis only to fix them up when the spring comes; all reckoned out neatly and accurately in advance, each piece with its number marked, not a door, not a window lacking, even to the colored glass for the veranda. And one day a cart comes up with a whole load of small stakes. What's them for? One of the settlers from lower down can tell them; he's from the south, and has seen the like before. " 'Tis for a garden fence," says he. So the new man is going to have a garden laid out in the wilds—a big garden.

All looked well; never before had there been such carting and traffic up over the moors, and there were many that earned good money letting out their horses for the work. This, again, was matter for discussion. There was the prospect of making money in the future; the trader would be getting his goods from different parts; inland or overseas, they would have to be carted up from the sea with teams of horses.

Aye, it looked as if things were going to be on a grander scale all around. Here was a young foreman or manager in charge of the carting-work; a lordly young spark he was, and grumbled at not getting horses enough, for all that there were not so many loads to come.

"But there can't be so much more to come now, with the houses all up," they said.

"Ho, and what about the goods?" he answered.

Sivert from Sellanraa came clattering up homeward, empty as usual, and the foreman called to him: "Hi, what are you coming up empty for? Why didn't you bring up a load for us here?"

"Why, I might have," said Sivert. "But I'd no knowledge of it."

"He's from Sellanraa; they've two horses there," someone whispered.

"What's that? You've got two horses?" says the foreman. "Bring them down, then, the pair of them, to help with the cartage here. We'll pay you well."

"Why," says Sivert, "that's none so bad, dare say. But we're pressed just now, and can't spare the time."

"What? Can't spare the time to make money!" says the foreman.

But they had not always time at Sellanraa, there was much to do on the place. They had hired men to help—the first time such a thing had ever been done at Sellanraa— two stoneworkers from the Swedish side, to get out stone for a new cowshed.

This had been Isak's great idea for years past, to build a proper cowshed. The turf hut where the cattle were housed at present was too small, and out of repair; he would have a stone-built shed with double walls and a proper dung-pit under. It was to be done now. But there were many other things to be done as well, one thing always leading to another; the building-work, at any rate, seemed never to be finished. He had a sawmill and a grain mill and a summer shed for the cattle; it was but reasonable he should have a smithy. Only a little place, for odd jobs as need arose; it was a long way to send down to the village when the sledge-hammer curled at the edge or a horseshoe or so wanted looking to. Just enough to manage with, that was all—and why shouldn't he? Altogether, there were many outbuildings, little and big, at Sellanraa.

The place is growing, getting bigger and bigger, a mighty big place at last. Impossible now to manage without a girl to help, and Jensine has to stay on. Her father, the blacksmith, asks after her now and again, if she isn't coming home soon; but he does not make a point of it, being an easygoing man, and maybe with his own reasons for letting her stay. And there is Sellanraa, farthest out of all the settlements, growing bigger and bigger all the time; the place, that is, the houses and the ground, only the folk are the same. The day is gone when wandering Lapps could come to the house and get all they wanted for the asking; they come but rarely now, seem rather to go a long way round and keep out of sight; none are ever seen inside the house, but wait without if they come at all. Lapps always keep to the outlying spots, in dark places; light and air distress them, they cannot thrive; 'tis with them as with maggots and vermin. Now and again a calf or a lamb disappears without a trace from the outskirts of Sellanraa, from the farthest edge of the land—there is no helping that. And Sellanraa can bear the loss. And even if Sivert could shoot, he has no gun, but anyway, he cannot shoot; a good-tempered fellow, nothing warlike; a born jester: "And, anyway, I doubt but there's a law against shooting Lapps," says he.

Aye, Sellanraa can bear the loss of a head or so of cattle here and there; it stands there, great and strong. But not without its troubles for all that. Inger is not altogether pleased with herself and with life all the year round, no;

once she made a journey to a place a long way off, and it seems to have left an ugly discontent behind. It may disappear for a time, but always it returns. She is clever and hard-working as in her best days, and a handsome, healthy wife for a man, for a barge of a man—but has she no memories of Trondhjem; does she never dream? Aye, and in winter most of all. Full of life and spirits at times, and wanting no end of things—but a woman cannot dance by herself, and so there was no dancing at Sellanraa. Heavy thoughts and books of devotion? Aye, well . . . But there's something, Heaven knows, in the other sort of life, something splendid and unequaled. She has learned to make do with little; the Swedish stoneworkers are something, at any rate; strange faces and new voices about the place, but they are quiet, elderly men, given to work rather than play. Still, better than nothing—and one of them sings beautifully at his work; Inger stops now and again to listen. Hjalmar is his name.

And that is not all the trouble at Sellanraa. There is Eleseus, for instance—a disappointment there. He had written to say that his place in the engineer's office was no longer open, but he was going to get another all right—only wait. Then came another letter; he was expecting something to turn up very shortly, a first-rate post; but meantime, he could not live on nothing at all, and when they sent him a hundred-krone note from home, he wrote back to say it was just enough to pay off some small debts he had. . . . "H'm," said Isak. "But we've these stoneworker folk to pay, and a deal of things. . . . Write and ask if he wouldn't rather come back here and lend a hand."

And Inger wrote, but Eleseus did not care about coming home again; no, no sense in making another journey all to no purpose; he would rather starve.

Well, perhaps there was no first-rate post vacant just then in the city, and Eleseus, perhaps, was not as sharp as a razor in pushing his way. Heaven knows—perhaps he wasn't over-clever at his work either. Write? Aye, he could write well enough, and quick and hard-working maybe, but there might be something lacking for all that. And if so, what was to become of him?

When he arrived from home with his two hundred kroner, the city was waiting for him with old accounts outstanding, and when those were paid, well, he had to get a proper walking-stick, and not the remains of an umbrella. There were other little things as well that were but reasonable—a fur cap for the winter, like all his companions wore, a pair of skates to go on the ice with as others did, a silver toothpick, which was a thing to clean one's teeth, and play with daintily when chatting with friends over a glass of this or that. And as long as he had money, he stood treat as far as he was able; at a festive evening held to celebrate his return to town, he ordered half a dozen bottles of beer, and had them opened sparingly, one after another. "What—twenty öre for the waitress?" said his friends. "Ten's quite enough."

"Doesn't do to be stingy," said Eleseus.

Nothing stingy nor mean about Eleseus, no; he come from a good home, from a big place, where his father the Margrave owned endless tracts of timber, and four horses and thirty cows and three mowing-machines. Eleseus was no liar, and it was not he who had spread abroad all the fantastic stories about the Sellanraa estate; 'twas the district surveyor who had amused himself talking grandly about it a long while back. But Eleseus was not displeased to find the stories taken more or less for truth. Being nothing in himself, it was just as well to be the son of somebody that counted for something; it gave him credit, and was useful that way. But it could not last forever; the day came when he could no longer put off paying, and what was he to do then? One of his friends came to his help, got him into his father's business, a general store where the peasants bought their wares—better than nothing. It was a poor thing for a grown lad to start at a beginner's wage in a little shop; no shortcut to the position of a Lensmand; still, it gave him enough to live on, helped him over the worst for the present —oh, 'twas not so bad, after all. Eleseus was willing and good-tempered here too, and people liked him; he wrote home to say he had gone into trade.

This was his mother's greatest disappointment. Eleseus serving in a shop—'twas not a whit better than being assistant at the store down in the village. Before, he had been something apart, something different from the rest; none of their neighbors had gone off to live in a town and work in an office. Had he lost sight of his great aim and end? Inger was no fool; she knew well enough that there was a difference between the ordinary and the uncommon, though perhaps she did not always think to reckon with it. Isak was simpler and slower of thought; he reckoned less and less with Eleseus now, when he reckoned at all; his eldest son was gradually slipping out of range. Isak no longer thought of Sellanraa divided between his two sons when he himself should be gone.

Some way on in spring came engineers and workmen from Sweden; going to build roads, put up hutments, work in various ways, blasting, leveling, getting up supplies of food, hiring teams of horses, making arrangements with owners of land by the waterside; what—what was it all about? This is in the wilds, where folk never came but those who lived there? Well, they were going to start that copper mine, that was all.

So it had come to something after all; Geissler had not been merely boasting.

It was not the same big men that had come with him that time—no, the two of them had stayed behind, having business elsewhere, no doubt. But the same engineer was there, and the mining expert that had come at first. They bought up all the sawn planks Isak could spare, bought food and drink and paid for it well, chatted in kindly fashion and were pleased with Sellanraa. "Aerial railway," they said. "Cable haulage from the top of the fjeld down to the waterside," they said.

"What, down over all this moorland here?" said Isak, being slow to think. But they laughed at that.

"No, on the other side, man; not this way, 'twould be miles to go. No, on the other side of the fjeld, straight down to the sea; a good fall, and no distance to speak of. Run the ore down through the air in iron tanks; oh, it'll work all right, you wait and see. But we'll have to cart it down at first; make a road, and have it hauled down in carts. We shall want fifty horses—you see, we'll get on finely. And we've more men on the works than these few here— that's nothing. There's more coming up from the other side, gangs of men, with huts all ready to put up, and stores of provisions and material and tools and things—then we meet and make connection with them halfway, on the top, you see? We'll make the thing go, never fear—and ship the ore to South America. There's millions to be made out of it."

"What about the other gentlemen," asked Isak, "that came up here before?"

"What? Oh, they've sold out. So you remember them? No, they've sold. And the people that bought them out have sold again. It's a big company now that owns the mine— any amount of money behind it."

"And Geissler, where'll he be now?" asks Isak.

"Geissler? Never heard of him. Who's he?"

"Lensmand Geissler, that sold you the place first of all."

"Oh, him! Geissler was his name? Heaven knows where he is now. So you remember him too?"

Blasting and working up in the hills, gangs of men at work all through the summer—there was plenty doing about the place. Inger did a busy trade in milk and farm produce, and it amused her—going into business, as it were, and seeing all the many folk coming and going. Isak tramped about with his lumbering tread, and worked on his land; nothing disturbed him. Sivert and the two stoneworkers got the new cowshed up. It was a fine building, but took a deal of time before it was finished, with only three men to the work, and Sivert, moreover, often called away to help in the fields. The mowing-machine was useful now; and a good thing, too, to have three active women that could take a turn at the haymaking.

All going well; there was life in the wilds now, and money growing, blossoming everywhere.

And look at Storborg, the new trader's place—there was a business on a proper scale! This Aron must be a wizard, a devil of a fellow; he had learned somehow beforehand of the mining operations to come, and was on the spot all ready, with his shop and store, to make the most of it. Business? He did business enough for a whole State—aye, enough for a king! To begin with, he sold all kinds of household utensils and workmen's clothes; but miners earning good money are not afraid to spend it; not content with buying necessaries only; they would buy anything and everything. And most of all on Saturday evenings, the trading-station at Storborg was crowded with folk, and Aron raking money in; his clerk and his wife were both called in to help behind the counter, and Aron himself serving and selling as hard as he could go at it—and even then the place would not be empty till late at night. And the owners of horse-flesh in the village, they were right; 'twas a mighty carting and hauling of wares up to Storborg; more than once they had to cut off corners of the old road and make new shortcuts—a fine new road it was at last, very different from Isak's first narrow path up through the wilds. Aron was a blessing and a benefactor, nothing less, with his store and his new road. His name was not Aron really, that being only his Christian name; properly, he was Aronsen, and so he called himself, and his wife called him the same. They were a family not to be looked down upon, and kept two servant-girls and a lad.

As for the land at Storborg, it remained untouched for the present. Aronsen had no time for working on the soil—where was the sense of digging up a barren moor? But Aronsen had a garden, with a fence all round, and currant bushes and asters and rowans and planted trees—aye, a real garden. There was a broad path down it, where Aronsen could walk o' Sundays and smoke his pipe, and in the background was the veranda of the house, with panes of colored glass, orange and red and blue. Storborg . . . And there were children—three pretty little things about the place. The girl was to learn to play her part as daughter of a wealthy trader, and the boys were to learn the business themselves—aye, three children with a future before them!

Aronsen was a man to take thought for the future, or he would not have come there at all. He might have stuck to his fishery, and like enough been lucky at that and made good money, but 'twas not like going into business; nothing so fine, a thing for common folk at best. People didn't take off their hats to a fisherman. Aronsen had rowed his boat before, pulling at the oars; now he was going to sail instead. There was a word he was always using: "Cash down." He used it all sorts of ways. When things went well, they were going "cash down." His children were to get on in the world, and live more "cash down" even than himself. That was how he put it, meaning that they should have an easier life of it than he had had.

And look you, things did go well; neighbors took notice of him, and of his wife—aye, even of the children. It was not the least remarkable thing, that folk took notice of the children. The miners came down from their work in the hills, and had not seen a child's face for many days; when they caught sight of Aronsen's little ones playing in the yard, they would talk kindly to them at once, as if they had met three puppies at play. They would have given them money, but seeing they were the trader's children, it would hardly do. So they played music for them on their mouth-organs instead. Young Gustaf came down, the wildest of them all, with his hat over one ear, and his lips ever ready with a merry word; aye, Gustaf it was that came and played with them for long at a time. The children knew him every time, and ran to meet him; he would pick them up and carry them on his back, all three of them, and dance with them. "Ho!" said Gustaf, and danced with them. And then he would take out his mouth-organ and play tunes and music for them, till the two servant-girls would come out and look at him, and listen, with tears in their eyes. Aye, a madcap was Gustaf, but he knew what he was doing!

Then after a bit he would go into the shop and throw his money about, buying up a whole knapsack full of things. And when he went back up the road again, it was with a whole little stock-in-trade of his own—and he would stop at Sellanraa on the way and open his pack and show them. Notepaper with a flower in the corner, and a new pipe and a new shirt, and a fringed neckerchief—sweets for the womenfolk, and shiny things, a watch-chain with a compass, a pocketknife—oh, a host of things. Aye, there were rockets he had bought to let off on Sunday, for everyone to see. Inger gave him milk, and he joked with Leopoldine, and picked up little Rebecca and swung her up in the air— "*Hoy huit!*"

"And how's the building getting on?" he asked the Swedes—Gustaf was a Swede himself, and made friends with them, too. The building was getting on as best it could, with but themselves to the work. Why, then, he'd come and give them a hand himself, would Gustaf, though that was only said in jest.

"Aye, if you only would," said Inger. For the cowshed ought to be ready by the autumn, when the cattle were brought in.

Gustaf let off a rocket, and having let off one, there was no sense in keeping the rest. As well let them off too—and so he did, half a dozen of them, and the women and children stood round breathless at the magic of the magician; and Inger had never seen a rocket before, but the wild fire of them somehow reminded her of the great world she had once seen. What was a sewing-machine to this? And when Gustaf finished up by playing his mouth-organ, Inger would have gone off along the road with him for sheer emotion. . . .

The mine is working now, and the ore is carted down by teams of horses to the sea; a steamer had loaded up one cargo and sailed away with it to South America, and another steamer waits already for the next load. Aye, 'tis a big concern. All the settlers have been up to look at the wonderful place, as many as can walk. Brede Olsen has been up, with his samples of stone, and got nothing for his pains, seeing that the mining expert was gone back to Sweden again. On Sundays, there was a crowd of people coming up all the way from the village; aye, even Axel Ström, who had no time to throw away, turned off from his proper road along the telegraph line to look at the place. Hardly a soul now but has seen the mine and its wonders. And at last Inger herself, Inger from Sellanraa, puts on her best, gold ring and all, and goes up to the hills.

What does she want there?

Nothing, does not even care to see how the work is done. Inger has come to show herself, that is all. When she saw the other women going up, she felt she must go too. A disfiguring scar on her upper lip, and grown children of her own, has Inger, but she must go as the others did. It irks her to think of the others, young women, aye . . . but she will try if she can't compete with them all the same. She has not begun to grow stout as yet, but has still a good figure enough, tall and natty enough; she can still look well. True, her coloring is not what it used to be, and her skin is not comparable to a golden peach—but they should see for all that; aye, they should say, after all, she was good enough!

They greet her kindly as she could wish; the workmen know her, she has given them many a drink of milk, and they show her over the mine, the huts, the stables and kitchens, the cellars and storesheds; the bolder men edge in close to her and take her lightly by the arm, but Inger does not feel hurt at all, it does her good. And where there are steps to go up or down, she lifts her skirts high, showing her legs a trifle; but she manages it quietly, as if without a thought. Aye, she's good enough, think the men to themselves.

Oh, but there is something touching about her, this woman getting on in years; plain to see that a glance from one of these warm-blooded menfolk came all unexpectedly to her; she was grateful for it, and returned it; she was a woman like other women, and it thrilled her to feel so. An honest woman she had been, but like enough 'twas for lack of opportunity.

Getting on in years . . .

Gustaf came up. Left two girls from the village, and a comrade, just to come. Gustaf knew what he was at, no doubt; he took Inger's hand with more warmth, more pressure than was needed, and thanked her for the last pleasant evening at Sellanraa, but he was careful not to plague her with attention.

"Well, Gustaf, and when are you coming to help us with the building?" says Inger, going red. And Gustaf says he will come sure enough before long. His comrades hear it, and put in a word that they'll all be coming down before long.

"Ho!" says Inger. "Aren't you going to stay on the mine, then, come winter?"

The men answer cautiously, that it doesn't look like it, but can't be sure. But Gustaf is bolder, and laughs and says, looks like they've scraped out the bit of copper there was.

"You'll not say that in earnest surely?" says Inger. And the other men put in that Gustaf had better be careful not to say any such thing.

But Gustaf was not going to be careful; he said a great deal more, and as for Inger, 'twas strange how he managed to win her for himself, for all that he never seemed to put himself forward that way. One of the other lads played a concertina, but 'twas not like Gustaf's mouth-organ; another lad again, and a smart fellow he was too, tried to draw attention to himself by singing a song off by heart to the music, but that was nothing either, for all that he had a fine rolling voice. And a little while after, there was Gustaf, and if he hadn't got Inger's gold ring on his little finger! And how had it come about, when he never plagued nor pushed himself forward? Oh, he was forward enough in his way, but quiet with it all, as Inger herself; they did not talk of things, and she let him play with her hand as if without noticing. Later on, when she sat in one of the huts drinking coffee, there was a noise outside, high words between the men, and she knew it was about herself, and it warmed her. A pleasant thing to hear, for one no longer young, for a woman getting on in years.

And how did she come home from the hills that Sunday evening? Ho, well enough, virtuous as she had come, no more and no less. There was a crowd of men to see her home, the crowd of them that would not turn back as long as Gustaf was there; would not leave her alone with him, not if they knew it! Inger had never had such a gay time, not even in the days when she had been out in the world.

"Hadn't Inger lost something?" they asked at last.

"Lost something? No."

"A gold ring, for instance?"

And at that Gustaf had to bring it out; he was one against all, a whole army.

"Oh, 'twas a good thing you found it," said Inger, and made haste to say good-bye to her escort.

She drew nearer Sellanraa, saw the many roofs of the buildings; it was her home that lay there. And she awoke once more, came back to herself, like the clever wife she was, and took a shortcut through to the summer shed to look to the cattle. On the way she passes by a place she knows; a little child had once lain buried there; she had patted down the earth with her hands, set up a tiny cross—oh, but it was long ago. Now, she was wondering if those girls had finished their milking in good time. . . .

The work at the mine goes on, but there are whisperings of something wrong, the yield is not as good as it had promised. The mining expert, who had gone back home, came out again with another expert to help him; they went about blasting and boring and examining all the ground. What was wrong? The copper is fine enough, nothing wrong with that, but thin, and no real depth in it; getting thicker to the southward, lying deep and fine just where the company's holding reached its limit—and beyond that was Almenning, the property of the State. Well, the first purchasers had perhaps not thought so much of the thing, anyway. It was a family affair, some relatives who had bought the place as a speculation; they had not troubled to secure the whole range, all the miles to the next valley, no; they had but taken over a patch of ground from Isak Sellanraa and Geissler, and then sold it again.

And what was to be done now? The leading men, with the experts and the foremen, know well enough; they must start negotiations with the State at once. So they send a messenger off at full speed to Sweden, with letters and plans and charts, and ride away themselves down to the Lensmand below, to get the rights of the fjeld south of the water. And here their difficulties begin; the law stands in their way; they are foreigners, and cannot be purchasers in their own right. They knew all about that, and had made arrangements. But the southern side of the fjeld was sold already—and that they did not know. "Sold?"

"Aye, long ago, years back."

"Who bought it then?"

"Geissler."

"What Geissler? Oh, that fellow—h'm."

"And the title-deeds approved and registered," says the Lensmand. " 'Twas bare rock, no more, and he got it for next to nothing."

"Who is this fellow Geissler that keeps cropping up? Where is he?"

"Heaven knows where he is now!"

And a new messenger is sent off to Sweden. They must find out all about this Geissler. Meanwhile, they could not keep on all the men; they must wait and see.

So Gustaf came down to Sellanraa, with all his worldly goods on his back, and here he was, he said. Aye, Gustaf had given up his work at the mine—that is to say, he had been a trifle too outspoken the Sunday before, about the mine and the copper in the mine; the foreman had heard of it, and the engineer, and Gustaf was given his discharge. Well, good-bye then, and maybe 'twas the very thing he wanted; there could be nothing suspicious now about his coming to Sellanraa. They set him to work at once on the cowshed.

They worked and worked at the stone walls, and when

a few days later another man came down from the mine, he was taken on too; now there were two spells, and the work went apace. Aye, they would have it ready by the autumn, never fear.

But now one after another of the miners came down, dismissed, and took the road to Sweden; the trial working was stopped for the present. There was something like a sigh from the folk in the village at the news; foolish folk, they did not understand what a trial working was, that it was only working on trial, but so it was. There were dark forebodings and discouragement among the village folk; money was scarcer, wages were reduced, things were very quiet at the trading-station at Storborg. What did it all mean? Just when everything was going on finely, and Aronsen had got a flagstaff and a flag, and had bought a fine white bearskin for a rug to have in the sledge for the winter, and fine clothes for all the family. . . . Little matters these, but there were greater things happening as well. Here were two new men had bought up land for clearing in the wilds; high up between Maaneland and Sellanraa, and that was no small event for the whole of that little outlying community. The two new settlers had built their turf huts and started clearing ground and digging. They were hard-working folk, and had done much in a little time. All that summer they had bought their provisions at Storborg, but when they came down now, last time, there was hardly anything to be had. Nothing in stock—and what did Aron want with heavy stocks of this and that now the work at the mine had stopped? He had hardly anything of any sort on the place now—only money. Of all the folk in the neighborhood, Aronsen was perhaps the most dejected; his reckoning was all upset. When someone urged him to cultivate his land and live on that till better times, he answered: "Cultivate the land? 'Twas not that I came and set up house here for."

At last Aronsen could stand it no longer; he must go up

to the mine and see for himself how things were. It was a Sunday. When he got to Sellanraa, he wanted Isak to go with him, but Isak had never yet set foot on the mine since they had started; he was more at home on the hillside below. Inger had to put in a word. "You might as well go with Aronsen, when he asks you," she said. And maybe Inger was not sorry to have him go; 'twas Sunday, and like as not she wanted to be rid of him for an hour or so. And so Isak went along.

There were strange things to be seen up there in the hills; Isak did not recognize the place at all now, with its huts and sheds, a whole town of them, and carts and wagons and great gaping holes in the ground. The engineer himself showed them round. Maybe he was not in the best of humor just now, that same engineer, but he had tried all along to keep away the feeling of gloom that had fallen upon the village folk and the settlers round—and here was his chance, with no less persons than the Margrave of Sellanraa and the great trader from Storborg on the spot.

He explained the nature of the ore and the rocks in which it was found. Copper, iron, and sulphur, all were there together. Aye, they knew exactly what there was in the rocks up there—even gold and silver was there, though not so much of it. A mining engineer, he knows a deal of things.

"And it's all going to shut down now?" asked Aronsen.

"Shut down?" repeated the engineer in astonishment. "A nice thing that'd be for South America if we did!" No, they were discontinuing their preliminary operations for a while, only for a short time; they had seen what the place was like, what it could produce; then they could build their aerial railway and get to work on the southern side of the fjeld. He turned to Isak: "You don't happen to know where this Geissler's got to?"

"No."

Well, no matter—they'd get hold of him all right. And then they'd start to work again. Shut down? The idea!

Isak is suddenly lost in wonder and delight over a little machine that works with a treadle—simply move your foot and it works. He understands it at once—'tis a little smithy to carry about on a cart and take down and set up anywhere you please.

"What's a thing like that cost, now?" he asks.

"That? Portable forge? Oh, nothing much." They had several of the same sort, it appeared, but nothing to what they had down at the sea; all sorts of machines and apparatus, huge big things. Isak was given to understand that mining, the making of valleys and enormous chasms in the rock, was not a business that could be done with your fingernails—ha ha!

They stroll about the place, and the engineer mentions that he himself will be going across to Sweden in a few days' time.

"But you'll be coming back again?" says Aronsen.

Why, of course. Knew of no reason why the Government or the police should try to keep him.

Isak managed to lead round to the portable forge once more and stopped, looking at it again. "And what might a bit of a machine like that cost?" he asked.

Cost? Couldn't say offhand—a deal of money, no doubt, but nothing to speak of in mining operations. Oh, a grand fellow was the engineer; not in the best of humor himself just then, perhaps, but he kept up appearances and played up rich and fine to the last. Did Isak want a forge? Well, he might take that one—the company would never trouble about a little thing like that—the company would make him a present of a portable forge!

An hour after, Aronsen and Isak were on their way down again. Aronsen something calmer in mind—there was hope after all. Isak trundles down the hillside with his precious forge on his back. Aye, a barge of a man, he could bear a load! The engineer had offered to send a couple of men down with it to Sellanraa next morning, but Isak thanked him—'twas more than worth his while. He was thinking of his own folk; 'twould be a fine surprise for them to see him come walking down with a smithy on his back.

But 'twas Isak was surprised after all.

A horse and cart turned into the courtyard just as he reached home. And a highly remarkable load it brought. The driver was a man from the village, but beside him walked a gentleman at whom Isak stared in astonishment —it was Geissler.

HERE were other things that might have given Isak matter for surprise, but he was no great hand at thinking of more than one thing at a time. "Where's Inger?" was all he said as he passed by the kitchen door. He was only anxious to see that Geissler was well received.

Inger? Inger was out plucking berries; had been out plucking berries ever since Isak started—she and Gustaf the Swede. Aye, getting on in years, and all in love again and wild with it; autumn and winter near, but she felt the warmth in herself again, flowers and blossoming again. "Come and show where there's cloudberries," said Gustaf; "cranberries," said he. And how could a woman say no? Inger ran into her little room and was both earnest and religious for several minutes; but there was Gustaf standing waiting outside, the world was at her heels, and all she did was to tidy her hair, look at herself carefully in the glass, and out again. And what if she did? Who would not have done the same? Oh, a woman cannot tell one man from another; not always—not often.

And they two go out plucking berries, plucking cloudberries on the moorland, stepping from tuft to tuft, and she lifts her skirts high, and has her neat legs to show. All quiet everywhere; the white grouse have their young ones grown already and do not fly up hissing any more; they are sheltered spots where bushes grow on the moors. Less than an hour since they started, and already they are sitting down to rest. Says Inger: "Oh, I didn't think you were like that?" Oh, she is all weakness towards him, and smiles piteously, being so deep in love—aye, a sweet and cruel thing to be in love, 'tis both! Right and proper to be on her guard—aye, but only to give in at last. Inger is so deep in love—desperately, mercilessly; her heart is full of kindliness towards him, she only cares to be close and precious to him.

Aye, a woman getting on in years. . . .

"When the work's finished, you'll be going off again," says she.

No, he wasn't going. Well, of course, some time, but not yet, not for a week or so.

"Hadn't we better be getting home?" says she.

"No."

They pluck more berries, and in a little while they find a sheltered place among the bushes, and Inger says: "Gustaf, you're mad to do it." And hours pass—they'll be sleeping now, belike, among the bushes. Sleeping? Wonderful—far out in the wilderness, in the Garden of Eden. Then suddenly Inger sits upright and listens: "Seems like I heard someone down on the road away off?"

The sun is setting, the tufts of heather darkening in shadow as they walk home. They pass by many sheltered spots, and Gustaf sees them, and Inger, she sees them too no doubt, but all the time she feels as if someone were driving ahead of them. Oh, but who could walk all the way home with a wild handsome lad, and be on her guard all the time? Inger is too weak, she can only smile and say: "I never knew such a one."

She comes home alone. And well that she came just then, a fortunate thing. A minute later had not been well at all. Isak had just come into the courtyard with his forge, and Aronsen—and there is a horse and cart just pulled up.

"*Goddag*," says Geissler, greeting Inger as well.

And there they stand, all looking one at another—couldn't be better. . . .

Geissler back again. Years now since he was there, but he is back again, aged a little, greyer a little, but bright and cheerful as ever. And finely dressed this time, with a white waistcoat and gold chain across. A man beyond understanding!

Had he an inkling, maybe, that something was going on up at the mine, and wanted to see for himself? Well, here he was. Very wide awake to look at, glancing round at the place, at the land, turning his head and using his eyes every way. There are great changes to note; the Margrave had extended his domains. And Geissler nods.

"What's that you're carrying?" he asks Isak. " 'Tis a load for one horse in itself," says he.

" 'Tis for a forge," explains Isak. "And a mighty useful thing to have on a bit of a farm," says he—aye, calling Sellanraa a bit of a farm, no more!

"Where did you get hold of it?"

"Up at the mine. Engineer, he gave me the thing for a present, he said."

"The company's engineer?" says Geissler, as if he had not understood.

And Geissler, was he to be outdone by an engineer on a copper mine? "I've heard you'd got a mowing-machine," says he, "and I've brought along a patent raker thing that's handy to have." And he points to the load on the cart. There it stood, red and blue, a huge comb, a hayrake to be driven with horses. They lifted it out of the cart and looked at it; Isak harnessed himself to the thing and tried it over the ground. No wonder his mouth opened wide! Marvel on marvel coming to Sellanraa!

They spoke of the mine, of the work up in the hills. "They were asking about you, quite a lot," said Isak.

"Who?"

"The engineer, and all the other gentlemen. 'Have to get hold of you somehow,' they said."

Oh, but here Isak was saying overmuch, it seemed. Geissler was offended, no doubt; he turned sharp and curt, and said: "Well, I'm here, if they want me."

Next day came the two messengers back from Sweden, and with them a couple of the mineowners; on horseback they were, fine gentlemen and portly; mighty rich folk, by the look of them. They hardly stopped at Sellanraa at all, simply asked a question or so about the road, without dismounting, and rode on up the hill. Geissler they pretended not to see, though he stood quite close. The messengers with their loaded packhorses rested for an hour, talked to the men at work on the building, learned that the old gentleman in the white waistcoat and gold chain was Geissler, and then they too went on again. But that same evening one of them came riding down to the place with a message by word of mouth for Geissler to come up to the gentlemen at the mines. "I'm here if they want me," was the answer Geissler sent back.

Geissler was grown an important personage, it seemed; thought himself a man of power, of all the power in the world; considered it, perhaps, beneath his dignity to be sent for by word of mouth. But how was it he had come to Sellanraa at all just then—just when he was most wanted? A great one he must be for knowing things, all manner of things. Anyway, when the gentlemen up at the mine had Geissler's answer, there was nothing for it but they must bestir themselves and come all the way down to Sellanraa again. The engineer and the two mining experts came with them.

So many crooked ways and turnings were there before that meeting was brought about. It looked ill to start with; aye, Geissler was over-lordly by far.

The gentlemen were polite enough this time; begged him to excuse their having sent a verbal message the day before, being tired out after their journey. Geissler was polite in return, and said he too was tired out after his journey, or he would have come. Well, and then, to get to business: Would Geissler sell the land south of the water?

"Do you wish to purchase on your own account, may I ask," said Geissler, "or are you acting as agents?"

Now this could be nothing but sheer contrariness on Geissler's part; he could surely see for himself that rich and portly gentlemen of their stamp would not be acting as agents. They went on to discuss terms. "What about the price?" said they.

"The price? Yes," said Geissler, and sat thinking it over. "A couple of million," said he.

"Indeed?" said the gentlemen, and smiled. But Geissler did not smile.

The engineer and the two experts had made a rough investigation of the ground, made a few boring and blastings, and here was their report: the occurrence of ore was due to eruption; it was irregular, and from their preliminary examination appeared to be deepest in the neighborhood of the boundary between the company's land and Geissler's, decreasing from there onwards. For the last mile or so there was no ore to be found worth working.

Geissler listened to all this with the greatest nonchalance. He took some papers from his pocket, and looked at them carefully; but the papers were not charts nor maps— like as not they were things no way connected with the mine at all.

"You haven't gone deep enough," said he, as if it were something he had read in his papers. The gentlemen admitted that at once, but the engineer asked how he knew that: "You haven't made borings yourself, I suppose?"

And Geissler smiled, as if he had bored hundreds of

miles down through the globe, and covered up the holes again after.

They kept at it till noon, talking it over this way and that, and at last began to look at their watches. They had brought Geissler down to half a million now, but not a hair's breadth farther. No; they must have put him out sorely some way or other. They seemed to think he was anxious to sell, obliged to sell, but he was not—ho, not a bit; there he sat, as easy and careless as themselves, and no mistaking it.

"Fifteen, say twenty thousand would be a decent price anyway," said they.

Geissler agreed that might be a decent price enough for anyone sorely in need of the money, but five-and-twenty thousand would be better. And then one of the gentlemen put in—saying it perhaps by way of keeping Geissler from soaring too far: "By the way, I've seen your wife's people in Sweden—they sent their kind regards."

"Thank you," said Geissler.

"Well," said the other gentleman, seeing Geissler was not to be won over that way, "a quarter of a million . . . it's not gold we're buying, but copper ore."

"Exactly," said Geissler. "It's copper ore."

And at that they lost patience, all of them, and five watch-cases were opened and snapped to again; no more time to fool away now; it was time for dinner. They did not ask for food at Sellanraa, but rode back to the mine to get their own.

And that was the end of the meeting.

Geissler was left alone.

What would be in his mind all this time—what was he pondering and speculating about? Nothing at all, maybe, but only idle and careless? No, indeed, he was thinking of something, but calm enough for all that. After dinner, he turned to Isak, and said: "I'm going for a long walk over my land up there; and I'd have liked to have Sivert with me, same as last time."

"Aye, so you shall," said Isak at once.

"No; he's other things to do, just now."

"He shall go with you at once," said Isak, and called to Sivert to leave his work. But Geissler held up his hand, and said shortly: "No."

He walked round the yard several times, came back and talked to the men at their work, chatting easily with them and going off and coming back again. And all the time with this weighty matter on his mind, yet talking as if it were nothing at all. Geissler had been for so long accustomed to changes of fortune, maybe he was past feeling there was anything at stake now, whatever might be in the air.

Here he was, the man he was, by the merest chance. He had sold the first little patch of land to his wife's relations, and what then? Gone off and bought up the whole tract south of the water—what for? Was it to annoy them by making himself their neighbor? At first, no doubt, he had only thought of taking over a little strip of the land there, just where the new village would have to be built if the workings came to anything, but in the end he had come to be owner of the whole fjeld. The land was to be had for next to nothing, and he did not want a lot of trouble with boundaries. So, from sheer idleness he had become a mining king, a lord of the mountains; he had thought of a site for huts and machine sheds, and it had become a kingdom, stretching right down to the sea.

In Sweden, the first little patch of land had passed from hand to hand, and Geissler had taken care to keep himself informed as to its fate. The first purchasers, of course, had bought foolishly, bought without sense or forethought; the family council were not mining experts, they had not secured enough land at first, thinking only of buying out a certain Geissler, and getting rid of him. But the new owners were no less to be laughed at; mighty men, no doubt, who could afford to indulge in a jest, and take up land for amusement's sake, for a drunken wager, or Heaven knows what. But when it came to trial workings, and exploiting the land in earnest, then suddenly they found themselves butting up against a wall—Geissler.

Children! thought Geissler, maybe, in his lofty mind; he felt his power now, felt strong enough to be short and abrupt with folk. The others had certainly done their best to take him down a peg; they imagined they were dealing with a man in need of money, and threw out hints of some fifteen or twenty thousand—aye, children. They did not know Geissler. And now here he stood.

They came down no more that day from the fjeld, thinking best, no doubt, not to show themselves overanxious. Next morning they came down, packhorses and all, on their way home. And lo—Geissler was not there.

Not there?

That put an end to any ideas they might have had of settling the manner in lordly wise, from the saddle; they had to dismount and wait. And where was Geissler, if you please? Nobody could tell them; he went about everywhere, did Geissler, took an interest in Sellanraa and all about it; the last they had seen of him was up at the sawmill. The messengers were sent out to look for him, but Geissler must have gone some distance, it seemed, for he gave no answer when they shouted. The gentlemen looked at their watches, and were plainly annoyed at first, and said: "We're not going to fool about here waiting like this. If Geissler wants to sell, he must be on the spot." Oh, but they changed their tone in a little while; showed no annoyance after a while, but even began to find something amusing in it all, to jest about it. Here were they in a desperate case; they would have to lie out there in the desolate hills all night. And get lost and starve to death in the wilds, and leave their bones to bleach undiscovered by their mourning kin—aye, they made a great jest of it all.

At last Geissler came. Had been looking round a bit— just come from the cattle enclosure. "Looks as if that'll be too small for you soon," said he to Isak. "How many head have you got up there now altogether?" Aye, he could talk like that, with those fine gentlemen standing there watch in hand. Curiously red in the face was Geissler, as if he had been drinking. "Puh!" said he. "I'm all hot, walking."

"We half expected you would be here when we came," said one of the gentlemen.

"I had no word of your wanting to see me at all," answered Geissler, "otherwise I might have been here on the spot."

Well, and what about the business now? Was Geissler prepared to accept a reasonable offer today? It wasn't every day he had a chance of fifteen or twenty thousand—what? Unless, of course . . . If the money were nothing to him, why, then . . .

This last suggestion was not to Geissler's taste at all; he was offended. A nice way to talk! Well, they would not have said it, perhaps, if they had not been annoyed at first; and Geissler, no doubt, would hardly have turned suddenly pale at their words if he had not been out somewhere by himself and got red. As it was, he paled, and answered coldly:

"I don't wish to make any suggestion as to what you, gentlemen, may be in a position to pay—but I know what I am willing to accept and what not. I've no use for more child's prattle about the mine. My price is the same as yesterday."

"A quarter of a million kroner?"

"Yes."

The gentlemen mounted their horses. "Look here," said one, "we'll go this far, and say twenty-five thousand."

"You're still inclined to joke, I see," said Geissler. "But I'll make *you* an offer in sober earnest: would you care to sell your bit of a mine up there?"

"Why," said they, somewhat taken aback, "why, we might do that, perhaps."

"I'm ready to buy it," said Geissler.

Oh, that Geissler! With the courtyard full of people now, listening to every word; all the Sellanraa folk, and the stone-workers and the messengers. Like as not, he could never have raised the money, nor anything near it, for such a deal; but, again, who could say? A man beyond under-standing was Geissler. Anyhow, his last words rather dis-concerted those gentlemen on horseback. Was it a trick? Did he reckon to make his own land seem worth more by his maneuver?

The gentlemen thought it over; aye, they even began to talk softly together about it; they got down from their horses again. Then the engineer put in a word; he thought, no doubt, it was getting beyond all bearing. And he seemed to have some power, some kind of authority here. And the yard was full of folk all listening to what was going on. "We'll not sell," said he.

"Not?" asked his companions.

"No."

They whispered together again, and they mounted their horses once more—in earnest this time. "Twenty-five thousand!" called out one of them. Geissler did not answer, but turned away, and went over to talk to the stoneworkers again.

And that was the end of their last meeting.

Geissler appeared to care nothing for what might come of it. He walked about talking of this, that, and the other; for the moment he seemed chiefly interested in the laying of some heavy beams across the shell of the new cowhouse. They were to get the work finished that week, with a temporary roof—a new fodder loft was to be built up over later on.

Isak kept Sivert away from the building-work now, and left him idle—and this he did with a purpose, that Geissler might find the lad ready at any time if he wanted to go exploring with him in the hills. But Isak might have saved himself the trouble; Geissler had given up the idea, or perhaps forgotten all about it. What he did was to get Inger to pack him up some food, and set off down the road. He stayed away till evening.

He passed the two new clearings that had been started below Sellanraa, and talked to the men there; went right down to Maaneland to see what Axel Ström had got done that year. Nothing very great, it seemed; not as much as he might have wished, but he had put in some good work on the land. Geissler took an interest in this place, too, and asked him: "Got a horse?"

"Aye."

"Well, I've a mowing-machine and a harrow down south, both new; I'll send them up, if you like."

"How?" asked Axel, unable to conceive such magnificence, and thinking vaguely of payment by installments.

"I mean I'll make you a present of them," said Geissler.

"'Tis hard to believe," said Axel.

"But you'll have to help those two neighbors of yours up above, breaking new land."

"Aye, never fear for that," said Axel; he could still hardly make out what Geissler meant by it all. "So you've machines and things down south?"

"I've a deal of things to look after," said Geissler. Now, as a matter of fact, Geissler had no great deal of things to look after, but he liked to make it appear so. As for a mowing-machine and a harrow, he could buy them in any of the towns, and send up from there.

He stayed talking a long while with Axel Ström about

the other settlers near; of Storborg, the trading-station; of Axel's brother, newly married, who had come to Breidablik, and had started draining the moors and getting the water out. Axel complained that it was impossible to get a woman anywhere to help; he had none but an old creature, by name Oline; not much good at the best of times, but he might be thankful to have her as long as she stayed. Axel had been working day and night part of that summer. He might, perhaps, have got a woman from his own parts, from Helgeland, but that would have meant paying for her journey, besides wages. A costly business all round. Axel further told how he had taken over the inspection of the telegraph line, but rather wished he had left it alone.

"That sort of thing's only fit for Brede and his like," said Geissler.

"Aye, that's a true word," Axel admitted. "But there was the money to think of."

"How many cows have you got?"

"Four. And a young bull. 'Twas too far to go up to Sellanraa to theirs."

But there was a far weightier matter Axel badly wanted to talk over with Geissler; Barbro's affair had come to light, somehow, and an investigation was in progress. Come to light? Of course it had. Barbro had been going about, evidently with child and plain to see, and she had left the place by herself all unencumbered and no child at all. How had it come about?

When Geissler understood what the matter was, he said quite shortly: "Come along with me." And he led Axel with him away from the house. Geissler put on an important air, as one in authority. They sat down at the edge of the wood, and Geissler said: "Now, then, tell me all about it."

Come to light? Of course it had; how could it be helped? The place was no longer a desert, with never a soul for miles; and moreover, Oline was there. What had Oline to do with it? Ho! And to make things worse, Brede Olsen had made an enemy of her himself. No means of getting round Oline now; here she was on the spot, and could worm things out of Axel a bit at a time. 'Twas just such underhand work she lived for; aye, lived by, in some degree. And here was the very thing for her—trust Oline for scenting it out! Truth to tell, Oline was grown too old now to keep house and tend cattle at Maaneland; she ought to have given it up. But how could she? How could she leave a place where a fine, deep mystery lay simply waiting to be brought to light? She managed the winter's work; aye, she got through the summer, too, and it was a marvel of strength she gained from the mere thought of being able one day to show up a daughter of Brede himself. The snow was not gone from the fields that spring before Oline began poking about. She found the little green mound by the stream, and saw at once that the turf had been laid down in squares. She had even had the luck to come upon Axel one day standing by the little grave, and treading it down. So Axel knew all about it! And Oline nodded her grey head —aye, it was her turn now!

Not but Axel was a kindly man enough to live with, but miserly; counted his cheeses, and kept good note of every tuft of wool; Oline could not do as she liked with things, not by a long way. And then that matter of the accident last year, when she had saved him—if Axel had been the right sort, he would have given her the credit for it all, and acknowledged his debt to her alone. But not a bit of it— Axel still held to the division he had made on the spot. Aye, he would say, if Oline hadn't happened to come along, he would have had to lie out there in the cold all night; but Brede, he'd been a good help too, on the way home. And that was all the thanks she got! Oline was full of indignation—surely the Lord Almighty must turn away His face

from His creatures! How easy it would have been for Axel
to lead out a cow from its stall, and bring it to her and say:
"Here's a cow for you, Oline." But no. Not a word of it.

Well, let him wait—wait and see if it might not come
to cost him more than the worth of a cow in the end!

All through that summer, Oline kept a lookout for every
passer-by, and whispered to them and nodded and con-
fided things to them in secret. "But never a word I've
said," so she charged them every time. Oline went down to
the village, too, more than once. And now there were rumors and talk of things about the place, aye, drifting like a
fog, settling on faces and getting into ears; even the children going to school at Breidablik began nodding secrets
among themselves. And at last the Lensmand had to take
it up; had to bestir himself and report it, and ask for instructions. Then he came up with a book to write in and an assistant to help him; came up to Maaneland one day and in-
vestigated things and wrote things down, and went back
again. But three weeks after, he came up once more, in-
vestigating and writing down again, and this time, he
opened a little green mound by the stream, and took out the
body of a child. Oline was an invaluable help to him; and
in return he had to answer a host of questions she put.
Among other things, he said yes, it might perhaps come to
having Axel arrested too. At that, Oline clasped her hands
in dismay at all the wickedness she had got mixed up with
here, and only wished she were out of the place, far away
from it all. "But the girl," she whispered, "what about
Barbro herself?"

"The girl Barbro," said the Lensmand, "she's under ar-
rest now in Bergen. The law must take its course," said
he. And he took the little body and went back again to the
village. . . .

Little wonder, then, that Axel Ström was anxious. He
had spoken out to the Lensmand and denied nothing; he

was in part responsible for the coming of the child at all, and in addition, he had dug a grave for it. And now he was asking Geissler what he had better do next. Would he have to go in to the town, to a new and worse examination, and be tortured there?

Geissler was not the man he had been—no; and the long story had wearied him, he seemed duller now, whatever might be the cause. He was not the bright and confident soul he had been that morning. He looked at his watch, got up, and said:

"This'll want thinking over. I'll go into it thoroughly and let you know before I leave."

And Geissler went off.

He came back to Sellanraa that evening, had a little supper, and went to bed. Slept till late next morning, slept, rested thoroughly; he was tired, no doubt, after his meeting with the Swedish mineowners. Not till two days after did he make ready to leave. He was his lordly self again by then, paid liberally for his keep, and gave little Rebecca a shining krone.

He made a speech to Isak, and said: "It doesn't matter in the least if nothing came of the deal this time, it'll come all right later on. For the present, I'm going to stop the working up there and leave it a bit. As for those fellows—children! Thought they would teach me, did they? Did you hear what they offered me? Twenty-five thousand!"

"Aye," said Isak.

"Well," said Geissler, and waved his hand as if dismissing all impertinent offers of insignificant sums from his mind, "well, it won't do any harm to the district if I do stop the working there a bit—on the contrary, it'll teach folk to stick to their land. But they'll feel it in the village. They made a pile of money there last summer; fine clothes and fine living for all—but there's an end of that now. Aye, it might have been worth their while, the good folks down there, to have kept in with me; things might have been different then. Now, it'll be as I please."

But for all that, he did not look much of a man to control the fate of villages, as he went away. He carried a parcel of food in his hand, and his white waistcoat was no longer altogether clean. His good wife might have equipped him for the journey up this time out of the rest of the forty thousand she had once got—who could say, perhaps she had. Anyhow, he was going back poor enough.

He did not forget to look in at Axel Ström on the way down, and give the results of his thinking over. "I've been looking at it every way," said he. "The matter's in abeyance for the present, so there's nothing to be done just yet. You'll be called up for a further examination, and you'll have to say how things are. . . ."

Words, nothing more. Geissler had probably never given the matter a thought at all. And Axel agreed dejectedly to all he said. But at last Geissler flickered up into a mighty man again, puckered his brows, and said thoughtfully: "Unless, perhaps, I could manage to come to town myself and watch the proceedings."

"Aye, if you'd be so good," said Axel.

Geissler decided in a moment. "I'll see if I can manage it, if I can get the time. But I've a heap of things to look after down south. I'll come if I can. Good-bye for now. I'll send you those machines all right."

And Geissler went.

Would he ever come again?

CHAPTER VI

THE REST of the workmen came down from the mine. Work is stopped. The fjeld lies dead again.

The building at Sellanraa, too, is finished now. There is a makeshift roof of turf put on for the winter; the great space beneath is divided into rooms, bright apartments, a great salon in the middle and large rooms at either end, as if it were for human beings. Here Isak once lived in a turf hut together with a few goats—there is no turf hut to be seen now at Sellanraa.

Loose boxes, mangers, and bins are fitted up. The two stoneworkers are still busy, kept on to get the whole thing finished as soon as possible, but Gustaf is no hand at wood-work, so he says, and he is leaving. Gustaf has been a splendid lad at the stonework, heaving and lifting like a bear; and in the evenings, a joy and delight to all, playing his mouth-organ, not to speak of helping the womenfolk, carrying heavy pails to and from the river. But he is going now. No, Gustaf is no hand at woodwork, so he says. It looks almost as if he were in a hurry to get away.

"Can't it wait till tomorrow?" says Inger.

No, it can't wait, he's no more work to do here, and besides, going now, he will have company across the hills, going over with the last gang from the mines.

"And who's to help me with my buckets now?" says Inger, smiling sadly.

But Gustaf is never at a loss, he has his answer ready, and says: "Hjalmar." Now Hjalmar was the younger of the two stoneworkers, but neither of them was young as Gustaf himself, none like him in any way.

"Hjalmar—huh!" says Inger contemptuously. Then suddenly she changes her tone, and turns to Gustaf, thinking to make him jealous. "Though, after all, he's nice to have on the place, is Hjalmar," says she, "and so prettily he sings and all."

"Don't think much of him, anyway," says Gustaf. He does not seem jealous in the least.

"But you might stay one more night at least?"

No, Gustaf couldn't stay one more night—he was going across with the others.

Aye, maybe Gustaf was getting tired of the game by now. 'Twas a fine thing to snap her up in front of all the rest, and have her for his own the few weeks he was there —but he was going elsewhere now, like as not to a sweetheart at home—he had other things in view. Was he to stay on loafing about here for the sake of her? He had reason enough for bringing the thing to an end, as she herself must know; but she was grown so bold, so thoughtless of any consequence, she seemed to care for nothing. No, things had not held for so very long between them—but long enough to last out the spell of his work there.

Inger is sad and downhearted enough; aye, so erringly faithful that she mourns for him. 'Tis hard for her; she is honestly in love, without any thought of vanity or conquest. And not ashamed, no; she is a strong woman full of weakness; she is but following the law of nature all about her; it is the glow of autumn in her as in all things else. Her breast heaves with feeling as she packs up food for Gustaf to take with him. No thought of whether she has the right, of whether she dare risk this or that; she gives herself up to it entirely, hungry to taste, to enjoy. Isak might lift her

up to the roof and thrust her to the floor again—aye, what of
that! It would not make her feel the less.

She goes out with the parcel to Gustaf.

Now she had set the bucket by the steps on purpose, in
case he should care to go with her to the river just once
more. Maybe she would like to say something, to give
him some little thing—her gold ring; Heaven knows, she
was in a state to do anything. But there must be an end of
it some time; Gustaf thanks her, says good-bye, and goes.

And there she stands.

"Hjalmar!" she calls out aloud—oh, so much louder
than she need. As if she were determined to be gay in spite
of all—or crying out in distress.

Gustaf goes on his way. . . .

All through that autumn there was the usual work in the
fields all round, right away down to the village: potatoes to
be taken up, corn to be got in, the horned cattle let loose
over the ground. Eight farms there are now and all are
busy; but at the trading-station, at Storborg, there are no
cattle, and no green lands, only a garden. And there is no
trade there now, and nothing for any to be busy about
there.

They have a new root crop at Sellanraa called turnips,
sending up a colossal growth of green waving leaves out
of the earth, and nothing can keep the cows away from
them—the beasts break down all hedgework, and storm in,
bellowing. Nothing for it but to set Leopoldine and little
Rebecca to keep guard over the turnip fields, and little
Rebecca walks about with a big stick in her hand and is a
wonder at driving cows away. Her father is at work close
by; now and again he comes up to feel her hands and feet,
and ask if she is cold. Leopoldine is big and grown up now;
she can knit stockings and mittens for the winter while she
is watching the herds. Born in Trondhjem, was Leopold-

ine, and came to Sellanraa five years old. But the memory of a great town with many people and of a long voyage on a steamer is slipping away from her now, growing more and more distant; she is a child of the wilds and knows nothing now of the great world beyond the village down below where she has been to church once or twice, and where she was confirmed the year before. . . .

And the little casual work of every day goes on, with this thing and that to be done beside; as, for instance, the road down below, that is getting bad one or two places. The ground is still workable, and Isak goes down one day with Sivert, ditching and draining the road. There are two patches of bog to be drained.

Axel Ström has promised to take part in the work, seeing that he has a horse and uses the road himself—but Axel had pressing business in the town just then. Heaven knows what it could be, but very pressing, he said it was. But he had asked his brother from Breidablik to work with them in his stead.

Fredrik was this brother's name. A young man, newly married, a lighthearted fellow who could make a jest, but none the worse for that; Sivert and he are something alike. Now Fredrik had looked in at Storborg on his way up that morning, Aronsen of Storborg being his nearest neighbor, and he is full of all the trader has been telling him. It began this way; Fredrik wanted a roll of tobacco. "I'll give you a roll of tobacco when I have one," said Aronsen.

"What, you've no tobacco in the place?"

"No, nor won't order any. There's nobody to buy it. What d'you think I make out of one roll of tobacco?"

Aye, Aronsen had been in a nasty humor that morning, sure enough; felt he had been cheated somehow by that Swedish mining concern. Here had he set up a store out in the wilds, and then they go and shut down the work altogether!

Fredrik smiles slyly at Aronsen, and makes fun of him now. "He's not so much as touched that land of his," says he, "and hasn't even feed for his beasts, but must go and buy it. Asked me if I'd any hay to sell. No, I'd no hay to sell. 'Ho, d'you mean you don't want to make money?' said Aronsen. Thinks money's everything in the world, seems like. Puts down a hundred-krone note on the counter, and says: 'Money!' 'Aye, money's well enough,' says I. 'Cash down,' says he. Aye, he's just a little bit touched that way, so to speak, and his wife she goes about with a watch and chain and all on weekdays—Lord He knows what can be she's so set on remembering to the minute."

Says Sivert: "Did Aronsen say anything about a man named Geissler?"

"Aye. Said something about he'd be wanting to sell some land he'd got. And Aronsen was wild about it, he was— 'fellow that used to be Lensmand and got turned out,' he said, and 'like as not without so much as a five-krone in his books, and ought to be shot!' 'Aye, but wait a bit,' says I, 'and maybe he'll sell after all.' 'Nay,' says Aronsen, 'don't you believe it. I'm a businessman,' says he, 'and I know— when one party puts up a price of two hundred and fifty thousand, and the other offers twenty-five thousand, there's too big a difference; there'll be no deal ever come out of that. Well, let 'em go their own way, and see what comes of it,' says he. 'I only wish I'd never set my foot in this hole, and a poor thing it's been for me and mine.' Then I asked him if he didn't think of selling out himself. 'Aye,' says he, 'that's just what I'm thinking of. This bit of bog-land,' says he, 'a hole and a desert—I'm not making a single krone the whole day now,' says he."

They laughed at Aronsen, and had no pity for him at all.

"Think he'll sell out?" asks Isak.

"Well, he did speak of it. And he's got rid of the lad he had already. Aye, a curious man, a queer sort of man, that

Aronsen, 'tis sure. Sends away his lad could be working on the place getting in winter fuel and carting hay with that horse of his, but keeps on his storeman—chief clerk, he calls him. 'Tis true enough, as he says, not selling so much as a krone all day, for he's no stock in the place at all. And what does he want with a chief clerk, then? I doubt it'll be just by way of looking grand and making a show, must have a man there to stand at a desk and write up things in books. Ha ha ha! Aye, looks like he's just a little bit touched that way, is Aronsen."

The three men worked till noon, ate food from their baskets, and talked a while. They had matters of their own to talk over, matters of good and ill to folk on the land; no trifles, to them, but things to be discussed warily; they are clear-minded folk, their nerves unworn, and not flying out where they should not. It is the autumn season now, a silence in the woods all round; the hills are there, the sun is there, and at evening the moon and the stars will come; all regular and certain, full of kindliness, an embrace. Men have time to rest here, to lie in the heather, with an arm for a pillow.

Fredrik talks of Breidablik, how 'tis but little he's got done there yet awhile.

"Nay," says Isak, "tis none so little already, I saw when I was down that way."

This was praise from the oldest among them, the giant himself, and Fredrik might well be pleased. He asks frankly enough: "Did you think so, now? Well, it'll be better before long. I've had a deal of things to hinder this year; the house to do up, being leaky and like to fall to pieces; hayloft to take down and put up again, and no sort of room in the turf hut for beasts, seeing I'd cow and heifer more than Brede he'd ever had in his time," says Fredrik proudly.

"And you're thriving like, up here?" asks Isak.

"Aye, I'll not say no. And wife, she's thriving too, why shouldn't we? There's good room and outlook all about; we can see up and down the road both ways. And a neat little copse by the house all pretty to look at, birch and willow—I'll plant a bit more other side of the house when I've time. And it's fine to see how the bogland's dried only since last year's ditching—'tis all a question now what'll grow on her this year. Aye, thrive? When we've house and home and land and all—'tis enough for the two of us surely."

"Ho," says Sivert slyly, "and the two of you—is that all there's ever to be?"

"Why, as to that," says Fredrik bravely, "'tis like enough there'll be more to come. And as to thriving—well, the wife's not falling off anyway, by the looks of her."

They work on until evening, drawing up now and again to straighten their backs, and exchange a word or so.

"And so you didn't get the tobacco?" says Sivert.

"No, that's true. But 'twas no loss, for I've no use for it, anyway," says Fredrik.

"No use for tobacco?"

"Nay. 'Twas but for to drop in at Aronsen's like, and hear what he'd got to say." And the two jesters laughed together at that.

On the way home, father and son talk little, as was their way; but Isak must have been thinking out something for himself; he says:

"Sivert?"

"Aye?" says Sivert again.

"Nay, 'twas nothing."

They walk on a good ways, and Isak begins again:

"How's he get on, then, with his trading, Aronsen, when he's nothing to trade with?"

"Nay," says Sivert. "But there's not folk enough here now for him to buy for."

"Ho, you think so? Why, I suppose 'tis so, aye, well . . ."

Sivert wondered a little at this. After a while his father went on again:

"There's but eight places now in all, but there might be more before long. More . . . well, I don't know . . ."

Sivert wondering more than ever—what can his father be getting at? The pair of them walk on a long way in silence; they are nearly home now.

"H'm," says Isak. "What you think Aronsen he'd ask for that place of his now?"

"Ho, that's it!" says Sivert. "Want to buy it, do you?" he asks jestingly. But suddenly he understands what it all means: 'tis Eleseus the old man has in mind. Oh, he's not forgotten him after all, but kept him faithfully in mind, just as his mother, only in his own way, nearer earth, and nearer to Sellanraa.

" 'Twill be going for a reasonable price, I doubt," says Sivert. And when Sivert says so much, his father knows the lad has read his thought. And as if in fear of having spoken out too clearly, he falls to talking of their road-mending; a good thing they had got it done at last.

For a couple of days after that, Sivert and his mother were putting their heads together and holding councils and whispering—aye, they even wrote a letter. And when Saturday came round Sivert suddenly wanted to go down to the village.

"What you want to go down village again for now?" said his father in displeasure. "Wearing boots to rags . . ." Oh, Isak was more bitter than need be; he knew well enough that Sivert was going to the post.

"Going to church," says Sivert.

'Twas all he could find by way of excuse, and his father muttered: "Well, what you want to go for . . . ?"

But if Sivert was going to church, why, he might harness up and take little Rebecca with him. Little Rebecca, aye, surely she might have that bit of a treat for once in her life, after being so clever guarding turnips and being always the pearl and blessing of them all, aye, that she was. And they harnessed up, and Rebecca had the maid Jensine to look after her on the way, and Sivert said never a word against that either.

While they are away, it so happens that Aronsen's man, his chief clerk, from Storborg, comes up the road. What does this mean? Why, nothing very much, 'tis only Andresen, the chief clerk from Storborg, come up for a bit of a walk this way—his master having sent him. Nothing more. And no great excitement among the folk at Sellanraa over that—'twas not as in the old days, when a stranger was a rare sight on their new land, and Inger made a great to-do. No, Inger's grown quieter now, and keeps to herself these days.

A strange thing that book of devotion, a guide upon the way, an arm round one's neck, no less. When Inger had lost hold of herself a little, lost her way a little out plucking berries, she found her way home again by the thought of her little chamber and the holy book; aye, she was humble now and a God-fearing soul. She can remember long years ago when she would say an evil word if she pricked her finger sewing—so she had learned to do from her fellow-workers round the big table in the Institute. But now she pricks her finger, and it bleeds, and she sucks the blood away in silence. 'Tis no little victory gained to change one's nature so. And Inger did more than that. When all the workmen were gone, and the stone building was finished, and Sellanraa was all forsaken and still, then came a critical time for Inger; she cried a deal, and suffered much. She blamed none but herself for it all, and she was deeply humbled. If only she could have spoken out to Isak, and relieved her mind, but that was not their way at Sellanraa;

there was none of them would talk their feelings and confess things. All she could do was to be extra careful in the
way she asked her husband to come in to meals, going right
up to him to say it nicely, instead of shouting from the
door. And in the evenings, she looked over his clothes, and
sewed buttons on. Aye, and even more she did. One night
she lifted up on her elbow and said:

"Isak?"

"What is it?" says Isak.

"Are you awake?"

"Aye."

"Nay, 'twas nothing," says Inger. "But I've not been all
as I ought."

"What?" says Isak. Aye, so much he said, and rose up
on his elbow in turn.

They lay there, and went on talking. Inger is a matchless woman, after all; and with a full heart: "I've not been
as I ought towards you," she says, "and I'm that sorry
about it."

The simple words move him; this barge of a man is
touched, aye, he wants to comfort her, knowing nothing
of what is the matter, but only that there is none like her.
"Naught to cry about, my dear," says Isak. "There's none
of us can be as we ought."

"Nay, 'tis true," she answers gratefully. Oh, Isak had a
strong, sound way of taking things; straightened them out,
he did when they turned crooked. "None of us can be as
we ought." Aye, he was right. The god of the heart—for
all that he is a god, he goes a deal of crooked ways, goes out
adventuring, the wild thing that he is, and we can see it in
his looks. One day rolling in a bed of roses and licking his
lips and remembering things; next day with a thorn in his
foot, desperately trying to get it out. Die of it? Never a bit,
he's as well as ever. A nice lookout it would be if he were
to die!

And Inger's trouble passed off too; she got over it, but she keeps on with her hours of devotion, and finds a merciful refuge there. Hard-working and patient and good she is now every day, knowing Isak different from all other men, and wanting none but him. No gay young spark of a singer, true, in his looks and ways, but good enough, aye, good enough indeed! And once more it is seen that the fear of the Lord and contentment therewith are a precious gain.

And now it was that the little chief clerk from Storborg, Andresen, came up to Sellanraa one Sunday, and Inger was not in the least affected, far from it; she did not so much as go in herself to give him a mug of milk, but sent Leopoldine in with it, by reason that Jensine the maid was out. And Leopoldine could carry a mug of milk as well as need be, and she gave it him and said: "Here you are," and blushed, for all she was wearing her Sunday clothes and had nothing to be ashamed of, anyway.

"Thanks, 'tis overkind of you," says Andresen. "Is your father at home?" says he.

"Aye; he'll be about the place somewhere."

Andresen drank and wiped his mouth with a handkerchief and looked at the time. "Is it far up to the mines?" he asked.

"No, 'tis an hour's walk, or hardly that."

"I'm going up to look over them, d'you see, for him, Aronsen—I'm his chief clerk."

"Ho!"

"You'll know me yourself, no doubt; I'm Aronsen's chief clerk. You've been down buying things at our place before."

"Aye."

"And I remember you well enough," says Andresen. "You've been down twice buying things."

" 'Tis more than could be thought, you'd remember that,"

says Leopoldine, and had no more strength after that, but stood holding by a chair.

But Andresen had strength enough, he went on, and said: "Remember you? Well, of course I should." And he said more:

"You wouldn't like to walk up to the mine with me?" said he.

And a little after something went wrong with Leopoldine's eyes; everything turned red and strange about her, and the floor was slipping away from under, and Chief Clerk Andresen was talking from somewhere ever so far off. Saying: "Couldn't you spare the time?"

"No," says she.

And Heaven knows how she managed to get out of the kitchen again. Her mother looked at her and asked what was the matter. "Nothing," said Leopoldine.

Nothing, no, of course. But now, look you, 'twas Leopoldine's turn to be affected, to begin the same eternal round. She was well fitted for the same, overgrown and pretty and newly confirmed; an excellent sacrifice she would make. A bird is fluttering in her young breast, her long hands are like her mother's, full of tenderness, full of sex. Could she dance? Aye, indeed she could. A marvel where she had managed to learn it, but learn it they did at Sellanraa as well as elsewhere. Sivert could dance, and Leopoldine too; a kind of dancing peculiar to the spot, growth of the new-cleared soil; a dance with energy and swing: schottische, mazurka, waltz, and polka in one. And could not Leopoldine deck herself out and fall in love and dream by daylight all awake? Aye, as well as any other! The day she stood in church she was allowed to borrow her mother's gold ring to wear; no sin in that, 'twas only neat and nice; and the day after, going to her communion, she did not get the ring on till it was over. Aye, she might well show herself in church with a gold ring on her finger, being the daughter of a great man on the place—the Margrave.

When Andresen came down from the mine, he found Isak at Sellanraa, and they asked him in, gave him dinner and a cup of coffee. All the folk on the place were in there together now, and took part in the conversation. Andresen explained that his master, Aronsen, had sent him up to see how things were at the mines, if there was any sign of beginning work there again soon. Heaven knows, maybe Andresen sat there lying all the time, about being sent by his master; he might just as well have hit on it for his own account—and anyway, he couldn't have been at the mines at all in the little time he'd been away.

" 'Tis none so easy to see from outside if they're going to start work again," said Isak.

No, Andresen admitted that was so; but Aronsen had sent him, and after all, two pair of eyes could see better than one.

But here Inger seemingly could contain herself no longer; she asked: "Is it true what they're saying, Aronsen is going to sell his place again?"

Andresen answers: "He's thinking of it. And a man like him can surely do as he likes, seeing all the means and riches he's got."

"Ho, is he so rich, then?"

"Aye," says Andresen, nodding his head; "rich enough, and that's a true word."

Again Inger cannot keep silence, but asks right out:

"I wonder, now, what he'd be asking for the place?"

Isak puts in a word here; like as not he's more curious to know than Inger herself, but it must not seem that the idea of buying Storborg is any thought of his; he makes himself a stranger to it, and says now:

"Why, what you want to know for, Inger?"

"I was but asking," says she. And both of them look at Andresen, waiting.

And he answers; answers cautiously enough that as to the price, he can say nothing of that, but he knows what Aronsen says the place has cost him.

"And how much is that?" asks Inger, having no strength to keep her peace and be silent.

" 'Tis sixteen hundred kroner," says Andresen.

Ho, and Inger claps her hands at once to hear it, for if there is one thing womenfolk have no sense nor thought of, 'tis the price of land and properties. But, anyway, sixteen hundred kroner is no small sum for folk in the wilds, and Inger has but one fear, that Isak may be frightened off the deal. But Isak, he sits there just exactly like a fjeld, and says only: "Aye, it's the big houses he's put up."

"Aye," says Andresen again, " 'tis just that. 'Tis the fine big houses and all."

Just when Andresen is making ready to go, Leopoldine slips out by the door. A strange thing, but somehow she cannot bring herself to think of shaking hands with him. So she has found a good place, standing in the new cowshed, looking out of a window. And with a blue silk ribbon round her neck, that she hadn't been wearing before, and a wonder she ever found time to put it on now. There he goes, a trifle short and stout, spry on his feet, with a light, full beard, eight or ten years older than herself. Aye, none so bad-looking to her mind!

And then the party came back from church late on Sunday night. All had gone well, little Rebecca had slept the last few hours of the way up, and was lifted from the cart and carried indoors without waking. Sivert has heard a deal of news, but when his mother asks: "Well, what you've got to tell?" he only says: "Nay, nothing much. Axel he's got a mowing-machine and a harrow."

"What's that?" says his father, all interested. "Did you see them?"

"Aye, I saw them right enough. Down on the quay."

"Ho! So that was what he must go into town for," says his father. And Sivert sits there swelling with pride at knowing better, but says never a word.

His father might just as well believe that Axel's pressing business in the town had been to buy machines; his mother too might think so for all that. Ho, but there was neither of them thought so in their hearts; they had heard whispers enough of what was the matter; of a new child-murder case in the wilds.

"Time for bed," says his father at last.

Sivert goes off to bed, swelling with knowledge. Axel had been summoned for examination; 'twas a big affair— the Lensmand had gone with him—so big indeed that the Lensmand's lady, who had just had another child, had left the baby and was gone into town with her husband. She had promised to put in a word to the jury herself.

Gossip and scandal all abroad in the village now, and Sivert saw well enough that a certain earlier crime of the same sort was being called to mind again. Outside the church, the groups would stop talking as he came up, and had he not been the man he was, perhaps some would have turned away from him. Good to be Sivert those days, a man from a big place to begin with, son of a wealthy landowner—and then beside, to be known as a clever fellow, a good worker; he ranked before others, and was looked up to for himself. Sivert had always been well liked among folk. If only Jensine did not learn too much before they got home that day! And Sivert had his own affairs to think of —aye, folk in the wilds can blush and pale as well as other. He had seen Jensine as she left the church with little Rebecca; she had seen him too, but went by. He waited a bit, and then drove over to the smith's to fetch them.

They were sitting at table, all the family at dinner. Sivert is asked to join them, but has had his dinner, thanks. They knew he would be coming, they might have waited that bit of a while for him—so they would have done at Sellanraa, but not here, it seemed.

"Nay, 'tis not what you're used to, I dare say," says the smith's wife. And: "What news from church?" says the smith, for all he had been at church himself.

When Jensine and little Rebecca were seated up in the cart again, says the smith's wife to her daughter: "Well, good-bye, Jensine; we'll be wanting you home again soon." And that could be taken two ways, thought Sivert, but he said nothing. If the speech had been more direct, more plain and outspoken, he might perhaps . . . He waits, with puckered brows, but no more is said.

They drive up homeward, and little Rebecca is the only one with a word to say; she is full of the wonder of going to church, the priest in his dress with a silver cross, and the lights and the organ music. After a long while Jensine says: " 'Tis a shameful thing about Barbro and all."

"What did your mother mean about you coming home soon?" asked Sivert.

"What she meant?"

"Aye. You thinking of leaving us, then?"

"Why, they'll be wanting me home some time, I doubt," says she.

"*Ptro!*" says Sivert, stopping his horse. "Like me to drive back with you now, perhaps?"

Jensine looks at him; he is pale as death.

"No," says she. And a little after she begins to cry.

Rebecca looks in surprise from one to the other. Oh, but little Rebecca was a good one to have on a journey like that; she took Jensine's part and patted her and made her smile again. And when little Rebecca looked threateningly at her brother and said she was going to jump down and find a big stick to beat him, Sivert had to smile too.

"But what did *you* mean, now, I'd like to know?" says Jensine.

Sivert answered straight out at once: "I meant, if you don't care to stay with us, why, we must manage without."

And a long while after, said Jensine: "Well, there's Leopoldine, she's big now, and fit and all to do my work, seems."

Aye, 'twas a sorrowful journey.

A MAN walks up the way through the hills. Wind and rain; the autumn downpour has begun, but the man cares little for that, he looks glad at heart, and glad he is. 'Tis Axel Ström, coming back from the town and the court and all—they have let him go free. Aye, a happy man—first of all, there's a mowing-machine and a harrow for him down at the quay, and more than that, he's free, and not guilty. Had taken no part in the killing of a child. Aye, so things can turn out!

But the times he had been through! Standing there as a witness, this toiler in the fields had known the hardest days of his life. 'Twas no gain to him to make Barbro's guilt seem greater, and for that reason he was careful not to say too much, he did not even say all he knew; every word had to be dragged out of him, and he answered mostly with but "Yes" and "No." Was it not enough? Was he to make more of it than there was already? Oh, but there were times when it looked serious indeed; there were the men of Law, black-robed and dangerous, easy enough for them, it seemed, just with a word or so, to turn the whole thing as they pleased, and have him sentenced. But they were kindly folk after all, and did not try to bring him to destruction. Also, as it happened, there were powerful influences at work trying to save Barbro, and it was all to his advantage as well.

Then what on earth was there for him to trouble about?

Barbro herself would hardly try to make things look worse than need be for her former master and lover; he knew terrible things about this and an earlier affair of the same sort; she could not be such a fool. No, Barbro was clever enough; she said a good word for Axel, and declared that he had known nothing of her having borne a child till after it was all over. He was different in some ways, perhaps, from other men, and they did not always get on well together, but a quiet man, and a good man in every way. No, it was true he had dug a new grave and buried the body away there, but that was long after, and by reason he had thought the first place was not dry enough, though indeed it was, and 'twas only Axel's odd way of thinking.

What need, then, for Axel to fear at all when Barbro took all the blame on herself that way? And as for Barbro herself, there were mighty influences at work.

Fru Lensmand Heyerdahl had taken up the case. She went about to high and low, never sparing herself, demanded to be called as a witness, and made a speech in court. When her turn came, she stood there before them all and was a great lady indeed; she took up the question of infanticide in all its aspects, and gave the court a long harangue on the subject—it almost seemed as if she had obtained permission beforehand to say what she pleased. Aye, folk might say what they would of Fru Lensmand Heyerdahl, but make a speech, that she could, and was learned in politics and social questions, no doubt about that. 'Twas a marvel where she found all her words. Now and again the presiding Justice seemed wishful to keep her to the point, but maybe he had not the heart to interrupt, and let her run on. And at the end of it all, she volunteered one or two useful items of information, and made a startling offer to the court.

Leaving out all legal technicalities, what took place was this:

"We women," said Fru Heyerdahl, "we are an unfortunate and oppressed moiety of humanity. It is the men who make the laws, and we women have not a word to say in the matter. But can any man put himself in the position of a woman in childbirth? Has he ever felt the dread of it, ever known the terrible pangs, ever cried aloud in the anguish of that hour?

"In the present instance, it is a servant-girl who has borne the child. A girl, unmarried, and consequently trying all through the critical time to hide her condition. And why must she seek to hide it? Because of society. Society despises the unmarried woman who bears a child. Not only does society offer her no protection, but it persecutes her, pursues her with contempt and disgrace. Atrocious! No human creature with any heart at all could help feeling indignant at such a state of things. Not only is the girl to bring a child into the world, a thing in itself surely hard enough, but she is to be treated as a criminal for that very fact. I will venture to say that it was well for the unfortunate girl now accused before the court that her child was born by accident when she fell into the water, and drowned. Well for herself and for the child. As long as society maintains its present attitude, an unmarried mother should be counted guiltless even if she does kill her child."

Here a slight murmur was heard from the presiding Justice.

"Or at any rate, her punishment should be merely nominal," said Fru Heyerdahl. "We are all agreed, of course," she went on, "that infant life should be preserved, but is that to mean that no law of simple humanity is to apply to the unfortunate mother? Think, consider what she has been through during all the period of pregnancy, what suffering she has endured in striving to hide her condition,

and all the time never knowing where to turn for herself
and the child when it comes. No man can imagine it," said
she. "The child is at least killed in kindness. The mother
tries to save herself and the child she loves from the misery
of its life. The shame is more than she can bear, and so the
plan gradually forms itself in her mind, to put the child out
of the way. The birth takes place in secret, and the mother
is for four-and-twenty hours in such a delirious state that at
the moment of killing the child she is simply not responsible for her actions. Practically speaking, she has not herself committed the act at all, being out of her senses at the
time. With every bone in her body aching still after her de-
livery, she has to take the little creature's life and hide
away the body—think what an effort of will is demanded
here! Naturally, we all wish all children to live; we are distressed at the thought that any should be exterminated in
such a way. But it is the fault of society that it is so; the
fault of a hopeless, merciless, scandalmongering, mischievous, and evil-minded society, ever on the watch to crush
an unmarried mother by every means in its power!

"But—even after such treatment at the hands of society,
the persecuted mother can rise up again. It often happens
that these girls, after one false step of the sort, are led by
that very fact to develop their best and noblest qualities.
Let the court inquire of the superintendents at refuge
homes, where unmarried mothers and their children are received, if this is not the case. And experience has shown
that it is just such girls who have—whom society has
forced to kill their own children, that make the best nurses.
Surely that was a matter for any and all to think seriously
about?

"Then there is another side of the question. Why is the
man to go free? The mother found guilty of infanticide is
thrust into prison and tortured, but the father, the seducer,
he is never touched. Yet being as he is the cause of the

child's existence, he is a party to the crime; his share in it, indeed, is greater than the mother's; had it not been for him, there would have been no crime. Then why should he be acquitted? Because the laws are made by men. There is the answer. The enormity of such man-made laws cries of itself to Heaven for intervention. And there can be no help for us women till we are allowed a say in the elections, and in the making of laws, ourselves.

"But," said Fru Heyerdahl, "if this is the terrible fate that is meted out to the guilty—or, let us say, the more clearly guilty—unmarried mother who has killed her child, what of the innocent one who is merely suspected of the crime, and has not committed it? What reparation does society offer to her? None at all! I can testify that I know the girl here accused; have known her since she was a child; she has been in my service, and her father is my husband's assistant. We women venture to think and feel directly in opposition to men's accusations and persecution; we dare to have our own opinion. The girl there has been arrested, deprived of her liberty, on suspicion of having in the first place concealed the birth of a child, and further of having killed the child so born. I have no doubt in my own mind that she is not guilty of either—the court will itself arrive at this self-evident conclusion. Concealment of birth—the child was born in the middle of the day. True, the mother is alone at the time—but who could have been with her in any case? The place is far away in the wilds, the only living soul within reach is a man—how could she send for a man at such a moment? Any woman will tell you it is impossible—not to be thought of. And then—it is alleged that she must have killed the child after. But the child was born in the water—the mother falls down in an icy stream, and the child is born. What was she doing by the water? She is a servant-girl, a slave, that is to say, and has her daily work to do; she is going to fetch juniper twigs for cleaning. And crossing the stream, she slips and falls in. And there she lies; the child is born, and is drowned in the water."

Fru Heyerdahl stopped. She could see from the look of the court and the spectators that she had spoken wonderfully well; there was a great silence in the place, only Barbro sat dabbing her eyes now and again for sheer emotion. And Fru Heyerdahl closed with these words: "We women have some heart, some feeling. I have left my own children in the care of strangers to travel all this way and appear as a witness on behalf of the unfortunate girl sitting there. Men's laws cannot prevent women from thinking; and I think this, that the girl there has been punished sufficiently for no crime. Acquit her, let her go free, and I will take charge of her myself. She will make the best nurse I have ever had."

And Fru Heyerdahl stepped down.

Says the Justice then: "But I think you said a moment ago that the best nurses were those who *had* killed their children?"

Oh, but the Justice was not of a mind to go against Fru Heyerdahl, not in the least—he was as humane as could be himself, a man as gentle as a priest. When the advocate for the Crown put a few questions to the witness afterwards, the Justice sat for the most part making notes on some papers.

The proceedings lasted only till a little over noon; there were few witnesses, and the case was clear enough. Axel Ström sat hoping for the best, then suddenly it seemed as if the advocate for the Crown and Fru Heyerdahl were joining forces to make things awkward for him, because he had buried the body instead of notifying the death. He was cross-examined somewhat sharply on this point, and would likely enough have come out badly if he had not all at once caught sight of Geissler sitting in the court. Aye, 'twas right enough, Geissler was there. This gave Axel courage, he no longer felt himself alone against the Law that was determined to beat him down. And Geissler nodded to him.

Aye, Geissler was come to town. He had not asked to be called as a witness, but he was there. He had also spent a couple of days before the case came on in going into the matter himself, and noting down what he remembered of Axel's own account given him at Maaneland. Most of the documents seemed to Geissler somewhat unsatisfactory; Lensmand Heyerdahl was evidently a narrow-minded person, who had throughout endeavored to prove complicity on Axel's part. Fool, idiot of a man—what did he know of life in the wilds, when he could see that the child was just what Axel had counted on to keep the woman, his help-meet, on the place!

Geissler spoke to the advocate for the Crown, but it seemed there was little need of intervention there; he wanted to help Axel back to his farm and his land, but Axel was in no need of help, from the looks of things. For the case was going well as far as Barbro herself was concerned, and if she were acquitted, then there could be no question of any complicity at all. It would depend on the testimony of the witnesses.

When the few witnesses had been heard—Oline had not been summoned, but only the Lensmand, Axel himself, the experts, a couple of girls from the village—when they had been heard, it was time to adjourn for the midday break, and Geissler went up to the advocate for the Crown once more. The advocate was of opinion that all was going well for the girl Barbro, and so much the better. Fru Lensmand Heyerdahl's words had carried great weight. All depended now upon the finding of the court.

"Are you at all interested in the girl?" asked the advocate.

"Why, to a certain extent," answered Geissler, "or rather, perhaps, in the man."

"Has she been in your service too?"

"No, he's never been in my service."

"I was speaking of the girl. It's she that has the sympathy of the court."

"No, she's never been in my service at all."

"The man—h'm, he doesn't seem to come out of it so well," said the advocate. "Goes off and buries the body all by himself in the wood—looks bad, very bad."

"He wanted to have it buried properly, I suppose," said Geissler. "It hadn't been really buried at all at first."

"Well, of course a woman hadn't the strength of a man to go digging. And in her state—she must have been done up already. Altogether," said the advocate, "I think we've come to take a more humane view of these infanticide cases generally, of late. If I were to judge, I should never venture to condemn the girl at all; and from what has appeared in this case, I shall not venture to demand a conviction."

"Very pleased to hear it," said Geissler, with a bow.

The advocate went on: "As a man, as a private person, I will even go further, and say: I would never condemn a single unmarried mother for killing her child."

"Most interesting," said Geissler, "to find the advocate for the Crown so entirely in agreement with what Fru Heyerdahl said before the court."

"Oh, Fru Heyerdahl! . . . Still, to my mind, there was a great deal in what she said. After all, what is the good of all these convictions? Unmarried mothers have suffered enough beforehand, and been brought so low in every human regard by the brutal and callous attitude of the world—the punishment ought to suffice."

Geissler rose, and said at last: "No doubt. But what about the children?"

"True," said the advocate, "it's a sad business about the children. Still, all things considered, perhaps it's just as well. Illegitimate children have a hard time, and turn out badly as often as not."

Geissler felt perhaps some touch of malice at the portly complacency of the man of law; he said:

"Erasmus was born out of wedlock."

"Erasmus . . . ?"

"Erasmus of Rotterdam."

"H'm."

"And Leonardo the same."

"Leonardo da Vinci? Really? Well, of course, there are exceptions, otherwise there would be no rule. But on the whole . . ."

"We pass protective measures for beast and bird," said Geissler; "seems rather strange, doesn't it, not to trouble about our own young?"

The advocate for the Crown reached out slowly and with dignity after some papers on the table, as a hint that he had not time to continue the discussion. "Yes . . ." said he absently. "Yes, yes, no doubt. . . ."

Geissler expressed his thanks for a most instructive conversation, and took his leave.

He sat down in the court-house again, to be there in good time. He was not ill pleased, maybe, to feel his power; he had knowledge of a certain piece of wrapping, a man's shirt cut across, to carry—let us say twigs for a broom; of the body of a child floating in the harbor at Bergen—aye, he could make matters awkward for the court if he chose; a word from him would be as effective as a thousand swords. But Geissler had doubtless no intention of uttering that word now unless it were needed. Things were going splendidly without; even the advocate for the Crown had declared himself on the side of the accused.

The room fills, and the court is sitting again.

An interesting comedy to watch in a little town. The warning gravity of the advocate for the Crown, the emotional eloquence of the advocate for the defense. The court sat listening to what appeared to be its duty in regard to the case of a girl named Barbro, and the death of her child.

For all that, it was no light matter after all to decide. The advocate for the Crown was a presentable man to look at, and doubtless also a man of heart, but something appeared to have annoyed him recently or possibly he had suddenly remembered that he held a certain office in the State and was bound to act from that point of view. An incomprehensible thing, but he was plainly less disposed to be lenient now than he had been during the morning; if the crime had been committed, he said, it was a serious matter, and things would look black indeed if they could with certainty be declared so black as would appear from the testimony of the witnesses already heard. That was a matter for the court to decide. He wished to draw attention to three points: firstly, whether they had before them a concealment of birth; whether this was clear to the court. He made some personal remarks on this head. The second point was the wrapping, the piece of a shirt—why had the accused taken this with her? Was it in order to make use of it for a certain purpose preconceived? He developed this suggestion further. His third point was the hurried and suspicious burial, without any notification of the death to either priest or Lensmand. Here, the man was the person chiefly responsible, and it was of the utmost importance that the court should come to the right conclusion in that respect. For it was obvious that if the man were an accomplice, and had therefore undertaken the burial himself, then his servant-girl must have committed a crime before he could be an accomplice in it.

"H'm," from someone in court.

Axel Ström felt himself again in danger. He looked up

without meeting a single glance; all eyes were fixed on the advocate speaking. But far down in the court sat Geissler again, looking highly supercilious, as if bursting with his own superiority, his underlip thrust forward, his face turned towards the ceiling. This enormous indifference to the solemnity of the court, and that "H'm," uttered loudly and without concealment, cheered Axel mightily; he felt himself no longer alone against the world.

And now things took a turn again for the better. This advocate for the Crown seemed at last to think he had done enough, had achieved all that was possible in the way of directing suspicion and ill-feeling towards the man; and now he stopped. He did more; he almost, as it were, faced round, and made no demand for a conviction. He ended by saying, in so many words, that after the testimony of the witnesses in the case, he on his part did not call upon the court to convict the accused.

This was well enough, thought Axel—the business was practically over.

Then came the turn of the advocate for the defense, a young man who had studied the law, and had now been entrusted with this most satisfactory case. His tone itself showed the view he took of it; never had a man been more certain of defending an innocent person than he. Truth to tell, this Fru Heyerdahl had taken the wind out of his sails beforehand, and used several of his own intended arguments that morning; he was annoyed at her having already exploited the "society" theme—oh, but he could have said some first-rate things about society himself. He was incensed at the mistaken leniency of the presiding Justice in not stopping her speech; it was a defense in itself, a brief prepared beforehand—and what was there left for him?

He began at the beginning of the life-story of the girl Barbro. Her people were not well off, albeit industrious and respectable; she had gone out to service at an early age, first of all to the Lensmand's. The court had heard that morning what her mistress, Fru Heyerdahl, thought of her —no one could wish for a finer recommendation. Barbro had then gone to Bergen. Here the advocate laid great stress on a most feelingly written testimonial from two young businessmen in whose employ Barbro had been while at Bergen—evidently in a position of trust. Barbro had come back to act as housekeeper for this unmarried man in an outlying district. And here her trouble began.

She found herself with child by this man. The learned counsel for the prosecution had already referred—in the most delicate and considerate manner, be it said—to the question of concealment of birth. Had Barbro attempted to conceal her condition; had she denied being with child? The two witnesses, girls from her own village, had been of opinion that she was in that condition; but when they had asked her, she had not denied it at all, she had merely passed the matter off. What would a young girl naturally do in such a case but pass it off? No one else had asked her about it at all. Go to her mistress and confess? She had no mistress; she was mistress on the place herself. She had a master, certainly, but a girl could not be expected to confide in a man upon such a matter; she bears her cross herself; does not sing, does not whisper, but is silent as a Trappist. Concealment? No, but she kept herself to herself.

The child is born—a sound and healthy boy; had lived and breathed after birth, but had been suffocated. The court had been made aware of the circumstances attending this birth: it had taken place in the water; the mother falls into the stream, and the child is born, but she is incapable of saving the child. She lies there, unable even to rise herself till some time after. No marks of violence were to be seen upon the body; there was nothing to indicate that it had been intentionally killed; it had been drowned by misadventure at birth, that was all. The most natural explanation in the world.

His learned colleague had made some mention of a cloth or wrapping, considering it something of a mystery why she should have taken half a shirt with her that day. The mystery was clear enough; she had taken the shirt to carry stripped juniper in. She might have taken—let us say, a pillowcase; as it was, she had taken this piece of a shirt. Something she must have, in any case; she could not carry the stuff back in her hands. No, there was surely no ground for making a mystery of this.

One point, however, was not quite so clear: had the accused been treated with the care and consideration which her condition at the time demanded? Had her master dealt kindly with her? It would be as well for him if it were found so. The girl herself had, under cross-examination, referred to the man in satisfactory terms; and this again was evidence in itself of her own nobility of character. The man, on his part, Axel Ström, had likewise in his depositions refrained from any attempt to add to the burden of the girl, or to blame her in any way. In this he had acted rightly—not to say wisely, seeing that his own case depended very largely upon how matters went with her. By laying the blame on her he would, if she were convicted, bring about his own downfall.

It was impossible to consider the documents and depositions in the present case without feeling the deepest sympathy for this young girl in her forsaken situation. And yet there was no need to appeal to mercy on her behalf, only to justice and human understanding. She and her master were in a way betrothed, but a certain dissimilarity of temperament and interests prevented them from marrying. The girl could not entrust her future to such a man. It was not a pleasant subject, but it might be well to return for a moment to the question of the wrapping that had been spoken of before; it should here be noted that the girl had taken, not one of her own undergarments, but one of her master's shirts. The question at once arose: had the man himself offered the material for the purpose? Here, one was at first inclined to see a possibility, at any rate, that the man, Axel, had had some part in the affair.

"H'm," from someone in court. Loud and hard—so much so, indeed, that the speaker paused, and all looked round to see who might be responsible for the interruption. The presiding Justice frowned.

But, went on the advocate for the defense, collecting himself again, in this respect, also, we can set our minds at rest, thanks to the accused herself. It might seem well to her advantage to divide the blame here, but she had not attempted to do so. She had entirely and without reserve absolved Axel Ström from any complicity whatever in the fact of her having taken his shirt instead of something of her own on her way to the water—that is, on her way to the woods to gather juniper. There was not the slightest reason for doubting the asseveration of the accused on this point; her depositions had throughout been found in accordance with the facts, and the same was evidently the case in this. Had the shirt been given her by the man, this would have been to presuppose a killing of the child already planned—the accused, truthful as she was, had not attempted to charge even this man with a crime that had never been committed. Her demeanor throughout had been commendably frank and open; she had made no endeavor to throw the blame on others. There were frequent instances before the court of this delicacy of feeling on the part of the accused, as, for instance, the fact that she had wrapped up the body of the child as well as she could, and put it away decently, as the Lensmand had found it.

Here the presiding Justice interposed, merely as a matter of form, observing that it was grave No. 2 which the

Lensmand had found—the grave in which Axel had buried
the body after its removal from the first.

"True, that is true. I stand corrected," said the advocate,
with all proper respect for the president of the court. Perfectly true. But—Axel had himself stated that he had only
carried the body from one grave and laid it in the other.
And there could be no doubt but that a woman was better
able to wrap up a child than was a man—and who best of
all? Surely a mother's tender hand?

The presiding Justice nods.

In any case—could not this girl—if she had been of another sort—have buried the child naked? One might even
go so far as to say that she might have thrown it into a
dustbin. She might have left it out under a tree in the open,
to freeze to death—that is to say, of course, if it had not
been dead already. She might have put it in the oven when
left alone, and burnt it up. She might have taken it up to
the river at Sellanraa and thrown it in there. But this
mother did none of these things; she wrapped the dead
child neatly in a cloth and buried it. And if the body had
been found wrapped neatly when the grave was opened, it
must be a woman and not a man who had so wrapped it.

And now, the advocate for the defense went on, it lay
with the court to determine what measure of guilt could
properly be attributed to the girl Barbro in the matter.
There was but little remaining for which she could be
blamed at all—indeed, in his, counsel's, opinion, there was
nothing. Unless the court found reason to convict on the
charge of having failed to notify the death. But here, again
—the child was dead, and nothing could alter that; the
place was far out in the wilds, many miles from either
priest or Lensmand; natural enough, surely, to let it sleep
the eternal sleep in a neat grave in the woods. And if it
were a crime to have buried it thus, then the accused was
not more guilty than the father of the child—as it was, the

misdemeanor was surely slight enough to be overlooked. Modern practice was growing more and more disposed to lay more stress on reforming the criminal than on punishing the crime. It was an antiquated system which sought to inflict punishment for every mortal thing—it was the *lex talionis* of the Old Testament, an eye for an eye and a tooth for a tooth. There was no longer the spirit of the law in modern times. The law of the present day was more humane, seeking to adjust itself according to the degree of criminal intent and purpose displayed in each case.

No! The court could never convict this girl. It was not the object of a trial to secure an addition to the number of criminals, but rather to restore to society a good and useful member. It should be noted that the accused had now the prospect of a new position where she would be under the best possible supervision. Fru Lensmand Heyerdahl had, from her intimate knowledge of the girl, and from her own valuable experience as a mother, thrown wide the doors of her own home to the girl; the court would bear in mind the weight of responsibility attaching to its decision here, and would then convict or acquit the accused. Finally, he wished to express his thanks to the learned counsel for the prosecution, who had generously refrained from demanding a conviction—a pleasing evidence of deep and humane understanding.

The advocate for the defense sat down.

The remainder of the proceedings did not take long. The summing-up was but a repetition of the same points, as viewed from opposite sides, a brief synopsis of the action of the play, dry, dull, and dignified. It had all been managed very satisfactorily all round; both the advocates had pointed out what the court should consider, and the presiding Justice found his task easy enough.

Lights were lit, a couple of lamps hanging from the ceiling—a miserable light it was; the Justice could hardly see

to read his notes. He mentioned with some severity the
point that the child's death had not been duly notified to the
proper authorities—but that, under the circumstances,
should be considered rather the duty of the father than of
the mother, owing to her weakness at the time. The court
had then to determine whether any case had been proved
with regard to concealment of birth and infanticide. Here
the evidence was again recapitulated from beginning to
end. Then came the usual injunction as to being duly conscious of responsibility, which the court had heard before,
and finally, the not uncommon reminder that in cases of
doubt, the scale should be allowed to turn in favor of the
accused.

And now all was clear and ready.

The judges left the room and went into another apart-
ment. They were to consider a paper with certain questions, which one of them had with him. They were away
five minutes, and returned with a "No" to all the questions.

No, the girl Barbro had not killed her child.

Then the presiding judge said a few more words, and declared that the girl Barbro was now free.

The court-house emptied, the comedy was over. . . .

Someone takes Axel Ström by the arm: it is Geissler.
"H'm," said he, "so you're done with that now!"

"Aye," said Axel.

"But they've wasted a lot of your time to no purpose."

"Aye," said Axel again. But he was coming to himself
again gradually, and after a moment he added: "None the
less, I'm glad it was no worse."

"No worse?" said Geissler. "I'd have liked to see them
try!" He spoke with emphasis, and Axel fancied Geissler
must have had something to do with the case himself; that
he had intervened. Heaven knows if, after all, it had not
been Geissler himself that had led the whole proceedings

and gained the result he wished. It was a mystery, any-way.

So much at least Axel understood, that Geissler had been on his side all through.

"I've a deal to thank you for," said he, offering his hand.

"What for?" asked Geissler.

"Why, for—for all this."

Geissler turned it off shortly. "I've done nothing at all. Didn't trouble to do anything—'twasn't worth while." But for all that, Geissler was not displeased, maybe, at being thanked; it was as if he had been waiting for it, and now it had come. "I've no time to stand talking now," he said. "Going back tomorrow, are you? Good. Good-bye, then, and good luck to you." And Geissler strolled off across the street.

On the boat going home Axel encountered the Lens-mand and his wife, Barbro, and the two girls called as wit-nesses.

"Well," said Fru Heyerdahl, "aren't you glad it turned out so well?"

Axel said: "Yes"; he was glad it had come out all right in the end.

The Lensmand himself put in a word, and said: "This is the second of these cases I've had while I've been here—first with Inger from Sellanraa, and now this. No, it's no good trying to countenance that sort of thing—justice must take its course."

But Fru Heyerdahl guessed, no doubt, that Axel was not over-pleased with her speech of the day before, and tried to smooth it over, to make up for it somehow now. "You understood, of course, why I had to say all that about you yesterday?"

"H'm—ye-es," said Axel.

"You understood, of course, I know. You didn't think

I wanted to make things harder for you in any way. I've always thought well of you, and I don't mind saying so."

"Aye," said Axel, no more. But he was pleased and touched at her words.

"Yes, I mean it," said Fru Heyerdahl. "But I was obliged to try and shift the blame a little your way, otherwise Barbro would have been convicted, and you too. It was all for the best, indeed it was."

"I thank you kindly," said Axel.

"And it was I and no other that went about from one to another through the place, trying to do what I could for you both. And you saw, of course, that we all had to do the same thing—make out that you were partly to blame, so as to get you both off in the end."

"Aye," said Axel.

"Surely you didn't imagine for a moment that I meant any harm to you? When I've always thought so well of you!"

Aye, this was good to hear after all the disgrace of it. Axel, at any rate, was so touched that he felt he must do something, give Fru Heyerdahl something or other, whatever he could find—a piece of meat perhaps, now autumn was come. He had a young bull. . . .

Fru Lensmand Heyerdahl kept her word; she took Barbro to live with her. On board the steamer, too, she looked after the girl, and saw that she was not cold, nor hungry; took care, also, that she did not get up to any nonsense with the mate from Bergen. The first time it occurred, she said nothing, but simply called Barbro to her. But a little while after there was Barbro with him again, her head on one side, talking Bergen dialect and smiling. Then her mistress called her up and said: "Really, Barbro, you ought not to be going on like that among the men now. Remember what you've just been through, and what you've come from."

"I was only talking to him a minute," said Barbro. "I could hear he was from Bergen."

Axel did not speak to her. He noticed that she was pale and clear-skinned now, and her teeth were better. She did not wear either of his rings. . . .

And now here is Axel tramping up to his own place once more. Wind and rain, but he is glad at heart; a mowing-machine and a harrow down at the quay; he had seen them. Oh, that Geissler! Never a word had he said in town about what he had sent. Aye, an unfathomable man was Geissler.

XEL had no long time to rest at home, as it turned out; the autumn gales led to fresh trouble and bothersome work that he had brought upon himself: the telegraph apparatus on his wall announced that the line was out of order.

Oh, but he had been thinking overmuch of the money, surely, when he took on that post. It had been a nuisance from the start. Brede Olsen had fairly threatened him when he went down to fetch the apparatus and tools; aye, had said to him in as many words: "You don't seem like remembering how I saved your life last winter!"

" 'Twas Oline saved my life," answered Axel.

"Ho, indeed! And didn't I carry you down myself on my own poor shoulders? Anyway, you were clever enough to buy up my place in summertime and leave me homeless in the winter." Aye, Brede was deeply offended; he went on:

"But you can take the telegraph for me, aye, all the rubble of it for me. I and mine we'll go down to the village and start on something there—you don't know what it'll be, but wait and see. What about a hotel place where folk can get coffee? You see but we'll manage all right. There's my wife can sell things to eat and drink as well as another, and I can go out on business and make a heap more than you ever did. But I don't mind telling you, Axel, I could make things awkward for you in many odd ways, seeing all I know about the telegraph and things; aye, 'twould be easy enough both to pull down poles and cut the line and all. And then you to go running out after it midway in the busy time. That's all I'll say to you, Axel, and you bear it in mind. . . ."

Now Axel should have been down and brought up the machines from the quay—all over gilt and coloring they were, like pictures to see. And he might have had them to look at all that day, and learn the manner of using them— but now they must wait. 'Twas none so pleasant to have to put aside all manner of necessary work to run and see after a telegraph line. But 'twas the money. . . .

Up on the top of the hill he meets Aronsen. Aye, Aronsen the trader standing there looking and gazing out into the storm, like a vision himself. What did he want there? No peace in his mind now, it seems, but he must go up the fjeld himself and look at the mine with his own eyes. And this, look you, Trader Aronsen had done from sheer earnest thought of his own and his family's future. Here he is, face to face with bare desolation on the forsaken hills, machines lying there to rust, carts and material of all sorts left out in the open—'twas dismal to see. Here and there on the walls of the huts were placards, notices written by hand, forbidding anyone to damage or remove the company's property—tools, carts, or buildings.

Axel stops for a few words with the mad trader, and asks if he has come out shooting.

"Shooting? Aye, if I could only get within reach of him!"

"Him? Who, then?"

"Why, him that's ruining me and all the rest of us hereabout. Him that won't sell his bit of fjeld and let things get to work again, and trade and money passing same as before."

"D'you mean him Geissler, then?"

"Aye, 'tis him I mean. Ought to be shot!"

Axel laughs at this, and says: "Geissler he was in town but a few days back; you should have talked to him there. But if I might be so bold as to say, I doubt you'd better leave him alone, after all."

"And why?" asks Aron angrily.

"Why? I've a mind he'd be overwise and mysterious for you in the end."

They argued over this for a while, and Aronsen grew more excited than ever. At last Axel asked jestingly: "Well, anyway, you'll not be so hard on us all to run away and leave us to ourselves in the wilds?"

"Huh! Think I'm going to stay fooling about here in your bogs and never so much as making the price of a pipe?" cried Aron indignantly. "Find me a buyer and I'll sell out."

"Sell out?" says Axel. "The land's good ordinary land if she's handled as should be—and what you've got's enough to keep a man."

"Haven't I just said I'll not touch it?" cried Aronsen again in the gale. "I can do better than that!"

Axel thought if that was so, 'twould be easy to find a buyer; but Aronsen laughed scornfully at the idea—there was nobody there in the wilds had money to buy him out.

"Not here in the wilds, maybe, but elsewhere."

"Here's naught but filth and poverty," said Aron bitterly.

"Why, that's as it may be," said Axel in some offense. "But Isak up at Sellanraa he could buy you out any day."

"Don't believe it," said Aronsen.

" 'Tis all one to me what you believe," said Axel, and turned to go.

Aronsen called after him: "Hi, wait a bit! What's that you say—Isak might take the place, was that what you said?"

"Aye," said Axel, "if 'twas only the money. He's means enough to buy up five of your Storborg and all!"

Aronsen had gone round keeping wide of Sellanraa on his way up, taking care not to be seen; but, going back, he called in and had a talk with Isak. But Isak only shook his head and said nay, 'twas a matter he'd never thought of, and didn't care to.

But when Eleseus came back home that Christmas, Isak was easier to deal with. True, he maintained that it was a mad idea to think of buying Storborg, 'twas nothing had ever been in his mind; still, if Eleseus thought he could do anything with the place, why, they might think it over.

Eleseus himself was midways between, as it were; not exactly eager for it, yet not altogether indifferent. If he did settle down here at home, then his career in one way was at an end. 'Twas not like being in a town. That autumn, when a lot of people from his parts had been up for cross-examination in a certain place, he had taken care not to show himself; he had no desire to meet any that knew him from that quarter; they belonged to another world. And was he now to go back to that same world himself?

His mother was all for buying the place; Sivert too, said it would be best. They stuck to Eleseus, both of them, and one day the three drove down to Storborg to see the wonder with their own eyes.

But once there was a prospect of selling, Aronsen became a different man; he wasn't pressed to get rid of it, not at all. If he did go away, the place could stand as it was; 'twas a first-rate holding, a "cash-down" place, there'd be no difficulty in selling it any time. "You'd not give my price," said Aronsen.

They went over the house and stores, the warehouse and sheds, inspected the miserable remains of the stock, consisting of a few mouth-organs, watch-chains, boxes of colored papers, lamps with hanging ornaments, all utterly unsalable to sensible folks that lived on their land. There were a few cases of nails and some cotton print, and that was all.

Eleseus was constrained to show off a bit, and looked over things with a knowing air. "I've no use for that sort of truck," said he.

"Why, then, you've no call to buy it," said Aronsen.

"Anyhow, I'll offer you fifteen hundred kroner for the place as it stands, with goods, livestock, and the rest," said Eleseus. Oh, he was careless enough; his offer was but a show, for something to say.

And they drove back home. No, there was no deal; Eleseus had made a ridiculous offer, that Aronsen regarded as an insult. "I don't think much of you, young man," said Aronsen; aye, calling him young man, considering him but a slip of a lad that had grown conceited in the town, and thought to teach him, Aronsen, the value of goods.

"I'll not be called 'young man' by you, if you please," said Eleseus, offended in his turn. They must be mortal enemies after that.

But how could it be that Aronsen had all along been so independent and so sure of not being forced to sell? There was a reason for it: Aronsen had a little hope at the back of his mind, after all.

A meeting had been held in the village to consider the position which had arisen owing to Geissler's refusal to sell his part of the mining tract. 'Twas not only the out-lying settlers who stood to lose by this, it would be fatal to the whole district.

Why could not folk go on living as well or as poorly now as before there had been any mine at all? Well, they could not, and that was all about it. They had grown accustomed to better food, finer bread, store-bought clothes and higher wages, general extravagance—aye, folk had learned to reckon with money more, that was the matter. And now the money was gone again, had slipped away like a shoal of herring out to sea—'twas dire distress for them all, and what was to be done?

There was no doubt about it: ex-Lensmand Geissler was taking his revenge upon the village because they had helped his superior to get him dismissed; equally clear was it that they had underestimated him at the time. He had not simply disappeared and left. By the simplest means, merely by demanding an unreasonable price for a mine, he had succeeded in checking the entire development of the district. Aye, a strong man! Axel Ström from Maaneland could bear them out in this; he was the one who had last met Geissler. Brede's girl Barbro had had a lawsuit in the town, and come home acquitted; but Geissler, he had been there in court all the time. And if anyone suggested that Geissler was dejected, and a broken man, why, he had only to look at the costly machines that same Geissler had sent up as a present to Axel Ström.

This man it was then, who held the fate of the district in his hand; they would have to come to some agreement with him. What price would Geissler ultimately be disposed to accept for his mine? They must ascertain in any case. The Swedes had offered him twenty-five thousand—Geissler had refused. But suppose the village here, the commune, were to make up the remainder, simply to get things going again? If it were not an altogether unheard-of amount, it might be worth while. Both the trader at the shore station and Aronsen up at Storborg would be willing to contribute privately and secretly; funds devoted to such a purpose now would be repaid in the long run.

The end of it was that two men were deputed to call on Geissler and take up the matter with him. And they were expected back shortly.

So it was, then, that Aronsen cherished a flicker of hope,

and thought he could afford to stand on his dignity with
any who offered to buy up Storborg. But it was not to last.

A week later the deputation returned home with a flat
refusal. Oh, they had done the worst thing possible at the
outset, in choosing Brede Olsen as one of the men they
sent—they had taken him as being one who best could
spare the time. They had found Geissler, but he had only
shaken his head and laughed. "Go back home again," he
had said. But Geissler had paid for their journey back.

Then the district was to be left to its fate?

After Aronsen had raged for a while, and grown more
and more desperate, he went up one day to Sellanraa and
closed the deal. Aye, Aronsen did. Eleseus got it for the
price he had offered; land and house and sheds, livestock
and goods, for fifteen hundred kroner. True, on going
through the inventory after, it was found that Aronsen's
wife had converted most of the cotton print to her own use;
but trifles of that sort were nothing to a man like Eleseus.
It didn't do to be mean, he said.

Nevertheless, Eleseus was not exactly delighted with
things as they had turned out—his future was settled now,
he was to bury himself in the wilds. He must give up his
great plans; he was no longer a young gentleman in an
office, he would never be a Lensmand, not even live in a
town at all. To his father and those at home he made it appear that he was proud at having secured Storborg at the
very price he had fixed—it would show them he knew what
he was about. But that small triumph did not go very far.
He had also the satisfaction of taking over Andresen, the
chief clerk, who was thus, as it were, included in the bargain. Aronsen had no longer any use for him, until he had
a new place going. It was a pleasant sensation to be Eleseus, when Andresen came up begging to be allowed to
stay; here it was Eleseus who was master and head of the
business—for the first time in his life.

"You can stay, yes," he said. "I shall be wanting an assistant to look after the place when I'm away on business —opening up connections in Bergen and Trondhjem," said he.

And Andresen was no bad man to have, as it soon proved; he was a good worker, and looked after things well when Eleseus was away. 'Twas only at first he had been somewhat inclined to show and play the fine gentleman, and that was the fault of his master Aronsen. It was different now. In the spring, when the bogs were thawed some depth, Sivert came down from Sellanraa to Storborg, to start a bit of ditching for his brother, and lo, Andresen himself went out on the land digging too. Heaven knows what possessed him to do it, for 'twas no work of his, but that was the sort of man he was. It was not thawed deep enough yet, and they could not get as far as they wanted by a long way, but it was something done, at any rate. It was Isak's old idea to drain the bogs at Storborg and till the land there properly; the bit of a store was only to be an extra, a convenience, to save folk going all the way down to the village for a reel of thread.

So Sivert and Andresen stood there digging, and talking now and again when they stopped for a rest. Andresen had also somehow or other managed to get hold of a gold piece, a twenty-krone piece, and Sivert would gladly have had the bright thing himself; but Andresen would not part with it —kept it wrapped up in tissue paper in his chest. Sivert proposed a wrestling-match for the money—see who could throw the other; but Andresen would not risk it. Sivert offered to stake twenty kroner in notes against the gold piece, and do all the digging himself into the bargain if he won; but Andresen took offense at that. "Ho," said he, "and you'd like to go back home, no doubt, and say I'm no good at working on the land!" At last they agreed to set twenty-five kroner in notes against the gold twenty-krone piece, and Sivert slipped home to Sellanraa that night to ask his father for the money.

A young man's trick, the pretty play of youth! A night's sleep thrown away, to walk miles up and miles down again, and work next day as usual—'twas nothing to a young man in his strength, and a bright gold piece was worth it all. Andresen was a little inclined to make fun of him over the deal, but Sivert was not at a loss; he had only to let fall a word of Leopoldine. "There! I was nearly forgetting. Leopoldine she asked after you. . . ." And Andresen stopped his work of a sudden and went very red.

Pleasant days for them both, draining and ditching, getting up long arguments for fun, and working, and arguing again. Now and then Eleseus would come out and lend a hand, but he soon tired. Eleseus was not strong either of body or will, but a thorough good fellow for all that. . . .

"Here's that Oline coming along," Sivert the jester would say. "Now you'll have to go in and sell her a paper of coffee." And Eleseus was glad enough to go. Selling Oline some trifle or other meant so many minutes' rest from throwing heavy clods.

And Oline, poor creature, she might well be needing a pinch of coffee now and again, whether by chance she managed to get the money from Axel to pay for it, or bartered a goats'-milk cheese in exchange. Oline was not altogether what she had been; the work at Maaneland was too hard for her; she was an old woman now, and it was leaving its mark. Not that she ever confessed to any weakness or ageing herself; ho! she would have found plenty to say if she had been dismissed. Tough and irrepressible was Oline; did her work, and found time to wander over to neighbors here or there for a real good gossip. 'Twas her plain right, and there was little gossiping at Maaneland. Axel himself was not given that way.

As for that Barbro case, Oline was displeased, aye, disappointed was Oline. Both of them acquitted! That Brede's girl Barbro should be let off when Inger Sellanraa had got eight years was not to Oline's taste at all; she felt an un-Christian annoyance at such favoritism. But the Almighty would look to things, no doubt, in His own good time! And Oline nodded, as if prophesying divine retribution at a later date. Naturally, also, Oline made no secret of her dissatisfaction with the finding of the court, more especially when she happened to fall out with her master, Axel, over any little trifle. Then she would deliver herself, in the old soft-spoken way, of much deep and bitter sarcasm. "Aye, 'tis strange how the law's changed these days, for all the wickedness of Sodom and Gomorrah; but the word of the Lord's my guide, as ever was, and a blessed refuge for the meek."

Oh, Axel was sick and tired of his housekeeper now, and wished her anywhere. And now with spring coming again, and all the season's work to do alone; haymaking to come, and what was he to do? 'Twas a poor lookout. His brother's wife at Breidablik had written home to Helgeland trying to find a decent woman to help him, but nothing had come of it as yet. And in any case, it would mean his having to pay for the journey.

Nay, 'twas a mean and wicked trick of Barbro to make away with the bit of a child and then run off herself. A summer and two winters now he had been forced to make do with Oline, and no saying how much longer it might be yet. And Barbro, the creature, did she care? He had had a few words with her down in the village one day that winter, but never a tear had trickled slowly from her eyes to freeze on her cheek.

"What you've done with rings I gave you?" asks he.

"Rings?"

"Aye, the rings."

"I haven't got them now."

"Ho, so you haven't got them now?"

" 'Twas all over between us," said she. "And I couldn't wear them after that. 'Tis not the way to go on wearing rings when it's all over between you."

"Well, I'd just like to know what you've done with them, that's all."

"Wanted me to give them back, maybe," said she. "Well, I never thought you'd have had me put you to that shame."

Axel thought for a moment, and said: "I could have made it up to you other ways. That you shouldn't lose by it, I mean."

But no, Barbro had got rid of the rings, and never so much as gave him the chance of buying back a gold ring and a silver ring at a reasonable price.

For all that, Barbro was not so thoroughly harsh and un-lovable, that she was not. She had a long apron thing that fastened over the shoulders and with tucks at the edge, and a strip of white stuff up round her neck—aye, she looked well. There were some said she'd found a lad already down in the village to go sweethearting with, though maybe 'twas but their talk, after all. Fru Heyerdahl kept a watchful eye on her at any rate, and took care not to let her go to the Christmas dances.

Aye, Fru Heyerdahl was careful enough, that she was; here was Axel standing talking to his former servant-girl about a matter of two rings, and suddenly Fru Heyerdahl comes right between them and says: "Barbro, I thought you were going to the store?" Off goes Barbro. And her mistress turns to Axel and says: "Have you come down with some meat, or something?"

"H'm," said Axel, just that, and touched his cap.

Now it was Fru Heyerdahl that had praised him up so that last autumn, saying he was a splendid fellow and she had always thought well of him; and one good turn was worth another, no doubt. Axel knew the way of doing things; 'twas an old story, when simple folk had dealing with their betters, with authority. And he had thought at once of a piece of butcher's meat, a bull he had, that might be useful there. But time went on, and month and month passed by and autumn was gone, and the bull was never killed. And what harm could it do, after all, if he kept it for himself? Give it away, and he would be so much poorer. And 'twas a fine beast, anyway.

"H'm, *goddag*. Nay," said Axel, shaking his head; he'd no meat with him today.

But Fru Heyerdahl seemed to be guessing his thoughts, for she said: "I've heard you've an ox, or what?"

"Aye, so I have," said Axel.

"Are you going to keep it?"

"Aye, I'll be keeping him yet."

"I see. You've no sheep to be killed?"

"Not now I haven't. 'Tis this way, I've never had but what's to be kept on the place."

"Oh, I see," said Fru Heyerdahl; "well, that was all." And she went on her way.

Axel drove up homeward, but he could not help thinking somewhat of what had passed; he rather feared he had made a false step somehow. The Lensmand's lady had been an important witness once; for and against him, but important anyway. He had been through an unpleasant time on that occasion, but, after all, he had got out of it in the end—got out of a very awkward business in connection with the body of a child found buried on his land. Perhaps, after all, he had better kill that sheep.

And, strangely enough, this thought was somehow connected with Barbro. If he came down bringing sheep for her mistress it could hardly fail to make a certain impression on Barbro herself.

But again the days went on, and nothing evil happened

for their going on. Next time he drove down to the village
he had no sheep on his cart, no, still no sheep. But at the
last moment he had taken a lamb. A big lamb, though; not
a miserable little one by any means, and he delivered it
with these words:

" 'Tis rare tough meat on a wether, and no sort of a gift
to bring. But this is none so bad."

But Fru Heyerdahl would not hear of taking it as a gift.
"Say what you want for it," she said. Oh, a fine lady, 'twas
not her way to take gifts from folk! And the end of it was
that Axel got a good price for his lamb.

He saw nothing of Barbro at all. Lensmand's lady had
seen him coming, and got her out of the way. And good
luck go with her—Barbro that had cheated him out of his
help for a year and a half!

THAT spring something unexpected happened—something of importance indeed; work at the mine was started again; Geissler had sold his land. Inconceivable! Oh, but Geissler was an unfathomable mind; he could make a bargain or refuse, shake his head for a "No," or nod the same for "Yes." Could make the whole village smile again.

Conscience had pricked him, maybe; he had no longer the heart to see the district where he had been Lensmand famishing on home-made gruel and short of money. Or had he got his quarter of a million? Possibly, again, Geissler himself had at last begun to feel the need of money, and had been forced to sell for what he could get. Twenty-five or fifty thousand was not to be despised, after all. As a matter of fact, there were rumors that it was his eldest son who had settled the business on his father's account.

Be that as it might, work was recommenced; the same engineer came again with his gangs of men, and the work went on anew. The same work, aye, but in a different fashion now, going backwards, as it were.

All seemed in regular order: the Swedish mineowners had brought their men, and dynamite and money—what could be wrong, anyway? Even Aronsen came back again, Aronsen the trader, who had set his mind on buying back Storborg from Eleseus.

"No," said Eleseus. "It's not for sale."

"You'll sell, I suppose, if you're offered enough?"

"No."

No, Eleseus was not going to sell Storborg. The truth was, he had changed his mind somewhat as to the position; it was none so bad, after all, to be owner of a trading-station in the hills; he had a fine veranda with colored glass windows, and a chief clerk to do all the work, while he himself went about the country traveling. Aye, traveling first class, with fine folks. One day, perhaps, he might be able to go as far as America—he often thought of that. Even these little journeys on business to the towns down in the south were something to live on for a long time after. Not that he let himself go altogether, and chartered a steamer of his own and held wild orgies on the way—orgies were not in his line. A strange fellow, was Eleseus; he no longer cared about girls, had given up such things altogether, lost all interest in them. No, but after all, he was the Margrave's son, and traveled first class and bought up loads of goods. And each time he came back a little finer than before, a greater man; the last time, he even wore galoshes to keep his feet dry. "What's that—you taken to wearing two pairs of shoes?" they said.

"I've been suffering from chilblains lately," says Eleseus.

And everyone sympathized with Eleseus and his chilblains.

Glorious days—a grand life, with no end of leisure. No, he was not going to sell Storborg. What, go back to a little town and stand behind the counter in a little shop, and no chief clerk of his own at all? Moreover, he had made up his mind now to develop the business on a grand scale. The Swedes had come back again and would flood the place with money; he would be a fool to sell out now. Aronsen was forced to go back each time with a flat refusal, more and more disgusted at his own lack of foresight in ever having given up the place.

Oh, but Aronsen might have saved himself a deal of self-reproach, and likewise Eleseus with his plans and intentions, that he might have kept in moderation. And more than all, the village would have done well to be less confident, instead of going about smiling and rubbing its hands like angels sure of being blessed—no call for them to do so if they had but known. For now came disappointment, and no little one at that. Who would ever have thought it; work at the mine commenced again, true enough—but at the other end of the fjeld, eight miles away, on the southern boundary of Geissler's holding, far off in another district altogether, a district with which they were in no way concerned. And from there the work was to make its way gradually northward to the original mine, Isak's mine, to be a blessing to folk in the wilds and in the village. At best, it would take years, any number of years, a generation.

The news came like a dynamite charge of the heaviest sort, with shock and stopping of ears. The village folk were overcome with grief. Some blamed Geissler; 'twas Geissler, that devil of a man, who had tricked them once more. Others huddled together at a meeting and sent out a new deputation of trusty men, this time to the mining company, to the engineer. But nothing came of it; the engineer explained that he was obliged to start work from the south because that was nearest the sea, and saved the need of an aerial railway, reduced the transport almost to nil. No, the work must begin that way: no more to be said.

Then it was that Aronsen at once rose up and set out for the new workings, the new promised land. He even tried to get Andresen to go with him: "What's the sense of you staying on here in the wilds?" said he. "Much better come with me." But Andresen would not leave; incomprehensible, but so it was, there was something which held him to the spot; he seemed to thrive there, had taken root. It must be Andresen who had changed, for the place was the same as ever. Folk and things were unaltered; the mining work had turned away to other tracts, but folk in the wilds had not lost their heads over that; they had their land to till, their crops, their cattle. No great wealth in money, true, but in all the necessaries of life, aye, absolutely all. Even Eleseus was not reduced to misery because the stream of gold was flowing elsewhere; the worst of it was that in his first exaltation he had bought great stocks of goods that were now unsalable. Well, they could stay there for the time being; it looked well, at any rate, to have plenty of wares in a store.

No, a man of the wilds did not lose his head. The air was not less healthy now than before; there were folk enough to admire new clothes; there was no need of diamonds. Wine was a thing he knew from the feast at Cana. A man of the wild was not put out by the thought of great things he could not get; art, newspapers, luxuries, politics and such-like were worth just what folk were willing to pay for them, no more. Growth of the soil was something different, a thing to be procured at any cost; the only source, the origin of all. A dull and desolate existence? Nay, least of all. A man had everything; his powers above, his dreams, his loves, his wealth of superstition. Sivert, walking one evening by the river, stops on a sudden; there on the water are a pair of ducks, male and female. They have sighted him: they are aware of man, and afraid; one of them says something, utters a little sound, a melody in three tones, and the other answers with the same. Then they rise, whirl off like two little wheels a stone's-throw up the river, and settle again. Then, as before, one speaks and the other answers; the same speech as at first, but mark a new delight: *it is set two octaves higher!* Sivert stands looking at the birds, looking past them, far into a dream. A sound had floated through him, a sweetness, and left him standing there with a delicate, thin recollection of something wild and splendid, something he had known before, and forgotten again. He walks home in silence, says no word of it, makes no boast of it, 'twas not for worldly speech. And it was but Sivert from Sellanraa, went out one evening, young and ordinary as he was, and met with this.

It was not the only thing he met with—there were more adventures beside. Another thing which happened was that Jensine left Sellanraa. And that made Sivert not a little perturbed in his mind.

Aye, it came to that: Jensine would leave, if you please; she wished it so. Oh, Jensine was not one of your common sort, none could say that. Sivert had once offered to drive her back home at once, and on that occasion she had cried, which was a pity; but afterwards she repented of that, and made it clear that she repented, and gave notice and would leave. Aye, a proper way to do.

Nothing could have suited Inger at Sellanraa better than this; Inger was beginning to grow dissatisfied with her maid. Strange; she had nothing to say against her, but the sight of the girl annoyed her, she could hardly endure to have her about the place. It all arose, no doubt, from Inger's state of mind; she had been heavy and religious all that winter, and it would not pass off. "Want to leave, do you? Why, then, well and good," said Inger. It was a blessing, the fulfillment of nightly prayers. Two grown women they were already, what did they want with this Jensine, fresh as could be and marriageable and all? Inger thought with a certain displeasure of that same marriageableness, thinking, maybe, how she had once been the same herself.

Her deep religiousness did not pass off. She was not full of vice; she had tasted, sipped, let us say, but 'twas not her intent to persevere in that way all through her old age, not by any means; Inger turned aside with horror from the thought. The mine and all its workmen were no longer there—and Heaven be praised. Virtue was not only tolerable, but inevitable, it was a necessary thing; aye, a necessary good, a special grace.

But the world was all awry. Look now, here was Leopoldine, little Leopoldine, a seedling, a slip of a child, going about bursting with sinful health; but an arm round her waist and she would fall helpless—oh, fie! There were spots on her face now, too—a sign in itself of wild blood; aye, her mother remembered well enough, 'twas the wild blood would out. Inger did not condemn her child for a matter of spots on her face; but it must stop, she would have an end of it. And what did that fellow Andresen want coming up to Sellanraa of Sundays, to talk field work with Isak? Did the two menfolk imagine the child was blind? Aye, young folk were young folk as they had ever been, thirty, forty years ago, but worse than ever now.

"Why, that's as it may be," said Isak, when they spoke of the matter. "But here's the spring come, and Jensine gone, and who's to manage the summer work?"

"Leopoldine and I can do the haymaking," said Inger. "Aye, I'd rather go raking night and day myself," said she bitterly, and on the point of crying.

Isak could not understand what there was to make such a fuss about; but he had his own ideas, no doubt, and off he went to the edge of the wood, with crowbar and pick, and fell to working at a stone. Nay, indeed, Isak could not see why Jensine should have left them; a good girl, and a worker. To tell the truth, Isak was often at a loss in all save the simplest things—his work, his lawful and natural doings. A broad-shouldered man, well filled out, nothing astral about him at all; he ate like a man and throve on it, and 'twas rarely he was thrown off his balance in any way.

Well, here was this stone. There were stones more in plenty, but here was one to begin with. Isak is looking ahead, to the time when he will need to build a little house here, a little home for himself and Inger, and as well to get to work a bit on the site, and clear it, while Sivert is down at Storborg. Otherwise the boy would be asking questions, and that was not to Isak's mind. The day must come, of course, when Sivert would need all there was of the place for himself—the old folks would be wanting a house apart. Aye, there was never an end of building at Sellanraa; that fodder loft above the cowshed was not done yet, though the beams and planks for it were there all ready.

Well, then, here was this stone. Nothing so big to look at above ground, but not to be moved at a touch for all that; it must be a heavy fellow. Isak dug round about it, and tried his crowbar, but would not move. He dug again and tried once more, but no. Back to the house for a spade then, and clear the earth away, then digging again, trying again —no. A mighty heavy beast to shift, thought Isak patiently enough. He dug away now for a steady while, but the stone seemed reaching ever deeper and deeper down, there was no getting a purchase on it. A nuisance it would be if he had to blast it, after all. The boring would make such a noise, and call up everyone on the place. He dug. Off again to fetch a levering-pole and tried that—no. He dug again. Isak was beginning to be annoyed with this stone; he frowned, and looked at the thing, as if he had just come along to make a general inspection of the stones in that neighborhood, and found this one particularly stupid. He criticized it; aye, it was a round-faced, idiotic stone, no getting hold of it any way—he was almost inclined to say it was deformed. Blasting? The thing wasn't worth a charge of powder. And was he to give it up, was he to consider the possibility of being beaten by a stone?

He dug. Hard work, that it was, but as to giving up . . . At last he got the nose of his lever down and tried it; the stone did not move. Technically speaking, there was nothing wrong with his method, but it did not work. What was the matter, then? He had got out stones before in his life. Was he getting old? Funny thing, he he he! Ridiculous, indeed. True, he had noticed lately that he was not so strong as he had been—that is to say, he had noticed nothing of the sort, never heeded it; 'twas only imagination. And he goes at the stone once more, with the best will in the world.

Oh, 'twas no little matter when Isak bore down on a levering-pole with all his weight. There he is now, hoisting and hoisting again, a Cyclops, enormous, with a torso that seems built in one to the knees. A certain pomp and splendor about him; his equator was astounding.

But the stone did not move.

No help for it; he must dig again. Try blasting? Not a word! No, dig again. He was intent on his work now. The stone should come up! It would be wrong to say there was anything at all perverse in this on Isak's part; it was the ingrown love of a worker on the soil, but altogether without tenderness. It was a foolish sight; first gathering, as it were, about the stone from all sides, then making a dash at it, then digging all round its sides and fumbling at it, throwing up the earth with his bare hands, aye, so he did. Yet there was nothing of a caress in it all. Warmth, yes, but the warmth of zeal alone.

Try the lever again? He thrust it down where there was best hold—no. An altogether remarkable instance of obstinacy and defiance on the part of the stone. But it seemed to be giving. Isak tries again, with a touch of hope; the earth-breaker has a feeling now that the stone is no longer invincible. Then the lever slipped, throwing him to the ground. "Devil!" said he. Aye, he said that. His cap had got thrust down over one ear as he fell, making him look like a robber, like a Spaniard. He spat.

Here comes Inger. "Isak, come in and have your food now," says she, kindly and pleasant as can be.

"Aye," says he, but will have her no nearer, and wants no questions.

Oh, but Inger, never dreaming, she comes nearer.

"What's in your mind now?" she asks, to soften him with a hint of the way he thinks out some new grand thing almost every day.

But Isak is sullen, terribly sullen and stern; he says: "Nay, I don't know."

And Inger again, foolish that she is—ugh, keeps on talking and asking and will not go.

"Seeing as you've seen it yourself," says he at last, "I'm getting up this stone here."

"Ho, going to get him up?"

"Aye."

"And couldn't I help a bit at all?" she asks.

Isak shakes his head. But it was a kindly thought, anyway, that she would have helped him, and he can hardly be harsh in return.

"If you just wait the least bit of a while," says he, and runs home for the hammers.

If he could only get the stone rough a bit, knocking off a flake or so in the right spot, it would give the lever a better hold. Inger holds the setting-hammer, and Isak strikes. Strikes, strikes. Aye, sure enough, off goes a flake. " 'Twas a good help," says Isak, "and thanks. But don't trouble about food for me this bit of a while, I must get this stone up first."

But Inger does not go. And to tell the truth, Isak is pleased enough to have her there watching him at his work; 'tis a thing has always pleased him, since their young days. And lo, he gets a fine purchase now on the lever, and puts his weight into it—the stone moves! "He's moving," says Inger.

" 'Tis but your nonsense," says Isak.

"Nonsense, indeed! But it is!"

Got so far, then—and that was something. The stone was, so to speak, converted now, was on his side; they were working together. Isak hoists and heaves with his lever, and the stone moves, but no more. He keeps at it a while, nothing more. All at once he understands that it is not merely a question of weight, the dead pull of his body; no, the fact is that he has no longer his old strength, he has lost the tough agility that makes all the difference. Weight? An easy matter enough to hang on with his weight and break an iron-shod pole. No, he was weakening, that was it. And the patient man is filled with bitterness at the thought—at least he might have been spared the shame of having Inger here to see it!

Suddenly he drops the lever and grasps the sledge. A fury takes him, he is minded to go at it violently now. And see, his cap still hangs on one ear, robber-fashion, and now he steps mightily, threateningly, round the stone, trying, as it were, to set himself in the proper light; ho, he will leave that stone a ruin and a wreck of what it had been. Why not? When a man is filled with mortal hatred of a stone, it is a mere formality to crush it. And suppose the stone resists, suppose it declines to be crushed? Why, let it try— and see which of the two survives!

But then it is that Inger speaks up, a little timidly, again; seeing, no doubt, what is troubling him: "What if we both hang on the stick there?" And the thing she calls a stick is the lever, nothing else.

"No!" cries Isak furiously. But after a moment's thought he says: "Well, well, since you're here—though you might as well have gone home. Let's try."

And they get the stone up on edge. Aye, they manage that. And "Puh!" says Isak.

But now comes a revelation, a strange thing to see. The underside of the stone is flat, mightily broad, finely cut, smooth and even as a floor. The stone is but the half of a stone, the other half is somewhere close by, no doubt. Isak knows well enough that two halves of the same stone may lie in different places; the frost, no doubt, that in course of time had shifted them apart. But he is all wonder and delight at the find; 'tis a useful stone of the best, a door-slab. A round sum of money would not have filled this field-worker's mind with such content. "A fine door-slab," says he proudly.

And Inger, simple creature: "Why! Now how on earth could you tell that beforehand?"

"H'm," says Isak. "Think I'd go here digging about for nothing?"

They walk home together, Isak enjoying new admiration on false pretenses; 'twas something he had not deserved, but it tasted but little different from the real thing. He lets it be understood that he has been looking out for a suitable door-slab for a long time, and had found it at last. After that, of course, there could be nothing in the least suspicious about his working there again; he could root about as much as he pleased on pretext of looking for the other half. And when Sivert came home, he could get him to help.

But if it had come to this, that he could no longer go out alone and heave up a stone, why, things were sorely changed; aye, 'twas a bad lookout, and the more need to get that site cleared quick as might be. Age was upon him, he was ripening for the chimney-corner. The triumph he had stolen in the matter of the door-slab faded away in a few days; 'twas a false thing, and not made to last. Isak stooped a little now in his walk.

Had he not once been so much of a man that he grew wakeful and attentive in a moment if one but said a word of stone, a word of digging? And 'twas no long time since, but a few years, no more. Aye, and in those days, folk that were shy of a bit of draining-work kept out of his way. Now he was beginning, little by little, to take such matters more calmly; eyah, *Herregud!* All things were changed, the land itself was different now, with broad telegraph roads up through the woods, that had not been there before, and rocks blasted and sundered up by the water, as they had not been before. And folk, too, were changed. They did not greet coming and going as in the old days, but nodded only, or maybe not even that.

But then—in the old days there had been no Sellanraa, but only a turf hut, while now . . . There had been no Margrave in the old days.

Aye, but Margrave, what was he now? A pitiful thing, nothing superhuman, but old and fading, going the way of all flesh. What though he had good bowels, and could eat well, when it gave him no strength? 'Twas Sivert had the strength now, and a mercy it was so—but think, if Isak had had it too! A sorry thing, to find his works running down. He had toiled like a man, carrying loads enough for any beast of burden; now, he could exercise his patience in resting.

Isak is ill pleased, heavy at heart.

Here lies an old hat, an old sou'wester, rotting on the ground. Carried there by the gale, maybe, or maybe the lads had brought it there to the edge of the wood years ago, when they were little ones. It lies there year after year, rotting and rotting away; but once it had been a new sou'-wester, all yellow and new. Isak remembers the day he came home with it from the store, and Inger had said it was a fine hat. A year or so after, he had taken it to a painter down in the village, and had it blacked and polished, and the brim done in green. And when he came home, Inger thought it a finer hat than before. Inger always thought everything was fine; aye, 'twas a good life those days, cutting faggots, with Inger to look on—his best days. And

when March and April came, Inger and he would be wild
after each other, just like the birds and beasts in the woods;
and when May was come, he would sow his grain and
plant potatoes, living and thriving from day to dawn. Work
and sleep, loving and dreaming, he was like the first big
ox, and that was a wonder to see, big and bright as a king.
But there was no such May to the years now. No such
thing.

Isak was sorely despondent for some days. Dark days
they were. He felt neither wish nor strength to start work
on the fodder loft—that could be left for Sivert to do some
day. The thing to be done now was the house for himself
—the last house to build. He could not long hide from
Sivert what he was doing; he was clearing the ground, and
plain to see what for. And one day he told.

"There's a good bit of stone if we'd any use for stonework," said he. "And there's another."

Sivert showed no surprise, and only said: "Aye, first-
rate stones."

"What you might think," said his father. "We've been
digging round here now to find that other door-slab piece;
might almost do to build here. I don't know. . . ."

"Aye, 'tis no bad place to build," said Sivert, looking
round.

"Think so? 'Twas none so bad, maybe, to have a bit of
a place to house folk if any should come along."

"Aye."

"A couple of rooms'd be as well. You saw how 'twas
when the Swedish gentlemen came, and no proper place
to house them. But what you think: a bit of a kitchen as
well, maybe, if 'twas any cooking to be done?"

"Aye, 'twould be a shame to build with never a bit of
kitchen," says Sivert.

"You think so?"

Isak said no more. But Sivert, he was a fine lad to grasp

things, and get into his head all at once just what was needed in a place to put up Swedish gentlemen that chanced to come along; never so much as asked a single question, but only said: "Doing it my way, now, you'd put up a bit of a shed on the north wall. Folks coming along, 'd be useful to have a shed place to hang up wet clothes and things."

And his father agrees at once: "Aye, the very thing."

They work at their stones again in silence. Then asks Isak. "Eleseus, he's not come home, I suppose?"

And Sivert answers evasively: "He'll be coming home soon."

'Twas that way with Eleseus: he was all for staying away, living away on journeys. Couldn't he have written for the goods? But he must go round and buy them on the spot. Got them so much cheaper. Aye, maybe, but what about cost of the journey? He had his own way of thinking, it seemed. And then, what did he want, anyway, with more cotton stuff, and colored ribbons for christening-caps, and black and white straw hats, and long tobacco pipes? No one ever bought such things up in the hills; and the village folk, they only came up to Storborg when they'd no money. Eleseus was clever enough in his way—only to see him write on a paper, or do sums with a bit of chalk! "Aye, with a head like yours," said folk, admiring him. And that was true enough; but he was spending overmuch. The village folk never paid their owings, and yet even a fellow like Brede Olsen could come up to Storborg that winter and get cotton print and coffee and molasses and paraffin on credit.

Isak has laid out a deal of money already for Eleseus, and his store and his long journeyings about; there's not overmuch left now out of the riches from the mine—and what then?

"How d'you think he's getting on, Eleseus?" asks Isak suddenly.

"Getting on?" says Sivert, to gain time.

"Doesn't seem to be doing so well."

"H'm. He says it'll go all right."

"You spoken to him about it?"

"Nay; but Andresen he says so."

Isak thought over this, and shook his head. "Nay, I doubt it's going ill," says he. " 'Tis a pity for the lad."

And Isak gloomier than ever now, for all he'd been none too bright before.

But then Sivert flashes out a bit of news: "There's more folk coming to live now."

"How d'you say? "

"Two new holdings. They've bought up close by us."

Isak stands still with his crowbar in hand; this was news, and good news, the best that could be. "That makes ten of us here," says he. And Isak learns exactly where the new men have bought, he knows the country all round in his head, and nods. "Aye, they've done well there; wood for firing in plenty, and some big timber here and there. Ground slopes down sou'west. Aye . . ."

Settlers—nothing could beat them, anyway—here were new folk coming to live. The mine had come to nothing, but so much the better for the land. A desert, a dying place? Far from it, all about was swarming with life; two new men, four new hands to work, fields and meadows and homes. Oh, the little green tracts in a forest, a hut and water, children and cattle about. Corn waving on the moorlands where naught but horsetail grew before, bluebells nodding on the fells, and yellow sunlight blazing in the ladyslipper flowers outside a house. And human beings living there, move and talk and think and are there with heaven and earth.

Here stands the first of them all, the first man in the wilds. He came that way, kneedeep in marsh-growth and heather, found a sunny slope and settled there. Others came after him, they trod a path across the waste Almenning; others again, and the path became a road; carts drove there now. Isak may be content, may start with a little thrill of pride; he was the founder of a district, the pioneer.

"Look here, we can't go wasting time on this bit of a house place if we're to get that fodder loft done this year," says he.

With a new brightness, new spirit; as it were, new courage and life.

A WOMAN tramping up along the road. A steady summer rain falls, wetting her, but she does not heed it; other things are in her mind—anxiety. Barbro it is, and no other—Brede's girl, Barbro. Anxious, aye; not knowing how the venture will end; she has gone from service at the Lensmand's, and left the village. That is the matter.

She keeps away from all the farms on the road up, unwilling to meet with folk; easy to see where she was going, with a bundle of clothing on her back. Aye, going to Maaneland, to take service there again.

Ten months she has been at the Lensmand's now, and 'tis no little time, reckoned out in days and nights, but an eternity reckoned in longing and oppression. It had been bearable at first, Fru Heyerdahl looking after her kindly, giving her aprons and neat things to wear; 'twas a joy to be sent on errands to the store with such fine clothes to wear. Barbro had been in the village as a child; she knew all the village folk from the days when she had played there, gone to school there, kissed the lads there, and joined in many games with stones and shells. Bearable enough for a month or so. But then Fru Heyerdahl had begun to be even more careful about her, and when the Christmas festivities began, she was strict. And what good could ever come of that? It was bound to spoil things. Barbro could never have endured it but that she had certain hours of the night to herself; from two to six in the morning she was more or less safe, and had stolen pleasures not a few. What about Cook, then, for not reporting her? A nice sort of woman she must be! Oh, an ordinary woman enough, as the world finds them; Cook went out without leave herself. They took it in turns.

And it was quite a long time before they were found out. Barbro was by no means so depraved that it showed in her face, impossible to accuse her of immorality. Immorality? She made all the resistance one could expect. When young men asked her to go to a Christmas dance, she said "No" once, said "No" twice, but the third time she would say: "I'll try and come from two to six." Just as a decent woman should, not trying to make herself out worse than she is, and making a display of daring. She was a servant-girl, serving all her time, and knew no other recreation than fooling with men. It was all she asked for. Fru Heyerdahl came and lectured her, lent her books—and a fool for her pains. Barbro had lived in Bergen and read the papers and been to the theater! She was no innocent lamb from the countryside.

But Fru Heyerdahl must have grown suspicious at last. One day she comes up at three in the morning to the maids' room and calls: "Barbro!"

"Yes," answers Cook.

"It's Barbro I want. Isn't she there? Open the door."

Cook opens the door and explains as agreed upon, that Barbro had had to run home for a minute about something. Home for a minute at this time of night? Fru Heyerdahl has a good deal to say about that. And in the morning there is a scene. Brede is sent for, and Fru Heyerdahl asks: "Was Barbro at home with you last night—at three o'clock?"

Brede is unprepared, but answers: "Three o'clock? Yes, yes, quite right. We sat up late, there was something we had to talk about," says Brede.

The Lensmand's lady then solemnly declares that Barbro shall go out no more at nights.

"No, no," says Brede.

"Not as long as she's in this house."

"No, no; there, you can see, Barbro, I told you so," says her father.

"You can go and see your parents now and then during the day," says her mistress.

But Fru Heyerdahl was wide awake enough, and her suspicion was not gone; she waited a week, and tried at four in the morning. "Barbro!" she called. Oh, but this time 'twas Cook's turn out, and Barbro was at home; the maids' room was a nest of innocence. Her mistress had to hit on something in a hurry.

"Did you take in the washing last night?"

"Yes."

"That's a good thing, it's blowing so hard. . . . Good night."

But it was not so pleasant for Fru Heyerdahl to get her husband to wake her in the middle of the night and go padding across herself to the servants' room to see if they were at home. They could do as they pleased, she would trouble herself no more.

And if it had not been for sheer ill-luck, Barbro might have stayed the year out in her place that way. But a few days ago the trouble had come.

It was in the kitchen, early one morning. Barbro had been having some words with Cook, and no light words either; they raised their voices, forgetting all about their mistress. Cook was a mean thing and a cheat, she had sneaked off last night out of her turn because it was Sunday. And what excuse had she to give? Going to say good-bye to her favorite sister that was off to America? Not a bit of it; Cook had made no excuse at all. but simply said that Sunday night was one had been owing to her for a long time.

"Oh, you've not an atom of truth nor decency in your body!" said Barbro.

And there was the mistress in the doorway.

She had come out, perhaps, with no more thought than that the girls were making too much noise, but now she stood looking very closely at Barbro, at Barbro's apron over her breast; aye, leaning forward and looking very closely indeed. It was a painful moment. And suddenly Fru Heyerdahl screams and draws back to the door. What on earth can it be? thinks Barbro, and looks down at herself. *Herregud!* a flea, nothing more. Barbro cannot help smiling, and being not unused to acting under critical circumstances, she flicks off the flea at once.

"On the floor!" cried Fru Heyerdahl. "Are you mad, girl? Pick it up at once!" Barbro begins looking about for it, and once more acts with presence of mind: she makes as if she had caught the creature, and drops it realistically into the fire.

"Where did you get it?" asks her mistress angrily.

"Where I got it?"

"Yes, that's what I want to know."

But here Barbro makes a bad mistake. "At the store," she ought to have said, of course—that would have been quite enough. As it was—she did not know where she had got the creature, but had an idea it must have been from Cook.

Cook at the height of passion at once: "From me! You'll please to keep your fleas to yourself, so there!"

"Anyway, 'twas you was out last night."

Another mistake—she should have said nothing about it. Cook has no longer any reason for keeping silence, and now she let out the whole thing, and told all about the nights Barbro had been out. Fru Heyerdahl mightily indignant; she cares nothing about Cook, 'tis Barbro she is after, the girl whose character she has answered for. And even then all might have been well if Barbro had bowed her head like a reed, and been cast down with shame, and promised all manner of things for the future—but no. Her mistress is forced to remind her of all she has done for her, and at that, if you please, Barbro falls to answering back, aye, so foolish was she, saying impertinent things. Or perhaps she was cleverer than might seem; trying on purpose, maybe, to bring the matter to a head, and get out of the place altogether? Says her mistress:

"After I've saved you from the clutches of the Law."

"As for that," answers Barbro, "I'd have been just as pleased if you hadn't."

"And that's all the thanks I get," says her mistress.

"Least said the better, perhaps," says Barbro. "I wouldn't have got more than a month or two, anyway, and done with it."

Fru Heyerdahl is speechless for a moment; aye, for a little while she stands saying nothing, only opening and closing her mouth. The first thing she says is to tell the girl to go; she will have no more of her.

"Just as you please," says Barbro.

For some days after that Barbro had been at home with her parents. But she could not go on staying there. True, her mother sold coffee, and there came a deal of folk to the house, but Barbro could not live on that—and maybe she had other reasons of her own for wanting to get into a settled position again. And so today she had taken a sack of clothes on her back, and started up along the road over the moors. Question now, whether Axel Ström would take her? But she had had the banns put up, anyway, the Sunday before.

Raining, and dirty underfoot, but Barbro tramps on. Evening is drawing on, but not dark yet at that season of

the year. Poor Barbro—she does not spare herself, but goes
on her errand like another; she is bound for a place, to com-
mence another struggle there. She has never spared herself,
to tell the truth, never been of a lazy sort, and that is why
she has her neat figure now and pretty shape. Barbro is
quick to learn things, and often to her own undoing; what
else could one expect? She had learned to save herself at a
pinch, to slip from one scrape to another, but keeping all
along some better qualities; a child's death is nothing to
her, but she can still give sweets to a child alive. Then she
has a fine musical ear, can strum softly and correctly on
a guitar, singing hoarsely the while; pleasant and slightly
mournful to hear. Spared herself? No; so little, indeed, that
she has thrown herself away altogether, and felt no loss.
Now and again she cries, and breaks her heart over this or
that in her life—but that is only natural, it goes with the
songs she sings, 'tis the poetry and friendly sweetness in
her; she had fooled herself and many another with the
same. Had she been able to bring the guitar with her this
evening she could have strummed a little for Axel when
she came.

She manages so as to arrive late in the evening; all is
quiet at Maaneland when she reaches there. See, Axel has
already begun haymaking, the grass is cut near the house,
and some of the hay already in. And then she reckons out
that Oline, being old, will be sleeping in the little room,
and Axel lying out in the hayshed, just as she herself had
done. She goes to the door she knows so well, breathless as
a thief, and calls softly: "Axel!"

"What's that?" asks Axel all at once.

"Nay, 'tis only me," says Barbro, and steps in. "You
couldn't house me for the night?" she says.

Axel looks at her and is slow to think, and sits there in
his underclothes, looking at her: "So 'tis you," says he.
"And where'll you be going?"

"Why, depends first of all if you've need of help to the summer work," says she.

Axel thinks over that, and says: "Aren't you going to stay where you were, then?"

"Nay; I've finished at the Lensmand's."

"I might be needing help, true enough, for the summer," said Axel. "But what's it mean, anyway, you wanting to come back?"

"Nay, never mind me," says Barbro, putting it off. "I'll go on again tomorrow. Go to Sellanraa and cross the hills. I've a place there."

"You've fixed up with someone there?"

"Aye."

"I might be needing summer help myself," says Axel again.

Barbro is wet through; she has other clothes in her sack, and must change. "Don't mind about me," says Axel, and moves a bit toward the door, no more.

Barbro takes off her wet clothes, they talking the while, and Axel turning his head pretty often towards her. "Now you'd better go out just a bit," says she.

"Out?" says he. And indeed 'twas no weather to go out in. He stands there, seeing her more and more stripped; 'tis hard to keep his eyes away; and Barbro is so thoughtless, she might well have put on dry things bit by bit as she took off the wet, but no. Her shift is thin and clings to her; she unfastens a button at one shoulder, and turns aside, 'tis nothing new for her. Axel dead silent then, and he sees how she makes but a touch or two with her hands and washes the last of her clothes from her. 'Twas splendidly done, to his mind. And there she stands, so utterly thoughtless of her. . . .

A while after, they lay talking together. Aye, he had need of help for the summer, no doubt about that.

"They said something that way," says Barbro.

He had begun his mowing and haymaking all alone again; Barbro could judge for herself how awkward it was for him now. Aye, Barbro understood. On the other hand, it was Barbro herself that had run away and left him before, without a soul to help him, he can't forget that. And taken her rings with her into the bargain. And on top of all that, shameful as it was, the paper that kept on coming, that Bergen newspaper it seemed he would never get rid of; he had had to go on paying for it a whole year after.

" 'Twas shameful mean of them," says Barbro, taking his part all the time.

But seeing her all submissive and gentle, Axel himself could not be altogether heartless towards her; he agreed that Barbro might have some reason to be angry with him in return for the way he had taken the telegraph business from her father. "But as for that," said he, "your father can have the telegraph business again for me; I'll have no more of it, 'tis but a waste of time."

"Aye," says Barbro.

Axel thought for a while, then asked straight out: "Well, what about it now, would you want to come for the summer and no more?"

"Nay," says Barbro, "let it be as you please."

"You mean that, and truly?"

"Aye, just as you please, and I'll be pleased with the same. You've no call to doubt about me any more."

"H'm."

"No, 'tis true. And I've ordered about the banns."

H'm. This was not so bad. Axel lay thinking it over a long time. If she meant it in earnest this time, and not shameful deceit again, then he'd a woman of his own and help for as long as might be.

"I could get a woman to come from our parts," said he,

"and she's written saying she'd come. But then I'd have to pay her fare from America."

Says Barbro: "Ho, she's in America, then?"

"Aye. Went over last year she did, but doesn't care to stay."

"Never mind about her," says Barbro. "And what'd become of me then?" says she, and begins to be soft and mournful.

"No. That's why I've not fixed up all certain with her."

And after that, Barbro must have something to show in return; she confessed about how she could have taken a lad in Bergen, and he was a carter in a big brewery, a mighty big concern, and a good position. "And he'll be sorrowing for me now, I doubt," says Barbro, and makes a little sob. "But you know how 'tis, Axel; when there's two been so much together as you and I, 'tis more than I could ever forget. And you can forget me as much as you please."

"What! me?" says Axel. "Nay, no need to lie there crying for that, my girl, for I've never forgot you."

"Well . . ."

Barbro feels a deal better after that confession, and says: "Anyway, paying her fare all the way from America when there's no need . . ." She advises him to have nothing to do with that business; 'twould be over-costly, and there was no need. Barbro seemed resolved to build up his happiness herself.

They came to agreement all round in the course of the night. 'Twas not as if they were strangers; they had talked over everything before. Even the necessary marriage ceremony was to take place before St. Olaf's Day and harvest; they had no need to hide things, and Barbro was now herself most eager to get it done at once. Axel was not any put out at her eagerness, and it did not make him any way suspicious; far from it, he was flattered and encouraged to find her so. Aye, he was a worker in the fields, no doubt, a thick-skinned fellow, not used to looking over-fine at things, nothing delicate beyond measure; there were things he was obliged to do, and he looked to what was useful first of all. Moreover, here was Barbro all new and pretty again, and nice to him, almost sweeter than before. Like an apple she was, and he bit at it. The banns were already put up.

As to the dead child and the trial, neither said a word of that.

But they did speak of Oline, of how they were to get rid of her. "Aye, she must go," said Barbro. "We've nothing to thank her for, anyway. She's naught but tale-bearing and malice."

But it proved no easy matter to get Oline to go.

The very first morning, when Barbro appeared, Oline was clear, no doubt, as to her fate. She was troubled at once, but tried not to show it, and brought out a chair. They had managed up to then at Maaneland. Axel had carried water and wood and done the heaviest work, and Oline doing the rest. And gradually she had come to reckon on staying the rest of her life on the place. Now came Barbro and upset it all.

"If we'd only a grain of coffee in the house you should have it," said she to Barbro. "Going farther up, maybe?"

"No," said Barbro.

"Ho! Not going farther?"

"No."

"Why, 'tis no business of mine, no," says Oline. "Going down again, maybe?"

"No. Nor going down again. I'm staying here for now."

"Staying here, are you?"

"Aye, staying here, I doubt."

Oline waits for a moment, using her old head, full of

policy. "Aye, well," says she. " 'Twill save me, then, no doubt. And glad I'll be for the same."

"Oho," says Barbro in jest, "has Axel here been so hard on you this while?"

"Hard on me? Axel! Oh, there's no call to turn an old body's words, there's naught but living on and waiting for the blessed end. Axel that's been as a father and a messenger from the Highest to me day and hour together, and gospel truth the same. But seeing I've none of my own folks here, and living alone and rejected under a stranger's roof, with all my kin over across the hills . . ."

But for all that, Oline stayed on. They could not get rid of her till after they were wed, and Oline made a deal of reluctance, but said "Yes" at last, and would stay so long to please them, and look to house and cattle while they went down to the church. It took two days. But when they came back wedded and all, Oline stayed on as before. She put off going; one day she was feeling poorly, she said; the next it looked like rain. She made up to Barbro with smooth words about the food. Oh, there was a mighty difference in the food now at Maaneland; 'twas different living now, and a mighty difference in the coffee now. Oh, she stopped at nothing, that Oline; asked Barbro's advice on things she knew better herself. "What you think now, should I milk cows as they stand in their place and order, or should I take Cow Bordelin first?"

"You can do as you please."

"Aye, 'tis as I always said," exclaims Oline. "You've been out in the world and lived among great folks and fine folks, and learned all and everything. 'Tis different with the likes of me."

Aye, Oline stopped at nothing, she was intriguing all day long. Sitting there telling Barbro how she herself was friends and on the best of terms with Barbro's father, with Brede Olsen! Ho, many a pleasant hour they'd had together, and a kindly man and rich and grand to boot was Brede, and never a hard word in his mouth.

But this could not go on forever; neither Axel nor Barbro cared to have Oline there any longer, and Barbro had taken over all her work. Oline made no complaint, but she flashed dangerous glances at her young mistress and changed her tone ever so little.

"Aye, great folk, 'tis true. Axel, he was in town a while last harvest-time—you didn't meet him there, maybe? Nay, that's true, you were in Bergen that time. But he went into town, he did; 'twas all to buy a mowing-machine and a harrow-machine. And what's folk at Sellanraa now beside you here? Nothing to compare!"

She was beginning to shoot out little pinpricks, but even that did not help her now; neither of them feared her. Axel told her straight out one day that she must go.

"Go?" says Oline. "And how? Crawling, belike?" No, she would not go, saying by way of excuse that she was poorly, and could not move her legs. And to make things bad as could be, when once they had taken the work off her hands, and she had nothing to do at all, she collapsed, and was thoroughly ill. She kept about for a week in spite of it, Axel looking furiously at her; but she stayed on from sheer malice, and at last she had to take to her bed.

And now she lay there, not in the least awaiting her blessed end, but counting the hours till she should be up and about again. She asked for a doctor, a piece of extravagance unheard of in the wilds.

"Doctor?" said Axel. "Are you out of your senses?"

"How d'you mean, then?" said Oline quite gently, as to something she could not understand. Aye, so gentle and smooth-tongued was she, so glad to think she need not be a burden to others; she could pay for the doctor herself.

"Ho, can you?" said Axel.

"Why, and couldn't I, then?" says Oline. "And, anyway, you'd not have me lie here and die like a dumb beast in the face of the Lord?"

Here Barbro put in a word, and was unwise enough to say:

"Well, what you've got to complain of, I'd like to know, when I bring you in your meals and all myself? As for coffee, I've said you're better without it, and meaning well."

"Is that Barbro?" says Oline, turning just her eyes and no more to look for her; aye, she is poorly, is Oline, and a pitiful sight with her eyes screwed round cornerways. "Aye, maybe 'tis as you say, Barbro, if a tiny drop of coffee'd do me any harm, a spoonful and no more."

"If 'twas me in your stead, I'd be thinking of other things than coffee at this hour," says Barbro.

"Aye, 'tis as I say," answers Oline. " 'Twas never your way to wish and desire a fellow-creature's end, but rather they should be converted and live. What . . . aye, I'm lying here and seeing things. . . . Is it with child you are now, Barbro?"

"What's that you say?" cries Barbro furiously; and goes on again: "Oh, 'twould serve you right if I took and heaved you out on the muck-heap for your wicked tongue."

And at that the invalid was silent for one thoughtful moment, her mouth trembling as if trying so hard to smile, but dare not.

"I heard a someone calling last night," says she.

"She's out of her senses," says Axel, whispering.

"Nay, out of my senses that I'm not. Like someone calling it was. From the woods, or maybe from the stream up yonder. Strange to hear—as it might be a bit of a child crying out. Was that Barbro went out?"

"Aye," says Axel. "Sick of your nonsense, and no wonder."

"Nonsense, you call it, and out of my senses, and all?

Ah, but not so far as you'd like to think," says Oline. "Nay, 'tis not the Almighty's will and decree I should come before the Throne and before the Lamb as yet, with all I know of goings-on here at Maaneland. I'll be up and about again, never fear; but you'd better be fetching a doctor, Axel, 'tis quicker that way. What about that cow you were going to give me?"

"Cow? What cow?"

"That cow you promised me. Was it Bordelin, maybe?"

"You're talking wild," says Axel.

"You know how you promised me a cow the day I saved your life."

"Nay, that I never knew."

At that Oline lifts up her head and looks at him. Grey and bald she is, a head standing up on a long, scraggy neck —ugly as a witch, as an ogress out of a story. And Axel starts at the sight, and fumbles with a hand behind his back for the latch of the door.

"Ho," says Oline, "so you're that sort! Aye, well—say no more of it now. I can live without the cow from this day forth, and never a word I'll say nor breathe of it again. But well that you've shown what sort and manner of man you are this day; I know it now. Aye, and I'll know it another time."

But Oline, she died that night—sometime in the night; anyway, she was cold next morning when they came in.

Oline—an aged creature. Born and died. . . .

'Twas no sorrow to Axel nor Barbro to bury her, and be quit of her forever; there was less to be on their guard against now, they could be at rest. Barbro is having trouble with her teeth again; save for that, all is well. But that everlasting woolen muffler over her face, and shifting it aside every time there's a word to say—'twas plaguy and troublesome enough, and all this toothache is something of a mystery to Axel. He has noticed, certainly, that she chews her food in a careful sort of way, but there's not a tooth missing in her head.

"Didn't you get new teeth?" he asks.

"Aye, so I did."

"And are they aching, too?"

"Ah, you with your nonsense!" says Barbro irritably, for all that Axel has asked innocently enough. And in her bitterness she lets out what is the matter. "You can see how 'tis with me, surely?"

How 'twas with her? Axel looks closer, and fancies she is stouter than need be.

"Why, you can't be—'tis surely not another child again?" says he.

"Why, you know it is," says she.

Axel stares foolishly at her. Slow of thought as he is, he sits there counting for a bit: one week, two weeks, getting on the third week. . . .

"Nay, how I should know . . ." says he.

But Barbro is losing all patience with this debate, and bursts out, crying aloud, crying like a deeply injured creature: "Nay, you can take and bury me, too, in the ground, and then you'll be rid of me."

Strange, what odd things a woman can find to cry for!

Axel had never a thought of burying her in the ground; he is a thick-skinned fellow, looking mainly to what is useful; a pathway carpeted with flowers is beyond his needs.

"Then you'll not be fit to work in the fields this summer?" says he.

"Not work?" says Barbro, all terrified again. And then —strange what odd things a woman can find to smile for! Axel, taking it that way, sent a flow of hysterical joy through Barbro, and she burst out: "I'll work for two! Oh, you wait and see, Axel; I'll do all you set me to, and more beyond. Wear myself to the bone, I will, and be thankful, if only you'll put up with me so!"

More tears and smiles and tenderness after that. Only the two of them in the wilds, none to disturb them; open doors and a humming of flies in the summer heat. All so tender and willing was Barbro; aye, he might do as he pleased with her, and she was willing.

After sunset he stands harnessing up to the mowing-machine; there's a bit he can still get done ready for tomorrow. Barbro comes hurrying out, as if she's something important, and says:

"Axel, how ever could you think of getting one home from America? She couldn't get here before winter, and what use of her then?" And that was something had just come into her head, and she must come running out with it as if 'twas something needful.

But 'twas no way needful; Axel had seen from the first that taking Barbro would mean getting help for all the year. No swaying and swinging with Axel, no thinking with his head among the stars. Now he's a woman of his own to look after the place, he can keep on the telegraph business for a bit. 'Tis a deal of money in the year, and good to reckon with as long as he's barely enough for his needs from the land, and little to sell. All sound and working well; all good reality. And little to fear from Brede about the telegraph line, seeing he's son-in-law to Brede now.

Aye, things are looking well, looking grand with Axel now.

CHAPTER XI

AND time goes on; winter is passed; spring comes again.

Isak has to go down to the village one day—and why not? What for? "Nay, I don't know," says he. But he gets the cart cleaned up all fine, puts in the seat, and drives off, and a deal of victuals and such put in, too—and why not? 'Twas for Eleseus at Storborg. Never a horse went out from Sellanraa but there was something taken down to Eleseus.

When Isak came driving down over the moors, 'twas no little event, for he came but rarely, Sivert going most ways in his stead. At the two farms nearest down, folk stand at the door of the huts and tell one another: " 'Tis Isak himself; and what'll he be going down after today?" And, coming down as far as to Maaneland, there's Barbro at the glass window with a child in her arms, and sees him, and says: " 'Tis Isak himself!"

He comes to Storborg and pulls up. "*Ptro!* Is Eleseus at home?"

Eleseus comes out. Aye, he's at home; not gone yet, but just going—off on his spring tour of the towns down south.

"Here's some things your mother sent down," says his father. "Don't know what it is, but nothing much, I doubt."

Eleseus takes the things, and thanks him, and asks:

"There wasn't a letter, I suppose, or anything that sort?"

"Aye," says his father, feeling in pockets, "there was. 'Tis from little Rebecca I think they said."

Eleseus takes the letter, 'tis that he has been waiting for. Feels it all nice and thick, and says to his father:

"Well, 'twas lucky you came in time—though 'tis two days before I'm off yet. If you'd like to stay a bit, you might take my trunk down."

Isak gets down and ties up his horse, and goes for a stroll over the ground. Little Andresen is no bad worker on the land in Eleseus's service; true, he has had Sivert from Sellanraa with horses, but he has done a deal of work on his own account, draining bogs, and hiring a man himself to set the ditches with stone. No need of buying fodder at Storborg that year, and next, like as not, Eleseus would be keeping a horse of his own. Thanks to Andresen and the way he worked on the land.

After a bit of a while, Eleseus calls down that he's ready with his trunk. Ready to go himself, too, by the look of it; in a fine blue suit, white collar, galoshes, and a walking-stick. True, he will have two days to wait for the boat, but no matter; he may just as well stay down in the village; 'tis all the same if he's here or there.

And father and son drive off. Andresen watches them from the door of the shop and wishes a pleasant journey.

Isak is all thought for his boy, and would give him the seat to himself; but Eleseus will have none of that, and sits up by his side. They come to Breidablik, and suddenly Eleseus has forgotten something. "*Ptro!* What is it?" asks his father.

Oh, his umbrella! Eleseus has forgotten his umbrella; but he can't explain all about it, and only says: "Never mind, drive on."

"Don't you want to turn back?"

"No; drive on."

But a nuisance it was; how on earth had he come to leave it? 'Twas all in a hurry, through his father being there waiting. Well, now he had better buy a new umbrella at Trondhjem when he got there. 'Twas no importance either way if he had one umbrella or two. But for all that, Eleseus is out of humor with himself; so much so that he jumps down and walks behind.

They could hardly talk much on the way down after that, seeing Isak had to turn round every time and speak over his shoulder. Says Isak: "How long you're going to be away?"

And Eleseus answers: "Oh, say three weeks, perhaps, or a month at the outside."

His father marvels how folk don't get lost in the big towns, and never find their way back. But Eleseus answers, as to that, he's used to living in towns, and never got lost, never had done in his life.

Isak thinks it a shame to be sitting up there all alone, and calls out: "Here, you come and drive a bit; I'm getting tired."

Eleseus won't hear of his father getting down, and gets up beside him again. But first they must have something to eat—out of Isak's well-filled pack. Then they drive on again.

They come to the two holdings farthest down; easy to see they are nearing the village now; both the houses have white curtains in the little window facing toward the road, and a flagpole stuck up on top of the hayloft for Constitution Day. " 'Tis Isak himself," said folk on the two new farms as the cart went by.

At last Eleseus gives over thinking of his own affairs and his own precious self enough to ask: "What you driving down for today?"

"H'm," says his father. " 'Twas nothing much today." But then, after all, Eleseus was going away; no harm, perhaps, in telling him. " 'Tis blacksmith's girl, Jensine, I'm going down for," says his father; aye, he admits so much.

"And you're going down yourself for that? Couldn't Sivert have gone?" says Eleseus. Aye, Eleseus knew no better, nothing better than to think Sivert would go down to the smith's to fetch Jensine, after she had thought so much of herself as to leave Sellanraa!

No, 'twas all awry with the haymaking the year before. Inger had put in all she could, as she had promised. Leopoldine did her share too, not to speak of having a machine for a horse to rake. But the hay was much of it heavy stuff, and the fields were big. Sellanraa was a sizable place now, and the women had other things to look to besides making hay; all the cattle to look to, and meals to be got, and all in proper time; butter and cheese to make, and clothes to wash, and baking of bread; mother and daughter working all they could. Isak was not going to have another summer like that; he decided without any fuss that Jensine should come back again if she could be got. Inger, too, had no longer a word against it; she had come to her senses again, and said: "Aye, do as you think best." Aye, Inger was grown reasonable now; 'tis no little thing to come to one's senses again after a spell. Inger was no longer full of heat that must out, no longer full of wild blood to be kept in check, the winter had cooled her; nothing beyond the needful warmth in her now. She was getting stouter, growing fine and stately. A wonderful woman to keep from fading, keep from dying off by degrees; like enough because she had bloomed so late in life. Who can say how things come about? Nothing comes from a single cause, but from many. Was Inger not in the best repute with the smith's wife? What could any smith's wife say against her? With her disfigurement, she had been cheated of her spring, and later, had been set in artificial air to lose six years of her summer; with life still in her, what wonder her autumn gave an errant growth? Inger was better than blacksmiths' wives—a little damaged, a little warped, but good by nature, clever by nature . . . aye. . . .

Father and son drive down, they come to Brede Olsen's lodging-house and set the horse in a shed. It is evening now. They go in themselves.

Brede Olsen has rented the house; an outbuilding it had been, belonging to the storekeeper, but done up now with two sitting-rooms and two bedrooms; none so bad, and in a good situation. The place is well frequented by coffee-drinkers and folk from roundabout the village going by the boat.

Brede seems to have been in luck for once, found something suited to him, and he may thank his wife for that. 'Twas Brede's wife had hit on the idea of a coffee-shop and lodging-house, the day she sat selling coffee at the auction at Breidablik; 'twas a pleasant enough thing to be selling something, to feel money in her fingers, ready cash. Since they had come down here they had managed nicely, selling coffee in earnest now, and housing a deal of folk with nowhere else to lay their heads. A blessing to travelers, is Brede's wife. She has a good helper, of course, in Katrine, her daughter, a big girl now and clever at waiting—though that is only for the time, of course; not long before little Katrine must have something better than waiting on folk in her parents' house. But for the present, they are making money fairly well, and that is the main thing. The start had been decidedly favorable, and might have been better if the storekeeper had not run short of cakes and sweet biscuits to serve with the coffee; here were all the feast-day folk calling for cakes with their coffee, biscuits and cakes! 'Twas a lesson to the storekeeper to lay in a good supply another time.

The family, and Brede himself, live as best they can on their takings. A good many meals are nothing but coffee and stale cakes left over, but it keeps them alive, and gives the children a delicate, sort of refined appearance. 'Tis not everyone has cakes with their coffee, say the village folk. Aye, Bredes are doing well, it seems; they even manage to keep a dog, that goes round begging among the customers and gets bits here and there and grows fat on it. A good fat dog about the place is a mighty fine advertisement for a lodging-house; it speaks for good feeding anywhere.

Brede, then, is husband and father in the house, and apart from that position, has got on variously beside. He had been once more installed as Lensmand's assistant and deputy, and had a good deal to do that way for a time. Unfortunately, his daughter Barbro had fallen out with the Lensmand's wife last autumn, about a trifling matter, a mere nothing—indeed, to tell the truth, a flea; and Brede himself is somewhat in disfavor there since. But Brede counts it no great loss, after all; there are other families that find work for him now on purpose to annoy the Lensmands; he is frequently called upon, for instance, to drive for the doctor, and as for the parsonage, they'd gladly send for Brede every time there's a pig to be killed, and more— Brede says so himself.

But for all that there are hard times now and again in Brede's house; 'tis not all the family are as fat and flourishing as the dog. Still, Heaven be praised, Brede is not a man to take things much to heart. "Here's the children growing up day by day," says he, though, for that matter, there's always new little ones coming to take their place. The ones that are grown up and out in the world can keep themselves, and send home a bit now and again. There's Barbro married at Maaneland, and Helge out at the herring fishery; they send home something in money or money's worth as often as they can; aye, even Katrine, doing waiting at home, managed, strangely enough, to slip a five-krone note into her father's hand last winter, when things were looking extra bad. "There's a girl for you," said Brede, and never asked her where she'd got the money, or what for. Aye, that was the way! Children with a heart to think of their parents and help them in time of need!

Brede is not altogether pleased with his boy Helge in that respect; he can be heard at times standing in the store with a little group about him, developing his theories as to children and their duty toward their parents. "Look you, now, my boy, Helge; if he smokes tobacco a bit, or takes a dram now and then, I've nothing against that, we've all been young in our time. But 'tis not right of him to go sending one letter home after another and nothing but words and wishes in. 'Tis not right to set his mother crying. 'Tis the wrong road for a lad. In days gone by, things were different. Children were no sooner grown than they went into service and started sending home a little to help. And quite right, too. Isn't it their father and mother had borne them under their breast first of all, and sweating blood to keep the life in them all their tender years? And then to forget it all!"

It almost seemed as if Helge had heard that speech of his father's, for there came a letter from him after with money in—fifty kroner, no less. And then Bredes had a great time; aye, in their endless extravagance they bought both meat and fish for dinner, and a lamp all hung about with lusters to hang from the ceiling in the best room.

They managed somehow, and what more could they ask? Bredes, they kept alive, lived from hand to mouth, but without great fear. What more could they wish for?

"Here's visitors indeed!" says Brede, showing Isak and Eleseus into the room with the new lamp. "And I'd never thought to see. Isak, you're never going away yourself, and all?"

"Nay, only to the smith's for something, 'tis no more."

"Ho! 'Tis Eleseus, then, going off south again?"

Eleseus is used to hotels; he makes himself at home, hangs up his coat and stick on the wall, and calls for coffee; as for something to eat, his father has things in a basket. Katrine brings the coffee.

"Pay? I'll not hear of it," says Brede. "I've had many a bite and sup at Sellanraa; and as for Eleseus, I'm in his books already. Don't take it, Katrine." But Eleseus pays all the same, takes out his purse and pays out the money, and twenty öre over; no nonsense about him.

Isak goes across to the smith's, and Eleseus stays where he is.

He says a few words, as in duty bound, to Katrine, but no more than is needed; he would rather talk to her father. No, Eleseus cares nothing for women; has been frightened off by them once, as it were, and takes no interest in them now. Like as not he'd never much inclination that way to speak of, seeing he's so completely out of it all now. A strange man to live in the wilds; a gentleman with thin writer's hands, and the sense of a woman for finery; for sticks and umbrellas and galoshes. Frightened off, and changed, incomprehensibly not a marrying man. Even his upper lip declines to put forth any brutal degree of growth. Yet it might be the lad had started well enough, come of good stock, but been turned thereafter into an artificial atmosphere, and warped, transformed? Had he worked so hard in an office, in a shop, that his whole originality was lost thereby? Aye maybe 'twas so. Anyway, here he is now, easy and passionless, a little weak, a little heedless, wandering farther and farther off the road. He might envy every soul among his fellows in the wilds, but has not even strength for that.

Katrine is used to jesting with her customers, and asks

him teasingly if he is off to see his sweetheart in the south again.

"I've other things to think of," says Eleseus. "I'm out on business—opening up connections."

"No call to be so free with your betters, Katrine," says her father reprovingly. Oh, Brede Olsen is all respect towards Eleseus, mighty respectful for him to be. And well he may, 'tis but wise of him, seeing he owes money up at Storborg, and here's his creditor before him. And Eleseus? Ho, all this deference pleases him, and he is kind and gracious in return; calls Brede "My dear sir," in jest, and goes on that way. He mentions that he has forgotten his umbrella: "Just as we were passing Breidablik, I thought of it; left my umbrella behind."

Brede asks: "You'll be going over to our little store this evening, belike, for a drink?"

Says Eleseus: "Aye, maybe, if 'twas only myself. But I've my father here."

Brede makes himself pleasant, and goes on gossiping: "There's a fellow coming in day after tomorrow that's on his way to America."

"Been home, d'you mean?"

"Aye. He's from up in the village a bit. Been away for ever so many years, and home for the winter. His trunk's come down already by cart—and a mighty fine trunk."

"I've thought of going to America myself once or twice," says Eleseus frankly.

"You?" cries Brede. "Why, there's little need for the likes of you going that way surely!"

"Well, 'twas not going over to stay forever I was thinking. But I've been traveling about so many places now, I might just as well make the trip over there."

"Aye, of course, and why not? And a heap of money and means and all, so they say, in America. Here's this fellow I spoke of before; he's paid for more feasting and parties than's easy to count this winter past, and comes in here and says to me: 'Let's have some coffee, a potful, and all the cakes you've got.' Like to see his trunk?"

They went out in the passage to look at the trunk. A wonder to look at on earth, flaming all sides and corners with metal and clasps and binding, and three flaps to hold it down, not to speak of a lock. "Burglar-proof," says Brede, as if he had tried it himself.

They went back into the room, but Eleseus was grown thoughtful. This American from up in the village had out-done him; he was nothing beside such a man. Going out on journeys like any high official; aye, natural enough that Brede should make a fuss of him. Eleseus ordered more coffee, and tried to play the rich man too; ordered cakes with his coffee and gave them to the dog—and all the time feeling worthless and dejected. What was his trunk beside that wonder out there? There it stood, black canvas with the corners all rubbed and worn; a handbag, nothing more —ho, but wait! He would buy a trunk when he got to the towns, a splendid one it should be, only wait!

" 'Tis a pity to feed the dog so," says Brede.

And Eleseus feels better at that, and ready to show off again. " 'Tis a marvel how a beast can get so fat," says he.

One thought leading to another: Eleseus breaks off his talk with Brede and goes out into the shed to look at the horse. And there he takes out a letter from his pocket and opens it. He had put it away at once, never troubling to look what money was in it; he had had letters of that sort from home before, and always a deal of notes inside— something to help him on the way. What was this? A big sheet of grey paper scrawled all over; little Rebecca to her brother Eleseus, and a few words from his mother. What else? Nothing else. No money at all.

His mother wrote that she could not ask his father for

more money again now, for there was none too much left of all they had got for the copper mine that time; the money had gone to buy Storborg, and pay for all the goods after, and Eleseus's traveling about. He must try and manage by himself this time, for the money that was left would have to be kept for his brother and sisters, not to leave them all without. And a pleasant journey and your loving mother.

No money.

Eleseus himself had not enough for his fare; he had cleaned out the cash box at Storborg, and that was not much. Oh, but he had been a fool to send that money to the dealers in Bergen on account; no hurry for that; he might have let it stand over. He ought, of course, to have opened the letter before starting out at all; he might have saved himself that journey down to the village with his miserable trunk and all. And here he was. . . .

His father comes back from the smith's after settling his business there; Jensine was to go back with him next morning. And Jensine, look you, had been nowise contrary and hard to persuade, but saw at once they wanted help at Sellanraa for the summer, and was ready to come. A proper way to do, again.

While his father is talking, Eleseus sits thinking of his own affairs. He shows him the American's trunk, and says: "Only wish I was where that's come from."

And his father answers: "Aye, 'twas none so bad, maybe."

Next morning Isak gets ready to start for home again; has his food, puts in the horse and drives round by the smith's to fetch Jensine and her box. Eleseus stands looking after them as they go; then when they are lost to sight in the woods, he pays his score at the lodging-house again, and something over. "You can leave my trunk here till I come back," he tells Katrine, and off he goes.

Eleseus—going where? Only one place to go; he turns

back, going back home again. So he too takes the road up
over the hills again, taking care to keep as near his father
and Jensine as he can without being seen. Walks on and
on. Beginning now to envy every soul of them in the wilds.

'Tis a pity about Eleseus, so changed he is and all.

Is he doing no business at Storborg? Such as it is; nothing to make a fortune out of there, and Eleseus is overmuch out and abroad, making pleasant journeys on business to open up connections, and it costs too much; he
does not travel cheaply. "Doesn't do to be mean," says
Eleseus, and gives twenty öre over where he might save
ten. The business cannot support a man of his tastes, he
must get subsidies from home. There's the farm at Storborg, with potatoes and corn and hay enough for the place
itself, but all provisions else must come from Sellanraa. Is
that all? Sivert must cart up his brother's goods from the
steamer all for nothing. And is that all? His mother must
get money out of his father to pay for his journeys. But is
that all?

The worst is to come.

Eleseus manages his business like a fool. It flatters him
to have folk coming up from the village to buy at Storborg,
so that he gives them credit as soon as asked; and when
this is noised abroad, there come still more of them to
buy the same way. The whole thing is going to rack and
ruin. Eleseus is an easy man, and lets it go; the store is
emptied and the store is filled again. All costs money. And
who pays it? His father.

At first, his mother had been a faithful spokesman for
him every way. Eleseus was the clever head of the family;
they must help him on and give him a start; then think
how cheaply he had got Storborg, and saying straight out
what he would give for it! When his father thought it was
going wrong somehow with the business, and naught but
foolery, she took him up. "How can you stand there and

say such things!" Aye, she reproved him for using such words about his son; Isak was forgetting his place, it seemed, to speak so of Eleseus.

For look you, his mother had been out in the world herself; she understood how hard it was for Eleseus to live in the wilds, being used to better things, and accustomed to move in society, and with none of his equals near. He risked too much in his dealings with folk that were none of the soundest; but even so, 'twas not done with any evil intent on his part of ruining his parents, but sheer goodness of heart and noble nature; 'twas his way to help those that were not so fine and grand as himself. Why, wasn't he the only man in those parts to use white handkerchiefs that were always having to be washed? When folk came trustingly to him and asked for credit, if he were to say "No," they might take it amiss, it might seem as if he were not the noble fellow they had thought, after all. Also, he had a certain duty towards his fellows, as the town-bred man, the genius among them all.

Aye, his mother bore all these things in mind.

But his father, never understanding it all in the least, opened her eyes and ears one day and said: "Look you here. Here's all that is left of the money from that mine."

"That's all?" said she. "And what's come of the rest?"

"Eleseus, he's had the rest."

And she clasped her hands at that and declared it was time Eleseus began to use his wits.

Poor Eleseus, all set on end and frittered away. Better, maybe, if he'd worked on the land all the time, but now he's a man that has learned to write and use letters; no grip in him, no depth. For all that, no pitch-black devil of a man, not in love, not ambitious, hardly nothing at all is Eleseus, not even a bad thing of any great dimensions.

Something unfortunate, ill-fated about this young man, as if something were rotting him from within. That engi-

neer from the town, good man—better perhaps, if he had
not discovered the lad in his youth and taken him up to
make something out of him; the child had lost his roothold,
and suffered thereby. All that he turns to now leads back
to something wanting in him, something dark against the
light. . . .

Eleseus goes on and on. The two in the cart ahead pass
by Storborg. Eleseus goes a long way round, and he too
passes by; what was he to do there, at home, at his trading-
station and store? The two in the cart get to Sellanraa at
nightfall; Eleseus is close at their heels. Sees Sivert come
out in the yard, all surprised to see Jensine, and the two
shake hands and laugh a little; then Sivert takes the horse
out and leads it to stable.

Eleseus ventures forward; the pride of the family, he
ventures up a little. Not walking up, but stealing up; he
comes on Sivert in the stable. " 'Tis only me," he says.

"What—you too?" says Sivert, all astonished again.

The two brothers begin talking quietly; about Sivert getting his mother to find some money; a last resource, the
money for a journey. Things can't go on this way; Eleseus
is weary of it; has been thinking of it a long time now, and
he must go tonight; a long journey, to America, and start
tonight.

"America?" says Sivert out loud.

"Sh! I've been thinking of it a long time, and you must
get her to do as I say; it can't go on like this, and I've been
thinking of going for ever so long."

"But America!" says Sivert. "No, don't you do it."

"I'm going. I've settled that. Going back now to catch
the boat."

"But you must have something to eat."

"I'm not hungry."

"But rest a bit, then?"

"No."

Sivert is trying to act for the best, and hold his brother back, but Eleseus is determined, aye, for once he is determined. Sivert himself is all taken aback; first of all it was a surprise to see Jensine again, and now here's Eleseus going to leave the place altogether, not to say the world. "What about Storborg?" says he. "What'll you do with it?"

"Andresen can have it," says Sivert.

"Andresen have it? How d'you mean?"

"Isn't he going to have Leopoldine?"

"Don't know about that. Aye, perhaps he is."

They talk quietly, keep on talking. Sivert thinks it would be best if his father came out and Eleseus could talk to him himself; but "No, no!" whispers Eleseus again; he was never much of a man to face a thing like that, but always must have a go-between.

Says Sivert: "Well, Mother, you know how 'tis with her. There'll be no getting any way with her for crying and talking on. She mustn't know."

"No," Eleseus agrees, "she mustn't know."

Sivert goes off, stays away for ages, and comes back with money, a heap of money. "Here, that's all he has; think it'll be enough? Count—he didn't count how much there was."

"What did he say—Father?"

"Nay, he didn't say much. Now you must wait a little, and I'll get some more clothes on and go down with you."

" 'Tis not worth while; you go and lie down."

"Ho, are you frightened of the dark that I mustn't go away?" says Sivert, trying a moment to be cheerful.

He is away a moment, and comes back dressed, and with his father's food basket over his shoulder. As they go out, there is their father standing outside. "So you're going all that way, seems?" says Isak.

"Aye," answered Eleseus; "but I'll be coming back again."

"I'll not be keeping you now—there's little time," mumbles the old man, and turns away. "Good luck," he croaks out in a strange voice, and goes off all hurriedly.

The two brothers walk down the road; a little way gone, they sit down to eat; Eleseus is hungry, can hardly eat enough. 'Tis a fine spring night, and the black grouse at play on the hilltops; the homely sound makes the emigrant lose courage for a moment. " 'Tis a fine night," says he. "You better turn back now, Sivert," says he.

"H'm," says Sivert, and goes on with him.

They pass by Storborg, by Breidablik, and the sound follows them all the way from the hills here and there; 'tis no military music like in the towns, nay, but voices—a proclamation: Spring has come. Then suddenly the first chirp of a bird is heard from a treetop, waking others, and a calling and answering on every side; more than a song, it is a hymn of praise. The emigrant feels homesick already, maybe, something weak and helpless in him; he is going off to America, and none could be more fitted to go than he.

"You turn back now, Sivert," says he.

"Aye, well," says his brother. "If you'd rather."

They sit down at the edge of the wood, and see the village just below them, the store and the quay, Brede's old lodging-house; some men are moving about by the steamer, getting ready.

"Well, no time to stay sitting here," says Eleseus, getting up again.

"Fancy you going all that way," says Sivert.

And Eleseus answers: "But I'll be coming back again. And I'll have a better sort of trunk that journey."

As they say good-bye, Sivert thrusts something into his brother's hand, a bit of something wrapped in paper. "What is it?" asks Eleseus.

"Don't forget to write often," says Sivert. And so he goes.

Eleseus opens the paper and looks; 'tis the gold piece, twenty-five kroner in gold. "Here, don't!" he calls out. "You mustn't do that!"

Sivert walks on.

Walks on a little, then turns round and sits down again at the edge of the wood. More folk astir now down by the steamer; passengers going on board, Eleseus going on board; the boat pushes off from the side and rows away. And Eleseus is gone to America.

He never came back.

A NOTABLE procession coming up to Sellanraa; something laughable to look at, maybe, but more than that. Three men with enormous burdens, with sacks hanging down from their shoulders, front and back. Walking one behind the other, and calling to one another with jesting words, but heavily laden. Little Andresen, chief clerk, is head of that procession; indeed, 'tis his procession; he has fitted out himself, and Sivert from Sellanraa, and one other Fredrik Ström from Breidablik, for the expedition. A notable little man is Andresen; his shoulder is weighed down slantwise on one side, and his jacket pulled all awry at the neck, the way he goes, but he carries his burden on and on.

Storborg and the business Eleseus had left—well, not bought it straight out on the spot, perhaps, 'tis more than Andresen could afford; better afford to wait a bit and get the whole maybe for nothing. Andresen is no fool; he has taken over the place on lease for the meanwhile, and manages the business himself.

Gone through the stock in hand, and found a deal of unsalable truck in Eleseus's store, even to such things as toothbrushes and embroidered table centers; aye, and stuffed birds on springs that squeaked when you pressed in the right place.

These are the things he has started out with now, going

to sell them to the miners on the other side of the hills. He knows from Aronsen's time that miners with money in their pockets will buy anything on earth. Only a pity he had to leave behind six rocking-horses that Eleseus had ordered on his last trip to Bergen.

The caravan turns into the yard at Sellanraa and sets down its load. No long wait here; they drink a mug of milk, and make pretense of trying to sell their wares on the spot, then shoulder their burdens and off again. They are not out for pretense. Off they go, trundling southward through the forest.

They march till noon, rest for a meal and on again till evening. Then they camp and make a fire, lie down, and sleep a while. Sivert sleeps resting on a boulder that he calls an armchair. Oh, Sivert knows what he is about; here's the sun been warming that boulder all day, till it's a good place to sit and sleep. His companions are not so wise, and will not take advice; they lie down in the heather, and wake up feeling cold, and sneezing. Then they have breakfast and start off again.

Listening now, for any sound of blasting about; they are hoping to come on the mine, and meet with folk sometime that day. The work should have got so far by now; a good way up from the water towards Sellanraa. But never a sound of blasting anywhere. They march till noon, meeting never a soul; but here and there they come upon holes in the ground, where men have been digging for trial. What can this mean? Means, no doubt, that the ore must be more commonly rich at the farther end of the tract; they are getting out pure heavy copper, and keeping to that end all the time.

In the afternoon they come upon several more mines, but no miners; they march on till evening, and already they can make out the sea below; marching through a wilderness of deserted mines, and never a sound. 'Tis all beyond

understanding, but nothing for it; they must camp and
sleep out again that night. They talk the matter over: Can
the work have stopped? Should they turn and go back
again? "Not a bit of it," says Andresen.

Next morning a man walks into their camp—a pale,
haggard man who looks at them frowningly, piercingly.
"That you, Andresen?" says the man. It is Aronsen, Aronsen the trader. He does not say "No" to a cup of hot coffee
and something to eat with the caravan, and settles down
at once. "I saw the smoke of your fire, and came up to see
what it was," says he. "I said to myself: 'Sure enough,
they're coming to their senses, and starting work again.'
And 'twas only you, after all! Where you making for,
then?"

"Here."

"What's that you've got with you?"

"Goods."

"Goods?" cries Aronsen. "Coming up here with goods
for sale? Who's to buy them? There's never a soul. They
left last Saturday gone."

"Left? Who left?"

"All the lot. Not a soul on the place now. And I've goods
enough myself, anyway. A whole store packed full. I'll sell
you anything you like."

Oh, Trader Aronsen in difficulties again! The mine has
shut down.

They ply him with coffee till he grows calmer, and asks
what it all means.

Aronsen shakes his head despairingly. " 'Tis beyond
understanding, there's no words for it," says he. All had
been going so well, and he had been selling goods, and
money pouring in; the village round all flourishing, and
using the finest meal, and a new schoolhouse, and hanging
lamps and town-made boots, and all! Then suddenly their
lordships up at the mine take it into their heads that the

thing isn't paying, and close down. Not paying? But it paid them before? Wasn't there clean copper there and plain to see at every blasting? 'Twas rank cheating, no less. "And never a thought of what it means to a man like me. Aye, I doubt it's as they say; 'tis that Geissler's at the bottom of it all, same as before. No sooner he'd come up than the work stopped; 'twas as if he'd smelt it out somehow."

"Geissler, is he here, then?"

"Is he not? Ought to be shot, he ought! Comes up one day by the steamer and says to the engineer: 'Well, how's things going?'—'All right, as far as I can see,' says the engineer. But Geissler he just stands there, and asks again: 'Ho, all right, is it?'—'Aye, as far as I know,' says the engineer. But as true as I'm here, no sooner the post comes up from that same boat Geissler had come by, than there's letter and telegram both to the engineer that the work wasn't paying, and he's to shut down at once."

The members of the expedition look at one another, but the leader, Andresen himself, has not lost courage yet.

"You may just as well turn back and go home again," is Aronsen's advice.

"We're not doing that," says Andresen, and packs up the coffee-pot.

Aronsen stares at the three of them in turn. "You're mad, then," says he.

Look you, Andresen he cares little now for what his master that was can say; he's master himself now, leader of an expedition equipped at his own expense for a journey to distant parts; 'twould lose him his prestige to turn back now where he is.

"Well, where will you go?" asks Aronsen irritably.

"Can't say," answers Andresen. But he's a notion of his own all the same, no doubt; thinking, maybe, of the natives, and coming down into the district three men strong, with glass beads and finger-rings. "We'll be getting on," says he to the rest.

Now, Aronsen had thought like enough to go farther up that morning, seeing he'd come so far, wanting, maybe, to see if all the place was quite deserted, if it could be true every man on the place was gone. But seeing these peddler-folk so set on going on, it hinders him, and he tells them again and again they're mad to try. Aronsen is furious himself, marches down in front of the caravan, turning round and shouting at them, barking at them, trying to keep them out of his district. And so they come down to the huts in the mining center.

A little town of huts, but empty and desolate. Most of the tools and implements are housed under cover, but poles and planks, broken carts and cases and barrels, lie all about in disorder; here and there a notice on a door declares: "No admittance."

"There you are," cries Aronsen. "What did I say? Not a soul in the place." And he threatens the caravan with disaster—he will send for the Lensmand; anyway, he's going to follow them every step now, and if he can catch them at any unlawful trading 'tis penal servitude and slavery, no mistake!

All at once somebody calls out for Sivert. The place is not altogether dead, after all, not utterly deserted; here is a man standing beckoning at the corner of a house. Sivert trundles over with his load, and sees at once who it is— Geissler.

"Funny meeting you here," says Geissler. His face is red and flourishing, but his eyes apparently cannot stand the glare of spring, he is wearing smoked glasses. He talks as brilliantly as ever. "Luckiest thing in the world," says he. "Save me going all the way up to Sellanraa; and I've a deal to look after. How many settlers are there in the Almenning now?"

"Ten."

"Ten new holdings. I'll agree. I'm satisfied. But 'tis two-and-thirty thousand men of your father's stamp the country wants. Aye, that's what I say, and I mean it; I've reckoned it out."

"Sivert, are you coming on?" The caravan is waiting.

Geissler hears, and calls back sharply: "No."

"I'll come on after," calls Sivert, and sets down his load.

The two men sit down and talk. Geissler is in the right mood today; the spirit moves him, and he talks all the time, only pausing when Sivert puts in a word or so in answer, and then going on again. "A mighty lucky thing—can't help saying it. Everything turned out just as I wanted all the way up, and now meeting you here and saving all the journey to Sellanraa. All well at home, what?"

"All well, and thank you kindly."

"Got up that hayloft yet, over the cowshed?"

"Aye, 'tis done."

"Well, well—I've a heap of things to look to, almost more than I can manage. Look at where we're sitting now, for instance. What d'you say to that, Sivert man? Ruined city, eh? Men gone about to build it all against their nature and well-being. Properly speaking, it's all my fault from the start—that is to say, I'm a humble agent in the workings of fate. It all began when your father picked up some bits of stone up in the hills, and gave you to play with when you were a child. That was how it started. I knew well enough those bits of stone were worth exactly as much as men would give for them, no more; well and good, I set a price on them myself, and bought them. Then the stones passed from hand to hand, and did no end of damage. Time went on. And now, a few days ago, I came up here again, and what for, d'you think? To buy those stones back again!"

Geissler stops for a moment, and looks at Sivert. Then suddenly he glances at the sack, and asks: "What's that you're carrying?"

"Goods," says Sivert. "We're taking them down to the village."

Geissler does not seem interested in the answer; has not even heard it, like as not. He goes on:

"Buy them back again—yes. Last time, I let my son manage the deal; he sold them then. Young fellow about your own age, that's all about him. He's the lightning in the family, I'm more a sort of fog. Know what's the right thing to do, but don't do it. But he's the lightning—and he's entered the service of industry for the time being. 'Twas he sold for me last time. I'm something and he's not, he's only the lightning; quick to act, modern type. But the lightning by itself's a barren thing. Look at you folk at Sellanraa, now; looking up at blue peaks every day of your lives; no new-fangled inventions about that, but fjeld and rocky peaks, rooted deep in the past—but you've them for companionship. There you are, living in touch with heaven and earth, one with them, one with all these wide, deep-rooted things. No need of a sword in your hands, you go through life bareheaded, barehanded, in the midst of a great kindliness. Look, Nature's there, for you and yours to have and enjoy. Man and Nature don't bombard each other, but agree; they don't compete, race one against the other, but go together. There's you Sellanraa folk, in all this, living there. Fjeld and forest, moors and meadow, and sky and stars—oh, 'tis not poor and sparingly counted out, but without measure. Listen to me, Sivert: you be content! You've everything to live on, everything to live for, everything to believe in; being born and bringing forth, you are the needful on earth. 'Tis not all that are so, but you are so; needful on earth. 'Tis you that maintain life. Generation to generation, breeding ever anew; and when you die, the new stock goes on. That's the meaning of eternal life. What do you get out of it? An existence innocently and properly set towards all. What you get out of it? Nothing can put you under orders and lord it over you Sellanraa folk, you've peace and authority and this great kindliness all round. That's what you get for it. You lie at a mother's breast and suck, and play with a mother's warm hand. There's your father now, he's one of the two-and-thirty thousand. What's to be said of many another? I'm something, I'm the fog, as it were, here and there, floating around, sometimes coming like rain on dry ground. But the others? There's my son, the lightning that's nothing in itself, a flash of barrenness; he can act. My son, aye, he's the modern type, a man of our time; he believes honestly enough all the age has taught him, all the Jew and the Yankee have taught him; I shake my head at it all. But there's nothing mythical about me; 'tis only in the family, so to speak, that I'm like a fog. Sit there shaking my head. Tell the truth—I've not the power of doing things and not regretting it. If I had, I could be lightning myself. Now I'm a fog."

Suddenly Geissler seems to recollect himself, and asks: "Got up that hayloft yet, above the cowshed?"

"Aye, that's done. And father's put up a new house."

"New house?"

" 'Tis in case anyone should come, he says—in case Geissler he should happen to come along."

Geissler thinks over this, and takes his decision: "Well, then, I'd better come. Yes, I'll come; you can tell your father that. But I've a heap of things to look to. Came up here and told the engineer to let his people in Sweden know I was ready to buy. And we'd see what happened. All the same to me, no hurry. You ought to have seen that engineer—here he's been going about and keeping it all up with men and horses and money and machines and any

amount of fuss; thought it was all right, knew no better.
The more bits of stone he can turn into money, the better;
he thinks he's doing something clever and deserving, bringing money to the place, to the country, and everything
nearing disaster more and more, and he's none the wiser.
'Tis not money the country wants, there's more than enough
of it already; 'tis men like your father there's not enough of.
Aye, turning the means to an end in itself and being proud
of it! They're mad, diseased; they don't work, they know
nothing of the plow, only the dice. Mighty deserving of
them, isn't it, working and wasting themselves to nothing
in their own mad way. Look at them—staking everything,
aren't they? There's but this much wrong with it all; they
forget that gambling isn't courage, 'tis not even foolhardy
courage, 'tis a horror. D'you know what gambling is? 'Tis
fear, with the sweat on your brow, that's what it is. What's
wrong with them is, they won't keep pace with life, but
want to go faster—race on, tear on ahead, driving themselves into life itself like wedges. And then the flanks of
them say: here, stop, there's something breaking, find a
remedy; stop, say the flanks! And then life crushes them,
politely but firmly crushes them. And then they set to
complaining about life, raging against life! Each to his own
taste; some may have ground to complain, others not,
but there's none should rage against life. Not be stern
and strict and just with life, but be merciful to it, and
take its part; only think of the gamblers life has to bear
with!"

Geissler recollects himself again, and says: "Well, all
that's as it may be; leave it!" He is evidently tired, beginning to breathe in little gasps. "Going down?" says he.

"Aye."

"There's no hurry. You owe me a long walk over the
hills, Sivert man, remember that? I remember it all. I remember from the time I was a year and a half; stood lean-

ing down from the barn bridge at Garmo, and noticed a smell. I can smell it again now. But all that's as it may be, that too; but we might have done that trip over the hills now if you hadn't got that sack. What's in it?"

"Goods. 'Tis Andresen is going to sell them."

"Well, then, I'm a man that knows what's the right thing to do, but doesn't do it," says Geissler. "I'm the fog. Now perhaps I'll buy that mine back again one of these days, it's not impossible; but if I do, it wouldn't be to go about staring up at the sky and saying: 'Aerial railway! South America!' No, leave that to the gamblers. Folk hereabout say I must be the devil himself because I knew beforehand this was going to break up. But there's nothing mystical about me, 'tis simple enough. The new copper mines in Montana, that's all. The Yankees are smarter than we are at that game; they are cutting us to death in South America—our ore here's too poor. My son's the lightning; he got the news, and I came floating up here. Simple, isn't it? I beat those fellows in Sweden by a few hours, that's all."

Geissler is short of breath again; he gets on his feet, and says: "If you're going down, let's get along."

They go on down together, Geissler dragging behind, all tired out. The caravan has stopped at the quay, and Fredrik Ström, cheerful as ever, is poking fun at Aronsen: "I'm clean out of tobacco; got any tobacco, what?"

"I'll give you tobacco," said Aronsen threateningly.

Fredrik laughs, and says comfortingly: "Nay, you've no call to take it all heavy-like and sad, Aronsen. We're just going to sell these things here before your eyes, and then we'll be off home again."

"Get away and wash your dirty mouth," says Aronsen furiously.

"Ha ha ha! Nay, you've no call to dance about that way; keep still and look like a picture!"

Geissler is tired, tired out, even his smoked glasses do not help him now, his eyes keep closing in the glare.

"Good-bye, Sivert man," says he all at once. "No, I can't get up to Sellanraa this time, after all; tell your father. I've a heap of things to see to. But I'll come later on—say that. . . ."

Aronsen spits after him, and says: "Ought to be shot!"

For three days the caravan peddles its wares, selling out the contents of the sacks, and getting good prices. It was a brilliant piece of business. The village folk were still well supplied with money after the downfall of the mine, and were excellently in form in the way of spending; those stuffed birds on springs were the very thing they wanted; they set them up on chests of drawers in their parlors, and also bought nice paper-knives, the very thing for cutting the leaves of an almanac. Aronsen was furious. "Just as if I hadn't things every bit as good in my store," said he.

Trader Aronsen was in a sorry way; he had made up his mind to keep with these peddlers and their sacks, watching them all the time; but they went separate ways about the village, each for himself, and Aronsen almost tore himself to pieces trying to follow all at once. First he gave up Fredrik Ström, who was quickest at saying unpleasant things; then Sivert, because he never said a word, but went on selling; at last he stuck to following his former clerk, and trying to set folk against him wherever he went in. Oh, but Andresen knew his master that was—knew him of old, and how little he knew of business and unlawful trading.

"Ho, you mean to say English thread's not prohibited?" said Aronsen, looking wise.

"I know it is," answered Andresen. "But I'm not carrying any this way; I can sell that elsewhere. I haven't a reel in my pack; look for yourself, if you like."

"That's as it may be," says Aronsen. "Anyway, I know

what's forbidden, and I've shown you, so don't try to teach me."

Aronsen stood it for a whole day, then he gave up Andresen, too, and went home. The peddlers had no one to watch them after that.

And then things began to go swimmingly. It was in the day when womenfolk used to wear loose plaits in their hair; and Andresen, he was the man to sell loose plaits. Aye, at a pinch he could sell fair plaits to dark girls, and be sorry he'd nothing lighter; no grey plaits, for instance, for that was the finest of all. And every evening the three young salesmen met at an appointed place and went over the day's trade, each borrowing from another anything he'd sold out of; and Andresen would sit down, often as not, and take out a file and file away the German trademark from a sportsman's whistle, or rub out "Faber" on the pens and pencils. Andresen was a trump, and always had been.

Sivert, on the other hand, was rather a disappointment. Not that he was any way slack, and failed to sell his goods —'twas he, indeed, sold most—but he did not get enough for them. "You don't put in enough patter with it," said Andresen.

No, Sivert was no hand at reeling off a lot of talk; he was a fieldworker, sure of what he said, and speaking calmly when he spoke at all. What was there to talk about here? Also, Sivert was anxious to be done with it and get back home, there was work to do in the fields.

" 'Tis that Jensine's calling him," Fredrik Ström explained. Fredrik, himself, by the way, had work on his own fields to be done that spring, and little time to waste; but for all that, he must look in on Aronsen the last day and get up an argument with him. "I'll sell him the empty sacks," said he.

Andresen and Sivert stayed outside while he went in. They heard grand goings-on inside the store, both talking at once, and Fredrik setting up a laugh now and again; then Aronsen threw open the door and showed his visitor out. Oh, but Fredrik didn't come out—no, he took his time, and talked a lot more. The last thing they heard from outside was Fredrik trying to sell Aronsen a lot of rocking-horses.

Then the caravan went home again—three young men full of life and health. They marched and sang, slept a few hours in the open, and went on again. When they got back to Sellanraa on the Monday, Isak had begun sowing. The weather was right for it; the air moist, with the sun peeping out now and again, and a mighty rainbow strung right across the heavens.

The caravan broke up—*Farvel, Farvel.* . . .

Isak at his sowing; a stump of a man, a barge of a man to look at, nothing more. Clad in homespun—wool from his own sheep, boots from the hide of his own cows and calves. Sowing—and he walks religiously bareheaded to that work; his head is bald just at the very top, but all the rest of him shamefully hairy; a fan, a wheel of hair and beard, stands out from his face. 'Tis Isak, the Margrave.

'Twas rarely he knew the day of the month—what need had he of that? He had no bills to be met on a certain date; the marks on his almanac were to show the time when each of the cows should bear. But he knew St. Olaf's Day in the autumn, that by then his hay must be in, and he knew Candlemas in spring, and that three weeks after then the bears came out of their winter quarters; all seed must be in the earth by then. He knew what was needful.

A tiller of the ground, body and soul; a worker on the land without respite. A ghost risen out of the past to point the future, a man from the earliest days of cultivation, a settler in the wilds, nine hundred years old, and, withal, a man of the day.

Nay, there was nothing left to him now of the copper mine and its riches—the money had vanished into air. And who had anything left of all that wealth when the working stopped, and the hills lay dead and deserted? But the Almenning was there still, and ten new holdings on that land, beckoning a hundred more.

Nothing growing there? All things growing there; men and beasts and fruit of the soil. Isak sowing his grain. The evening sunlight falls on the grain that flashes out in an arc from his hand, and falls like a dropping of gold to the ground. Here comes Sivert to the harrowing; after that the roller, and then the harrow again. Forest and field look on. All is majesty and power—a sequence and purpose of things.

Kling . . . eling . . . say the cow-bells far up on the hillside, coming nearer and nearer; the cattle are coming home for the night. Fifteen head of them, and five-and-forty sheep and goats besides; threescore in all. There go the women out with their milkpails, carried on yokes from the shoulder: Leopoldine, Jensine, and little Rebecca. All three barefooted. The Margravine, Inger herself, is not with them; she is indoors preparing the meal. Tall and stately, as she moves about her house, a Vestal tending the fire of a kitchen stove. Inger has made her stormy voyage, 'tis true, has lived in a city a while, but now she is home; the world is wide, swarming with tiny specks—Inger has been one of them. All but nothing in all humanity, only one speck.

Then comes the evening.